SECOND SIGHT

MEG NAPIER

NAPIERPRESS

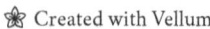 Created with Vellum

To my beautiful, talented, kind, and beloved daughter, Alexandra, who is the most gifted writer in our family. You have never hesitated to share your love for writing with the world, and your courage and dedication has been an inspiration to me.

And to my mother, who hates the colorful language my characters insist on using, but who nonetheless promotes my books to everyone she meets. Thanks, Mom.

PROLOGUE

Present Day

Giza, Egypt

How in hell could it be so hot this early in the morning? Sweating in the fierce morning sun, Etienne watched tourists from all parts of the world gaze in marvel at the Great Pyramid. No doubt they, too, had hoped to beat the heat with an early start. He had photographed the pyramids innumerable times, but it was still refreshing to watch the awe in others' eyes and see them try to manage selfies that captured both themselves and one of the world's greatest structures.

He glanced at his watch. He had arrived ahead of time, as always, but his contact from the ministry should be arriving any minute. The piece *GeoMonde* had planned was important to the Egyptian government as it tried to maintain international interest in its history despite the ever-present threat of terrorism and violence.

The glare of the August sun was relentless, and the diesel smell from the tourist buses mingled with the babel of languages and the gritty fine sand that seemed to give everything a just-out-of-focus appearance.

While he waited, he snapped photos of the more unusual faces around him, but his eyes kept following a young couple who seemed as equally enthralled by each other as they were by their surroundings.

Etienne's parents had behaved like that, before his father's death. He himself had avoided relationships that presaged any threat of long-term attachments. He loved his ability to travel wherever he wanted whenever he wanted, his camera and his laptop his chosen companions. Yet his eyes kept returning to the couple. The young man reached out and tenderly pushed some hair aside that was blowing into the young woman's face, and Etienne felt a tightening in his solar plexus.

He looked away and searched for the figure of the teenaged Egyptian entrepreneur he had photographed earlier. The eager young man was enticing tourists in a variety of languages to pose for pictures with his camel.

As he lifted his camera, a deafening explosion shattered the scene. Etienne felt himself knocked from his feet. Deafening noise, pain, and a suffocating haze of smoke and dust overwhelmed his senses.

Etienne realized he was on the ground, his arms over his head. He pushed himself awkwardly to a crouch and scanned the area, trying to get his bearings and ascertain what had happened. His body hurt everywhere from having hit the ground so hard, but he didn't think anything was broken.

Thick smoke and sand seemed to hover everywhere, and

he struggled to take a breath. Thank God his camera was still on its strap around his neck. He hoped it hadn't been damaged. He moved closer to where he thought the blast had originated, snapping photos rapidly and trying not to think about the carnage he was recording even while tears ran down his face from the acrid fumes and his ears rang from the noise all around him.

Another burst of horrendous sound amidst the cacophony of cries and sirens, and Etienne was thrown. Pain such as he had never known engulfed him.

CHAPTER ONE

Tarrytown, (The Tarry Towns) Colony of New York,
Fall, 1774

"More ale, Sir?" she asked politely, trying hard not to stare at the familiar hands while she lifted the empty tankard from the table.

"No, Miss Rynick, thank you. But please tell your mother that her apple cobbler was particularly fine today."

"I will, Sir. Thank you. She'll be happy to hear it."

"Meet me outside, *please*," he whispered fiercely as she turned to go.

She felt his fingers on the folds of her skirt as he whispered again, "Katrina, *please*. I have to see you."

She nodded, glancing around the now almost empty tavern to make sure no one had seen them, and headed behind the bar with the dirty crockery.

Looking around once more, she pulled her shawl from

the hook and stole out the door. Stephen was waiting for her by the hitching post, and he grabbed her hand and pulled her back towards the stable. Once they were out of sight of the door, his mouth descended hungrily on her own.

"Kat, what are you doing to me?" he groaned, running his hands up and down her back and pulling her hard against him. "You haven't spoken to me in days. Look at me, My Angel. Have your courses come?"

"No," she whispered against his chest.

"No? *No*? Do you know what that means? You *have* to marry me now, my love. You have to."

"Stephen, we cannot. My parents won't allow it. Your parents won't allow it."

"My parents will be happy I have found someone so wonderful to love. My mother has long despaired at my reluctance to find a suitable young lady to give her grand-children."

"Stephen, please. Be reasonable!"

"I am being reasonable. I love you. You love me and are carrying our child. Of course we shall marry."

"Stephen, you are an officer in His Majesty's army. The same *His Majesty* that my family and I, and most of my world, have come to hate. You live in a castle. I help my mother with the young ones and serve table at our tavern. Oh, Stephen, I do love you, and of course I want to be with you, but our lives are too different. This is all my fault. You were the gentleman and I was the trollop, but I promise you, I will make sure our child is loved. I am so sorry."

She turned away, hoping he would not see the tears slipping from her eyes.

Stephen caught her face between his strong hands and pushed the tears aside with his thumbs before bending again and kissing her gently. His words, though, were fierce.

"You will not apologize, ever, and you will never again speak of yourself with such words. This is our child, Katrina, *ours*. I most certainly do not live in a castle, as I have told you before, and I never will. I am free to choose my own path in this world. And Katrina, my dearest heart, *you* are that path."

"Stephen, before you came here, you never even had to lace up your own boots. How can you think of marrying someone such as me? We come from completely different worlds."

"I do quite well with my boots now, thank you very much. And I am not thinking of marrying someone such as you. It is you and only you, Katrina. You are more lovely, more generous, and far more intelligent than any ninny prancing around London. You've even read more books than I have. The time is past for being afraid of what is between us, my love. Let me go and speak with your father."

"He hates you, Stephen. Not you, personally, and God knows my mother has taken a secret fancy to you, but they both hate all the British soldiers who come through town. And my father says that true war will break out soon between us."

He pulled her tightly against him again and kissed the top of her cap. She lifted her head and stared into his piercing blue eyes, eyes that looked back at her with fierce determination. She had fallen under the spell of those eyes the first time he had walked into her father's tavern. He had politely asked how many families lived in the area and which homes might have space to house his men, should the need arise. He had turned then and seen her standing by a table with a cleaning rag in her hand. He had smiled at her, and she had felt riveted by his beautiful, clear gaze.

A few days later Katrina had gone for an early morning walk near the river on one of the first warm days of spring.

She brought the bound paper journal she kept for scribbling her thoughts and short stories and had nearly walked into him, not seeing him seated on a horse blanket, sketching. Curiosity overrode propriety, since the idea of a British officer drawing what looked like a family of beavers seemed incomprehensible to her.

"Are those beavers?"

He came swiftly to his feet, reddening slightly as he looked down at his own pad.

"I suppose they must be, although I assumed I was looking at muskrats. I've been watching this family for several days, and I wanted to capture their sense of community."

"A community of beavers? My goodness. The weekly gazette is always seeking stories about extended family members. Perhaps I should alert Mr. Hiscock to the presence right here by the river of potential material that he has somehow missed."

She laughed, her delight in the early spring with its musical harmony of the rushing water and the insistent bird chatter overcoming her instinctive distrust of his uniform. "You are new to the area, Major, are you not?"

"Yes. Major Stephen Howard at your service, Mistress," he said, bowing slightly. "And your father is the tavern owner, is he not?"

"Lord Philipse is the true owner, but my family has provided service at the tavern for almost twenty years, and we live in the quarters above."

"Your mother's cooking is delicious. Or perhaps the praise is due you?"

She laughed again. "Oh no. I am quite the nuisance in the kitchen. My mother will readily attest to that."

"Well, Miss . . .?" he looked at her with eyebrows raised.

"Rynick."

"Miss Rynick. Your absence from the kitchen allows you to grace the diners with your lovely presence."

At his words she grew pink and tried to hide her smile.

"Sir, I see you are as skilled with words as you are with charcoal."

"I speak only the truth, Miss Rynick."

"Oh my. That sounds so old-fashioned. Everyone calls me Katrina."

"But I assume the *everyone* you speak of has known you all your life. I am a newcomer and would not want to cause insult or appear impolite."

She looked up at him. "'Twill not be calling me by my Christian name that will cause distress, Sir. It is your uniform and your continued presence here in our town. Do you mean to be long amongst us?"

"My dear Miss Rynick, you have already threatened to alert the town paper about the heretofore secret behavior of the Hudson's coastal inhabitants, so I do not think it wise to provide information concerning His Majesty's plans for my presence, continued or otherwise."

Katrina's eyes narrowed in suspicion, but she smiled in spite of herself when she saw the corners of his own lips moving ever so slightly in an attempt to hide a smile.

"Well then," she said, arching her brows and giving him a look of mock severity. "You may address me as Katrina for the duration of your stay, however long it may be, although we all hope you will leave soon."

He reached for her hand and bowed deeply before brushing the back of her hand lightly with his lips.

"Miss Katrina Rynick, it is a delight to make your acquaintance. I am, as I said, Major Stephen Howard, at your service. And I hope, most sincerely, that I will not be leaving anytime soon."

He continued to hold her fingers lightly in his own, and Katrina felt a blush spread across her face.

"A pleasure to meet you, Major Howard." She dropped a perfunctory courtesy.

"As you've caught me doing something altogether unaffiliated with my military duties, please call me Stephen, at least while in the presence of muskrats."

"Beavers."

"Beavers, then. I appear to have interrupted your walk. Will you continue, or would you care to join me here for a bit to enjoy this beautiful morning in company?"

"It is exquisite, is it not? I thought spring would never arrive, and now it has burst forth so spectacularly. I need to get back soon to prepare for the noon-day meal, but I couldn't resist just a short respite in the open air. Please do not let me interrupt your sketching, Major Howard. Your picture is very life-like."

"Stephen," he said, still holding her hand. "And the company of a lovely young woman could never be termed an interruption. Sit for a few minutes, and I will finish, and then we can walk back to the tavern together."

Katrina knew she should refuse, but she felt herself drawn to this man whom she would normally regard with distaste. He looked at her with apparent respect and admiration and hardly seemed an agent of the tyranny spoken about in the tavern of late. And his eyes were so compellingly attractive as they crinkled in continued amusement.

She sat carefully down on the edge of the blanket, several feet from Major Howard, and gazed out towards the gently moving water. The Hudson was so wide at this point that the early settlers had named it a sea, and the whole area was still sometimes called by its original Dutch name, the "Tappan Zee."

It truly was a glorious morning, and everywhere she

looked she could see green shoots pushing up. The chatter of the birds in the still early morning was insistent and loud, as if the various flocks on the branches were trying to drown out the ever-present whoosh of the river. Should she tell her family about meeting the British major when she returned, or would it be better not to mention him? As soon as the thought crossed her mind, she knew she would not speak of this meeting. In all her twenty-one years, she could not remember a more perfect morning, and she certainly would not want the censure of her family to spoil its memory.

She glanced over at the major and saw he was returning his charcoal to a pouch and slipping it into his pocket. He loosened the page he had been working on from its binding and stood up gracefully, turning to hold out a hand to help her rise.

"This is for you, Miss Rynick. A keepsake of a most unforgettable spring morning." He held out the sheet and Katrina gasped. Where a scant few moments earlier there had been only the barest hint of a river with a few animals near the shore, he had managed to enhance the contours of the riverbank and outline the figure of a young woman walking with her face raised towards the sun. The drawing was simple, but even so, Katrina could recognize her own features, however quickly sketched. And the picture was lovely. *She* looked lovely in it. How had he done something so miraculous so quickly, and was that really how he saw her?

She looked up at him in astonishment. "It's extraordinary. Thank you. But . . . don't you want to keep it?"

He looked down at the drawing and then into her eyes. "Verily, Katrina, I *would* like to keep it. That is most rude of me, is it not? But I would like nothing more than to see your image before my eyes when I wake in the morning."

Katrina felt a wave of color sweep over her. She scrambled to her feet and bobbed a quick half curtsy before moving swiftly to make her way back towards town, turning as she reached the top of the hill to see him gazing after her.

KATRINA STOLE down to the riverbank again early the next day, telling herself she was just seeking some fresh morning air, and blushed with happiness when she came upon him once more. By unspoken agreement they continued to cross paths, seemingly by accident, for several days, whenever the weather was fair.

Their conversations were friendly and polite, but as time went on they began to banter as political and philosophical matters were touched upon.

On the fourth morning that they met, she carried a pamphlet that had recently arrived. "Major Howard, I pray you consider the injustices that we here in the colonies have had to endure of late," and she read aloud to him a persuasive call to resist payment of taxes while he sketched the fauna closest to the riverbank.

"He is our sovereign," Stephen answered her quietly but firmly, "and as such he has the right to impose taxes and regulations where and when he deems it necessary."

"If we were subjects of a *responsible* monarch, we would have the right to fair and just representation and to privileges equal to any enjoyed elsewhere in the empire, including your beloved London! Have *your* parents ever been asked to make room in their castle for soldiers to stay with them?"

"I shall take you with me on my next visit to London and arrange a private audience for you with His Majesty," Stephen answered with a smile. "You may present the colonists' complaints to him directly. And I most certainly do not live in a castle. Katrina, I truly do not understand your vehemence. Lord Philipse has been extraordinarily welcoming to me, and he has told me that this entire area is peaceful and loyal."

Katrina blew out her breath in frustration, crossing her arms across her chest and scowling out at the river. She then turned to him and spoke with a steely, level tone that betrayed how hard she was working to maintain control.

"Lord Frederick Philipse is, indeed, a loyal puppet of His Majesty. His family was granted the land for miles around in every direction to hold and use as they see fit. He does not have to lift a finger to receive his daily bread. We do all the lifting. The lifting, the milling, the tanning, the farming, the fishing, the ferrying, and the tavern running. He and his family reap all the profits, and the small incomes we get to keep are then siphoned away on taxes for necessities like sugar. Then we are told we may have to share our homes with the King's enforcers. My vehemence, as you so sweetly put it, is justified."

Stephen stared at her, his smile disappearing as he seemed to ponder her words.

"One might think that the crofters on my uncle's estate would express the same indignant objections as your pamphleteers, but many of them are unschooled and accept their lot in life. There must be something in the air in this wide land of yours that inspires a tendency toward rebellion."

"But do you not agree, Major Howard, that an individual should be able to enjoy the fruits of his own labor without losing a great share of it to a monarch who cares naught for his subjects?"

He reached out and brushed back a curl that had slipped from her cap in her agitation.

"I cannot help but think you are judging King George harshly, Miss Rynick. The expense of maintaining an empire is enormous. The cost of his army alone, spread out as it is here in the New World and in the Orient, is immense."

She glared at him, her hands coming to her hips. "Then take yourselves home and tell the King he must learn to economize. That way my mother will not have to sacrifice so much of our income just to buy sugar for her pies."

"Do you wish me gone so soon? I was hoping to see your river valley in the summertime."

Katrina looked up at him, stricken. The reality of all she had just said to him—to a British officer—washed over her, and she felt a flush run up her neck and her cheeks grow warm. She self-consciously bobbed a curtsy. "I apologize, Major Howard. I spoke out of turn."

"I've told you my name is Stephen, have I not? At least here by the river where we are friends, not adversaries. In truth, I wish never to be an adversary to anyone here in the colonies. And for better or worse, it seems I will remain here for the foreseeable future. It would be a more agreeable stay if I could think we were able to stay friends despite our differences."

Katrina knew she did not want him gone. But she realized how foolishly she had allowed her infatuation to get the better of her. She most certainly should not have brought the pamphlet with her and should never have spoken so intemperately. She pulled her cloak more tightly about her and turned to go.

Stephen reached out his hand and touched her arm. "Katrina? Can we not remain friends despite our differences?" He held out his sketch pad and showed her the picture he had drawn of a girl in an apron and bonnet curtsying to a king.

She stared at it in wonder. The girl in the picture was indeed curtsying, but her head was held high and the expression on her face was determined. And Katrina saw instantly that the girl's features greatly resembled her own.

Suddenly an impish grin spread over her features. "Mayhap you will decide to throw your lot in with us after you have tasted our apples at harvest time."

"Oh, Katrina, once again a beautiful lass seeks to tempt a man with an apple. Have you no shame, woman?"

They both laughed at his words, and the tension broke. They continued to smile at each other for a moment, happy in their youth, the spring sunshine, and their temporary escape from reality.

"I do not know when I last laughed thus, Miss Rynick. You have an uncanny knack for putting things in perspective. Perhaps you should indeed put your quill to paper and send your thoughts to the King."

"WOULD you *please* stop tossing and turning," Katrina's sister, Anna, grumbled sleepily as Katrina tried for the hundredth time that night to settle comfortably on the bed they shared in the loft area where the three girls slept.

Stop thinking about him, she admonished herself. *You know nothing can or should come of this.* But when she closed her eyes and tried to quiet her thoughts, Stephen's face was all she could see. The light brown hair that curled just a bit when tendrils escaped the tail he wore neatly tied in back. His strong jaw and firm brow above the bluest eyes she had ever seen. Eyes that always looked so intently into her own.

He was the first man to have ever paid attention just to her. Of course she spoke daily with her father and her brothers, and she had conversed with scores of tavern patrons over the years. But she had always been Johann and Susanna's daughter.

To the young men of the Tarry Towns she was a pretty serving maid with whom they flirted and occasionally tried to court, but she had never felt strongly attracted to any of them. Her parents had not tried to push her: her mother reassuring her that she would know when the right man appeared, and her father grousing that until the King left them in peace, there was no sense in starting a family of her own.

But Stephen spoke directly to her. He listened to her ideas and arguments and seemed to care naught for the differences in their backgrounds. He had most certainly not tried to take liberties with her person, but she knew by the joy in his smile and the way his eyes brightened when he looked at her that he found her comely.

Do not think of him as Stephen! He is Major Howard, a British officer, and you would be wise to put him from your mind!

But as she tried yet again to quiet her breathing and settle her mind, she found herself hoping desperately that the morrow would again be fair and that she would be able to slip down to the riverbank.

ON THEIR SEVENTH or eighth morning together, she ran up breathlessly and told him she could not stay as her mother had enquired about her frequent absences. He reached for her hands just as she turned to leave, determined to finally follow her conscience and end their pointless dalliance.

"Katrina, stop for just a moment. I have to go to Manhattan for a few days, and I find myself loath to say good-bye for even a short time." He gazed into her eyes, his thumbs caressing her hands as he held them, and she gazed back at him, crestfallen, instantly forgetting her earlier resolution.

"This fortnight has been the most delightful time I can remember, not only from my stay here in the colonies, but . .

. somehow in my entire life. I fear you have become as essential to me as the morning sun itself."

She looked up at him as he spoke, her heart pulsing with joy at his words but her eyes filling with tears.

"Oh Stephen, *I* fear that our time together will lead to misfortune. Aside from my mother wondering what I am about early in the morning, my parents are both aggravated by your continued presence in the area, and many of the townspeople whisper about plans to drive you away. How I wish they could know you for who you are and not just see your uniform."

He brushed back the bits of hair that had come loose from under her bonnet in the brisk morning breeze. "My little one, do not fret. These troubles between the crown and the colonies will pass, and all will be well. I came to these shores with warnings of wild savages and uncivilized colonists, and I have found you, instead. We will find a way to mend these conflicts. We must. Please tell me you will come to the river again when I return?"

Their fingers still entwined, she smiled at him through her tears and nodded slowly. He bent his head and brushed her lips lightly with his own. Katrina's eyes closed as her mouth softened under his, and he groaned softly and pulled her close, deepening the kiss. She rose on tiptoe, her arms going up to encircle his neck.

STEPHEN FELT the earth shift under him. Her lips were so surprisingly sweet and giving. He was like an explorer in the desert tasting water for the first time in days, unable to turn from the honeyed nectar. Neither his earlier awkward fumbles with society debutantes nor his brother's carefully arranged brothel visits in London had prepared him for the tidal wave of passion and tenderness that swept over him at the touch of Katrina's warm body. He did not want to let her return to the tavern that morning, let alone not see or touch her for several days.

He pulled her closer and deepened the kiss. Her lips parted and her tongue shyly met his own. Time seemed to stop as he was engulfed by a wave of desire.

"My Kat," he whispered, lifting his head at last. "I pray the next few days will fly past. I will stop at the tavern when I return and ask your parents for permission to call on you."

"No! You must not," she cried, putting her fingers to his lips. "They will not look kindly on such an idea, I assure you. Just come in for a meal, and I will know you are back, and I will come the following morning. I promise."

"But Katrina, I do not want to sneak behind their backs. I want to court you openly with the respect and attention you deserve."

"Oh, Stephen, I must run now, truly. We will discuss this matter when you return. Please travel safely and promise me you will say nothing." She rose on tiptoe and brushed a last, soft kiss against his lips and then was gone.

WHEN STEPHEN ENTERED the tavern five days later, Katrina was stirring the large pot at the hearth. Before she saw him, she felt the atmosphere in the room change, a tense quiet settling over the crowded room.

"Please go see what our guest desires," her father said coldly.

"Good evening, Major Howard. Will you be having a meal or just an ale, Sir?"

"A meal, please, Miss Rynick." Seemingly by accident, his elbow hit the plumed cap he had set on the table, causing it to fall. They both bent down to pick it up, and he said quietly, "Have you changed your mind? May I speak with your parents?"

She shook her head quickly but reached out to squeeze his fingers for just a second under the table before standing.

"We have venison stew this evening, Sir. Will that be acceptable?"

"Of course. Your mother's stew is always delicious."

When she brought him his bowl a few minutes later, she whispered, "My parents will be busy this evening. It will probably be pleasant by the river."

She blushed as his face broke into a joyful smile. "Stop!" she whispered anxiously, and turned away quickly, a feeling of happiness nevertheless sweeping over her.

The town elders were meeting that night to read aloud the pamphlets that had arrived that afternoon from Philadelphia. Normally she would stay, but she hoped that given the level of interest over each new bit of news, her brief absence would go unnoticed.

The days were getting longer, and she felt herself almost skipping with joy in the filtered light as she approached the river. She slowed and tried to assume an air of nonchalance when she caught sight of his red coat through the trees, but he saw her at almost the same instant and opened his arms wide.

Going into them was as natural as breathing, and their lips met hungrily.

"Oh, how I missed you," he said, brushing kisses over her eyebrows and temple.

"And I you," she said shyly. But then his lips returned to hers, and her shyness disappeared. She was flooded by a sense of both contentment and wanting. She reached up to fit herself more closely against him, modesty forgotten as his arms tightened and his hands pulled her buttocks firmly against him.

She gasped in delight at feeling him pressed against her and wound her arms around him. He reached up with one hand to pull his cap off, and her fingers found and loosened the thong binding his hair. She did not know what these sensations overtaking her meant, but she needed more of them, more of him.

Their kiss went on for what could have been minutes or hours, but at last he lifted his head.

"Kat. This is not right. I am going to speak to your father and ask his permission for your hand."

"My hand? What do you mean?"

"You know very well what I mean. I want you to be my wife. Please, darling Katrina, will you marry me? I never want to be apart from you again without knowing you are mine."

"Stephen, no. You must listen. We hardly even know each other, and I am only here tonight because my people, *my people*, Stephen, are discussing what should be done about the continued oppression you are helping to enforce."

"I am not oppressing anyone! Your people are *my* people, too, Kat. We are all British subjects, and I have no hostility to anyone here in the Tarry Towns. You *know* that. We are all better served with order and with measured application for change. The King will not reverse his decisions overnight, but parliament is aware of the colonies' concerns and pays them heed, I am sure."

She tried to speak again, but he put his fingers over her lips before removing them to kiss her gently one more time.

"And Katrina, my beautiful, wise, wonderful Katrina. How can you say we hardly know each other? I feel like my life began when you walked down to the river that morning. I want you to be my wife. Today, tomorrow, and forever."

DAYS WENT by and Katrina continued to demure, insisting that the differences in their backgrounds were too great and that her family would never come to accept a British officer. Seven weeks later she was still fearful of Stephen approaching her parents, but now the prospect was unavoidable.

She had tried staying away from him, but her days that had once seemed so busy and normal felt both empty and endless without his gentle teasing and their thoughtful discussions. Every moment they spent together strengthened the bond between them. When he was absent fulfilling his duties in other regions, she worried for his safety and listened anxiously for news of his return.

And Stephen, during those same absences, found his thoughts returning again and again to the beacon of peace and joy she had come to be for him. Her quiet beauty was his last conscious image when he closed his eyes, and he found himself thinking how next to make her laugh. During a trip to Manhattan he had learned of a litter of puppies about to be put down, and he had instantly thought of the smile that would brighten her eyes if he brought one back with him. It had not been an easy trip, but the small bundle of fur had indeed brought forth a cry of delight as soon as Katrina laid eyes on the little devil. They had laughingly agreed to call the dog Hudson since it was near the river that all three enjoyed the rare freedom to experience unrestrained happiness in each other's existence.

Now, though, it had been more than a month since her courses should have come but hadn't. Worse yet, each day seemed to herald news from somewhere in the colonies of deteriorating relations between the colonists and the crown's representatives.

"Katrina. I know the situation appears overwhelming. But we have to retain hope that conflict will be averted. And if it comes, I will do my duty. But you, my beloved, are a part of me. We belong together. Always. Somehow, we will find a way. Now let me go speak with your father."

CHAPTER TWO

Arlington
Present Day

Engrossed in work at her kitchen table, Catherine glanced at the clock and realized it was later than she had thought. She had fought off the lingering malaise from her dream and spent hours working on the article she was editing. But if she didn't get moving, the people she needed to see at the office would already be at lunch by the time she got there.

She gulped down the last of her tea and gave a quick look around. Things were so much easier to keep tidy now that she was single. When Catherine's grandmother had died shortly after her college graduation, Catherine had been surprised to learn she had inherited her beloved grandma's house. She and her college boyfriend, Bob, had been renting an apartment together, so having a home to move into without a mortgage had seemed like a miracle. Catherine had felt slightly guilty, however, at bringing Bob with her into the house. Her grandma had met him several times but never seemed completely at ease with him.

She had shaken her head at her grandmother's words to her shortly before she died: "You'll have to wait a while longer before you find him this time, Catherine."

"Find who, Grandma? I'm not looking for anyone. I've got great friends and a job I like. I've got everything I need, and you like Bob, remember?"

Her grandmother opened her eyes and focused intently on Catherine's face, then spoke slowly through her pain.

"Don't be silly, girl. Life is not about endless happy hours, brunches, and an illustrious job. You'll find him again. I am certain. And when you do, pay attention and hold on tightly."

Those were the last words her grandmother had spoken to her. At the time, Catherine and Bob had been together for more than four years. Their first tentative explorations of a physical relationship had been fun and . . . comfortable. Bob had never rushed her, and in fact, it had often been she who had initiated intimacy.

"Ha. I wonder why?" she now asked herself, remembering the night they had first slept together. Bob had been sweet and gentle, asking several times if he was hurting her, and Catherine telling him everything was fine.

And it *had* been fine. Pleasant, sweet, and . . . fine. Nothing like the ridiculous passion she read about in some of her mother's romance books, but most definitely okay. They were great friends, after all, and she didn't believe in, or want, any of the stupid happily-ever-after stuff.

She had thought life close to perfect. Yes, in their last year (years, probably, but she tried not to think about it all too much) they had made love far less frequently, but the demands of two full-time jobs and Bob's long hours working on his dissertation had seemed like a reasonable explanation for their abstinence. But no, she hadn't seen what in hindsight should have been more than obvious. After almost five years together, Bob told her gently and lovingly that he was terribly sorry, but that he was in love with their best friend, Rafael.

Blind as a bat, she thought, for the hundredth time, and although she tried to make light of it all, she couldn't completely rid herself of the nagging sense of inadequacy she carried around. Inadequacy, but no real sorrow. Bob had moved out months ago, and while she at times missed the company, she didn't really miss him. Instead, she sometimes found herself almost missing someone she had never met. Most probably the result of too many Disney movies as a child, every once in a while, she woke up and found herself reaching for someone who wasn't there and who never had been.

Get a grip, nitwit, she told herself sternly. She had a life she was happy with and no need to worry about the comings and goings of anyone other than herself. She had her job, the novel she hoped to write someday, friends she saw whenever she wanted, and her volunteer time at the animal shelter to keep her busy. And her mother, God bless her, never harped on about grandchildren or her lack thereof. Catherine's life was pretty darn perfect. But if she didn't get going, she'd be late for her appointments at work.

***

ETIENNE BENT DOWN and checked the harness again. Today would be his first foray onto the metro system on his own with only Jake to guide him. He had practiced twice with Tony, the guide dog facilitator, and Etienne was confident he could handle it. He didn't want to, though. He didn't want to deal with any of the damn day-to-day crap he had to deal with. He wanted his sight back, and he wanted to throw off the steely discipline that had him constantly presenting a calm and accepting demeanor to the world around him.

"Yes, of course, I'll be fine," he had repeated endlessly, to whatever question well-meaning helpers had asked him. "*Oui, Maman. Tout va bien,*" he told his mother each afternoon when she called from Brittany to say good night.

But he wasn't fine. He was angry and impatient with the crazy turn of events his life had taken. When the first explosion had reverberated amongst the crowds of tourists visiting the Great Pyramid, he had quickly focused his camera on the chaos. But the second explosion had gone off somewhere behind him, and he had been thrown several feet and felt a sharp blast of pain that seemed to split his skull. No wonder. It *had* split his skull.

He had come to a few minutes, or perhaps a few hours later, clutching his head and hearing the shouting and sirens but unable to see anything. He had stayed crouched, hoping not to get stepped on or run over, until someone had grasped him by the shoulders and said in thickly accented English: "You must come with me, Mister. You need to move."

His memories from the hospital were a swirling mix of sounds and smells. Women wailing, people shouting in Arabic, English, and German about their injuries, and others, probably hospital employees, yelling out instructions. "Are you British?" someone had asked him, and he had whispered, "No. American."

The excruciating pain in his head had swept over him in waves, and he vomited to the side of the chair he had somehow landed in, hoping through the fog of agony that he was not hitting anyone. After that, he remembered very little. Movement, pain, voices, some he could understand and some he couldn't. A sensation of being carried, the sharp smell of alcohol, a needle in his arm, and more noise.

When he finally heard a voice he recognized, saying his name, he had struggled to sit up.

"You're awake. Oh, thank God. Stop trying to move. I'll put the bed up."

Etienne turned his head toward his boss' voice. David normally worked in the D.C. offices of *GeoMonde*. Was he back in the States?

"David. Where am I? What happened?"

"You're home. Well, you're in Bethesda. We got you on an emergency medevac as quickly as we could. You took a piece of shrapnel directly in the head."

Etienne could swear his eyes were open, but he couldn't see anything. He reached up and touched his face. He could feel his eyes, and nothing was covering them. He reached higher and felt bandages around his head.

"I can't see, David. Am I blind?"

There was silence for a moment.

"Well, yes. At least for now. They keep telling me they're not permitted to release medical information, but since I'm the one who got you here, they're sort of playing it both ways. Officially telling me they can't tell me anything and then quietly slipping me little bits of information. How bad are you feeling?"

"I actually don't feel anything right now. My head feels a bit heavy, and I'm thirsty, but that's all."

"Here, drink some water."

Looking back, Etienne grimaced at that first introduction to his awkward, new reality. He had reached out while David was trying to bring a cup to his lips, and their hands had collided, spilling water onto his chest. David apologized and both men clumsily tried to hold the cup while David mumbled about getting something to soak up the water.

"Don't worry. It's nothing," Etienne had said. "Tell me, please. What are they saying?"

"I'm sorry, Etienne. It seems a very small piece of shrapnel – a fragment, they keep calling it -- penetrated your left temple and lodged directly inside your brain. From what a nurse told me yesterday, one or two of the doctors said surgery might be possible, but some big shot neurologist says it would be too risky. As I said, no one will speak to me officially since I'm not next of kin. But your mother says they've said the same to her."

"Oh God, my mother? Is she here?"

"Yes, of course she is. I called her myself as soon as I heard. She's been at the hospital since yesterday. She'll probably be back any moment. I think she just went down to get more coffee."

THAT HAD BEEN six weeks ago. Etienne had finally managed to convince his mother to fly back home to France, and David had helped him settle into his condo in Arlington. Etienne refused the urgings of his "case workers" who wanted him to move into a more accessible apartment, but he had grudgingly accepted the company of Jake. Everyone kept repeating how serendipitous Jake was: he had been flown east to work with a teenager, also in Arlington, but something hadn't worked out, and *voila!* Etienne had skipped the long waiting list for a service dog.

He couldn't help but wonder if part of the something was Jake's rather . . . free spirited nature. He was a Golden Retriever, a light one they told him, and so far he had behaved well whenever the harness was on. Somehow, though, whenever Etienne removed the harness (and yes, the facilitators had recommended keeping the harness on at all times), Jake seemed to revert instantly to a normal, playful puppy who thought nothing of the "off the bed" command Etienne half-heartedly gave him every evening.

Today they were heading into the *GeoMonde* office, where Etienne would discuss his future with the magazine's HR department. But first he had an appointment with a recommended neurologist at Washington General. One of the residents at Bethesda had served in the military and believed it might be possible to restore Etienne's sight, but the chief neurologist had suggested that the risks were too great. Etienne hoped Dr. Abrams would prove to be the fearless sort and settle the question. From what he had found on the Internet, she had trained in the military and had an excellent reputation.

He left his apartment at 9:30, hoping the bulk of rush-hour traffic was finished for the morning. He and Jake walked the seven blocks to the metro and Jake brought him to the handicapped seat once the train came. It sounded like the train had a fair number of people on it, but he didn't have to push through a throng to get to his seat. He wondered how many people were staring at him and shuddered. Better to think as little as possible. He needed all his attention focused on just carrying on.

CATHERINE JUMPED into the metro car just as the doors started to close. She looked around for a seat. The only spot empty was the seat perpendicular and adjacent to the handicapped spot, currently occupied by a blind man and his dog. She thought about standing, but she was tired; between sleeping poorly and the long run she had taken last night, she really just wanted to sit for a few minutes before she had to switch trains and then walk the several blocks from the Dupont Circle station.

Gingerly she sat on the edge of the seat and looked down at the guide dog. It was a beautiful Golden Retriever. Their eyes met and the dog's tail started thumping. Catherine laughed, and the dog's tail thumped more quickly. She saw the man reach down and touch the dog's head.

"What's up, Jake?" he asked quietly.

"I'm sorry. I seem to have disturbed him," Catherine said. "I thought they weren't supposed to pay attention to other people."

"They're not," Etienne responded dryly. "But Jake here seems to have skipped that chapter in the manual. I think he skipped a lot of them, in fact."

"May I pet him?"

"I'm pretty sure I'm supposed to say 'no' to that, but as you can probably tell, I wasn't able to read much of the manual myself. So go ahead."

She reached down and patted the Golden behind his ears, and the dog stretched out his neck as if begging for more.

Catherine laughed again. "I'm not sure he takes his work seriously," she said.

"Yes, well, we're both still adjusting to our new roles in life," he answered and turned his head away slightly.

Catherine stared at the man. He was blind, right? So she could get away with what was probably impolite curiosity. His hair was very short, as if he were growing out a crew cut, but his features were handsome – a strong jaw and neck and a sensitive mouth. He wore large dark glasses, so his eyes weren't visible, and had on a nondescript jacket over a pair of jeans. Poor guy. He looked kind of lonely sitting there with his fist clenched tightly on the dog's harness. And his words had made it sound like the whole guide-dog thing was new to him.

She patted the dog one last time and then pulled out her reader and tried to focus on her story. When the metro stopped at Foggy Bottom, the man touched the dog, and the two made their way to the doors and left.

———

ETIENNE HAD PURPOSELY TURNED AWAY from the woman on the train, not wanting to encourage any further conversation. He hated knowing that people were staring at him, no doubt with pity and curiosity in their eyes. He didn't want to think of himself as a blind man. He was a photographer, a wanderer – never wanting to stay too long in any one place. He had never even bothered to fully furnish his condo in Arlington. Hell, he had thought often in the past of selling it, but inertia and the convenience of not having to use a hotel had kept him from putting it on the market. And of course, the prime reason for keeping it had been to house his books and his piano – a lot of good they were to him now.

He wondered morosely if he would ever seek out female companionship again. His mother had been dropping unsubtle hints for years about her desire for a daughter-in-law and grandchildren, but he had always laughed and told her he was having too much fun to settle down. "Soon enough, *Maman*," he always said.

After his one and only semi-serious girlfriend had broken up with him via email during his first extended trip, he had kept his commitments to a minimum. His mother's dinner parties when he visited her in Brittany often seemed to include old family friends with young daughters. It was astonishing that these "old" friends were often strangers to him, and he laughingly chided his mother that her attempts at manipulation were far too transparent.

"Besides, *Maman*, you know I'm more American than French. But even American women have no patience for the life I lead. A mademoiselle from St. Brieuc would certainly grow tired of my lifestyle *très vite*."

"You could always change your lifestyle, then," she would say softly. "Think how nice it would be to have a true home and love of your own and little ones to grow old with. You're too alone, Etienne, *mon coeur*."

"We have lots of time, *Maman*," he would answer. He didn't bother reminding her that he hoped to never settle down. He had mentioned it before and she had gone on and on about love being the only thing that mattered. She and his dad had loved each other, but she had now spent over ten years as a lonely widow. Life was better unencumbered, and he had embraced traveling the world without attachments.

Now it looked like the joke had been on him. What woman in the world would want an unemployable, blind photographer anyway? Thank God he had never been so stupid as to tie someone to him.

DR. ABRAMS SPENT a few minutes examining Etienne physically, shining a light in his eyes (or so Etienne assumed when he felt the doctor's fingertips spreading his eyes) and checking his reflexes and balance. Jake had obediently remained still, lying quietly when Etienne commanded and moving with him into the doctor's office after the exam.

"The way I look at it, were we to do surgery, you'd have a small chance of regaining your sight," Dr. Abrams said. "Unfortunately, the flip side of that small chance could leave you considerably worse off than you are now. It's pretty close to a miracle that you survived as well as you did. I've looked at all your records. The fragment that went through your skull lodged directly on your optic chiasm. If the doctors hadn't acted quickly to reduce the pressure and swelling, you would never have lived to discuss further surgery. Going that far into the brain is risky – extremely risky. There's no guarantee you would come out of it with either your sight or the brain functions you have now." Her voice was kind but direct.

Etienne chewed on his lip for a moment. "What brain functions are you saying I could lose?"

"Almost anything is possible. We've learned enormous amounts about the brain in the past few years, but some of its intricacies still perplex us. Deep brain surgery, no matter how carefully done, still sometimes results in paralysis, memory loss, or vast decreases in mental capacities. And while we do our best to avoid it, patients die on the table far more often than we would like."

"So you're saying I could end up dead, or else paralyzed, stupid, and still blind?"

"I suppose that's a direct way of putting it, yes. Although stupid is certainly not the word I'd ever choose. But diminished mental capacity is a real possibility," the doctor answered.

"Would you have it done?" Etienne asked.

"I don't know. You've been sightless for only . . . what, two months? It's easy to see how you're still reluctant to accept it. The fact is, millions of visually-impaired people lead full and satisfying lives."

"Not many photographers."

"Well, no, obviously, photography would not be the career of choice for adjusting to your new needs. But certainly, there are other lines of work you could pursue."

"How soon could you do the surgery?" he asked.

The room stayed quiet for a few moments.

"Mr. Seton, I understand your frustration, but what you're considering is enormously risky. I'd advise you to spend a few months adjusting to your current situation. See how it goes. Talk to your family. Are you married? Do you have any children?"

"No," Etienne answered. "I'm free and unattached. Free to travel the world and work where I want in my chosen profession, except now I'm not."

"Well," the doctor answered, "I'm not prepared to schedule anything just yet. You still strike me as a young, healthy man, with a well-functioning brain. Give it a few months. Have you been doing the occupational therapy that was prescribed?"

She waited, and when Etienne said nothing, she continued. "I'd advise you to do so. Come back to see me in the new year if you want to explore this further. We'll do more scans and see if anything's shifted on its own. Do I have your contact information?"

When Etienne nodded, Dr. Abrams added, "I'll send you an audio link with contact information for an organization I know that does great work with the vision impaired. I see you've got a dog already. How is that working out?"

Etienne laughed. "Jake's the best friend I've got right now. I'm pretty sure they were ready to flunk him out of the program, which is why he was available so quickly. But we're doing fine together."

"That's great," Dr. Abrams said. "Call the numbers I send you. I'm sure you'll come to understand that there are more options out there than you think."

———

ETIENNE LEFT the hospital and waited for his ride on the far side of 23rd St. When his phone signaled its arrival, he reached out to find the door handle.

"Your dog's not going to make a mess, is he?" the driver asked.

"Not at all," Etienne promised, hoping it was true. He verified the address of the *GeoMonde* headquarters and leaned back against the seat, trying to get his frustration and anger under control. That the doctor thought he should *adjust* instead of immediately pursuing the only path that would restore his life, was beyond comprehension.

Half an hour later he entered the building, yet again exhausted from what should have been the easiest of endeavors. The driver's words had reminded him that Jake was probably due for some relief of his own, as they had curtailed their walk outside that morning to make his appointment on time. When they exited the car, Etienne had tried from memory to move down the street from the office to a slightly less congested spot. He gave the commands the facilitator had taught him, and as taught, Jake did his business right where Etienne could find it. Now that he had his bag, though, he was uncertain what to do with it. It was a beautiful October morning, and the downtown streets were full of people as the noon hour approached. Feeling like an absolute fool, he tried to make his way back to where he hoped the entrance was.

"Do you need help?" A man's voice spoke to Etienne's right.

"Thank you," Etienne answered. "I'm trying to get to the entrance of 4800, but I need to find a trash can first."

"You're right in front of the building," the man answered. "Just continue on about three steps and then turn to your left, and you'll be there. And let me take that bag."

Feeling highly embarrassed, Etienne held out his left hand with the bag and felt it taken from him.

"Thank you," he said. "That's very kind of you."

"No problem at all," the man answered. "I've got a dog of my own at home."

Etienne and Jake entered the lobby, and the noise of the

street was replaced by the murmur of videos playing on the monitors around the lobby. Once in the elevator, he grimaced at the now commonplace opportunity to use Braille. He had resisted when they first introduced the skill, but the rehab staff had insisted he at least master numbers, and so he now was able to identify elevator buttons with relative ease. *Wasn't he a genius?*His preference would have been to go straight to David's office, his usual destination when he was in town, but he had an appointment today with HR, and he mentally braced himself.

The elevator stopped, and Etienne felt a moment of panic. He was confident that he had pushed the right button, but what floor had they stopped at? He felt someone brush against him, and bizarrely, Jake's tale started thumping against the elevator floor. He heard and felt the sound of laughter by his shoulder and then a voice came from close to the ground as a woman spoke from down near Jake. "Fancy meeting you again, Beautiful."

It was the woman from the metro. Etienne recognized her quiet but clear voice and a whiff of an evocative scent: a light musk with just the slightest touch of citrus that seemed to have unknowingly registered with him earlier.

He wasn't sure what to do or say, but as the unexpected seemed his new norm, he forced himself to pretend civility.

"Hello again. My dog seems to think you're a new friend."

"That's good. We all need friends, right?" Her voice still seemed to be coming from down near Jake's level. "What's his name?"

"Jake."

"Well, Jake. What brings you here? I saw you get off the train at Foggy Bottom."

"I'm sorry, but could you tell me what floor we're at?" Etienne asked quickly as the doors opened again.

"Fifth. I'm getting off here."

"We are, too," Etienne said as he signaled Jake to move.

"Do you work here?" she asked, sounding surprised.

Etienne stepped into the lobby of the fifth floor and hesitated.

"I guess you'd have to say I used to work here. I'm here to speak with the HR department about . . . uh . . . about not working here, at least for the time being."

"Oh. That doesn't sound like fun," she said quietly. "Mrs. Jenkins, the office manager, is just a few steps ahead on the left. Take care."

Through the leash Etienne again felt the vibration of Jake's thumping tale and assumed the woman had bent yet again towards the dog. The thumping stopped and he guessed she had moved off.

FORTY-FIVE MINUTES later Etienne knocked against the wall by David's open door.

"Etienne! How did it go?"

He heard David's voice getting closer and then felt his friend and former boss touch his shoulder.

"Come in and sit down."

"Hey, David," he said, sinking gratefully into a chair. "I guess all things considered, it went well. Personnel said that my health insurance will continue until the end of the year, and in theory, I'll be able to get COBRA coverage for 18 months after that. Apparently, I was one of only about five people on staff getting benefits without a set salary, but since I've completed so many assignments in the past eight years, Jo Anne said I'd accrued leave and would continue to get paid through the end of the calendar year. Plus, because I was hurt on the job, insurance will be sending me a generous settlement, so at least I won't have to worry about funds for a while. If I get my sight back and want to work again, she said all I had to do was call. I think I owe you, David. I sense you had a hand in keeping their attitude so generous. Of course, she told me that I was eligible for Social Security disability and some form of Medicare, as well, but frankly, I'm not ready to sign up for pity payments yet, especially since I don't need them, financially."

"They wouldn't be pity payments, Etienne. Catastrophic events are why the system exists."

"Yeah, well. I'm not ready to go there yet. Even thinking about it gives me a headache."

"How are your headaches?" David asked. "Have they gotten any better?"

"They're not so bad," Etienne answered, and David seemed to get the hint and let the subject drop.

"How about I close up here for today and we get some lunch, and then I'll give you a lift home? My car's in the parking garage downstairs."

"You drive in?" Etienne asked in surprise.

"Not normally, no, but Susan wanted me to pick up Danny from play rehearsal on my way home. I'll play hooky and hang out with you for a little while and then go and get him."

"What play is he in?" Etienne asked.

"*Music Man*. You want to come? The show's next week and we're supposed to be doing the good parent thing and encouraging friends and family to buy tickets."

"Thanks, but I think I'll skip this one," Etienne answered. The idea of attending a high school musical would have filled him with mild horror under normal circumstances, but now the idea seemed preposterous.

"You're welcome to come if you change your mind," David said. "It would probably be good to get out and try new things."

"Thanks, David. Right now, every day is a try-new-things-day. But I think theater outings can wait a bit."

David shut down his computer and stepped out to tell someone he was leaving early. They entered the elevator to go down to the garage, and absurdly, Jake's tale started thumping again.

"Hey, Catherine," David said. "What brings you into the office today?"

"Oh hello, David. I had to come and pick up the new laptop they've been promising me for months, and I spent some time with Jaiya going over the copy for the Bolivia story. Are you friends with my new friend Jake?"

"Who?"

"My dog, David," Etienne said.

"Oh, I didn't know you knew each other," David said.

"We don't," Catherine laughed. "I only know Jake."

"I'm sorry. You've lost me," said David.

"My dog seems to have found his soul mate. They keep meeting up and seem to have become fast friends."

The elevator stopped at what must have been the ground floor, and David said quickly, "Catherine, wait. Don't you live out near Ballston? We're just leaving and I'm driving Etienne home after we get some lunch. Why don't you join us?"

She looked at him quizzically. "You're leaving now? Isn't it pretty early for you?"

"He's pretending fatigue on my account," Etienne interrupted. "I'm not sure he trusts me to make it home on my own."

The elevator was moving again and the silence conveyed their unspoken conversation. *God, how he hated not being able to watch peoples' faces.* But David seemed to sense Etienne's unease and spoke up quickly.

"Etienne lives near Ballston as well. You might as well

keep us company as we're going that way, anyway. But I'm still confused. Do you two know each other or not?"

"Not," they both answered simultaneously as the doors opened onto the parking garage, and they all laughed. Etienne was momentarily shocked at how unfamiliar laughing had become. They stepped out and David turned to them.

"Well, then, introduce yourselves while I go get the car and pull it up. It will be easier that way."

"I'm Etienne Seton," Etienne obeyed, transferring the harness lead to his left hand and holding out his right, mentally scolding himself for forgetting yet again that the leash was supposed to stay in his left hand.

"Oh – you're the photographer who got injured, aren't you? I'm so sorry. I had no idea it was you when I saw you on the metro this morning, or I would have said something. I'm Catherine Reynolds." She reached out and shook Etienne's hand.

"I read a bit about the attack when it happened. It must have been terrible. Were you badly hurt?"

"Given the fact that eleven people died, and I'm here walking and talking, I guess I was one of the lucky ones," Etienne answered quietly.

"But you're blind now. How . . . horrible for you," she finally mumbled. "You've been a photographer for *GeoMonde* for a while, haven't you?"

"On and off for the past several years," Etienne answered. "I started while I was still in school, and I've been more or less full time for about eight years. But that's over now, I guess."

Catherine didn't answer, and Etienne assumed the conversation was making her uncomfortable.

"So, I guess you work here, too?" he asked.

"I'm a copy editor. I work mostly from home, but I had to

come in today to pick up a laptop and meet with a couple people. I've known David ever since I started because his brother was one of my professors. He introduced us right after I graduated and helped me get a job with the magazine."

Etienne heard the car pull up and David's voice. "Do you want the front or the back, Etienne?"

"Jake and I will get in back, if that's okay."

Once they were out of the garage, David spoke to Catherine.

"Etienne lives off of Washington Blvd, but I thought we could stop at the Silver Diner for lunch. Where exactly do you live?"

"Not far from there. I'll just walk home from the diner. I expected to be walking a lot today, anyway, so you're doing me a huge favor as it is."

"Have you lived in the area long, Etienne?" The sound of her voice indicated she had turned part way around from the front seat.

"I've had a home base here for several years. But I've never lived here year-round. You?"

"I grew up in the area, and my grandmother left her house to me when she died a few years ago, so I'm one of the truly lucky ones. Not many people my age can afford a house all for herself."

"Are you and Bob on good terms?" David asked. "Or is that a question I shouldn't be asking?"

Catherine gave a rueful laugh. "Yup. Best buds. Sorry, Etienne. He's talking about the man I lived with for a few years. He came to a lot of work-related events with me, so David, like everyone else, probably assumed we were a long-term thing. But he . . . uh, well, we split up recently so that he could be with one of our best friends. One of our male best friends."

The car fell silent except for Jake's quiet panting.

41

"Ouch," Etienne said uncertainly. "That must be pretty uncomfortable."

"Yeah, well, what's done is done. Does Jake like riding in a car?"

"I have no idea. I guess he's doing okay, right?" He rubbed his hand along Jake's side and the dog turned his head and licked him.

"He really is a beautiful dog," Catherine said.

The car grew quiet again and Etienne took off his dark glasses and leaned back to rest his head against the back seat.

CATHERINE WATCHED Etienne silently from the front of the car. The man looked exhausted, even more so with the pale skin around his eyes revealed. She couldn't begin to imagine the upheaval his life had undergone. She had never met him before, but she had been aware of his work in the magazine for years. He had traveled all over the world, photographing natural and man-made wonders, yet his work almost always showed a human perspective.

Even his pictures taken just before the explosions had captured the wildly divergent groups of people gathered by the Great Pyramid on a normal summer morning. The assignment had coincided with the newest thermal scans being conducted by the Paris based Heritage Innovation Preservation Institute, and it made sense that *GeoMonde* had sent Etienne. But his pictures had, as always, spoken more of humanity than of current events, science, or history. The picture she remembered best from the recent files had been of what looked like a poor Egyptian youth, smiling as he held a cell-phone up to photograph a group of blond, well-fed tourists posing near the base of the pyramid.

Etienne had somehow managed to capture it all: the

magnificence of the pyramid, the welcoming enthusiasm of the local entrepreneur, and the wonder in the faces of the visitors. Catherine tried to imagine briefly what had happened to them. Somehow the memory stick in Etienne's camera had survived the blast unscathed, but who knew what might have become of the smiling Egyptian boy or the eager tourists.

And now that magnificent photographer was blind, forced to rely on a gorgeous but somewhat silly dog to get around. Obviously being jilted for a boyfriend's best friend was lightyears down the list of bad things that could happen in life.

"How's the Bolivia story coming?" David asked, and Catherine saw Etienne lift his head and put his glasses back in place. She turned her head back as she answered.

"Fine. Jaiya's got it all blocked out beautifully, and they're just waiting on the clarification from the photographer on one of the captions."

"Was that Andrew's piece?" Etienne asked.

"Yes," Catherine answered, startled. "Do you two know each other?"

"Of course. Andrew and I have fought over assignments for years. I thought about challenging him for the Bolivia piece, but then Cairo came up, and they called me immediately."

"I guess that was an unfortunate roll of the dice," David muttered. "But for what it's worth, the pictures you got were terrific."

Etienne said nothing, but Catherine saw him take a deep breath and let it out slowly.

"Which diner did you say we're going to?" she asked.

"The one on Wilson. That sound good to you both?"

"Sure," Etienne said from the back, and Catherine nodded as David shot her a quick glance.

43

THE YOUNG MAN with the menus started to say something when he saw the dog, but Catherine caught his eye and shook her head vigorously while pointing to the harness. He nodded and then went to speak with someone behind the counter before returning to ask if they were only three.

The meal passed pleasantly, but Catherine noticed that both she and David worked hard at maintaining a constant flow of conversation while surreptitiously watching Etienne's every movement. Finding herself staring as he lifted a burger towards his mouth, Catherine was surprised to feel a sense of both shame and sorrow, but she couldn't look away. He was blind, but he seemed somehow to be even more detached from their company than that horrible fact alone might entail; he seemed to have a wall around himself that she wasn't sure was offensive or defensive in nature.

She worked for an international travel magazine, yet paradoxically, she usually paid little attention to politics, international or domestic. Now she was having lunch with a colleague whose life had been irrevocably changed by politically charged events completely beyond his control. His entire livelihood had been thrown off course, so she supposed learning to get food into his mouth successfully was one of his less pressing concerns.

As she watched him eat, she felt the oddest sense of wanting to protect him. She kept up a cheerful conversation with David about office politics and tried to shake off the weird feeling. She had never met him before and would likely never meet him again.

They returned to the car, and David looked at her uncertainly. "You said you wanted to walk, but it's no trouble driving you the rest of the way."

"Why don't I just get out at Etienne's?" Catherine heard

herself say. "That way I'll know where he lives, so maybe I can drop by sometime and play with my new friend. Would that be okay with you and Jake?" she asked, turning towards Etienne as they stood in the parking lot.

The dog's tail started again at the mention of his name, and he looked adoringly up at her.

"I guess you've got your answer," Etienne answered ruefully.

When they pulled up in front of the high rise, David looked towards Etienne in the rearview mirror. "Would you like me to come up? Is there anything I can help with?"

"Thanks, David. Everything's working out fine, really. Go get Danny and enjoy an afternoon at home for a change."

"Thanks for the ride, David," Catherine echoed as she got out of the front seat. "I'll see you when I come in next week."

David pulled out of the circular drive in front of the building, and Catherine looked up and around.

"This is a pretty nice place. I've always wondered what the units look like."

"You're welcome to come in and look around if you'd like. Do you live far from here?"

"Not at all. My house is probably less than half a mile away. You have to cross Glebe, walk east a few blocks, turn right, and then I'm about another block in. Sounds like the perfect distance for a dog walk."

What in the world was she going on about? He would think her crazy, and he wouldn't be far off the mark. She barely knew this man, but here she was, attempting to prolong their time together.

"I'm pretty sure Jake would be happy to learn the route," Etienne answered, laughing, and Catherine exhaled, realizing belatedly that she had been holding her breath. He hadn't seemed taken aback by her words and didn't think she was some deranged stalker.

"But you're welcome to come up if you'd like. I'm just going to take off my jacket and then leave again to take Jake out."

"Okay—you show me your place, and then I'll show you both how to get to my house." Her mouth seemed to have a will totally of its own, since this was *not* how she normally behaved with strangers.

They walked in and Etienne and the dog moved unhesitatingly towards the elevator. He pushed the button for the 8th floor.

"You and David seem to know each other well," she commented as the doors closed.

"We've been friends for years. And he probably saved my life after the accident, literally and figuratively. He had me medevaced out of Egypt in hours, flew my mother over, and then did all the hard work necessary for me to return to some semblance of independent life."

"Was your mother in Egypt, too?"

"No. She lives in Europe."

Jake turned eagerly to the left as soon as the doors opened.

"I guess he knows his way," Catherine laughed as the dog almost pulled Etienne the several steps to the door of 811.

Etienne fitted the key without a problem and stood back politely for her to precede him in. She did so, moving quickly to the side so that Etienne and Jake could enter and close the door. The entrance led immediately into a kitchen area on the left with a living room beyond and two open doors on the right—the first into a small bathroom, and the second into what looked like a spacious bedroom. The windows at the back end of the living room opened onto a narrow balcony and offered a magnificent view that included the top of the Washington Monument far in the distance.

"This is so beautiful," Catherine exclaimed, moving toward the windows.

"Yeah, that was one of the selling points when I bought it. Kind of wasted now, though."

She turned her head swiftly to look at him, but his face remained expressionless, dark glasses firmly in place.

"You said in the car that you'd been based here for a while, right?"

"I bought this condo about four years ago during a small break in the crazy housing market. I figured it was a good investment and close enough to the metro that it would always be easy to sell. And as you noticed, it does have a nice view. Before I left in July, the early morning sun in here was spectacular."

"But you're here by yourself, now?" Catherine hoped her voice sounded neutral. The thought of him here alone in this optimal location was somehow heartbreaking. Alone and blind. She found herself staring at him intently, wanting desperately for him to reassure her that he wasn't alone and yet, bizarrely, dreading it at the same time.

"When I got out of the hospital, David moved furniture, helped get all the vision impaired equipment in place, and installed apps on my laptop and phone that make surviving possible. He even helped keep my mother under control and convinced her I really could manage without her constant attendance. I think moving in the deep freezer she insisted on buying to keep all the meals she cooked for me was what finally persuaded her she could leave."

She had been quietly looking around while he spoke, taking note of the numerous bookshelves lining the walls and the upright piano pushed into the corner by the window.

"You play the piano?"

"I *played* the piano. I was never very good, and I rarely played without music, which means I don't play at all, now."

His face showed no change, and Catherine marveled at his apparent lack of emotion. His walls were good.

"Do you miss it?" she asked quietly.

"It's not an option at the moment, so it's not something I bother thinking about."

"Huh," was all she managed to utter ineloquently. "Well, I should probably head home. Would you still like to walk with me and see where I live? I mean, know where I live? I'm sorry, of course you can't see. That was dumb of me."

She cursed herself for her inane babbling. "Do stupid mistakes like that bother you?"

"No, of course not. I use the word all the time myself without thinking about it."

Etienne had taken his jacket off while they were talking and put it carefully on the back of a chair at the small table.

"Give me just a minute and we'll walk with you. It's warmer than it was this morning, and Jake and I can certainly use the exercise."

Etienne walked slowly but unhesitatingly into the bedroom and closed the door behind him. Jake sat patiently by the door, evidently knowing that he would be leaving again soon. Catherine moved closer to the bookshelves and scanned the spines. The titles were mixed: a lot of history, both American and international, several classics, and a nice assortment of popular and suspense titles. He obviously had enjoyed reading. And of course, several exquisite, framed photographs hung on the walls above the books.

Life was bizarre. Here she was, alone in the home of an attractive, talented, and intelligent single man, who played the piano and appreciated books. Maggie, her one really close remaining friend from high school, would be bouncing up and down with excitement, urging her to jump him. Too bad he seemed so reserved and impersonal. Something about him, though, seemed oddly familiar.

She'd probably seen his picture next to his photo credits at one time or another. She shook her head and then turned away from the shelves when the bedroom door opened.

"If you'd ever like me to read to you, I'd be happy to," she heard herself say without thinking. "It must be annoying to have so many books and not be able to read them." *God in heaven but her mouth was out of control today!*

"It is, a bit. But I'm really lucky that there are so many audio books available. They help pass the time. Should we go?"

Again, he seemed unconcerned, but Catherine noticed that he hadn't responded directly to her offer. She hoped he didn't think she was one of those women with a fetish for blind people, assuming there were such creatures. But given her uncharacteristic behavior, she fervently hoped she wasn't, in fact, turning out to be such a deviant.

They took the elevator back down and walked out of the building, down the path, and along the sidewalk to the busy intersection at the corner. Catherine walked beside Etienne but hesitated to offer her arm or even suggest doing so. Jake walked confidently a step ahead and to Etienne's left and stopped expectantly at the corner.

"We'll cross Glebe here and then continue a couple blocks on this side before turning right," she said into the silence. He had seemed friendlier somehow before they had gone up to his place. Maybe all her babbling had, in fact, bothered him.

"I'll keep track of the blocks as we walk," he answered.

Traffic hadn't reached rush hour craziness yet, so they crossed easily.

"Do you and Jake ride the metro often?" Catherine asked, searching for a neutral topic.

"Not at all. In fact, today was our first major outing alone.

Jake's only been with me for two weeks, so everything is still pretty new to us."

"Have you owned dogs before?"

"There was one when I was little. We moved around a lot when I was young, so it made keeping a dog difficult. We had cats, or cats had us – I'm not sure they would have appreciated being referred to as possessions."

So, he had at least some sense of humor, she thought as they came to her street. "We turn right here," she said, "and then my house is about half-way down on the left."

"On the other side of the street?"

"Oh yes, sorry. I guess it's best to cross now. I didn't think. My ex-boyfriend always used to yell at me for jaywalking."

"You're kidding, right? Jaywalking? Is that really still a thing?"

"Well, he thought so. Here's my walkway."

She moved ahead of him. "There are three steps up with a railing on both sides."

"We don't need to come in. I really should let you get on with your day." Etienne spoke calmly and quietly, but Jake sat looking up at her with bright eyes and his tail wagging back and forth on the top step.

"Why don't you come in for a cup of tea? Or a beer? I could certainly use one, and it looks like Jake would like to make himself at home." *Wait, damn. Would that make it sound like she needed a beer?*

Etienne hesitated a minute and then nodded. "Okay, thanks. A cup of tea would be nice."

Catherine opened the door and moved in, looking around to make sure there were no obstacles on the floor. "Just walk straight ahead. We're walking through the living room into the kitchen and there's a table with chairs to your right. Make yourself comfortable."

Etienne sat down and Jake sat at his side, but his head turned as he watched Catherine walk into the kitchen.

"Is tea really all right, or would you rather have a beer?"

"Tea's fine, if that's what you're going to have."

"Is Jake allowed off the harness?" Catherine asked, amused at the dog's keen interest in her movements.

"I think officially I'm supposed to say 'no,' but it's your house. It's okay with me if you don't mind."

"Let him off, then. He's been so good."

Etienne bent to unstrap Jake, and the dog exuberantly bounded over to Catherine. He jumped up with his paws on her chest and she burst out laughing while rubbing his head and trying to avoid his wet nose. Then he turned and took off, smelling his way around the kitchen and living room.

"Oh God, is he going to destroy the place?" Etienne asked, tilting his head towards Jake's noises.

"Of course not. I love dogs."

"I gathered that. Why don't you have one of your own?"

"Bob wanted to wait until we were more settled. I'm not sure what that was supposed to mean, but I went along with it."

"It sounds like he had a lot of issues."

"Yeah, I suppose in retrospect, he did."

Catherine carried in the cups. "Milk? Sugar?"

"Just as it is, is fine. But you grew up with dogs?"

"Oh yes. In fact, I really can't believe I've survived so long without one of my own. I spend time at the animal shelter and try hard not to fall in love with any of them. When I was little, my mom used to take me and the dogs together to the park to burn off energy. Hey—why don't we take Jake to a dog park? There's a really nice one by a creek less than ten minutes from here. I bet he'd love it." *God almighty, could there have been some drug in the food she'd had at lunchtime?* She never acted like this, even with friends.

Etienne sat quietly, his hands resting on the table, the teacup held loosely between them.

"I'm sorry," she said quickly. "Am I getting carried away?"

Etienne's face was impassive, but she was sure she had seen . . .what? a grimace? pass quickly over his features. He probably thought she was a raging lunatic. She reached out her hand and touched his shoulder.

Etienne sat perfectly still. Catherine stared at his face, hating the fact that she couldn't read his thoughts. Why was she letting him get to her like this? Why was she touching him?

Finally he answered. "Thank you. That sounds like fun. But not today. I have some research I have to do from my appointment this morning, and we've already taken up far too much of your time."

"Let's do it tomorrow, then. This wonderful weather won't last much longer, and I know Jake would like it." *What was she doing? Had she lost her mind entirely?*

"You're not busy tomorrow?"

"I work from home most days, so I can set my own schedule. Why don't I pick you up about 10? That way I can get a run in and get a little work done, and after that I'll be more than ready to drop everything and play."

"You run?" he asked, and Catherine was sure she heard a wistful note in his question.

"Not well. And definitely not fast. But I do it to stay in shape and blow off steam. Do you—I mean, did you run? You probably still could, you know. I ran a half-marathon last year, and there was a blind woman running with someone alongside her. I thought it was great she was brave enough to be out there. If it's something you enjoy, you should go for it." *Shit. She was again babbling on like an idiot.*

Etienne laughed.

"Somehow I don't see myself running a race with Jake by

my side. I think I'll stick to the treadmill in my building if I feel the urge."

"Well, if you change your mind, I'm willing to give it a try. You're probably a lot faster than I am anyway, so being blind might cut down on your advantage." She gasped. "Oh God. That was a horrible thing to say."

Etienne laughed again. "Don't worry about it. Let's give the dog park a try before we sign up for a marathon, shall we? Ten tomorrow morning would be fine."

As HE AND Jake walked the several blocks home, Etienne realized his whole face felt different. Today had been the first time he had smiled, let alone laughed, in more than two months.

Catherine was a bit like a shaken bottle of soda—words seemed to just bubble out of her. He hadn't thought seriously of running since the explosion. During the few weeks he had been back in the condo, he had taken to forcing himself through endless push-ups, sit-ups and squats, all in a desperate attempt to make falling asleep at night a little easier.

But listening to her almost made him think things like running might be possible. A sudden desire to run hard and fast swept over him, and he took a deep breath and tried to focus on just walking with Jake. The effort it took to walk confidently when a large part of him still wanted to curl up in a ball and howl was mentally taxing enough.

Later that night he lay awake and wished again for the exhaustion brought about by a long run. There was no difference, now, between night and day. His body was supine, but the world was the same: black and empty. He supposed he would have to bite the bullet and actually attempt to master Braille so that he could read in bed the way he used to. He had embraced e-readers early in their development due to his constant travel, but he had no desire now to lie in bed and listen to a disembodied voice or fall asleep while listening and then have to find his way backwards in a narrative.

Catherine had offered to read to him, he remembered, and he wondered what that would be like. He doubted she had children's bedtime stories in mind, so it would be interesting to learn what kinds of books she enjoyed. His body stirred involuntarily at the idea of her in bed with him. *Idiot*, he thought to himself savagely. A: You're blind. B: You're unemployed and essentially unemployable. C: You have no idea what she looks like or anything about her, really. And then D, of course, which was a given and now more important than ever: don't encourage women in general. Ties bind, and bindings lead to dependence. And he had always somehow known, that deep down, he wasn't the type anyone should grow to depend on.

He should have said no to her offer. Hell, he shouldn't even have walked with her back to her house. His life was in shambles enough as it was. He certainly didn't need to drag anyone else into his darkness.

But she was, somehow, the brightest presence he had encountered since his world went dark. He could still feel the touch of her hand on his shoulder, and here in the desolate bleakness of night, he allowed himself for just a moment to fantasize about burying himself in her—and not just his engorged dick, which seemed suddenly to be demanding recompense for months of inattention. He unaccountably wanted to wrap his arms around her and bury his face in her hair. Her hair, which he had never seen but somehow he *could* see with its golden auburn color and thick luster. He was obviously now going insane on top of everything else.

He had caught the scent of her perfume again as she led him to the door, and now he imagined breathing it in while he nuzzled her neck.

His hand moved to his aching groin, and Jake's collar chimed as he lifted his head and thumped his tail. Etienne gave a groan of frustration and despair. "Go to sleep, boy," he said and rolled over, forcing himself to think about the intricacies of brain surgery he had spent the afternoon trying to absorb. *Fuck, fuck, fuck!*

CHAPTER THREE

"Good afternoon, Mr. Rynick. Might I speak with you for a moment?"

Katrina's father turned from the tankards he had been replacing on the shelf after the mid-day meal. He gave Major Howard a malevolent look and then rearranged his expression to unconvincingly convey polite attention.

"Of course. How may I help you?"

"Mr. Rynick, I need to speak to you about a personal matter."

"Personal?"

"Yes, Sir. Might there be somewhere we could speak in private?"

Katrina had been wiping down the long tables, but she turned to follow the two men as they moved toward the storage room in the back of the tavern.

"Katrina, tend to the crockery," her father instructed with a glare.

Stephen gave her a furtive smile. "Don't worry," he mouthed as he turned to follow her father.

"Don't worry," she muttered to herself as the door closed

behind them. "Dear God, please, please, *please* let my father be reasonable."

Johann turned toward Stephen with a skeptical look on his face. "What would be the nature of this personal matter?"

"Mr. Rynick, Sir, I'd like your permission and blessing to marry your daughter."

Johann's eyes grew enormous and his breath quickened. "Marry my daughter? My Katrina? Mein Gott, my daughter will not marry an English d—" he cut off his words abruptly. "You have no right to even speak to my daughter."

"Please, Sir, hear me. We love each other." Stephen hesitated and then continued. "And Sir, we are going to have a child together."

Johann reached for the back of the door and skewered the British soldier with a look of absolute disdain. "You have dared to dishonor my daughter? It wasn't enough that you and your men have taken over our towns, have occupied our homes, and have tried to control our every action? Now you have defiled my beloved daughter?"

"Please, Sir, I love Katrina. And she loves me. I know it was wrong to anticipate our wedding vows, but I am filled with joy at the prospect of becoming her husband and the father of our child."

"You are an English officer, occupying our land and denying us our rights and privileges. My daughter should be ashamed to tie her fortune to you!"

"Mr. Rynick, we are both subjects of His Majesty, and I am confident that the disagreements between you, here in the colonies, and the crown can be resolved peacefully. But even if they cannot, I love Katrina. I will do everything in my power, today and always, to cherish and protect her."

"And take her away from her family? From her home? You have ruined her! You have disgraced her and destroyed her future!"

"No, Sir, please. We acted precipitously, but we love each other. I will do everything I can to make her happy."

Johann stared at him with disgust. "Be gone for now. I must speak with my wife. And stay away from my daughter!" He pushed out ahead of Stephen and spoke harshly to Katrina. "Girl, go upstairs now and do not come down until your mother or I come to you."

Katrina looked behind him towards Stephen with fear visible on her face. "Go," he mouthed silently. "It will be well. I love you." She saw determination in his eyes and nodded before turning and heading towards the stairs.

KATRINA SAT HUDDLED with her knees drawn up against her chest and rocked back and forth in silent misery. She had never wished to bring pain or shame to her parents, but neither could she regret for even a moment the joy she had come to know in Stephen's arms. They understood each other on such an elemental level. Conversation never flagged between them, whether they were discussing the plant life by the river or the taxes that made even simple commodities like sugar near impossible for the colonists to find or afford.

Stephen listened to her arguments with respect and attention, but his rebuttal was always the same: the colonists must have patience. The crown's resources had been stretched thin by the French and Indian Wars and by the need to keep so many troops posted to the Americas to maintain order.

"If it costs too much to keep soldiers posted here, then let them all leave! We would not miss them, and look at all the money His Majesty could save."

"You would have me leave, then?" he teased, looking down at her upturned face from where she sat cradled on his lap.

They were seated on a small rock formation that rested at the top of a hill about thirty yards from the water's edge.

"Oh no, Stephen, not you. You can stay here and become an American artist, sending paintings of our beautiful land back to the King to make him regret his cruelty and short-sighted laws."

"So my angel has a vindictive streak, does she?" he laughed, kissing her nose. "But no, my love, were the soldiers to be sent back to England, I would have to bundle you up and take you with me to meet the King yourself, so you could explain in detail the extent of his folly."

He had kissed her then, laughing, but their laughter had quickly died as the fire between them had sparked yet again.

Tears dripped quietly down her face as she remembered the giddy happiness of their first physical encounter. That morning on the rocks Stephen's hands had moved to her breasts and her bottom and had held her pressed tightly against his hardness, but it had been she who had reached to undo the laces of his britches. His hand had stilled her fingers, holding her hand trapped as he let out a soft groan, but making an attempt, nonetheless, to still her progress.

"No, my love, We must not. 'Tis not fitting."

But the breeze had been blowing softly from the river and the birds filled the air with the glory of their song.

"I am yours, Stephen," she had said. "I always will be. If you do not want me, I will understand, but I care not for 'fitting.'"

His lips had returned to hers, then, unable to resist. He had been gentle and so magnificently patient, lying back against the rocks to bear the hardness himself, and pulling her ever so slowly down on top of him until he filled her completely, leaning up to kiss away her gasp of pain at the last moment. He had then kept still, gentling her, planting soft kisses all about her face and circling her nipples gently

59

with his fingers until her hips began to move of their own accord. The rough, hurtful sense of impalement faded as a strange urgency began, and her muscles tightened around him. All of a sudden, an unimaginable sensation of pleasure overcame her, and she collapsed against him.

"Stephen!" she cried, and he grasped her buttocks tightly against him, gave a few desperate, hard thrusts, and let out his own groan of pleasure.

Now the tips of her wondrously enlarged breasts were tender as she hugged her knees to her chest and the enormity of what they had done threatened to overwhelm her.

There was a baby growing inside her. A baby that was the result of a passion she had been unable to resist, even while she had put off Stephen's words of a future together. Now that act, which had seemed so beautiful, so natural, and so right, had brought a new life into existence, and the simple inevitability of their love was suddenly a harsh reality that would forever cause a rift between her and her parents.

It must be near an hour since her father had sent her up here. She had expected to hear raised voices or to be summoned down for punishment. But she had not expected silence. As was occurring so frequently of late, she felt an urgent need to relieve herself. She would have to go down and risk increasing her father's anger, but she wasn't going to humiliate herself further by carrying a chamber pot down in the middle of the day.

Going quietly down the narrow stairs, she peeked around the curtain into the kitchen area. Her parents were sitting together at the worn oaken table where the family gathered for their private meals and where her mother, sisters, and the serving girls worked to prepare food for the tavern guests. She was pretty sure she had never in her life seen her parents sitting alone together in daylight, let alone with their hands clasped tightly together. She slipped out the back door, ran quickly to the outhouse, and returned as quietly as she could, hoping to move back up the stairs without disturbing them.

"Katrina." Her father's voice was not raised, but it was definitely a command and not a question.

"Yes, Papa?"

"Come here, daughter."

Katrina's eyes flew to her mother's face. Susanna Rynick gave her daughter a smile and beckoned her into the room, tears still visible on her care-worn cheeks.

"Katrina, you have brought shame to this family," her father said quietly, looking down at his folded hands. "But this Englishman seeks to do the honorable thing, so you will marry him posthaste."

"Oh Father, thank you." The words burst from her lips as a smile swept over her face. "He is a good man, truly."

"A good man." Her father's voice was bitter. "He is no friend to our family or our land. Nor has he treated you with the respect you deserve. But you have bound yourself to him through this immoral act, and once you wed him, you, too, will cease to be one of us."

Her smile faded as she looked in bewilderment from her mother to her father.

"Not be one of you? What do you mean, Papa?"

Her mother rose and moved to take Katrina's hands in hers as her father continued.

"You will always be our beloved daughter, Katrina. We understand that you and the major have already started a family of your own, and therefore you must say good-bye to your childhood as all new brides must do, though for you there is no time. But you must also appreciate that an English officer is not the husband we hoped for you. Your mother tells me that you find Major Howard handsome, and she tells me he behaves kindly to her and others in our community. I also understand that when one is young, one believes love

61

more important than any other consideration. But the work we have chosen to do here in the tavern is important, too. In truth, it is far more important than any foolish romantic notions. The major is not welcome here, as you well know. He must not be privy to what is discussed here, and therefore, as his wife, you, too, must now and forever be outside our confidence, at least until these scurrilous Redcoats are gone from our shores."

Katrina looked back and forth between her parents, a part of her dying from the resolute firmness in their eyes.

"But Stephen is certain the difficulties between the colonies and the crown will soon be resolved."

"Daughter. You have attended meetings and listened to discussions here at the tavern since you were old enough to walk. Do you believe in your heart that these differences will soon be resolved?"

"No, Father." She whispered the words she knew to be true, and she felt tears begin to well again as she looked at the two people who until recently had been the most important people in her world.

Katrina's mother reached for her then and pulled her into a tight embrace.

"You are still my little girl, and now you carry my grand-baby inside of you. So somehow, we must find a way for you to leave this home and yet still know we are your family. It will work out, my child, but it will not be easy. Go and find your major. We will have to speak to the pastor and arrange a wedding. What's done is done."

CHAPTER FOUR

Catherine had spread a sheet across the back seat of her Prius, and she left the car running in front of the entrance while she got out to ring the buzzer.

"Catherine?" came Etienne's voice.

"Yup. I'm here. Do you want me to come up?"

"No thanks. We'll be right down."

Minutes later Etienne and Jake walked out the front door. Standing by the open passenger and rear doors, she watched him walk towards her and was surprised again at how attractive he was and at how natural it seemed to be doing something with him. She didn't spend time with people she barely knew and was pretty much a loner in general. Etienne was tall and slim, with closely cropped light brown hair and a confident stride despite his handicap. His eyes were again covered by a large pair of dark glasses. But the structure of his face around the glasses was strong and arresting: a firm chin and well-defined cheekbones under a clear, medium-toned complexion. She saw evidence of a tiny area of stubble close to his jaw that he had obviously missed while shaving and was struck by how hard the simplest of tasks must be for him.

"Good morning!" she said as he reached the car. "And hello, Sweetheart," she said to Jake as the dog gave an excited but controlled toss of his head at the sight of her. She walked around and helped Etienne guide Jake into the rear seat, reaching out to stroke him behind the ears as she did so.

"You're sure you have time for this?" Etienne asked.

"Are you kidding? I feel like a kid playing hooky from school. I haven't been to the dog park in years. I ran that way this morning to make sure it was still there, and they have it nicely separated from the rest of the park."

"You are a serious runner, then."

"Nope. Just a serious lover of the last good days before winter sets in. I hate the cold and absolutely refuse to run outside in bad weather."

"You're welcome to come here anytime and use my fitness center," Etienne said, and only because Catherine had been watching his face so intently did she notice the lift of his brow and the tightening of his lips, as if he instantly regretted his words.

"Thanks. Maybe I'll take you up on that."

THE DRIVE TOOK ONLY a few minutes, and Catherine seemed to find a parking spot easily.

"We're here already?"

"Yes. I told you it was nearby."

"Huh. I guess there are lots of places around here I never knew about. I never kept a car and usually got around by foot or metro."

"This part of the world is great for dogs. There's so much money around here that they end up just as spoiled as the kids, and from what I hear, doggie daycare is almost as hard to get into as child daycare."

"*Doggie* daycare?"

They had left the car and were walking slowly along what felt like a dirt path. Jake was still walking at his side, but Etienne could feel a slight tension in the lead, and he sensed that the dog was assessing the new possibilities in their surroundings.

"You're kidding, right?"

"Nope. I have one friend who tells me she sometimes pays $200 a week, since they charge extra for overtime."

"Why have a dog if you can't take care of it?"

"So if you had a kid, would you stay home with it full time? Or expect your wife to do so?"

"Hmm. Maybe I should keep my mouth shut. Are there swings and slides for the dogs in this playground?"

"Ha ha. You've really never heard of a dog park before? Here – careful – we have to walk through this gate and over a bridge."

"A bridge?"

"Yes. We're crossing a creek. Or maybe it's a stream. I really have no idea. But the dog park is on the other side, and they can run around off leash and play in the water if they want."

She had grasped his arm as they crossed the bridge and now let go. Suddenly he felt Jake bump into his leg and heard unfamiliar barking close at hand.

"There's another dog trying to get at Jake," Catherine said. "May I let him off the leash?"

"I guess so," he said, wondering exactly what they had gotten into. He felt Catherine bend down and her weight brushed against him as she unhooked Jake.

"He doesn't seem to know whether to go or not," Catherine said, straightening up and hooking her arm through his.

"Well, like everything else, this is all new to both of us. It's okay, Jake, go play. Go, boy."

"Here. Let's move over a bit away from the bridge. Jake's sniffing a black standard poodle that seems friendly."

"How many dogs are here?"

"I see two others closer to the water. One looks like your average-sized tan mutt, and the other one is one of those small furry ones."

"Small and furry. I guess that means not small and spindly or small and hairless."

"Okay, so maybe my descriptive skills could use a little work. It's one of those dogs that looks like it yaps a lot."

He could hear the moving water and the noises of numerous dogs and felt what he assumed was Jake bump into his legs every few minutes. The weather seemed perfect – he could feel warm sunlight on his face and a light breeze against his skin.

"Is he having fun?"

"I think so. But he seems a little unsure of what to do or hesitant to leave you. I'm not sure which."

A sound of high-pitched barking grew suddenly louder.

"It's the little dog coming towards Jake," Catherine said, sounding a bit anxious. "I hate those small dogs. They always think they have something to prove."

Etienne felt a hard nudge against his legs and felt himself pushed off balance, and he instinctively reached out and found what he hoped was Catherine's arm.

"Jake, Jake, it's okay," he heard her say, as Jake's barks and growls joined the mix.

"Oh dear. Maybe this wasn't such a good idea. Jake can't seem to decide whether he needs to defend you or play like a dog."

"Then let's harness him and just walk in the regular section of the park. Come here, Jake. Let's go, boy."

The cacophony grew louder as Jake's barking joined that of the smaller dog and a woman called frantically, "Scooter, come back!"

Catherine had let go of his arm, presumably to fasten Jake's harness, but Etienne now felt animals bumping into his legs from both sides. A mild feeling of panic rose up within him that he did his best to ignore as he struggled to keep his balance.

"I'm sorry, Etienne. I'm having trouble getting at Jake with these other dogs pushing at him. I'll have him in just a sec."

A third dog's bark seemed to have joined the chorus, and Etienne assumed it was the poodle, back for more attention. Suddenly he felt himself falling, caught off balance as something or someone crashed against his midsection. Instinctively he reached to grab onto something and felt what must have been Catherine's hair slip through his hands as he landed hard on top of another body.

"Oh God," he heard her cry out in what was obviously pain.

"Catherine? Are you okay? What's happened?"

"SCOOTER! Come here now!" A voice came from above them. "Oh my. Are you both all right? Scooter, get over here."

Etienne struggled to sit upright and felt for Catherine next to him. She seemed to be taking quick, ragged breaths. "Are you okay?" he asked again. "Where's Jake?"

"Jake's here. I got his harness on just as he reared up to avoid the little dog jumping at him. But the way we landed – my ankle went. It, uh, really hurts."

A string of colorful oaths ran through Etienne's mind, but he somehow kept his tongue. Of all the stupid predicaments he had gotten into over the years, this had to be one of the dumbest. What had they been thinking?

"Put Jake's lead in my right hand, and let me try to get up first."

"Oh dear me. Is there anything I can do?" came Scooter's person's voice. "I know my little one didn't mean any harm, did you, Sweetums?"

"It's okay, ma'am," Catherine said from below. "If you could maybe get Scooter away, then we'll be fine. Thank you."

"Are you sure?"

"Yes. Sure. Thanks." Catherine's voice was tense.

"Here, girl!" came what sounded like an older man's voice. "Oh heavens. Is there anything I can do to help?"

"No, We're fine. Thanks."

"I'm so sorry about all this. Winny and I come here almost every day and usually have the area all to ourselves."

"Don't worry," Catherine answered, and Etienne could only guess that the man and the poodle belonged to each other. "We'll just take Jake and be on our way."

Etienne could hear pain in her voice. He spread his feet a bit wider to make sure he wouldn't tip over and moved Jake's lead to his left hand, holding out his right.

"Kat, here, grasp my arm." He felt her grab onto his fingers with one hand and his forearm with the other and braced himself as he levered her up and then felt her lean against him. He was conscious of her slender form and instinctively inhaled deeply as her fresh scent enveloped him.

"How bad is it?" he asked quietly.

"Pretty bad, I think. I can't seem to put any weight on it."

"Put your arm around my waist and lean into me." Etienne reached awkwardly and tried to find a way to wrap his arm around her without either grabbing on too tightly or making her uncomfortable. She was smaller than he had imagined, and as they tried to take a few steps with him supporting her weight against him, he felt an overwhelming sense of protectiveness sweep over him. They fumbled a few more feet, Jake's lead held clumsily in his left hand until Etienne had had enough.

"This is ridiculous. You're obviously not very big and you're in a lot of pain. Just get on my back and I'll give you a piggyback to the car. Do you think you'll be able to drive?"

"Yes, it's my left foot, thank God. But you can't carry me – I'm far too heavy."

"Yeah – somehow I don't think so. I've spent half my life carrying camera equipment around on my back, which was no small feat before the world went digital, remember? Just move around and climb on." He held on to her as she hopped to get behind him and then bent down to allow her to reach his shoulders.

"Oh God. This is embarrassing," she said as he reached around and behind to grasp her under her buttocks and lift her high onto his back, feeling her legs wrap around his middle.

For just an instant as she settled against him, her scent washed over him once more. He inhaled sharply, and a vision of a pair of laughing brown eyes crossed his imagination.

"You're in luck, then, because I can't see you blush, right? It's all going to be okay, Kat. Tell me which way to go so we can get across that bridge. Then we'll pretend that this never happened and we somehow levitated ourselves to the car."

He adjusted her weight with both hands and felt soft bare skin against his own. He closed his stupid, useless eyes which for some reason insisted on staying open, and inhaled quietly. This whole situation was farcical enough—he couldn't make things worse by making her feel objectified. She must have on shorts or a short skirt. Her legs around him sent a wave of pleasure shooting down his spine, and Etienne steeled himself to get his mind out of the gutter.

"The poor dog," Catherine said. "He must be utterly confused."

"What's he doing?" Etienne asked, more than a bit confused himself.

"He's licking my leg. Maybe he thinks this is all part of some crazy game."

Given where his own thoughts had instinctively strayed, Etienne could only feel sympathy for the besotted canine.

"Crazy is definitely the word of the morning, I'd say. Jake, with me, now. By the way, what color are your eyes?"

"My eyes? They're brown. Why?"

"No reason. I just never gave a piggyback to someone I couldn't pick out of a crowd."

He started to move, glad she couldn't see how chagrined he felt at his inane comment.

Catherine gave him directions as he walked slowly but steadily, Jake now obediently at his side. He held the lead loosely with the fingers of his left hand, keeping his wrist and forearm braced against Catherine's leg. Her knees were pressed tightly against his midriff, but he could tell that the jostling was causing her pain by her occasional small gasps. Her arms had come up and were wrapped around his shoulders and neck. A small and obviously insane part of him wished the car were much further away, but he knew they had to figure out what to do quickly.

When they finally reached the car, he slid her down slowly and carefully, keeping a tight hold on her until he could tell she was balanced against the car. "We're on the driver's side, right?" he asked as she got her keys out of her pocket and unlocked the doors. "I'll put Jake in the back here and walk around."

"Are you sure you're okay to drive?" he asked once they were both seated.

"Yeah. I'm okay. I don't think it would work so well for you to drive with me giving you directions."

"You're probably right," he answered wryly. "But still. We could call 911 and then somehow come back for your car later."

"No, it's okay. I just have to figure out what's the best thing to do."

"Do you have family in the area? Are you on good terms with your ex?" Even as he asked the question, a fierce hope shot through him that she wouldn't call her ex.

"God, no. I'm not calling Bob. What I'm trying to figure out is whether to try to go to a hospital here, or call my mom and have her come get me – although saying it out loud makes me think I'm being ridiculous – of course I'll call my mom. My step-dad's an orthopedic surgeon, so it would be dumb not to call."

"Where do they live?"

"Fair Lakes – about an hour out – less during the day when there's not much traffic."

"So if you're sure you can drive, why don't you call your mom right now, before we leave here, have her come straight to your house, and I'll stay with you until she gets there."

"You don't have to do that. I can just take you back to your place and then get home by myself."

He turned in the seat and reached out until he found her arm and worked his way down to take her hand.

"Don't be silly, Kat. I feel so bad about what's happened. It's all my fault."

"No, no, Etienne, it's not. This was my idea, remember? And seriously, it wasn't one of my better ones."

He could still hear the pain in her voice, but he could hear sincerity and a bit of humor there, as well.

"It's okay, really." She entwined her fingers momentarily with his and squeezed gently. "I'll be fine. But I have to ask you something: why are you calling me Cat? No one's ever called me that before."

"I . . .I have no idea. I didn't even realize I had. I'm sorry – what do most people call you? Are you always Catherine?"

"Usually, yes. I hated it when people tried to call me Cathy when I was little. But Cat's kind of nice."

She slipped her hand from his. "I'm going to call my mom. Let's hope she doesn't go all mother-crazy on us."

He sat waiting patiently as she told her mother briefly that she had gone to a dog park with a friend and been knocked over, and yes, hurt just a little bit.

"I think I probably need to get my foot x-rayed, so I thought maybe Darren would be able to look at it. . . . Yeah, I think it might be . . . yes, I'm at home, and I was hoping you might be able to drive in . . . Thanks, Mom. See you in a little while."

"You're home, huh? Catherine, I'm truly so sorry. I wish I could drive you. Are you sure you don't want me to call a taxi, and we can get the car later?"

"No, I'm fine. Let's go."

He heard her start the car, and they drove quietly for a few minutes.

"Go straight to your house," he reminded her. "Jake and I will get ourselves home after your mom gets there."

When the car finally came to a stop and she turned the engine off, he spoke quickly. "Don't move yet. Am I next to the curb or are we in a garage or driveway?"

"We're in my driveway."

"Okay. You stay put. I'm going to get out and walk around the car until I get to you." Her silence brought home to him how much she must be hurting.

When he reached her side, she had the door open, and he

felt her brush against him as she got out and tried to turn herself around on one leg.

"Do you need anything from the car?"

"Yes. My purse is in the trunk. I just popped the lid. If I could just hold on to you and . . ."

"No. Stay here and lean against the car. I'll find it."

As he walked slowly around towards the back of the car, he heard her start to laugh, and he suddenly found himself smiling, too. "I guess we're like something out of a slapstick comedy at the moment, aren't we?"

"I'm sorry, Etienne. I shouldn't be laughing, and I'm definitely not laughing at you, but this is really right up there as one of the most ridiculous messes I've ever gotten into. And here I've dragged you into it as well, as if you didn't have enough on your plate already."

He felt around until he touched what he assumed was her purse, slipped the strap over his shoulder, reached up and pushed the lid of the trunk down, and made his way carefully back to where Catherine stood. He reached out and made contact with her hair. It felt soft and thick beneath his fingers, and he moved his hand down to the ends, finding curls that went to the top of her shoulders. He reached up again and ran his fingertips lightly over her forehead and then down to her cheekbones.

"Do you mind?" he asked and felt her head move ever so slightly back and forth in reply.

"You have absolutely nothing to apologize for," he said softly. "It was incredibly kind of you to suggest an outing like this for me and Jake. We're the ones who should be apologizing to you." He leaned down and brushed her lips with his own. He meant for it to be a light token of gratitude, but the moment he felt her soft lips under him, a jolt of joy shot through him. Instinctively, he increased the pressure of the kiss and felt her lips part sweetly beneath his. Jake gave a small whine from the back of the car, and Etienne suddenly realized what he was doing. He lifted his head and cradled hers gently against his chest and stroked her hair again.

"I am so sorry about your foot, Catherine." He released his hold on her, moved aside to open the back door, and felt for the lead to Jake's harness. Once he felt the dog was out, he carefully shut the door and then turned and reached again for Catherine.

"Okay, up you go again," he said, squatting slightly to lift her onto his back. "You push the door shut and lock it, then tell me where to walk."

"Etienne, it's okay. I can walk if you put me down."

"Just tell me where to go." They moved slowly around the car and towards the entrance, and she let him know when they were at the steps.

"Three, right?" he asked.

"Etienne, let me down. I'm too heavy!"

"You hardly weigh anything," he said truthfully as he grasped the rail with his left hand and felt her move her injured foot further around his front to avoid bumping it. "Can you reach the lock or do you want me to try?"

"I've got it." Her hair brushed against his face as she leaned around him to work the lock, and he felt the strangest sense of warmth pass up his torso. She pushed the door open, and Jake moved in ahead of them. Etienne dropped the lead and turned so that Catherine could push the door shut.

"Okay. Where to?" he asked.

"Here's fine. I'm going to hop to the bathroom and then sit on the couch."

He let her down gently and heard her move a few steps and then close a door.

Not that I'd be able to see anything, anyway, he thought grimly to himself. He moved gingerly forward, finding the table and chair he had sat in yesterday, then called Jake and unhooked the lead from the harness. He stood and waited until he heard the bathroom door open.

"The kitchen's over here to the right, isn't it? You tell me where to go, and I'm going to get you some ice. Any frozen peas in the freezer by any chance?"

She laughed. "No, but you and my mother would get along well. She always kept frozen peas for bumps and bruises. There's an ice dispenser on the refrigerator door, and you can get a plastic bag from the drawer to the left of the fridge. Second drawer down."

He found the plastic bag and then felt along the front of the fridge, finding the dispenser. "Can you see my hands from where you are? Which button do I press?"

"There are three across the top. Press the middle one."

He did and felt ice fall into the bag he was holding open with his left hand. Once he thought it sufficiently full, he turned around and moved back carefully to where Catherine was standing beside the table. "You take this," he said, holding it out to her. "Then put your arm around me and lean into me while you direct me to the couch."

They awkwardly made their way until he felt the edge of the sofa. He turned and bumped his shin hard against something. His "ouch" was involuntary, and Catherine's head came up and this time he felt her hair brush against the side of his neck.

"That was the coffee table. Sorry. I didn't think."

"Don't worry. I've gotten quite used to bumping into things."

Catherine maneuvered herself down onto the couch and reached up to take Etienne's hand. "You can leave if you want. I'm terribly grateful for all you've done, and I'm really sorry I caused all of this."

Etienne held onto her hand and lowered himself down next to her.

"Please stop blaming yourself. You had a fun idea and things worked out differently than we expected. I'm just sorry your foot's messed up."

"I guess you know all about days turning out differently than expected," she said quietly. "I can't even imagine how horrible that explosion must have been. Do you remember much of it?"

"I remember how it started, but I didn't see the bomber, and there was no advance warning. All of a sudden everything just blew up, and bodies were thrown in all directions."

She didn't speak for a moment, and Etienne knew she was looking at him.

"Is there any chance you'll be able to see again?"

He laughed ruefully. "When you saw us yesterday on the metro, I was on my way to speak with a neurosurgeon at the hospital. She said there *is* surgery she could try, but that the odds wouldn't be great. She thinks I should give living as a blind person a go for a while. Too bad I made my living as a photographer."

Their fingers were still entwined, and she raised his hand to her lips and kissed it. "It will be all right," she whispered.

Etienne gave a harsh laugh, detached his hand, and got up. "It's all right now," he said. "I just have to get used to things. Come on, Jake. Let's get going. Please call me and let me know what the doctors say, okay?"

"I will. Be careful walking home. "

Etienne grunted, and he and Jake made their way slowly to the front door. He should never have agreed to spend the day outside, never have touched her so intimately, never have let her do something so ridiculously stupid as kiss his hand. He was blind and his life was a fucking disaster. He had no business dragging a beautiful woman down into his mess.

CHAPTER FIVE

"I do."

Katrina's barely audible vow was nonetheless full of love and promise, and Stephen felt a tide of joy sweep over him as he gazed down into her eyes. Those beautiful brown eyes now filled with tears as she looked up at him and gave a shaky smile. They had done it, and he was now legally bound to the loveliest and most loving woman in the New World. He couldn't believe his good fortune. He had accepted his assignment to the colony of New York with resignation and tried unsuccessfully to reassure his mother that it wouldn't be the "God forsaken land of barbarians and savages" she and her friends believed the Americas to be.

His mother had also fretted that his time away would prevent him from meeting and marrying an eligible young society maiden. But his parents would love Katrina; he was sure of it. It might take them a while to adjust to the idea of an "American" daughter-in-law, and he would postpone as long as possible their learning that Katrina's family ran a tavern, but Katrina, herself, they would love. There was no way they could not, for she was all he had ever dreamed of and more. He would send his mother a sketch of her in his next letter.

The simple church was nothing like the cathedral his family members usually married in, but it had a rustic beauty of its own with the backless but sturdy oak benches gleaming from the light of the small, square windows high off the ground. Catherine had pointed to the inscription on the belfry that had been installed almost a hundred years earlier: *"Si Deus Pro Nobis, Quis Contra Nos?"* Stephen certainly hoped that God would be for them, and no one would be against them, but nothing could be taken for granted in these turbulent times.

The somber Dutch Reformed marriage ceremony included no kissing of the bride, but he held her two hands in his and lifted them to his lips, kissing first one and then the other. They both turned, then, and walked with their hands tightly clasped down the aisle to the back of the small church, out the door, and into the crisp autumn sunlight. A chilly breeze was blowing, and Katrina's mother hurried after them and put Katrina's black woolen shawl over her, covering up the simple but lovely caramel colored dress that Stephen knew Katrina, her sisters, and her cousins had worked hard to put together quickly. The full skirt was embroidered with flowers, and Katrina had told him how her father had frowned while her mother worked long into the night on the pink, red, and yellow blossoms.

The church stood on a small hill just to the side of the Albany Post Road, and the carriage that Katrina's father had grudgingly borrowed from the doctor was behind the church, not far from the graves of Katrina's grandparents. Stephen had walked to the service that morning, not wanting to call more attention than necessary to himself by arriving on horseback, although by now the whole town was abuzz at the news of revolutionary Johann Rynick's daughter marrying a British officer. Most of the church attendees usually walked the mile or so from the town center and the spread-out residences, but today Katrina had been driven in the carriage borrowed by her parents. The newlyweds would ride back to the tavern with her mother, who was anxious to see to the wedding dinner.

"Now that's all taken care of," she said matter-of-factly, giving them a kind smile as the carriage started off. "Your brother will have us home in no time, and we'll have a nice meal before we move your things over to the major's cottage."

"Please, Mrs. Rynick, call me Stephen. I have just given my vow to honor and cherish your daughter for the rest of my life, have I not?"

"Yes, you have, Stephen. And I, for one, believe you meant those words. I do warn you, though, not to expect any great change in my husband's demeanor. It still pains him greatly to think of Katrina bound to you. But his own parents were none too happy when he married me, a Scottish lass newly arrived in the colony. I expect he'll come around once the babe is born. And now you must call me Mother or Mother Rynick. I am truly sorry your own parents were not present to see you wed."

"I expect they have not yet received my letter, but I am certain they will love Katrina as I do. And my sister will be so happy to have a sister of her own at last."

"Yes, well, pray do not even think of taking our Katrina back to England any time soon. We must accustom ourselves to this unexpected change in our lives gradually."

While Stephen had been speaking with his new mother-in-law, his fingers had been laced tightly with Katrina's, his thumb gently caressing the back of her hand. It seemed like months since they had been alone together, and he could not wait for the day to be over so that he could have her in his arms again at last.

When the carriage pulled up behind the tavern, Stephen jumped down and helped his mother-in-law descend, then reached up and grasped Katrina around her still slim waist. He could feel the definite bump of her tummy, though, under her skirt, and it gave him a frisson of pride and joy. He glanced around quickly, but Katrina's brother was busy with the horse and her mother was hurrying inside. Katrina looked up at him as he set her down and gave him a joyous smile. "I cannot believe I am your wife!" she said with delight.

"You most certainly are. And I cannot wait to finally make love to you properly, oh wife of mine," he whispered. "No more hiding nor pretending." His lips came down on hers, and passion quickened instantly between them, as it had the first day they had walked together along the river. Her arms came up to encircle his neck and their lips and tongues danced together in joyful reunion.

Katrina's brother Martin coughed loudly, and Stephen reluctantly released her. "Don't let Father see you doing that," he warned. "He was still predicting fire and brimstone as we dressed this morning."

Katrina giggled. "He will come around. He stopped glowering for at least twenty seconds or so to embrace me before we walked into the church."

"Yes, but his glare was back in place as you walked out," Martin assured her. "I think a large part of that was directed at some of our neighbors who have been none too happy about you marrying a Redcoat. Begging your pardon, Stephen."

"No need, Martin. I know that my men and I are pariahs in this town. My only hope is that the townsfolk do not shun your sister."

"I'm pretty sure Father believes they will. I heard him

arguing with the town elders at the meeting the other night." Martin stopped abruptly and colored slightly. Katrina moved quickly between them and pulled Stephen towards the tavern entrance.

"Let's go in. Mother has been cooking for three days in spite of Father's ill temper, and I know she wants us to enjoy it."

The wedding dinner was delicious: roasted venison with baked potatoes, carrots, and onions in a rich brown gravy, Mother Rynick's delicious bread and creamy butter, and two bottles of decent red wine, which Stephen knew was now extremely difficult to come by. He couldn't help but feel a bit amused watching the conflict play out across the face of his mother-in-law when she unwrapped the packet of tea he gave her just before she brought the cake and pies to the table. "Maybe just for today, to celebrate," she said quietly, glancing apprehensively at her husband.

"None for me," he said gruffly. "I wouldn't want His Majesty to think we had changed our minds."

The Bride's Cake was a thick, rich, spiced cake, soaked for several days in rum and loaded with dried fruits and nuts. Stephen knew the Rynick women had been extraordinarily busy trying to prepare for the wedding as if all were normal, and their beloved Katrina was not marrying an enemy, while at the same time carrying out the daily operations of the town's single tavern. Only Katrina's parents, her brother Martin, younger sisters Anna and Christina, and her paternal grandmother were with them at the celebration, though. Katrina had told him how most of the town had gathered to celebrate when her older brother, Paul, had wed a local girl two years before. They had since moved to Manhattan, where Paul was working in a law office. But Stephen understood that many in the town now looked upon Katrina as a traitor for marrying him. How he wished they could understand how much he loved her, and how desperately he hoped to help alleviate some of the tensions between the colonists and the King's forces.

When the meal was over at last, Martin offered to help carry Katrina's things from the room above where she had shared a bed with her sister and the room itself with all her siblings. The articles she had packed didn't amount to much: three bags with a few dresses, her winter cloak and boots, her nightdress and hairbrush. Martin stood by the door while Katrina said her goodbyes. Tears were falling from her mother's eyes, but she smiled at them both. "Oh, my little one," she said. "This is not how I dreamed it would be for you, but I hope you will be happy."

"I will, Mama. *I am*. And we won't be far away."

Mrs. Rynick glanced anxiously again at her husband. "It is important for a young couple to have time on their own without outside interference," she said diplomatically, and Stephen knew she was suggesting they stay away from the tavern. He understood her wishes and would do all he could to maintain peace between Katrina and her family, but he would never neglect his duty, and the tavern was still the only commercial eating establishment for several miles.

"Thank you for the most delicious dinner," he said, taking her hand in his. "And for all you did to prepare for today. I know my mother would have liked to have been here and to have met you, but I will certainly write and tell her of your kindness." He bent and kissed her work-worn knuckles, and she reached out and touched his cheek.

"Take care of her, please, Stephen," she whispered. "I fear dark days are ahead of us." He nodded and turned towards Katrina's father.

"Thank you, again, Sir, for permitting me to marry your daughter."

Johann grunted and gave his daughter a fierce embrace

before turning away. Stephen gave a brief courteous bow and took Katrina's arm. Martin walked out behind them with the bags, and Stephen helped Katrina back into the carriage. Martin would drive them as far as the small cottage on the manor grounds Stephen had been using as his private quarters and then return the borrowed vehicle to the doctor.

When they arrived at the cottage, Katrina hugged her brother, who grinned down at her. "I know I'm not supposed to know about the babe, but I'm looking forward to having a niece or nephew I can see once in a while. We haven't seen Paul and Emma's baby in months. And in the meantime, just send word if you need anything." Martin shook Stephen's hand and drove off.

Stephen and Katrina stood together in the late afternoon sunlight. The leaves were a canvas of red and gold around them, and the river could be heard in the distance. It was a Sunday, the gristmills were closed, and for the moment, a sense of peace and quiet prevailed.

"Shall we walk a bit, or would you like to go in and rest?" Stephen asked, suddenly nervous.

Katrina looked up at him with love shining from her eyes. "Perhaps we could rest together, and then take a walk?"'

He saw the flush creeping up her cheeks and laughed, reaching out to pull her against him. "Oh, my wise, beautiful girl. Do you have any idea how much I love you?"

"I hope so, Major Howard. I believe I just pledged you my troth until death do us part."

"Then let's go inside, and you can examine the way I've set up our new home. I was able to purchase some decent linen from a friend who supplies the governor's household. I hope you'll like it."

Katrina reached up to stroke the worry lines stretching across Stephen's brow and gazed into his sapphire blue eyes. "We're together, at last. That's all that matters to me."

CHAPTER SIX

"I still cannot believe you took a blind man you just met yesterday to the dog park. Whatever possessed you? I've been trying to get you to go out and do something different for months, and then you go and do something crazy, totally out of the blue."

"I don't know, Mom. It seemed like a good idea when I suggested it. And for whatever reason, Etienne doesn't feel like someone I just met yesterday. I just felt so horribly sad for him and wanted to give him something new to think about."

"It sounds like you succeeded. I suppose he must have been terrified when you both ended up on the ground with dogs barking all around you."

"I didn't get the sense that he was terrified at all. I got us into the mess, and all he seemed to care about was helping me."

Catherine's mom took her eyes off the road briefly to glance at her daughter's face. "Okay," she said slowly. "So this is a *nice* blind man. What else do you know about him?"

"Well, everybody at work heard about him getting hurt in

August. Somehow or other it was the first time in years that anyone from the magazine has been hurt on the job. Aside from the usual travel-related parasites, of course. But I'm pretty sure I never actually met him before yesterday, though as I said, he seems familiar, somehow. "

"Does he have family in the area?"

"I don't think so. He mentioned that his mother lives in Europe, and I know he's been traveling for *GeoMonde* for years. He talks like someone who doesn't really have roots anywhere. "

"Probably best not to get involved, then."

"Mom! I'm not *getting involved*. We spent a few hours together, and I ended up with what's probably a broken ankle. It could have happened anytime with anyone."

They pulled off the highway and said little for the next ten minutes while Ellen navigated the busy traffic before turning into the hospital's entrance. "I'll let you off in front of the E.R. and park the car. Use my phone to text Darren that we're here. He said he'd come and meet you."

Catherine did as she was told and then put her mom's phone on the console as the car came to a stop. "Thanks, Mom. I'll see you inside."

"Can you manage, honey, or do you need me to get out and help you?"

"I'll be fine. I'll just stand here and wait for Darren to come out."

Three hours later, Catherine was exhausted but happy that at least this step in her ordeal was coming to an end. The injury had indeed been a break, but a clean one, and since Darren was both the chief of orthopedic surgery and her step-father, she had been taken care of quickly. Her ankle had been set, put in a temporary cast, and the pain medications he had brought her had begun to take effect. She would sleep at her mom's house and worry about adjusting to life on her own with crutches tomorrow.

When they pulled into the garage, Catherine got out carefully and maneuvered the short walk to the door, climbed awkwardly up the two steps with her new crutches, and entered her mom's spotless kitchen.

"Let me get you something to eat, Catherine, and then let's get you to bed."

Catherine gratefully let her mom fuss around her. It had been a long time since she had had anybody take care of her. Bob had always been a good friend, but they had lived companionable, independent lives throughout their years together. Maybe she should have caught on earlier that his passion was directed elsewhere, she thought to herself for the thousandth time. But no matter. She'd given a supposedly committed relationship a try and now could focus on getting on with her life.

Once the bedroom door had closed, Catherine picked up her phone but then hesitated. Etienne had asked her to call, but was he just being polite? Was it too late? Did blind people go to bed earlier or later than sighted people? Was that an absolutely ridiculous question? Visually impaired people were probably just like everybody else – some went to bed early, some late. God, she was being stupid! But she had no idea what kind of person Etienne was. All she knew for sure was that he had seemed to express genuine concern for her earlier, so he deserved the courtesy of a call.

He answered instantly. "Catherine, is that you? How are you?"

"I'm fine, Etienne. My ankle's broken, but they've already put it in a make-shift cast, and it doesn't hurt at all. I have a feeling my armpits will end up hurting more than my foot, at least for a while."

"Did they say how long you'd be in a cast?"

"Probably about six weeks after they put the hard one on later in the week. So that should just about take care of any good running weather before the cold sets in."

"Oh damn. That really sucks."

"It'll be all right. Maybe I will get you to go out with me when I start up again, after all. We can go super slow and prop each other up."

"I'll hold you to that. Catherine, listen. I told you I was sorry about how things turned out, and I am, but it was incredibly thoughtful of you to take a chance on Jake and me. Today was the most. . . . out of my own head I've been since the explosion."

"Enough apologizing! My grandmother always used to say that everything happens for a reason. So for whatever reason, I'm meant to be on crutches for a few weeks. No big deal. My mother will be driving me home tomorrow and will probably stay for a while fussing about food and stuff, but why don't you come over later for dinner? We can order something and get it delivered, and then I can read to you."

There was silence for a minute and Catherine realized that she was asking a guy she barely knew over for dinner and blithely assuming he'd want her to read to him. What had happened to her common sense? He'd probably think she was after him or was some kind of compulsive freak.

"I'll call you tomorrow afternoon and see how you're feeling. We can decide then. You probably need sleep now – did they give you pain pills?"

"Yes, they did. And you're right, I am sleepy." She found herself yawning even as she said the words.

"Don't do that! You'll get me yawning, too. Get some sleep, Kat. I'll talk to you tomorrow."

They hung up, and as Catherine tried to find a comfortable position to sleep in, she heard his words repeating in her head. He had called her Cat again. Strange. But as she started to doze off, it was the memory of his lips on hers that she fell asleep with.

———

Etienne moved towards his bedroom. He had spoken truthfully to Catherine: today was probably the first day since the explosion that he had spent large chunks of time thinking about someone else or something other than his own predicament. But he didn't want to drag Kat – *Catherine*, he reminded himself—down into the dark abyss that his life had become. And why in the world did he keep thinking of her as Kat? But God, her lips had tasted delicious. He couldn't remember a kiss ever feeling so . . . right. But he also couldn't remember ever before acting quite so impulsively. What the hell had he been thinking?

He heard and felt Jake jump on the bed and laughed at the dog's continued assumption that the bed was theirs to share. Jake was all he needed now, and if he were smart, he wouldn't even allow himself to get close to the silly dog. Because no matter what Dr. Abrams advised, Etienne was going to have surgery as soon as he could convince the doctor to operate. Chances were he'd either get his sight back and not need a companion dog, or he'd end up beyond the help of poor Jake's limited skills. Either way, it would be ridiculous to drag an innocent woman, no matter how familiar and alluring she seemed, along with him. Serious relationships led to pain and disappointment—he knew this in his gut—and he wasn't going to hurt Catherine Reynolds.

CHAPTER SEVEN

As the days grew shorter and colder, Katrina reveled in the changes that were occurring in her body. Her breasts were fuller than they had ever been, and Stephen loved cupping, caressing, and licking them whenever they had a few quiet moments. But he frequently moved his lips tenderly over her belly while playing with her breasts, whispering nonsensical things to the baby and promising that he was taking good care of Mama's bubbies so that they would be ready for the young master as soon as he needed them.

"Or the young lady," she reminded him for the hundredth time, giggling.

"Yes, yes, dear. Whatever you say. But young Master Howard and I have matters well under control, so you need not worry. Just lie back and think peaceful thoughts."

She giggled again. How could she possibly think peaceful thoughts while his lips were moving so diabolically down below the ever-growing bulge of her belly to the sensitive flesh between her legs? He had made it clear very quickly after their wedding that he had no intention of yielding to her modest cries that to touch her anywhere "down there" was improper.

"Improper be damned, my sweet love. You are as beautiful 'down there' as a bouquet of flowers. Silky and beautiful and delightful to nuzzle." He had done just that, repeatedly, and she had grown to love him even more as he had taught her the myriad ways they could pleasure each other.

But sadly, their quiet times together were becoming harder to come by. Neighbors were turning against neighbor, with most of the townspeople supporting the militias training to fight the crown, while others supported Lord Philipse and his insistence on complete and total loyalty to the King. Stephen had been officially ordered to join Admiral Graves' troops in Boston, but once Governor General Gage had been apprised of Stephen's personal situation, and relying on Lord Philipse's continued support, he had agreed that having a high-ranking officer readily visible in the strategic area north of Manhattan was a good idea. Gage was confident that the rebellion would soon be quashed, but in the meantime, he was eager for a regular stream of reliable information concerning the locals' activities, especially in light of the restlessness aroused by the Orangetown Resolutions passed in July.

The residents of the Tarry Towns were still predominantly of Dutch origin or descent, but there were several English families that had moved into the area more recently, as well as a small number of Scots, Germans, and Negroes, some free and some enslaved. Some who lived in this beautiful hilly land 25 miles north of Manhattan accepted and supported the Philipse family's steadfast allegiance to the crown, but many more were growing impatient with the perceived tyranny of parliamentarians thousands of miles away. When Stephen rode off the manor's residential lands, he knew that his safety was increasingly in jeopardy, and Katrina knew it, too.

Katrina had grown up secure in her position as a beloved daughter of a respected family. She had willingly helped out in the tavern, even as a young girl, had gone to church regularly, and had attended classes with her brothers and sisters in the schoolhouse. Now conversations stopped when she walked into a shop, and soon after her wedding, she had seen how uncomfortable the congregation had become when she and Stephen entered the church on Sunday mornings. They had gone to sit on the bench next to her parents, but the family sitting in the row behind them had gotten up and moved. The church was small, so isolating her family in one area had led to crowding in other spots. Even though it broke her heart, Katrina decided to forgo services until the unrest had passed.

Her love for Stephen, however, had continued to grow and fill her with joy. He was unfailingly kind and considerate, witty and intelligent. They would read together in the evenings and he would regale her with tales of his childhood: idyllic stays at his family's country estate, difficult but enriching years away at school, and his more recent adventures as a young man in London. He told her of his many travels and promised that someday, she, too, would visit the great cities of Europe.

Stephen usually sketched or painted in the evenings while she knitted, sewed, or read aloud, and often he asked her to read the short little stories she continued to write about the personalities and wildlife inhabiting the Hudson Valley. His watercolors and drawings were hung on the walls of their simple cottage, and Katrina blushed when she saw the picture he had made of her recently, showing her bulging belly as she stood by the hearth.

"I need to capture every stage of your beauty," he had said in response to her cries of protest.

"Stephen, NO! That is indecent! You must not draw me thus, please!"

"Kat, you grow more beautiful every day. Do not call our child growing inside of you indecent, I beg you. I promise no one but us will ever see this."

Even in her embarrassed confusion, Katrina could see the love in the simple sketch: the wonder and hope in her expression and the care and tenderness of the artist. How she loved him!

The baby was moving frequently now, and sometimes at night they would lie together, both their hands positioned at different parts of her belly, waiting to see whose hand got pushed up first. They would dissolve in giggles, and Stephen would pull her into his arms and kiss her deeply. Occasionally, though, tears would follow the laughter and lovemaking, as every day Katrina grew more fearful of the upcoming birth and what would follow amidst the political unrest that surrounded them.

STEPHEN HATED LEAVING HER ALONE, but his duties required him to spend much of his time riding around the settlements to the north and south along the Old Post Road and monitoring traffic along the Hudson River. And he still needed to report frequently to headquarters in Manhattan.

One night in mid-November, though, he headed home with excitement, hoping to make Katrina forget all about the ever-festering turmoil in the colonies, at least for a short time. On this latest trip to Manhattan he had dined at the governor's mansion with the acting governor, Cadwallader Colden, and his wife, Alice. A mother of many children of her own, Mrs. Colden had insisted he return to Katrina with a bundle of baby clothes and a beautiful dressing gown and had encouraged him to bring her to Manhattan for a visit.

He rode down the path to the cottage, and Hudson, their rapidly growing puppy, came bounding up to greet him, his tail wagging frantically. Stephen dismounted and bent to pat the high-spirited dog before catching sight of Katrina coming out the door. He ran to her and caught her up in his arms, spinning around with the sheer joy of holding her.

"Stephen! Put me down! I'm far too heavy for you to lift."

"Nonsense. You are still as light as a feather." He kissed her as he set her back on her feet, and she rose on her toes to wrap her arms around his neck.

"It is you who speaks nonsense. I am growing as fat as a cow and soon will not even be able to fit through the door."

"You," he punctuated his dialogue with kisses, "and this little pumpkin," his hand moved to gently press against her belly, "are just perfect. Now, inside with you, out of the chill, and let me see to the horse."

He opened the door fifteen minutes later and inhaled deeply, overcome with contentment at being back where he was happiest. It was just a simple cottage, nothing like the grand estate where he had grown up, but it smelled like home. Katrina had found colorful braided rugs to cover the floors and had centered an arrangement of pinecones and holly on the table. A fragrant stew of some sort or other was on the hearth and his mouth watered in anticipation. She smiled at him as he entered, and he quickly doffed his cloak and boots.

"How would you like to take a trip to Manhattan?" he asked.

Katrina stared at him in bewilderment. "I have never been there," she said. "It's so far and . . . "

"Your brother lives there, does he not? Does no one from your family ever visit him there?"

"No, never. Mama and Papa have the tavern to run, and there has never been time or money to warrant such a journey."

"Well, the time has come, for you at least. The acting governor and his wife are lovely people, and Mrs. Colden is eager to make your acquaintance. Look, she has sent you this parcel."

Katrina unwrapped the bundle and gasped in delight. "Stephen, these are beautiful. Look at this dressing gown! I have never even touched anything so elegant. And these clothes for the babe! But she doesn't even know me. Why in the world would she send such magnificent gifts?"

"As I told you, they are truly kind people, and I have been fortunate to get to know them better each time I've traveled there. Because of the unrest, there are officers posted to their residence at all times, but I think Mrs. Colden is as eager as you are to focus her attention on non-confrontational issues. She and the governor are parents to ten children, and she said you deserved some adventure before you begin your life as a mother."

"Ten children! Are they all living at the governor's mansion?"

"Heavens no. The Coldens are in their 80s now. I think some of their children may be here with children of their own, since I was aware of at least a few young ones about. They are both interested in art and science, and Mr. Colden is writing a book on local botany. When I saw his drawings, I showed him some of my sketches of the plants by the river and told him of the stories you have written. That was when Mrs. Colden insisted I bring you down to meet them."

"Oh how I would love to see Manhattan. From Emma's letters it seems like an extraordinary city, with people coming and going at all hours of the day and night. Can we really go there together?"

Stephen took her hands in his own and drew her close, bending his head to kiss her lips. "I haven't spoken of this before, Sweetheart, but I was hoping you might consider staying in Manhattan until after the baby is born."

She looked up at him in confusion. "I cannot have the baby there, Stephen. My family is here. My mother and Genny, the midwife, are here in Tarrytown. I do not want to give birth amidst strangers."

"But your brother and sister-in-law are there, and I've told you how kind the Coldens are."

"Yes, but Stephen, this is my home. Even with half the people in the Hudson Valley angry that I have married an English officer, this is still my home."

CHAPTER EIGHT

Catherine stood, one crutch propped loosely under her left arm, and sipped her tea as she looked out her kitchen window. Her mother had finally left, after going through the house like a dorm monitor checking for contraband. Except her mother was checking to make sure Catherine had everything she needed: sufficient toilet paper in both bathrooms, laundry from the dryer folded and put away, and innumerable frozen items loaded into the freezer after a stop at the grocery store on the way to Catherine's house.

"Don't forget to microwave them in a safe dish," her mother said as she kissed Catherine on the forehead before leaving. "You don't need cancer on top of a broken ankle."

"MOTHER! I'm twenty-seven years old, and I know how to microwave frozen food. And stop assuming the worst all the time."

"I don't assume the worst. I just worry about you living alone, getting older, with my prospects for grandmother-hood growing dimmer and dimmer . . ."

Catherine and her mother both burst into laughter. It was

a familiar refrain that Catherine swore her mother had begun before she had even finished middle school.

"I'm NEVER having kids," she would say, returning from her regular babysitting job.

"Of course you will," her mother would answer.

"Nope. Too much trouble. I'm not going to bother."

The topic of children had never even come up during her time with Bob, and her mind had certainly not changed since he had gone his merry way with Rafael. She felt an occasional twinge of . . . . something or other when one of her friends joyfully announced a pregnancy, but she always shoved the feeling aside quickly, happy that she was free and unencumbered. She was fairly sure she wasn't the motherly type.

"Mom, go home and read a nice happily-ever-after book, and don't worry about me. Thank you for everything you and Darren did yesterday and today. I couldn't have been in better hands. But I'll be fine, really. I've got plenty of work to do, enough food to last a lifetime, and remember this?" She held up her phone. "They do all kinds of things these days, despite your refusal to try anything more complicated than phoning and texting."

Her mom laughed. "Yes, dear. I'll use mine to call you tonight, but you call me if you need anything before then. Did you say you're going to be seeing that man again?"

"Mother, I told you his name and you repeated it enough times while attempting to analyze his entire history. I have no idea whether I'll be seeing Etienne again. I certainly assume so. We work for the same company, and he's kind of in a bad way right now."

"Well, I'd say you're in a bad way, too, and you wouldn't be if you hadn't come up with such a harebrained idea. I'm sure he has enough to worry about now, anyway."

"Yes, Mom. Whatever you say. Drive home safely, and thanks again for all your help."

Her mom laughed as she bent down to kiss her only daughter. "You always do what you want anyway, no matter what I say. Just be careful, darling. I don't want you getting in over your head."

Catherine had settled down and worked for a while after her mother had left, but part of her kept waiting for the phone to ring. Etienne had said he would call, hadn't he?

Maybe he had changed his mind about spending time together after yesterday's fiasco? Or maybe something had happened? What if he had fallen? Or gotten lost?

For heaven's sake, she admonished herself. He's a grown man with a guide dog and an all-powerful smartphone. And falling was statistically unlikely after yesterday. Just which one of them had ended up on crutches anyway?

Her phone rang and she grabbed it off the coffee table, relieved to see his name. "Hi, Etienne."

"Hey, Catherine. How's the foot feeling today?"

"It's fine, thanks. How are you doing?"

"Everything's great. Listen, I know we talked about getting together, but you probably have enough going on, so I figured we'd leave you in peace. "

Everything was great? Leave her in peace? "Etienne, is something wrong? Did we get our signals crossed somehow?"

"No, of course not. I'm just sure that you're busy between your work and your ankle, and I don't want to add to that."

"Etienne, listen. If you don't want to get together, that's fine, but don't imagine that I suggested doing so out of pity or anything stupid like that. I'm stuck at home, you live nearby, and I like your dog." As she spoke, Catherine actually felt herself getting angry. What did he think – that she was taking him on as a charity case? Or, even worse, that she was trying to come on to him? *But God in heaven, was she?*

There was silence for a moment, giving Catherine just enough time to worry whether she had sounded more like a condescending bitch or a tart.

"Well, if you put it that way, I guess Jake and I will come by. We could use the walk anyway. Would you like me to pick up anything from the sandwich shop?"

"Oh please, no. Thanks. I have enough food to feed an army or two, so plan on eating here if you haven't done so already."

"Okay. Sounds good. We can be there in twenty minutes or so. Is the door unlocked? I don't want you to have to get up."

She laughed. "My mother was the last one out, and she would NEVER leave the door unlocked. But I'm on my feet at the moment, anyway," she lied, "so I'll unlock it now. Are you sure you'll know which house it is?"

She felt uncomfortable the moment the words came out. Was she insulting him by implying he'd get confused?

"I think between the three of us: Jake, my phone, and I, we will find you. He's not the world's best-behaved dog, but he's done a pretty good job so far of getting me where I need to be. See you in a bit."

The phone went dead and Catherine stared at it for a moment. Why had she gotten angry so quickly with him? She didn't usually react that way. He probably really did think she was pitying him. Or coming on to him. But for the life of her, she didn't know what the heck she was doing. She did feel sorry for him, and he was damn good looking. But in reality he didn't seem like someone who needed pity, no matter how rotten his circumstances. And after all, in a way he had rescued her, carrying her to the car when she couldn't walk.

And as far as coming on to him – that was ridiculous. She pushed the thought aside. She had been steering clear of even thinking about men since Bob had left, but if she *were* to get back in the game, a guy with all the baggage Etienne was probably carrying would be a dumb idea. She was sure that kiss yesterday had been just a fluke – the result of the overwhelming tension and anxiety they had experienced, nothing more.

But it had been a rather spectacular kiss, hadn't it? One she had been unable to get out of her mind each time moving in bed had woken her. She had tried to push the memory of it out of her head, but that kiss had been . . . so different than anything she had ever experienced. Soft, but somehow familiar, and alarmingly sensual. Maybe she shouldn't have encouraged him to come over. She didn't want to give him the wrong idea, because she most definitely was *not* looking for a relationship.

She picked up her crutches and awkwardly made her way to the front door, where she stood, anxiously peering out through the screen door. *Why was she standing there? What was she doing?* Did she mean to send him away before he even came in? No, she couldn't do that. God, she had to get a grip on herself and stop blowing everything out of proportion. He was a friend, and the crazy events of yesterday had led to a uniquely emotional reaction from both of them – nothing more. People with similar interests often became friends quickly. There was nothing that remarkable there. Just because it had been uncommon in her life didn't mean it was impossible. They would have supper tonight, chat for a while, and that would be that.

She gazed up and down the street through her screen door. It was far darker than it should be for four in the afternoon in early October. There had been talk earlier in the week of a tropical storm off the Carolinas, but she hadn't paid it much attention and certainly hadn't checked the weather since her fall yesterday. She had left her phone on the coffee table when she got up – should she hobble back and check the weather or wait here by the door? She didn't want it to look like she didn't trust him to make it this far.

She turned and made her way back into the living room and was just reaching down for her phone when she heard a knock and then the sound of her door opening.

"Catherine? It's Etienne and Jake. Should we come in?"

"Of course," she said, turning towards them. She watched as they moved together down the short entry hallway. He had a bouquet of flowers in his left hand with Jake's leash in his right.

"Etienne, those are beautiful. However did you manage to find flowers in the last twenty minutes?"

He raised his eyebrows above the dark glasses that covered his eyes.

"I've only lost my sight, Catherine, not my sense of decency. These are for you, of course, but if you tell me what to do, I can try to put them in water."

"No, that's okay. I'll do it." She maneuvered close to him, took the flowers, and reached up to kiss him on the cheek.

"Thank you, Etienne. They really are lovely." She made her way awkwardly to the kitchen and set the flowers on the counter while she bent down to find a vase. She saw the label of the expensive gift shop near the metro entrance on the plastic wrapping and realized he had to have purchased the flowers earlier in the day. So he *had* planned on coming and then changed his mind before calling her.

"What did you guys do today?"

"I spent some time on the computer; not much else."

She imagined the trip to get the flowers had been time and energy consuming in and of itself, but didn't say anything.

"It's nice and cool outside, with quite a breeze blowing," he added.

"Yes, I was just noticing that it's fairly dark outside for this early. You didn't hear a weather report today, did you?"

"No, I can't say that I did. I was trying to listen to some medical articles and only checked the headlines on CNN and BBC. I'm still getting used to manipulating everything around the Internet by voice, so there's a lot of hit and miss and wasted time."

"Are you hungry? As I told you, my mom left more than enough food."

"I'm fine for the moment, thanks." Silence fell and Catherine realized he was still standing, holding Jake's leash, unsure what to do.

"I'm sorry, Etienne. Please make yourself at home. Let Jake off and have a seat on the couch. No, wait, come here if you can, and I'll hand you a couple beers to carry in."

He bent to unclip Jake's harness and the dog set off around the living room, sniffing at corners. Etienne made his way carefully towards her, walking with a firm, upright confidence even as he swept the area in front and around himself with his hands to avoid bumping into anything. He really was incredibly good looking, she thought as she watched him approach. Probably just as well he was blind, or she *would* start getting silly about him.

He reached the refrigerator and she put two bottles into his hands. "Stand here while I open them, and then you can carry them back to the coffee table, okay? Are you picky about your beer?"

He laughed. "Not really. It's cold and wet, right?"

She laughed as well and they made their way carefully back into the living room and settled down onto the couch. Catherine turned so that she was partially facing him with her right leg bent and the cast resting on the edge of the couch. "Cheers," she said, reaching over and gently tapping the bottom of her bottle against his.

"Cheers," he echoed and settled back against the cushion behind him.

"I'm kind of at a disadvantage," he said quietly. "This is where I'd look around your living room and ask polite questions about . . . I don't know . . . a picture or an interesting piece of furniture. How about you describe it to me instead?"

Catherine gazed around the rather nondescript living room. When her grandmother had left her the house, she had given away most of the outdated furniture and knick-knacks, and she and Bob had bought simple, utilitarian stuff on sale, whenever the need arose, keeping only a few unique pieces that weren't true antiques but were too nice to surrender. There was a TV in the corner, bookshelves against two walls, and her rapidly growing antiquated collection of DVDs and CDs on the mantel over the fireplace.

"You know, as I look at it, I'm kind of ashamed to say that there's not much of interest. It's just a living room."

"Wow. And here I thought you were good at words, working as a copy editor and all."

Catherine laughed. "All right, all right. We're sitting on a blue canvas sofa and there's a dark wooden square coffee table, of sorts, in front of us. The table was my grandmother's because she liked to do jigsaw puzzles and regular coffee tables weren't the right size. There's a maroon colored upholstered arm chair that also belonged to my grandmother in the corner, a medium sized TV, and a fireplace."

"Real or gas?"

"Real. Though I've never used it much. I was thinking of having it cleaned out this fall so I could enjoy it this winter."

"Let me guess, your ex didn't like fireplaces?"

Catherine laughed. "You got it. He said they made things dusty and our heat was perfectly adequate."

"Forgive me for prying, but from all I've heard, it sounds

like you two were mismatched from the get-go. What brought you together?"

"I'm afraid it's a pretty boring story. We got together in college, stayed together after graduating, and he finally realized last year that he prefers men. Well, he might have realized it earlier, but he decided to announce it to the world last spring."

"Huh. That must have hurt you to some degree. Did you love him?" Etienne seemed to realize as he spoke the words that he had probably overstepped polite conversational boundaries and quickly apologized. "I'm sorry. That's none of my business."

"No, it's okay," Catherine answered after a moment. "It's a legitimate question, but I'm not sure I even know the answer. I thought I did, and we were always comfortable together, but I think I felt more like I'd been kicked than actually heart-broken. How about you? Have you a true love tucked away somewhere?"

Etienne laughed ruefully. "No, Thank God. That would be the last thing I need right now."

"Why do you say that?"

"I would think that's pretty obvious. I'm not the person I was three months ago, and I have no idea who or what I'll be six months from now."

"What in the world does that mean?" As she spoke, she caught sight of a jagged streak of lightning out the living room window, followed by a loud clap of thunder.

"God, that was close," she said.

"I should probably go now if there's going to be a storm," he said.

"I think it's too late for that. It's gotten really dark out there all of a sudden and it looks like it's going to start pouring any second." Even as she spoke, the rain began to fall. "And I was right. It's started already."

"Let me know when it seems to be stopping, okay?"

"There's no need. I told you I have lots of food, so there's no reason to hurry. Let me check my phone and see what's forecast."

She was quiet for a moment or two and then looked over towards Etienne. "Well, for two technologically savvy adults, we seem to have missed the warnings for a pretty major storm. According to my phone, this is the remnants of tropical storm Jessie, and it's likely to be bad until sometime tomorrow."

Thunder boomed again, and the lights flickered but came back on. Catherine's phone rang and she answered immediately.

"Hi, Mom. Yup, everything's fine. Yes, but I've got everything I need. Even if the power goes out, I'll be fine. It's not too hot and not too cold, so we don't have to worry about heat or air conditioning . . . Yes, uh-huh. Yup. I have no idea, Mom. . . Yes, I'm sure. Love you, too. "

She hung up. "Sorry about that," she said.

"Not at all. I've got one, too."

"One . . . ?"

"A mother who worries. Only mine is several thousand miles away and horribly frustrated that she can't be here holding my hand on a daily basis."

"That's right. You said she lived in Europe. Is she in France?"

"Brittany. In Northern France."

"Ah. That's why your name is Etienne, right? But you're American, aren't you?"

"*Mais oui, ma chérie.* My dad was an American diplomat, so I pretty much grew up traveling the world as an American kid with a French mother."

"That must have been quite the childhood. How many languages do you speak?"

105

"Only English and French fluently. But I know a smattering of Italian, German, Spanish, and Portuguese, and over the years I've picked up a very small amount of Arabic and Hebrew."

"Oh my. I suddenly feel very inadequate."

"No need. Traveling was a major part of my life, and exposure to languages was part of the package, that's all."

"Where do you think of as home?"

There was quiet for a few moments, and Catherine watched Etienne's face, although in the increasing darkness it was harder than ever to read his expression, especially around the large dark glasses.

"Well, up until this year, I'd have said that home was wherever I hung my proverbial hat."

He said nothing after that, and after waiting a bit, Catherine prompted, "And now?"

"I think the whole concept of home is rather over-inflated, don't you? You just told me your living room was just a living room—nothing special. And you have no pet, even though you claim to love dogs, so it sounds like the concept of home doesn't mean that much to you, either."

"Whoa there. I just asked a question. There's no need to go into attack mode."

Again he stayed silent before saying softly, "You're right. And I'm sorry. That was totally uncalled for."

She reached out and touched his shoulder, and he turned his face more in her direction. "It's okay, Etienne. I kind of do understand. And you're probably right."

Thunder roared close by again, and the sound of the rain on the roof grew louder.

"I hate storms," Catherine said abruptly.

"Why?"

"I don't know. I always have."

"Is that why your mother was worried?"

"Yes. Well, no, she probably thinks I outgrew it years ago. She was asking if you had come over."

"Oh. Is that a cause for her worry?"

"To the mother of an unmarried twenty-seven-year-old daughter living alone, everything is cause for worry."

Lightning sizzled outside the window again, and before the almost instantaneous sound of thunder, the lights went out. The rain pounding on the roof and the gusts of wind through the trees were loud in the silence of the house, with even the hum of the refrigerator now mute.

"Did the power go out?" Etienne asked, sensing the change.

"Yeah."

"Are you okay?" he asked gently.

"Yes, of course, I'm just being childish. Having the lights go out must seem a bit meaningless to you, I guess. Is it truly awful?"

"Not being able to see?"

"Yes."

"It is, actually. Sorry if that sounds pathetic, but it is. You know that silly expression that says you don't truly appreciate something until it's gone? Well, it's not like that for me. My eyes were my life. I've loved art and photography for as long as I can remember. I probably got my first camera when I was about three, and my mother still has the off-centered photographs I took of her and my dad in front of the Christmas tree. And when I wasn't taking pictures, I read. It was how I stayed sane during all my traveling. A good book can make an uncomfortable train ride or an endless delay at an airport bearable. Yes, I can listen to books now and even surf the internet, albeit slowly, and I feel incredibly grateful that it's the early 21st century and not even twenty or thirty years ago, but it's still not the same thing."

He paused before continuing with evident embarrassment. "I'm sorry, you didn't need to hear all that."

"Hey, I asked, didn't I?" She reached out and took the hand that was lying fisted tightly against his thigh. She felt his grip loosen slowly, and after a moment he laced his fingers through hers.

He seemed to sit up straighter and visibly decide to change the subject. "So you didn't really tell me before. Why *do* you hate storms?"

"I'm not sure. I just get this feeling of impending doom. It's stupid; I know."

"Has anything really bad ever happened to you during a storm?"

"Not that I can remember. Just stupid, as I said."

They sat quietly for a few minutes, his thumb lightly caressing the side of her hand.

"Have you found anything helpful or encouraging during your research these last couple days?"

"Yes and no. The general consensus seems to be that though there have been phenomenal breakthroughs in the understanding of how the brain works, and more complicated surgery goes on now than ever before, there's still a huge gap in terms of knowledge and risk analysis. And there are ads galore on whichever site I come to for mechanical and cyber accommodations of one sort or another for the visually impaired. "

She noticed that his tone sounded bitter. "So does that mean you're discouraged about the idea of surgery or just annoyed at the information you've been able to find?"

"Both, I guess. Or maybe not. Because I'm *not* discouraged. I want to have the surgery. I can't stay like this for the rest of my life."

She stared at him. "But Etienne, what if it doesn't work? I know it sucks, but there are thousands, or more likely millions, of people in the world who can't see, but who manage somehow or other. You're young and smart; you'll be able to build a life again, even if it seems impossible right now."

He pulled his hand from her grasp and looked like he was getting ready to get up.

"I didn't bring an umbrella, so I should probably call Uber."

"No, please, don't go," she said, reaching out to grab back his hand. "I'm sorry. I know it's none of my business, and I have no right to interfere. But I know you, and I know . . . " Her voice trailed off as she wondered at the words she had just spoken. "That sounds ridiculous, doesn't it? I don't know why I'm saying I know you, seeing as we just met two days ago. I'm interfering and I have no right to."

Etienne made no further attempt to get up, but his head was turned slightly away from her. He was breathing in slow, quiet breaths, as though trying to control his emotions.

"Etienne?" Catherine reached out with her other hand and gently turned his chin in her direction. "Would you mind taking off your glasses? I keep thinking that I *do* know you from somewhere, but I can't remember where."

"Kat," he began, but she interrupted.

"See? You keep calling me Cat as if it's an old nickname or something, but no one's ever called me that, at least not that I can remember."

"Sorry. Catherine. Better? I'll take them off to humor you, but in general, I'm happier keeping them on. I've spent half my life photographing peoples' faces—their eyes, and I can't stand the idea of anyone looking into my face and seeing. . . nothing." He removed the dark glasses and turned towards her.

Catherine stared into Etienne's deep blue eyes and felt a wrenching twist in her gut. The room was darkened due to the storm and the power outage, but his eyes were visible and appeared completely normal. She reached up with both hands and held his face as she moved her own closer to his. Those eyes, those beautiful blue eyes, seemed to be looking directly at her, drawing her still closer. She ran her thumbs gently under each eye, and they closed in pleasure, a smile turning up his lips. The pull between them intensified, and she moved her lips towards his, her own eyes closing in surrender.

At first the touch was soft and gentle: a brush of greeting like the flutter of butterfly wings. But then Etienne brought his own hands up to pull her even closer, and the kiss deepened. Their tongues met and danced, and Catherine felt herself drowning in a sea of escalating sensations. Etienne pulled her even closer against him so that she lay halfway across his lap.

No kiss had ever done anything like this to her before. She felt at once incredibly turned on, heat shooting through to her very core and down, and at the same time she felt a wave of contentment sweep over her. A feeling of safety, of belonging, of rightness, enveloped her, and when Etienne at last lifted his lips, she instinctively reached back towards them.

He nipped lightly at her top lip and then worked his way over to the crook of her neck.

"You smell wonderful," he said softly, nuzzling against her hair just below her ear.

Catherine reached up and took both his hands in her own, staring intently into his face.

"Etienne? I'm thinking that maybe you're better off keeping your eyes covered. I'd hate to think of women all over the Washington area trying to crawl into your lap and kiss you every time you took your glasses off."

He chuckled and wrapped his arms around her shoulders

and the back of her head, holding her tightly against his thudding heart.

"So what's the verdict? Do we know each other from some forgotten dinner party?"

"I'm pretty sure we don't. I think if I had met you at a dinner party, I would have spent all my time watching you and not paying attention to anyone else."

Etienne laughed and Catherine became aware of something nudging against her leg. She lifted her head to see Jake trying to stick his nose between their partly entwined bodies.

"I take it we have company. Lie down, Jake," he said gently.

"He's got to be totally confused, the poor dog. This undoubtedly wasn't the scenario they taught in guide dog school."

Etienne laughed again. "You're probably right, and I should definitely be going."

"Wait. You're just going to leave? Did I say something wrong? I kind of thought we were enjoying each other's company."

"We were. We are. But I don't want . . .I can't . . .Catherine, I'm blind. I'm not boyfriend material. "

"That's the most ridiculous thing I've ever heard. Besides, who even said I wanted a boyfriend?"

"Why wouldn't you? You're young and beautiful, and it sounds like you wasted several years with someone who was never right for you. You deserve a real boyfriend at the very least, or better still, someone willing to make a life-long commitment."

"First of all, Mr. Know it All, I'm not into life-long commitments. It's all a lot of nonsense. Second of all, you have no idea what I look like, and I'm most certainly not beautiful. But more importantly, what right do you have to just brush something away that might be really nice, at least for now? Have you been so busy gallivanting around the world that you've never heard of friends with benefits?"

"Kat, I'm thirty-one years old. I have no job, can't see, and am planning on having surgery that might as soon kill me as cure me. I think your mother's very wise to advise you to keep away from me."

"Well, then, I guess it's good my mother's not here at the moment, isn't it?" As she spoke she reached up and pulled his head gently towards hers again. Their lips met as if drawn together by a magnetic force.

Etienne seemed about to pull away again, but then he appeared to surrender, and after a moment his hands moved between their bodies to gently cup her breasts. They both emitted soft moans as he caressed her. Catherine stretched her fingers down to encircle the bulge in his jeans, and Etienne drew in a sharp gasp of pleasure.

"Are you sure this is what you want? It can't mean anything."

"Fine," she whispered, continuing to stroke him as she spoke into the hollow below his Adam's apple. "I agree. It means nothing."

He sucked in his breath and arched upwards under her continued caress, and his hand moved beneath her shirt and reached up under her bra to thumb her taut nipple.

"I don't suppose you have a condom handy, do you?" he asked.

"No. I used to be on the pill, but I stopped when Bob moved out. You don't have one?"

"I did, in my old wallet. But that never made it home after the explosion, and it's not something I've given a whole lot of thought to in the last couple months."

Her breathing came in uneven hiccups as she continued to stroke him, feeling him grow even bigger against the straining fabric. Her own excitement from his touch and his from hers seemed almost inseparable.

"Wait – I *do* have one. My friend Maggie bought me a big box when Bob left and told me she expected them all to go to good use. I forgot about them, but they're upstairs."

"Thank God," he groaned, still arching into her touch. "Okay, we can manage this, right? Just because we're blind and crippled, there shouldn't be any reason we can't get upstairs for a night of wild sex, should there?"

She giggled and then reluctantly pulled away from him and moved towards the edge of the couch, reaching for her crutches.

"Let's go for it. I'm getting up, and you can move behind me and hold on while we climb the stairs."

"Do you care which part of you I hold on to?" he muttered, getting up and pressing his entire length briefly up against her back, his arms sliding between her crutches and wrapping around her middle, pressing her bottom to him.

"We'll never get anywhere at this rate." But she rested her head back against his neck and inhaled deeply before pulling away and starting towards the stairs.

Jake jumped up and came to walk next to Etienne, who was following a step behind her, his arms extended to hold on to her waist.

"Oh great," he grumbled. "A threesome. Just what I always wanted."

Catherine giggled again, leaning against the wall momentarily and halting her ungainly hop up the stairs. Etienne's hands moved down to caress her hips.

"Get going, girl. This is no time for dawdling."

She continued to laugh as she restarted her clumsy ascent. "Somehow this is nothing like any seduction scene I've ever seen on TV or in the movies, and certainly not like anything I've ever read about."

"Who said anything about seduction? I thought we were on a hunt for condoms so that I could make you forget about the storm." His hand moved over her butt and thigh as she hopped up the next step, and Catherine felt a shiver run through her entire body.

She reached the top of the stairs and turned to look at Etienne standing a step behind her. The magnitude of what she was about to do struck her, and she spoke more quietly.

"One more step and then my bedroom is to the left, but the bathroom is to the right after you go through the bedroom door. I'll be in there a minute and come back with a condom. There's another bathroom about ten steps to the right if you need one, or you can wait 'til I'm done in this one."

What in the world was she doing, having a pre-sex bathroom conversation with a man she had met – what? could it possibly be only two days ago? She wondered briefly if he would need help in an unfamiliar bathroom but then decided to keep her mouth shut.

Catherine leaned against the sink while she worked her cut-offs down over her cast. She hated the idea of taking her panties off and going to him naked as if she couldn't wait, but the idea of one or the other of them trying to get them down and around her cast once in bed seemed equally appalling. And heaven help her, she did want him desperately. She could not remember ever truly wanting to feel a man inside her the way she craved Etienne. *In for a penny, in for a pound*, she thought grimly and stripped completely. She glanced in the mirror and found herself hoping that she'd at least *feel* good to him, if nothing else.

ETIENNE ORIENTED himself in the small guest bathroom, Jake waiting outside the door. What the hell was he doing? But God, he wanted her so badly, more than he could ever remember desiring a woman in his life. Should he wait to undress until he got to the bedroom? What if she had changed her mind and he bumped his way in, bare-ass naked, his erection leading the way? But no. He knew, knew somehow without any room for doubt, that she wouldn't change her mind. He stripped as quickly as he could, left his clothes hanging on the hook he found on the back of the door, and made his way carefully back to her bedroom, Jake again at his side.

"I'm here," he heard her say as he felt his way through the door. "Just turn about 45 degrees and walk five or six steps, and you'll come to the bed." Etienne followed her directions and felt her hands reach out to take his just as his shin touched the side of the bed.

"Lie down, good boy," he said quietly to Jake.

CHAPTER NINE

Katrina lay on her side, Stephen's arm securely around what was left of her waist and his legs tucked up against hers. She could tell from his deep breathing that he was fast asleep. The cottage was quiet with Hudson curled up on his rug near the hearth and only the very slight whisper of the wind audible in the darkness.

They had made love slowly and tenderly, and Stephen's last words as he drifted off to sleep were his customary, "I love you, sweet Kat." And heaven above, how she loved him in return. But she could not stop the silent tears that slipped down her face and dampened her pillow.

He wanted her to leave her home and family to give birth in a strange place with people she didn't know. She knew his desire was based on concern, but how could she explain the terror that sometimes threatened to overwhelm her? Every day brought fresh news of skirmishes somewhere in the colonies, and she knew that her own brother was engaged in surreptitious training with local rabble-rousers. Martin had spoken of it with pride when she saw him on one of her increasingly rare visits to the tavern.

"Your grand and glorious major might want to think about sailing home to jolly old England," he had said to her, partly in jest, she could tell, but she recognized a subtle warning in his eyes as well. "There's plenty of room for you and the babe here at the tavern."

"Martin! He is my husband!"

"Husband he may be, but while he wears that damn red coat of his, he's no friend to you and yours."

"Martin, why do you speak so to me? I thought you liked Stephen!"

Her brother heard the anguish in her voice and his frown dissolved into remorse.

"Oh Katrina, I am sorry. Truly. I do know you love him, lass, but they've all got to go. Have you not seen the pamphlets that arrived this week? No, I suppose you have not. That bastard Gage is suffocating the good people of Boston, and your husband works for the man. I beg your pardon for my harsh language, but it is God's truth."

Worse still, when she had rested for a spell with her younger sister before returning to the cottage, she had seen a letter from Paul's wife, Emma. She had picked it up eagerly and read the first few lines, her heart clenching when Emma mentioned Paul rising early every morning to meet with his fellow patriots before reporting to work. When Anna saw the letter in Katrina's hand, she took it from her, blushing. "All's fine with Paul and Emma, Katrina," she said and then changed the subject.

Dear Stephen. He was so strong and idealistic, but Katrina was coming to fear that his faith in a peaceful resolution to the unrest was naïve. How could she stay with the British governor in New York when her own brother was training to confront him just a short distance away? Why didn't Stephen understand how virulent the hatred was becoming against the British oppression?

She and Stephen were perfect together. They saw the same beauty in life, shared a love of words, and burned for each other's touch. But what would their life be like once they had a son or daughter to raise while hostilities escalated between their homelands?

The baby moved within her and Katrina felt Stephen's arm tighten instinctively around her in his sleep. His love was true and steadfast, but so was his sense of honor and duty.

The wind seemed to grow stronger outside, but in her heightened state of anxiety, it now sounded more threatening than pleasant. She pushed herself deeper against Stephen's sleeping strength as the tears trickled silently down her face. In the morning she would try to explain why she could not travel with him to New York. She knew he would accept her decision, no matter how it saddened or angered him, but she desperately hoped he would *truly* understand and not just credit her fears to pregnant emotions.

THE NEXT SEVERAL weeks passed slowly. Stephen desisted in trying to convince her to travel to Manhattan when he came to understand how important having her mother near for the birth was to her. "We will go in the springtime," he said, "and you and the babe will share your first great journey."

The weather was cold and damp, but it never got quite cold enough for the crisp chill that might accompany a snowfall. Stephen took short trips up and down the valley, trying to minimize his nights away to those times it was necessary to get a message to Boston or New York. Neither side trusted the established means of forwarding post, so correspondence was hand delivered at pre-arranged meeting times from one trusted carrier to another.

Katrina knew their cottage and the manor house were being watched. She could sometimes hear the sound of musket fire in the distance and knew the local men were gathering for militia practice, but the noise never started until Stephen had been gone for at least an hour, and she never spoke of it when he returned.

Stephen's father had fought in the Seven Years' War, and Katrina knew that Stephen held his own commission as a sacred duty. Yet in his drawings she saw that he sympathized with the Americans, seeing their day-to-day struggles as honorable, too.

One cold December afternoon when she was moving things around the cottage to make room for the cradle Martin had brought from their parents, she took a moment to sit down and rest with Stephen's sketchbook.

She leafed through it and saw a charcoal drawing of an old man chopping wood and another of a young man about Martin's age cleaning a musket. The young man's features were indistinct, and Katrina understood immediately that Stephen was trying to capture the youth's dedication and commitment and not his identity.

A chill passed through her, though, as she studied the picture. The artistry was impressive, as always, but the musket seemed to grow more menacing the more she regarded it. The baby gave a hard kick against her belly, and the book slipped from her hands.

"Oh, my dear little one," Katrina said, propelling herself to her feet as she rubbed her fingers protectively over her belly. "I hope our world will be at peace when you are old enough to hold a musket."

CHAPTER TEN

Etienne lay on his back, Catherine's head on his shoulder, and wondered what the hell had just happened. How had he ended up in bed with a woman he barely knew, and how had it come to pass that he had just experienced the most phenomenal sexual satisfaction of his life?

Catherine was quiet, her fingers lightly caressing his chest. He wished desperately that he could see her, but even without sight, he was pretty sure that she, too, had felt something extraordinary. In the end she had been gripping his buttocks so tightly as they climaxed together that he was pretty sure there were bruises – not that he minded.

Nothing about their encounter had been normal: her movements were hampered by her left foot in a cast, his clumsy, blind fumbling with the condom before and after had led to shared laughter rather than embarrassment or irritation, and the sex itself. . . it had been so far beyond normal that he was having trouble believing it had been real.

How could this have happened? He had to get out of here, had to put an end to what could only end in unhappiness. He didn't *do* relationships, and he certainly wasn't going to start one now when his life was a total disaster. But this woman lying in his arms felt so perfect, felt as if she had been a part of him forever. The sensation of entering her had been like coming home, and for the first time since the explosion he had actually forgotten that he was blind. He was, and she was, and they were together, and there had been nothing beyond that . . . that *everything*.

Ridiculous. And inconceivable. His physical reactions must simply have been enhanced somehow by the months of sensual deprivation. He had to extract himself—both from her arms and from the situation, had to put things in perspective. Had to go back to being a blind man with iffy prospects, at best, for a future.

"I'd better get up and see to Jake. He's been remarkably patient, but it's past his dinner time and he probably needs to go out."

He brushed a kiss against the top of her head and almost flinched at the wrench he felt in his gut. God but she was beautiful. He could not see her, but he knew. The scent and feel of her was so warm and enveloping, and he felt himself hardening again despite his best intentions.

"Jake seems okay for the moment. Are you sure you need to go right now?" As she spoke, Catherine's hand drifted down, instantly encountering his already more than eager erection.

"You're not very coordinated, are you?" she continued. "Your mouth keeps saying one thing . . . well, actually, your voice keeps saying one thing, but the rest of you . . . " She reached up and kissed him, his own lips opening instantly under hers. After a moment she drew back. "The rest of you, including your mouth, seems to be saying something else entirely."

"News flash: I'm just one more guy on this planet who lets

his dick do his thinking. But my brain is pretty sure this is a bad idea." His words ended in a groan as her hand continued to play with him.

He felt her shift away slightly and had the feeling she was studying him. Then she blew out a breath, conveying surrender. "Okay, you win. After tonight we'll be friends only. No benefits. Deal? But before you go . . ."

Etienne was still lying on his back and felt her moving up awkwardly. Before he realized what she was doing, she had straddled him. She sank down, slowly but surely, until he was completely sheathed within her.

"*Jesus.*"

A HALF HOUR later Catherine moved to the edge of the bed and got up carefully, reaching for the crutches she had left against the wall near the headboard.

"I'm pretty sure it's still raining, but it sounds a little less torrential right now if you want to head out with Jake. I've still got food if you change your mind and want to stay."

"Thank you, but I should get him home. I hear dogs are pretty pampered in this part of the world, so I don't want to get picked up for pet abuse if I keep him waiting too long for a meal."

"Very funny. I'm going into the bathroom for a couple minutes, but I'll meet you downstairs, all right?"

"Sure."

Catherine closed the bathroom door behind her and leaned back against it for a moment. She hoped she had *sounded* calm, because she certainly didn't feel that way. What in the world had happened here tonight? Making love to Etienne had been unlike anything she had ever experienced before, and somehow she had allowed herself to be so swept away with the absolute magic of it all that she had completely forgotten about a condom before climbing on top of him. What an idiot!

He probably thought her some kind of sex-crazed lonely woman. But oh, God, the feeling of him inside her had been so . . . so mind-blowingly delicious. She wanted to just curl up in a ball and hug the memories tightly to herself and never let them go.

Bob obviously hadn't ever had a clue, which made sense in retrospect, and she guessed she hadn't either. But the condom! How could she have forgotten? She reached for the box she had stupidly left on the bathroom counter. Spermicide. They had spermicide. That meant she was probably okay, right? There had to have been some left over from the first time, didn't there? She was pretty sure she had never before had sex twice in one day, let alone in an hour, so no wonder she hadn't thought to bring in an extra.

Pull yourself together. Get your clothes on, go downstairs, and be the friend you promised to be. What difference did it make if she'd never be able to look at her bed again without thinking about what they had just done there? Etienne was a colleague. He was going through hard times, and she had just told him they were friends.

When she got down the stairs a few minutes later, Etienne was clipping Jake to his harness.

"You're sure about food?"

"Yes. Thanks."

"It's not raining hard at the moment, but I could still drive you if you'd like."

"No need, but thanks. We'll be fine."

"What will you do if the power is out at your place? You won't be able to use the elevator."

"I'm sure it won't be. It's a big place, and there's probably a backup generator. Will you be okay?"

"Of course. Call me if it's out, though, and you can come back here."

"It will be fine, really."

They stood awkwardly for a minute or two, and then Etienne reached out a hand. "Catherine? Can you come here?"

She hobbled the few steps it took to reach him and took his hand. He laced his fingers with hers and brought the back of her hand to his lips.

"I'm sorry about all this. I really am. If things were different . . ."

Catherine looked up at him, but his damn glasses were back in place, not that she could have seen much in the darkness anyway. Grateful that at least she didn't have to paste on a fake smile, she answered him honestly.

"I'm sorry, too. Maybe in another time and place we could have made a go of this, but you're right. It's not what either of us wants or needs right now."

She reached up and kissed his cheek, just to the side of his mouth. "It never hurts to have friends in this world, though, does it? I'll give you a call in a day or two or you call me. We're still blind and crippled, right? So we need to stick together."

"Absolutely. I hope your power comes back on soon. Good night, Catherine."

Catherine stood for a while at the door, watching Etienne and Jake make their way down the darkened street. Did the talking "walk" signs work if the lights were out at the intersection? Probably not. Should she call him in a bit and make sure he had gotten home? *God no.* That would definitely be a terrible idea.

Etienne had made it perfectly clear he didn't want anything to do with a romance, and so had she. She had never truly imagined herself head over heels in love with

Bob, but the end of even that low-key relationship had left her wounded. It would be supremely stupid to get involved with anyone like Etienne. He was right. Better just to stay friends.

She moved slowly back into the kitchen and found the flashlight on top of the fridge and matches inside a kitchen drawer. Thank the modern appliance gods for gas stoves: at least she could make a cup of tea and heat something up.

Sleep was a while coming that night. The sheets had been a crumpled mess and the bed held his particular woodsy scent and the echoes of their passionate encounters. Catherine grabbed one of the pillows and wrapped herself around it as if trying to pretend she wasn't alone in the bed. Memories of their lovemaking flooded her mind. Her body had come alive in a way she had never before experienced – as if their bodies knew each other instinctively—knew how to give and receive pleasure such as she had never known.

She fell asleep hoping the memories would be enough to last a lifetime, since she doubted very much that lightning like that would ever strike again.

THE STORM RAGED on and on, and little Anne fretted and whimpered. Why didn't he come back? She paced back and forth across the small room, patting the baby, both of them growing more frantic. She sat down in a rocking chair and tried to nurse her little girl, but Anne seemed to sense her tension and continued to cry. Where could he be?

CATHERINE JOLTED AWAKE, pushing herself up and gasping for breath. The baby had a name: Anne. That somehow made it all worse. She crossed her arms over her sweat drenched chest but then let go and pulled out the collar of her nightshirt and stared at her naked breasts. Just a moment ago she had been nursing a crying child – she, who had hardly ever even babysat for young babies, let alone had one of her own.

She had dreamt before of a child crying in her arms, but it had never been so vivid or replete with memorable details. Was it the fear that had crossed her mind earlier after forgetting the condom that had put an ailing baby in her arms again? She shook her head, trying to dispel the sense of despair that gripped her, reached for her crutches, and made her way to the bathroom. She stared at herself in the mirror. Just herself: Catherine Reynolds. No crying baby, no phantom husband or father to a child she didn't have.

She splashed cold water on her face. *Stop being melodramatic,* she scolded herself. She would have thought that after all that fabulous sex, she would have wonderful, erotic dreams, not more nightmares. Time to go back to bed and remember how it had felt when Etienne had moved on top of her the first time. She shivered with the memory. Probably not the best thing to think about now that she had agreed that their. . . friendship would stay platonic. But given the weather, her broken ankle, and a nagging fear that she would have many years of drought ahead of her, she was going to cling to the vestiges of those sensations no matter how hard the rain pounded on the roof. Her bad dream had been the stupid storm's fault.

God, how she hated storms.

CHAPTER ELEVEN

K atrina felt the draft of cold air hit her before she opened her eyes. She stretched her legs and clumsily pushed herself over to get to the side of the bed. This latest version of their morning routine allowed her a few moments of privacy to use the chamber pot while Stephen walked outside with Hudson and attended to his own needs in the privy. It was still dark, but Stephen had lit the lamp before going out.

Pulling up her nightdress while awkwardly attempting to squat, she marveled at the immense expanse of her belly. A protrusion of what she presumed was a foot jutted out sharply just to the right of her belly button and Katrina giggled. The baby was getting its morning stretch in, too. How did he or she relieve itself in there, she wondered, and then decided she really didn't want to think about it. She had enough to do to haul herself up again.

Making her way over to the corner, she washed quickly and pulled on the only shift she had left that still fit. Her green dress hugged her tightly even with all the laces barely touching and rode up a bit too much at her ankles, but it was the prettiest one she owned. She stared at her reflection in the small mirror hanging over the basin and attempted to tame her unruly locks into something a little less wild. They would be dining at the Manor House that afternoon, and she wanted to look her best.

The door opened and the bitter cold swept in before Stephen pushed the door shut. Hudson shook himself vigorously and then ran over to nuzzle against Katrina's legs.

"That darn dog always gets to you before I do," Stephen grumbled, hanging his cloak by the door and pulling off his boots. He tucked his hands under his arms to warm them as he walked over to Katrina.

"Good morning, Sweetheart. Happy Christmas." He bent his head and kissed her, one hand going to her back and the other gently caressing her stomach. "How are you both this morning?"

"Happy Christmas, Stephen. We're fine this morning, thank you. Bigger than yesterday, though, I fear."

"And more beautiful." He kissed her again, and Hudson whined and tried to push between them.

"Away, you blasted cur." His words were harsh but his tone was affectionate, and Hudson pushed his head one last time up against the bottom of Katrina's bulge before he padded off to plop down before the hearth.

Katrina reached up to cup Stephen's cheeks. "You're so cold!"

"Not anymore," he whispered, turning slightly and pulling her against him. "You are like a walking bundle of embers." He nuzzled his lips and nose into the curve of her neck, inhaling deeply. "And you smell delicious. Just like a winter's nap and a hot toddy all rolled into one."

Katrina laughed at the tickling sensation.

"No Christmas snow yet?"

"Just a dusting. We won't have any problems getting to church, if you still want to go."

"Of course I want to go. It's Christmas. Surely today of all days we can hope for a civil reception."

"You think they won't see me as an enemy amongst them just because it's Christmas?"

"Stephen, don't. Please. You're not the enemy."

He sighed. "I certainly never wanted to be. But never mind. Come sit down and I'll get the tea ready."

"Peppermint for me."

"Yes, dear. I know." Stephen sighed again. "You're certainly not getting less stubborn. I hope our little one is more biddable."

"I pray it will be a strong and brave little boy just like his father."

"And I have changed my mind and am secretly hoping for a beautiful and clever little girl, just like her mother." He held his finger up to his lips and pantomimed sharing a secret. "Now stay still for a moment. I have to find something."

Stephen went over to the heavy chest of drawers that was among the several pieces the Philipse family had moved into the cottage for them. He rifled through the second drawer and brought out a small velvet pouch and some papers. Returning to the rocker, he knelt down at Katrina's feet.

"Happy Christmas, my darling Kat."

Katrina looked at him, astonished. She pulled at the black ribbon that closed the dark blue package. When it was at last open, a beautiful garnet ring surrounded by small diamonds lay in her hand.

"Stephen, it is exquisite! Where in the world did it come from?"

"It was my grandmother's. I wrote my mother last August and it finally made its way to the governor's office last week, just when I happened to be there."

"Oh Stephen, I cannot believe how beautiful it is. Your poor mother must have been horrified."

"Horrified? She wrote me of how happy she was to have you in our family. And she sent a note for you as well." Stephen handed over the folded stationery.

My dearest Katrina. Stephen has written us of your gentle heart and your great beauty. If you have brought joy and love to my son, you are all I could ever hope for in a daughter-in-law. I hope this letter finds you well. I look forward to the news of my new grandson or granddaughter and to meeting you both in the not too distant future. All my best to you and your family. Eveline Howard.

Katrina looked up at Stephen, tears in her eyes.

"She is so kind. And the ring is beautiful. But are you sure you do not want to keep it in your family?"

"Katrina, you goose, you *are* my family. I did not know what true happiness was before I met you. We are one, now and forever."

He reached out and stroked the side of her cheek and she turned instinctively to push closer into his caress. His other hand came up and held her head still as he brought his lips gently down on hers.

Katrina luxuriated in the warmth of his mouth and tongue. He somehow got to his feet without breaking the kiss and pulled her up against him. His right hand moved to cup her breast and his other reached around her hip, pulling the side of her against his arousal.

She squirmed against him, wanting to be closer but unable even to reach him around her own bulk. Stephen laughed and loosened the ties on her dress she had just recently secured.

"It's Christmas morning, my love. Services begin at ten, do they not? Any objection to a little celebrating of our own before we set out? I know I promised you tea, but I'm willing to wait a few minutes if you are."

Katrina moaned softly in pleasure as his hands continued their wandering. He relieved her of her dress and shift and drew her back towards the bed, shedding his breeches and shirt as he moved to join her.

Gently he turned her on her side and pressed his throbbing erection against her buttocks. He moved slightly down in the bed to ease the angle and slipped inside her slowly, his hand reaching around to tease her sensitive nipples in turn as his lips moved across her shoulders and nape.

Katrina pushed back against him in answer to his gentle thrusts, and as he reached down to caress her mons, she gasped.

"Stephen!" she cried sharply, unable to hold back the sensations that were overtaking her.

He laughed softly, his fingers continuing to brush her curls.

"My hot little minx. You cannot wait for your husband even on Christmas morning?"

Katrina arched back against him again and shifted slightly so his bottom hand was no longer pressed tightly to her breast. She pulled his hand up and took his index finger in her mouth and sucked hard as she ground back against him.

Now it was Stephen's turn to groan. His thrusting quickened, though Katrina could tell he was doing his best not to press too deeply. "Little witch," he whispered breathlessly between kisses. His fingers found her sensitive bud once more just as he climaxed, and Katrina felt herself convulsing around him again, her own hand reaching down to cover his and her fingertips just able to brush softly against his rock-hard tightened testicles between their bodies.

"Oh Sweetheart. You are so perfect." His words were quiet. He slipped out of her carefully and pulled her as tightly against him as he could, his hand coming up to rest on her belly. "And this is by far the best Christmas morning I have ever experienced."

Katrina sighed in pleasure as she snuggled against him. "If anyone had told me a year ago that a person could be this happy, I never would have believed it."

They remained quiet a few more minutes, and then Stephen rolled away, stretched, and pulled the quilt up over Katrina as he got out of the bed.

"Stay warm a few more minutes while I heat the water," he said. "And then we shall set forth and hope for some Christmas welcome from your kin."

CHAPTER TWELVE

Etienne spent the next two days going for long walks with Jake, listening to a John Grisham novel, and sifting through research articles on trauma induced blindness. He thought wistfully of the days when he had found visually scrolling through articles and clicking on links tedious; now he had to listen through endless mechanized readings of site after site, often wasting valuable time while he waited to hear if the information pertained to him or not. He shook his head at his own self-inflated impatience. Just how was his time valuable?

Etienne had loved his job. He was always eager to investigate and come to appreciate new environments, landscapes, and cultures, and he had looked upon his work almost as a mission: through his pictures he could bring his own sense of wonder and delight to others.

Now he sat alone in a high-rise apartment building, unable to see even his own photographs that adorned his walls. Jake, at least, was proving to be a trusted companion in innumerable ways, staying close to Etienne's feet even when off the harness during Etienne's endlessly redundant searches on his laptop.

Etienne tried to keep his mind on what he was hearing, but memories of travels, conversations, and experiences would flit across his consciousness with annoying frequency. So, too, did memories of his time with Catherine. He was now having to go back and restart this God-awful boring article on deep brain activity for the third time because somehow his own brain kept imagining a slim, warm, and fragrant woman slipping down on top of him and gripping him tightly.

He sighed and stopped the audio in disgust. It wasn't as if he was going to operate on himself, so he probably didn't need to know exactly where the division between the sensory cortex and the parietal lobe was, after all. *Jesus*, but she had felt good.

It wouldn't be such a bad idea to call her, would it? Regardless of what had happened afterward, he was still at least partly responsible for her broken ankle. And they had agreed to be friends, and friends checked in on each other, right? For the hundredth time he took in a breath to voice activate his phone, and for the hundredth time, he stopped himself.

But what if his hesitance to call was just another form of self-pity? Was he going to pine and pout in silence because he couldn't be more to her than a friend, or was he going to act like a responsible man who could deal with reality in a rational manner?

Yes, that was it. He could be mature about things and maintain a friendly and responsive relationship without wallowing in regret for what couldn't be. He grabbed his phone quickly before he could change his mind again and put the call through. It rang twice and then stopped.

That meant what? Her phone was off? She had declined

the call? Etienne groaned in frustration. Served him right for having waited so long.

He got up and made his way to the kitchen, intending to have a beer and force himself to think about other things. David had suggested he write a piece about his experiences in Egypt before the bombing and his life since, but he had been hesitant to start such a project, pretty sure that his friend was just clutching at straws in an attempt to find him something to do.

His phone rang on the desk and in his haste to get to it, he misjudged, and slammed his knee against the desk chair. Hissing in pain, his "hello" came out more as a strangled choke than anything coherent.

"Are you all right, Etienne? Is something wrong?"

"Catherine! Hi. No, no, everything's fine. I just bumped my knee."

"Ouch. Sorry. And sorry I missed your call. I was just paying at the grocery store, and between the bags and my crutches, I couldn't handle the phone as well."

"No worries. And if this is a bad time, I can call again later. I just wanted to see how you were doing."

"Now's fine. I'm in the car in the parking lot, but I'm not in any hurry. How have you been?"

"Fine, thanks. Everything's good. How about you?"

"Fine, too. I had to get out and get some shopping done so I could convince my mom I didn't need her to drive in and take care of me."

Etienne laughed, and they were both quiet for a moment.

"How's Jake doing? Has he been behaving?"

"Absolutely. His head is on my feet as we speak."

The ensuing silence lasted a beat too long.

"Hey Etienne, listen. I'm going to a lecture at the library tomorrow night, and I thought you might like to go. In fact, I'd been planning on giving you a call later tonight to suggest it. One of the reporters from *The Times* got back recently from two years in the Middle East, and he's giving a talk based on the book he's just written."

Etienne hesitated a moment. He was firm in his resolution to keep things casual between the two of them, but he was pretty certain her proposal could hardly be construed as a date.

"Yeah, that sounds like it might be interesting, thanks. Is it at a local library or one in D.C.?

"The one right here in Arlington. They have a great schedule of all kinds of events."

"Even better. Do you want me to meet you there?"

Another silence.

"Well, you could, if that's what you'd prefer. But I'm driving, so it would be no trouble for me to come by and pick you up. I promise I won't get us attacked by strange dogs this time."

Etienne laughed. "I absolutely guarantee that never crossed my mind. I just didn't want to put you out."

"You wouldn't be putting me out. I'm driving anyway, and you're certainly not far away."

"Okay, thanks. What time should I be ready?"

"It starts at 7:30, but there will probably be a crowd, so we should try to get there by seven, or a little before to find a parking spot. Do you want to grab something to eat on the way?"

Etienne hesitated again. He was torn between a desperate desire to spend time with her and an equally strong desire to put up impenetrable walls. But they were adults. They should certainly be able to eat a meal together without attacking each other, shouldn't they?

"That sounds good, if we can keep it to something simple."

"I know a place pretty close that makes great sandwiches and salads. Does that sound okay?"

"Sounds perfect. So . . . about six, do you think?"

"Yeah, or maybe a little before. I'll give you a call when I leave so you'll know I'm on my way."

"Great. Thanks. I'll be ready." *Think of something else to say —something normal and friendly.* "How long was your power out?" *Better yet, get off the phone, idiot. You've already gotten in deeper than you intended.*

"It was back on by the time I woke up the next morning, thank God. Although it would have been the perfect excuse to play hooky and not get any work done. But I've got a deadline to finish editing a piece on Zika, so it's just as well I had power. How about you? Was everything okay at your place?"

"Yup. Jake and I got a little wet walking home, but it was kind of refreshing." *And fortunately, it gave me something to concentrate on besides how hard it was to leave your bed.* "And it gave me laundry to stay busy with the next day after all the towels I used to dry him."

"I can imagine. He is pretty hairy, isn't he?"

"Yes, he is."

More silence.

"Well, I'm sure you'd prefer to bring your groceries home, instead of spending the evening in the parking lot on the phone." *Brilliant. He sounded like an old man.* "I'll be ready a little before six tomorrow night."

"I'm glad. I promise I won't try to jump your bones."

"Damn. There goes that fantasy. Good night, Kat."

"Night, Etienne. Thanks for calling. Really."

She disconnected before he had time to say anything else.

Etienne sank into the desk chair, absently rubbing the knee that still smarted from his mad dash to the phone. *God, but he was a fool.* Catherine had gone out of her way to reassure him that she was on board with his limitations on their relationship, and he had to throw back a provocative retort.

Weren't there horribly nasty names for women who behaved like he himself had just behaved? He was proof positive there needed to be equally pejorative terms for jerks like him.

"It's not enough that I'm blind, unemployed, and without anything resembling a future, but now I'm an asshole and a tease on top of it all."

Jake lifted his head at Etienne's voice, somehow sensing that the words were no longer directed into a phone. He sat up and nudged Etienne's hand, arching his neck as Etienne reached down and stroked him.

"Want to take a walk with an asshole, boy? And maybe tomorrow night you should put a leash on me. Better yet, a muzzle."

CATHERINE SAT for a few minutes in the parking lot before starting the car. She didn't want to care for that annoying man, she really didn't. But the husky tone of his voice when he had said those few simple words, "There goes that fantasy," calling her 'Cat' again, had somehow reached deep inside her and twisted her heart—and evoked twinges in other parts as well.

She had tried very hard to push thoughts of him and what they had done together out of her mind the thousand or so times they had come to her over the last two days. Now it had taken just a few short minutes to line up another night of having to resist the forces that seemed to pull them together. *Damn, but she wanted to be pulled together with him.* Together, on top of, underneath. . . . But she had given her word, both at her house the other day and just now on the phone.

They would go out and get some supper and then listen to the talk at the library like two mature adults. She could hardly rationalize where the idea of attending the lecture had even come from as she almost always ignored political topics, but when she had seen the flyer, she had instantly thought that Etienne might be interested. *But*, she told herself sternly, she would not make any more jokes about sexual contact, nor would she encourage, or God forbid, initiate, any physical overtures. Etienne had made it clear he wanted them to be no more than friends, and friends they would be.

———

IT WAS POURING AGAIN when Catherine set out to pick up Etienne on Thursday evening. She had called when she left her house, and he was standing with Jake in the well-lit lobby as she pulled into the circular drive. Something about his posture struck a deep chord of awareness in her—he stood so tall and defiantly straight, determined to face whatever life handed him without flinching. She saw his head turn as she put the car in park, although she thought it unlikely he had actually heard anything through the heavy glass. But Jake, too, seemed instantly aware of her arrival, and Catherine was overcome by the strangest sense of rightness —as if these two creatures were somehow hers, and they all belonged together.

The two stepped out as Catherine put the window down. "I'm here, Etienne," she said. "If you walk straight ahead you'll be at the passenger door. I've got a towel on the back seat for Jake to lie on."

"I didn't think about the rain when you called," he said as he got into the car. "Are you sure you want to do all this, given how bad the weather is? It can't make being on crutches any easier."

"I've got a big umbrella back there, which I figure you can hold with the hand not holding the lead, and it should cover us both. With luck, the weather will cut down on the crowd at the library."

"Okay. You're in charge."

She smiled at the feigned deference of his words.

"You're not used to anyone else being in charge, are you?"

He turned his head sharply as if to rebut her assumption but then laughed.

"Am I that obvious? It's not that I mind so much someone else being in charge. It's just that I'm used to doing things on my own."

The sandwich shop had few customers, so they were able to get their food quickly, allowing them time to eat without rushing. Catherine was aware of what a magnet to curious eyes they must be: she on her crutches and he with a guide dog. She watched Etienne's face and understood from the way he subtly tilted his head that he was constantly trying to perceive who was around him and how they were reacting to him.

"Does it bother you to think that people are watching you?"

"A bit."

"I bet women always watched you before, anyway."

Etienne snorted on the coffee he had just sipped.

"Come on, you know they did. I see how you carry yourself, even now, as if you always know exactly where you're going and what you're doing. And you're certainly not bad in the eye candy department."

"Good Lord, woman, do you always say whatever comes to your mind?" he asked, laughing.

"Yup. Pretty much. Just stick with me, though, and we can be an Abbot and Costello routine for the world to watch. And I'll keep you apprised of the audience's reactions."

"That bad, huh? Okay then, tell me about this café and what kind of attention we're attracting."

"Well, to start with, Jake is truly gorgeous, so he's probably the first thing people stare at. Then there's you, of course, the brave, blinded, handsome hero. Then there's the wind-blown, frizzled hair girl on crutches – most likely his sister, the older couple by the window are probably thinking."

"Sister, huh? Do you think I ought to shock them and show them just how not my sister you are?"

They both laughed, and Catherine was glad to see that some of the tenseness had left his shoulders and that he couldn't see how his comment had thrown her. Why did he seem to be flirting when he had insisted they avoid that slippery slope?

"The café itself is a neat little place that opened here about three years ago." She struggled to keep her tone light and unaffected. "They tend to be super busy at lunchtime, but not so much in the evenings when people go to either the more upscale restaurants or ethnic places in the area for dinner. I fell in love with their pumpkin soup last year, though, so it's stayed one of my favorites ever since."

"You're a loyal customer, then?"

"Yup. When I find something I like, I tend to stick with it. I'm not always looking for the next newest thing."

Etienne smiled and continued eating his roast turkey sandwich.

"How about you? Did you have favorite places to eat around the world you liked to revisit?"

"A couple, I guess. Although I was always ready to try new places and new foods. You never know where you're going to find something unexpected. For instance, I had great Indian food in India, of course. But a friend from the French embassy in Prague took me out to dinner when I was in town to an Indian restaurant, and it was one of the best

Indian meals I've ever had. Always good to keep an open mind."

"Indian food in Prague, huh? I'll have to remember that if I ever make the grand tour."

"Have you traveled much?"

"Nope. I'm the most boring person on the planet. Born and bred here in Virginia, went to college here, and now brave enough to commute all the way into the District a few days a month. I get my adventure from books from the comfort of my couch and from refereeing dog skirmishes when I volunteer at the shelter."

"Are you serious? Not even a year abroad while you were at school?"

"As I said, boring. I did a double major in English and history, and I always found there were more courses I wanted to take than I could fit in my schedule as it was."

"I guess if I have my surgery and get my sight back, I'll have to talk you into taking a trip somewhere."

Catherine felt a surge of fear shoot unexpectedly through her at his words.

"You still want to have surgery?"

"Absolutely."

They were silent for a few minutes, Catherine a bit confused by the unease that seemed to envelope her.

"If you're done, we should probably get going. This is such a nerdy part of the world that events like this at the library tend to be popular."

"Yes, ma'am. See? No problem with you being in charge."

"Yeah, right." Catherine laughed. "You just put on a good front."

THERE WERE ALREADY several seats filled when they arrived at the library, but a few of the back rows still had spots, and Catherine said as much to Etienne as they walked in.

"Good. We don't want our celebrity canine and our own – what did you call us? Abbot and Costello—routine to detract from the speaker."

She found them seats in the very last row where there was room for Jake to lie down and her to stretch her leg out and lay the crutches on the floor.

The speaker spoke passionately about the time he had spent in Syria and Lebanon, sharing the intimate details of people he had gotten to know and talking about how the ever-escalating violence made it impossible for them to live anything resembling a normal life. As he spoke, Catherine noticed that Etienne seemed to grow tenser by the moment, and she was suddenly appalled by her own insensitivity. What had she been thinking to bring him to a talk about unrest in the Middle East when his own life had been forever changed by part of that violence?

His hands were clenched tightly on his lap, and Catherine reached out with her right hand and covered his left fist, then reached underneath to open his fingers and entwine them with her own. After a few seconds, she felt him relax slightly, and a minute or two later, his fingers held hers, his thumb gently caressing the back of her hand.

Catherine stared at their hands, the speaker's voice fading from her attention as a wave of . . . . she had no idea what, swept over her. Their hands, linked together on his lap, looked and felt so familiar. They had kissed, he had carried her piggyback, and they had had wonderful, passionate sex, but somehow seeing their fingers laced together seemed wrenchingly intimate.

Her hand in his felt like it was where it had always belonged. His long, strong fingers held and sheltered her, and his thumb rubbed the back of her hand in a gentle caress that seemed almost absentmindedly instinctive. She had been the one to reach out to offer comfort to him, but now she felt as if every part of her was at peace. She closed her eyes for a moment and concentrated on breathing, allowing the sense of contentment to wash over her in gentle waves.

They stayed that way until the end of the talk, another twenty minutes or so. Catherine would have liked to have left immediately, before questions and answers got underway, but she didn't want to disrupt the other attendees. Given their encumbrances, it would be close to impossible to slip out unnoticed.

Momentarily lost in thought, she was startled to notice Etienne raising his right hand. When the speaker acknowledged 'the gentleman in the dark glasses,' Etienne's voice was clear and steady across the crowded room.

"Do you believe the August bombings in Egypt increased public support for the insurgents or the government?"

"As with so many acts of terrorism, public reaction was polarized. Not many Egyptians were physically injured in the explosions, and although the drastic decrease in tourism has been disastrous for the Egyptian economy, the terrorists won approval for injuring and killing the so-called unwelcome infidels." He went on to answer more questions for another few minutes and then thanked the audience for coming.

"If you don't mind, I'd like to speak to him for a moment before we leave," Etienne said as the rows of people in front of them began to file out. "I think we may have met a few years ago in Damascus."

"Of course, I don't mind. Do you want me to go with you, or should I stay out of the way?"

He turned his head instantly towards her. "You would never be in the way, Kat. Please come up if you'd like."

They made their way towards the speaker, who turned to

them as soon as an elderly couple thanking him took their leave.

"Etienne, isn't it?" he asked, reaching out his hand. "It took me a moment or two after you started speaking, but I recognized your voice and just had to sift through the memory files until I could put a name to it. I guess, sadly, that you were the journalist blinded in the explosions."

"Yes, that was me, unfortunately. It's Jim, isn't it? But good memory and a great talk. I'd say 'it's good to see you again,' but I'm reduced to voice recognition at the moment myself."

Catherine inhaled softly as she observed Jim awkwardly realize that Etienne couldn't see his outstretched hand.

"That was a very interesting talk," she said. "Like so many people here tonight, I'm a little familiar with what's been going on, but you truly helped me understand it from a more personal perspective."

"Jim, this is my good friend, Catherine Reynolds," Etienne said. "She's a copy-editor for *GeoMonde*."

"Nice to meet you. And thank you for coming out on such a dreary evening. It looks like it's rather an ordeal for you both to get out and about, so I'm doubly appreciative."

"I'm glad Catherine suggested coming. I've been slow to take any initiative to get out and do things, so I wouldn't have known you were giving a talk if she hadn't suggested it."

"You were in the field more recently than I, so you probably could have added to what I had to say."

"Perhaps. But my job was to get good pictures, not provide cogent analysis."

"Neither one works well without the other. And I always depend on people like you, Catherine, to make sure my words make sense."

Catherine smiled at Jim. She could tell he was being polite, but he seemed sincere nonetheless. He also looked exhausted and old. Etienne had had the misfortune to suffer

145

a blatantly obvious and quantitative injury, but it certainly appeared like time in dangerous war zones had taken a toll on this man in other ways.

Jim was closing up his laptop and gathering his things as he spoke: "I wish I had known you would be here, Etienne. We could have gotten a drink or dinner, but I'm catching the last shuttle back to New York tonight, so I have to run."

They said goodnight, and Catherine and Etienne moved slowly out to the parking lot. The rain had stopped at last, and the temperature had dropped.

"I guess fall's finally getting serious," Catherine muttered, shivering slightly as she got the car going.

"Not a fan of winter, then?"

"Not really, no. Though it will be easier to get long pants on when I get this damn cast off."

"Ah. You're out without pants, then? Sounds like I picked a bad night to be blind."

"Very funny." She gave him a quick glance. The light was dim since they were several feet from a streetlight, but even in the shadows, Catherine could tell he wasn't smiling.

"You okay, Etienne?"

"Me? Of course."

They were silent for a few minutes more as Catherine exited the lot and drove through the quiet streets.

"Do you think he really had to leave, or did I make him uncomfortable?" Etienne asked abruptly.

"Why in the world would you think that?"

"I don't know. Just a feeling I had. I'm not in his league anymore. It's not like I'll be on a lecture tour of my own anytime soon."

"That's absurd. He said himself that you could have added to his talk. You're more than welcome to feel sorry for yourself because you're blind, but don't go acting like an ass on top of it. Your brain still works just fine, and you have years of experience and insight that will serve you well whatever you end up doing."

Etienne didn't answer and Catherine continued to drive, pulling into the entrance of his building sooner than she might have wanted.

As she slowed and put the car into park, he moved to release his seat belt and reach for the door.

Catherine reached out and grabbed his left hand, forestalling the automatic words of thanks he was starting to utter.

"Etienne, don't."

"Don't what?"

"Don't let it all get to you. I know it must seem utterly hopeless right now, but I just can't believe that things aren't going to get better, somehow."

Etienne's profile was bleak in the dim glow of the streetlights, but he didn't pull away from her hand.

"Catherine, listen, because I don't want you to take this the wrong way. I had to sit there tonight and listen to Jim talk about places I've been to and situations I've known, and for moments I was so caught up in what he was saying that I completely forgot my own mess. I have you to thank for that, truly, because I never even would have known about him being there, if you hadn't invited me. It's rare that I forget my situation, even for a minute or two.

"But listening to him also brought home to me how totally useless my life is right now. My pictures made events in other parts of the world real to people. I served a purpose, or at least I convinced myself that I was serving a purpose. Now I'm not even sure what the point was in crawling away from that damn explosion."

Catherine's insides twisted as a feeling of panic and fear swept over her. Confused by the unexpected sensations, she gripped his hand tighter and spoke without thinking.

"Etienne. Stop. Don't you dare say that or even think it. There damn well was a point in your living through that horror, and just because you can't see that point—literally, I guess, sorry—doesn't mean there isn't one. Just don't think that way. Please." Tears filled her eyes as she spoke, and one slipped loose and trickled down her cheek.

Once again their fingers seemed to be having their own private dialogue as they clung tightly to each other, their thumbs speaking words too intimate for either of them to voice.

They sat in silence for a few moments, the low purr of the car engine the only sound. Finally Etienne shifted towards her, his right hand coming up unerringly to touch the side of her face, and his fingers met the dampness on her cheek.

"Oh, Sweetheart, I'm sorry. Forgive me. You've given me the nicest night out—the only night out—I've had since August, and I've made you cry. I didn't mean to spoil it. Just ignore me, please. My self-pity is my own problem, not something you have to deal with."

She rubbed her face against his palm, wanting somehow to crawl inside him and comfort him at the same time.

"It's okay," she whispered. "I understand. Just don't say shit like that again, all right?"

"I promise." He leaned over and kissed her lightly, his lips landing softly on her left cheekbone. Calling on all her willpower, Catherine resisted the urge to search for his lips with her own, remembering her promise to keep things on a "friendly" basis.

After a few muted seconds, she pulled away and inserted a false brightness in her tone.

"So. How about a concert next time? My friend Maggie plays in an orchestra that's giving a concert on Saturday night at George Mason. Usually I go with my mom, since she's known Maggie since she was a kid, but she and Darren are going to Boston for a medical convention, and I have an extra ticket."

"Am I your new project? Is this the 'pull Etienne out of his cave campaign?'"

"Yup. That's it. You found me out. I figured if I couldn't train for a race with my foot in a cast, I had to do something else challenging, right?"

Etienne was silent for a moment and then sighed. "Okay, Kat. You win. I will attempt to gird up my loins for another adventure. You seem determined to keep me from wallowing in my den of misery."

"Yeah, well. Either that, or I'll have to think of something else for your loins to do."

They both laughed, but Etienne's fingers tightened on hers again, and he reached across for one more quick kiss.

"Enough, temptress. Get thee back to your witch's lair and leave me and my dog to our nighttime walk and our beauty sleep. I'll call you tomorrow about the concert." He paused. "And thanks again for tonight. I mean it."

———

AS CATHERINE DROVE AWAY and Etienne moved with Jake to walk behind the building for the dog to do his business, he thought about the flood of emotions that had swept over him in the last several hours.

He had been the one to adamantly insist on boundaries between them, but from the moment Catherine had arrived tonight, he had been suffused with a gentle peace that seemed to accompany her proximity. The sandwich he had eaten in the café had tasted better than anything he had eaten in a long time, and he had meant what he said about momentarily forgetting his own plight during Jim's talk.

Of course what he hadn't said was that the only other

time since August that he had forgotten his blindness had been during the hour or so of bliss in her bed. That put it at two for two. And it wasn't like he hadn't spent the entire evening tonight wishing he could get her back in bed, eyesight or no eyesight. Seemed like only when he was with Catherine could he let go of his own preoccupation with misery.

"What should I deduce from that, boy?"

Jake didn't pause in his slow meanderings about the property, obviously aware that his opinion wasn't actually anticipated.

"It would seem to indicate that I either need to get my sight back, or I need to spend all my time with Catherine, my own loins firmly girdled up, not girded up. And doesn't that sound like an appealing proposition for a young lady: physical and mental distraction for a blind, reclusive, has-been?"

He shook his head at his own black humor but refused to consider the irrational fantasy that kept trying to break through the wall he steadfastly reinforced: *What if he could get his sight back and still spend his life with Catherine?*

CHAPTER THIRTEEN

Katrina awoke to a dull, dragging pain in her back. The cottage was cold, and she knew it had only been an hour or so since she had last gotten up to use the chamber pot. She had been sleeping so fitfully that it almost seemed silly to bank the hearth at night, but she had done so anyway, and now she shivered as she stood and tried to ease the cramping. Her beloved Hudson looked up from his spot near the fireplace and wagged his tail. Pulling a shawl tightly around her shoulders, Katrina walked stiffly to the door and let the pup out.

Abbie, the serving girl from the manor whom Stephen had arranged to stay with her during his absence, stirred from her pallet on the floor.

"Madam? Is all well with you?"

"I'm not sure, Abbie. I feel a bit strange."

"Oh, Madam," she cried, jumping to her feet and reaching for her cloak. "The major said I was to get help immediately if your time came."

Katina felt a wave of discomfort sweep over her, not

unlike the cramps she sometimes suffered with her menses, but more intense. Her hands went instinctively around her swollen belly and felt the familiar jutting of what she assumed was a heel against her palm. She smiled in spite of herself in the midst of her anxiety. The baby always felt so strong and determined—almost as if he or she wanted to kick its way out. But seconds later a soft moan escaped her throat. It felt horrible to stand, but it had been the pain she felt lying down that had woken her and impelled her to her feet.

"I think the babe may make an appearance soon, after all," she said with an attempt at a smile. "Let's hope the major gets home early today as he promised."

"I will run to the manor and have someone send for the midwife," the girl said, quickly lacing her boots. "Thank heavens there is no new snow."

She ran from the cottage, and Katrina turned from the door, uncertain what to do. How she wished Stephen were here, but equally urgent was the wish for her mother. Would Abbie send word to town for someone to fetch her? What if no one made it back to her in time, and the baby came while she was all alone? *Please God, let Stephen come back soon.*

Katrina moved slowly over to the fireplace and clumsily bent to add a log from the pile Stephen had left inside. *Damn.* She wasn't thinking straight. The log would never catch without something to get the fire going, but now somehow the thought of bending yet again in order to get the wood-chips from the copper bucket seemed impossible. She sank into the rocking chair near the hearth and hugged her belly as another wave of cramping passed through her.

"Mistress Howard, how do you fare?" came Abbie's breathless voice as she burst back in through the door. "The lads have gone for the midwife and for your mother, so all will be well. Should you not return to your bed?"

"I do not know, Abbie. I don't think I want to lie down again for the moment. Can you see about getting the fire going?"

She rocked back and forth slowly, huddling into herself in cold misery. A bark came from the door, and she roused herself for a moment, happy that the dog, at least, was here to attend her. Abbie let the pup in, and he ran to her side, shoving his nuzzle against her elbow.

Katrina smiled wanly and reached out to fondle the dog's head. Her mother had expressed dismay at the dog living so intimately with them inside the cottage, but he had proven a true and steadfast comfort during Stephen's frequent absences.

"Do you think he'll make it home soon, sweet boy?" she said to the dog. His tail thumped in response to her attention and she forced another smile in his direction. "Let's hope you are right."

"What else can I do, Madam?" Abbie asked, looking about uncertainly.

Abbie was young, probably only thirteen or fourteen, and no doubt almost as nervous as she was herself, Katrina thought.

"Maybe bring in some extra water? The major made sure all the kettles were full before he left, but we didn't refill them yesterday evening, I fear."

Abbie grabbed the kettles and hurried out again, no doubt happy to escape the tension in the small cottage.

Katrina continued to rock slowly as the pains came and went. Feeling the need to relieve herself, she pushed up gingerly to her feet and felt a stream of warm liquid trail down her legs. *Oh God. Had she wet herself?* But no, she was sure she hadn't, as she still felt the need. She tried to remember what her mother and the midwife, Genny, had talked about during their recent visits, but another wave of pain overtook her and she held on

153

tightly to the back of the rocker. How in the world was she going to manage the chamber pot when she could barely stand?

Abbie pushed through the door with the two heavy kettles and looked at Katrina in dismay. "Do you need my assistance, Madam?"

"Hang a kettle over the fire, Abbie, and leave the others in front of the hearth," Katrina gasped out. "And then maybe you can help me. Do you know what time it is?"

"I heard the church bells ring while I was outside, so it is just past eight, I believe."

"Oh yes. 'Tis Sunday morning, is it not?" Katrina felt another wave of despair wash over her. The church was closer to the manor than the tavern was, but if her mother then had to get the midwife, who not being Dutch, did not attend their church, more time would be lost.

Just as the tears welling in her eyes began to fall, she heard the sound of hoof beats. It couldn't be Stephen, not this early in the morning, could it?

Abbie heard the noise and ran to the door, opening just the top to look out. "Oh God be praised! The major is back!"

Still anxious to relieve herself and fearing that she might vomit as well, Katrina nevertheless felt an enormous sense of relief sweep over her. Stephen would be able to help, some-how, even if men were not supposed to be anywhere in the vicinity of childbirth. Another wave of pain washed over her, and she squeezed her eyes shut. He would make the necessary decisions, and he would not let her die.

STEPHEN BURST through the door and swiftly took in the scene. "Have you called for the midwife?"

"Yes, sir. Peter left nigh on an hour ago."

He shed his cloak quickly and came to Katrina's side. "How are you, my love? I woke at two and knew I must leave immediately."

"You rode through the dark? Oh Stephen, you could have been hurt!"

"Thank God the roads here have fewer vagabonds about than those in England in the dark of night. I knew, somehow, that I had to come quickly." He pulled her gently against him and Katrina relaxed momentarily in his arms.

"Tell me what you need, my love."

"You must not look, Stephen, but I need help to the chamber pot, and I fear I have made a mess of the floor."

Stephen looked around and assessed the space. As he held her against him, another wave of pain gripped her, but even in her misery she saw fear on his face give way to fierce determination.

"Abbie, set the chamber pot on top of the stool there, please, and come help Katrina. I will not look, Kat dearest, I promise, but I will support you under your arms from behind as Abbie helps you."

Somehow they achieved the awkward maneuver, Katrina embarrassed beyond measure but still grateful for the slight sense of relief.

"The rocker or the bed, Sweetheart? Where would you be more comfortable?"

Another contraction tore through her and Katrina gripped Stephen's hand tightly. "I don't know," she whimpered. "I just want it to stop."

"It will be over soon, my love, and then we will have a fine new babe to make us a family." Stephen gazed into her eyes, and she could see how he wished he could do more to help. The room was still chilly, but beads of perspiration stood out on her upper lip and temples. He bent and kissed her softly

155

on the forehead. "Be brave, Kat. The midwife will be here soon."

And miracle of miracles, she was. The tiny woman, whom townspeople said was more Iroquois than British, bustled into the cottage just a few minutes later.

"I was on my way before young Peter got halfway to my home. I had a sense that you were needing me," she said gently to Katrina, pushing Stephen firmly aside. "Make yourself useful, young man. Go bring in more water and then build up the fire. And I believe I saw a horse outside that needs tending to."

Knowing he was dismissed, Stephen reached out and cupped Katrina's face between his hands. "Look at me, My Dearest Heart. All will be well, I promise. And I will be here if you need me. I love you." A tick of serenity in the midst of chaos, and Katrina gained a momentary sense of respite and reassurance, gazing into the deep blue depths of Stephen's eyes.

"Thank you for coming home. As long as you're here, I know it will be all right."

He kissed her quickly on the mouth and then turned to follow the midwife's orders. As he left the cottage, she heard the sound of a carriage turning into the lane—probably the same carriage they had ridden in on their wedding day.

———

STEPHEN RAN OVER and helped his mother-in-law descend.

"Oh, Stephen, I was afraid you would not be here."

"I just returned a short while ago, but the midwife is with Katrina now and made it obvious that I should stay out. Though I'm supposed to fetch more water and firewood."

"Quite right. We will find you when there's a wee bairn. It can sometimes take a while, you know."

"Yes, I know. But I hope it comes quickly. I don't want Katrina to suffer."

"Most certainly you do not. But all you can do is pray for a speedy and safe delivery. Off with you now, but stay close."

Stephen set about bringing in more wood and water, the dog following him faithfully about. The poor pup had been evicted faster than Stephen and now seemed equally unsure of how to occupy himself.

Stephen went and stabled the horse that had served him so well during his early morning journey. The road up from New York was heavily traveled during daylight hours, but this morning's trip had been daunting as he had needed to go slowly enough to manage the lantern and the reigns while trying to reach the manor as quickly as possible. Fortunately, the bandits that haunted British roads at night were still relatively scarce in the colonies.

He busied himself for as long as possible in the stables, played fetch with the dog in the snow, and then walked up to the manor house. Frederick III, the latest Lord Philipse to own the house, lived most of the year at his estate in the Yonkers, but the Tarrytown mansion was kept staffed and running and was at times used by William Pugsley, who leased and ran the mills that employed much of the local population.

Stephen made his way to the kitchen and was greeted by the warm comforting smells that reminded him of home.

"Major Howard, welcome back," the cook said, smiling up at him from the great table where she worked. "I hear the babe is on its way. Come have some tea and biscuits while you wait."

Unlike elsewhere in the area, tea was still plentiful in the manor house, where allegiance to the crown was unwavering, and Stephen was grateful for the hot, sugary drink. He had been outside in the cold for more than seven hours now, and he found himself refilling his cup several times. He was unable to sit still, though, and paced around the kitchen, going frequently to peer out the window.

"Never fear. They will come for you soon enough, and then you and your lady will have your hands full. Now sit down, Sir, for heaven's sake. You are tiring me out watching you."

Stephen sat again, and tried to quiet his racing thoughts. He wanted desperately to be back at Katrina's side but feared the women's wrath if he dared return uninvited. Finally the warmth of the kitchen seeped into his cold and tense muscles, and he realized with a start that he had actually dozed off. He shook himself awake, thanked the cook, and went out to pace in front of the cottage.

He looked at his pocket watch and saw that it was almost three. Surely it shouldn't take this long, should it? He wandered down towards the stables again and had just turned back towards the manor house when the top half of the cottage door opened and Abbie caught sight of him.

"Major Howard, Sir, you are a father," she called to him, and Stephen ran to the door.

His beautiful Katrina lay in the bed, propped up on a few pillows, a tightly swaddled bundle in her arms. She looked up as he came in, and Stephen was dazzled yet again by her lustrous smile and the love in her eyes.

"Come see your little girl," she said quietly and held up the baby for him to see.

"She's lovely. Just like her mother," he whispered and bent down to kiss the baby softly on the forehead. He then leaned in and kissed Katrina gently on the lips.

"Are you well, Kat?" he asked, gazing into her winsome brown eyes, his own suddenly brimming with tears. "You are both so precious to me."

"Oh, Stephen. We have done it. We are a true family now."

Her voice was raspy, but he could hear the joy behind her words, and he bent down and kissed her again, pulled to her as if by a magnet.

"Yes, my love. We are, indeed, a family." He was a father now, he thought to himself with amazement. A father!

CHAPTER FOURTEEN

C atherine stared again at the calendar, trying hard not to give way to panic. The last several weeks had gone by quickly, and she and Etienne were now what anyone observing them would consider close friends. They spent time together a few days a week and spoke often on the phone. Several times he had walked over in the afternoon and stayed for supper. They kept things simple: tacos or spaghetti, Etienne keeping her company in the kitchen and proving adept at opening and pouring wine but not trying to prove anything by offering to chop or slice. They had even fallen into a pattern of reading together when they discovered they both liked mysteries. He introduced her to Ian Rankin and the dark environs of Edinburgh and then became equally engrossed in the P.D. James novel she chose.

They would sit on the couch, close but not quite touching, and she would read aloud until one of them began yawning. She had always loved reading, but sharing a book in this way was a new and somehow intimate experience. They talked about the writers when she wasn't reading, discussing style and plot and reminiscing about past books read.

They often kissed upon greeting and parting, but it was a quick kiss on both cheeks. He had done so instinctively when she had picked him up to attend Maggie's concert, and she had teased him for showing his French roots. He had laughed in acknowledgement.

"You're absolutely right. Without sight I've obviously reverted to ingrained behavior I don't even think about. I'm pretty sure I've never in my life greeted an American woman that way."

"Should I be flattered or insulted?"

"It was most definitely not meant as an insult, so let's go with flattered."

They had both laughed, but aside from those chaste pecks, Etienne and Catherine each took care not to allow any real physical contact. Whenever they were out, her hands were busy with her crutches and he always had Jake's lead to hold.

But Catherine shamelessly took advantage of Etienne's blindness and watched him constantly. He was quite the most beautiful man she had ever seen: tall, perfectly proportioned, well-defined muscles, and a firmly sculptured face with thick light brown hair that had started to curl just a bit at the ends. He was undoubtedly the kind who kept his hair short and was probably due for a haircut, but she certainly wasn't going to mention it.

And so she stared at him whenever they were alone, drinking in his gestures and facial expressions and watching his ass whenever he walked in front of her. She remembered clutching those divine buttocks as he had filled her, and she would find herself breathless and disoriented – how the hell had something so perfect ended up so completely off limits?

But today her mind dwelled not on the pleasure that isolated day had brought, but on her stupid, irresponsible passion and its apparent consequences. She had climbed on top of him with no protection between them, and now she was late. At least four, horrible, indisputable weeks late. She had never been more than a day or two late in her life. She glared again at the innocent calendar. No matter how many times she counted, it had been 61 days since the start of her last period.

Prickles of fear had skimmed across her consciousness occasionally in the last few weeks, but she had steadfastly ignored them, assuming somewhat irrationally that injuring her foot had messed up her cycle. This morning, though, she had needed to call Darren's office to confirm when she would come in to have her cast removed, and staring at the accusing numbers on her phone's calendar had finally driven her to count. And to count again. And then to count a third time.

"Oh God. What have I done?"

She could only stare helplessly at the calendar, frozen in fear.

"Fuck, fuck, fuck!"

She would see her mother tomorrow after the appointment. Should she tell her? Should she tell Etienne?

She nixed that last thought instantly.

He would, presumably, maybe, have to be told, but not now, and not by phone.

Today was Wednesday. She would get her cast off tomorrow, and Etienne wasn't going to come by until Friday afternoon because she had assumed she would eat with her parents after her appointment.

"Oh God, what am I going to do?" For the first time in her life, she desperately wished she had a sister. But her own father had died in an accident when she was very young, and her mother hadn't married Darren until Catherine was in her teens, so she had gotten used to keeping her own company. She and Maggie were close, and she had a few other friends from high school and college she kept in touch with and went out with occasionally, but she had always been comfortable on her own. Wednesdays were all-day workdays for Maggie, anyway, so that option was out.

As her mind searched irrationally for someone she could turn to, someone she could dump this horrible predicament on who would find a way to make it all okay, the irony struck her. The person she was now somehow closest to was the absolutely last person she wanted to turn to.

Was there any possible way this could all be okay?

She was twenty-seven years old, had a good job, a good home, a good brain, and a loving mother and stepfather. She could be a mother. She could be a good mother, couldn't she?

Disjointed images from her dreams over the years passed through her mind: a baby crying, fear, confusion, sorrow— the same horrible dream had haunted her for years, and she knew in her heart that it had been to some degree those recurring dreams that had kept her from ever seriously contemplating children during her time with Bob. Mother-hood was something she had instinctively wanted to avoid, and until today, its possibility had been something she had kept out of her neat, tidy, life.

She stared at the calendar once more and decided she needed to count again. She turned back to September and started counting weeks. How many weeks did the whole ghastly process take? 38? 40? Forty weeks from her last period would put her in the beginning of July. Etienne had said he wanted to have surgery early in the new year. Surgery that could give him back his sight. Or surgery that could leave him a vegetable. Or kill him. And unless her body had gone completely askew and she was just late, she was carrying his baby. Their baby. A baby they had made during the most mind-blowing sex she had ever had, with a guy she had come to adore, who had made it crystal clear he wanted nothing to do with anything resembling a romantic commitment.

Catherine rocked back and forth in misery. What the hell had she done?

———

THE NEXT AFTERNOON Catherine walked carefully into her mother's kitchen. The technician had told her to wean herself gradually from her crutches and given her a set of exercises to start doing. Her foot and ankle felt weak but not painful, and she had accepted the prescription for six weeks of physical therapy though she doubted she would use it.

Her mother was standing at the sink preparing salad, but she turned off the water and came over to embrace Catherine as she entered.

"How does it feel, Honey?"

"It's not bad. Darren looked again at the x-rays from October and said he expected I'd have no trouble. And he said to tell you he'd try hard to be home by six."

Her mother laughed. "I've heard that one before. We'll plan on dinner for about seven, and he'll rush in sometime after that, full of apologies. Good thing he's still cute."

Catherine rolled her eyes. "When are you two going to stop acting like newlyweds?"

"Never, I hope. And I would wish the same for you, young lady. Speaking of which, are you still seeing that blind guy?"

"Jeez, Mom! Not feeling very diplomatic tonight, are you? His name is Etienne, remember? And I never said I was seeing him."

Ellen stared at her daughter intently, and Catherine felt her cheeks flush slightly under the scrutiny.

They looked at each other, some unspoken question and answer passing between them, and Catherine sighed.

"Mom, can we talk for a minute?"

"Of course, Sweetheart. Let's go sit in the living room. I was thinking it was just cold enough to light a fire for the first time. That sound good to you?"

"Yes. Thanks."

"You want some coffee or juice? Maybe hot chocolate? Or a glass of wine?"

Catherine laughed. "I guess if I'm going to pour my heart out to you, hot chocolate and a fire are just what the doctor ordered. I'd tell you to add something extra to the hot chocolate, but I have to drive home." *And I guess adding anything to anything is off the table for a while, anyway.* "I'll turn the fire on while you make the cocoa."

Catherine turned on the gas flame, and her mom came in just a few minutes later carrying a tray with two steaming mugs and a plate of brownies. "I had defrosted these for after dinner tonight, but there's no reason we can't have one now. Dinner's a while off, anyway." She put the tray down on the coffee table after moving aside some newspapers and tucked her legs under herself, like a teenager, on an armchair. Catherine seated herself in the opposite chair and started to do the same but winced when her ankle expressed surprise at such a thoughtless demand.

"Guess I better remember to go gently for a bit," she said, adjusting herself to a more conventional position.

"Oh Honey, I should have thought." Her mother got up and moved a footstool up close to Catherine's legs. "Put your foot up. It's going to take a while, you know." She reached for one of the mugs and handed it to Catherine and then held out the plate of brownies, dropping a napkin on Catherine's lap as if she were a five-year-old. "Take one now and then you can sit peacefully for as long as you want."

Catherine smiled, bit into the chewy chocolate brownie, and closed her eyes with a sigh of gratitude.

"Delicious. As always, Mom. How did you know I'd need chocolate today?"

Her mother stilled the hand that had been raising a cup of cocoa to her lips.

"What is it, Catherine? What's wrong?"

"I'm pregnant, Mom." The words came out without thought or lead-up. Catherine hadn't even been entirely sure she was going to tell her mother the pertinent detail today but instead had been mulling over different ways to discuss the whole issue of Etienne in a rational manner. Because somehow, even without the now stunning prospect of a baby to consider, Etienne had become a major part of her life—of even her daily consciousness, and she needed her mother, her closest confidant, to understand and help her figure out the situation.

Ellen sat quietly, gazing intently at Catherine and then reaching down to settle her cup on the table.

"Is it Etienne's baby?"

"Yes."

"Does he know?"

"No."

"Are you going to keep it?"

Catherine's eyes widened in shock.

"Of course. I could never get rid of my baby." Her left hand moved instinctively to her still completely flat abdomen, and Catherine realized with astonishment that she had somehow just acknowledged her baby as a real being and made a commitment to protect him or her.

Her mother smiled.

"I didn't mean to imply anything bad, Catherine. I just asked. Now I understand. In some cases a pregnancy is an impossible dilemma, but I see that you love the little critter already, and I'm so glad. You'll be a wonderful mother."

Tears fell unbidden down Catherine's cheeks.

"Oh Mom, thank you. I've been so scared and so confused."

Her mother came over and sat on the arm of the chair, pulling Catherine against her in a tight hug.

"We'll get through this, my love. When your father died I thought the future was nothing but an abyss of darkness and misery, but you were there, a demanding bundle of light and joy, greeting each morning with an air of anticipation. And you taught me that every day brings new opportunities for happiness. This little boy or girl growing inside you will do the same, regardless of how complicated things get."

Catherine buried her head deeper into her mother's embrace.

"Oh, Mom. I think I love him. I really do. But he wants nothing to do with love and he's so uncertain about his future. And I really, really, really did not want to fall in love with him or anybody, and I definitely never wanted to have a baby!"

Her mother continued to hold her, rocking gently and caressing her head.

"That's just life's way of showing that there's more going on than we understand. We're riding the bike, balancing well and staying on course, but the path veers off in ways we never expect." After a moment she straightened and tilted Catherine's face up to see her eyes.

"Are you feeling okay? How far along are you? Have you been to a doctor yet? Wait, you didn't have more x-rays today, did you?"

Catherine laughed. Her mother had moved directly into no-nonsense mode, completely skipping the what-ifs and recriminations. This poor baby's parents might be useless, but at least it would have a grandmother who could think straight.

"No, Mom. They said it had been a clean break, and they

saw no need for a second set of x-rays, so I didn't even have to say anything. Although I'm not sure I would have thought about it. I'm not quite used to the whole idea yet, myself."

"And how far along are you?"

"I think about six weeks?"

"That's how long your cast was on. Was that how you broke your ankle? Oh God, is this guy some kind of monster?"

Catherine laughed again.

"No, Mother. He's a perfect gentleman. You'd like him, I'm sure. No, unfortunately, the whole ridiculous story of what happened at the dog park is all true, every embarrassing little detail. I was an absolute ninny to propose it, and we were probably lucky a broken ankle was all that came of it."

Her mother peered at her suspiciously. "Then maybe I don't want to know just how you ended up pregnant. There are some things that are none of a mother's business, anyway. But back to the important issue: Are you still seeing him, and how are you going to tell him?"

"Well . . . there's no easy answer to any of that. We're technically friends, and we see each other fairly often, but we've both agreed that we're not going to get romantically involved."

"Again, my thoughts stray to wondering how on earth you ended up pregnant, but I will valiantly attempt to not think about it. You're sure it's his baby?"

"Yes, Mother! I don't have a string of men I'm sleeping with!"

"Okay, okay. I just thought that maybe Bob had come back and . . . "

"No, Mom. I think he's pretty definite now about where his preferences lie. We've barely even spoken the last couple of months."

"All right, then. You and this *gentleman*, Etienne, are good friends. Neither one of you wants to be in a relationship, but somehow or other you've fallen in love and now you're pregnant. Am I missing anything?"

Catherine closed her eyes and grimaced.

"Nope. That about covers it all, I'm afraid. Well, no, actually, that doesn't even begin to cover it all. Because Etienne feels his life is worthless since he can no longer work as a photographer, and he's planning on having surgery that has a slight chance of restoring his sight but has an equal chance of leaving him much worse off or killing him."

Ellen stared at her daughter in dismay. After a moment she took a deep breath and forced a smile to her lips.

"Let's look at the bright side. Summer babies are so much easier than winter babies. By the time it gets cold enough to bundle them up, you're no longer afraid they're going to break if you do something wrong."

Catherine smiled and then began to laugh. She could not remember her mother ever being overwhelmed. No matter what the problem, she always found some humor in it somewhere, and then got on with solving it. Catherine herself wasn't at all sure that there was a solution to her predicament, but her mother's reliance on humor sure beat her own inclination to panic.

"Thanks, Mom. I came here thinking I might not have the nerve to tell you, but I guess I knew inside that I needed you to tell me everything would be okay."

"Just part of the job, darling. Something you'll have to start doing eventually, too. Now tell me about this surgery. Is it necessary? Is his condition worsening?"

"No, I don't think so. But I know very little, really. Etienne is an incredibly private person, so it's almost surprising I know the little I do know. But he feels that the chance to see again is worth any risk."

"It might be worth any risk to a single, unencumbered young man, but would it be worth it to a new father?"

"I'm not going to tell him."

"WHAT? How can you not tell him? This is the 21st century. He has a legal and moral right to know and a responsibility to you and the baby that he needs to be aware of."

"No, Mom. I can't add that to what he's already dealing with. He's hoping to have surgery in January, so I'll barely even be showing by then, and besides, he's blind, remember?"

Ellen sat silent for a few minutes, gazing at her daughter.

"Are you sure that's what you want to do, Catherine? Doesn't he have the right to know before he takes such a risky step?"

"No. Well, maybe yes, probably yes, but I'm sticking with no. I don't want him to second-guess what he decides, and I don't want him to spend the rest of his life regretting *not* trying, and hating me for it. I mean, it doesn't really matter whether he hates me or not. The fact of the matter is that he hates his life as it is now, and he'd be even more unhappy if he felt obligated by guilt to forego the surgery."

"That all sounds pretty convoluted to me. Whether either one of you likes it or not, as long as you've decided to keep the baby, there's someone else who has to be taken into consideration."

"No. A baby is the last thing he needs to think about. If he goes through with the surgery and comes out of it okay, of course I'll tell him. And if not, well, then I'll raise him or her as best I can, and try to do as good a job as you did."

Her mother sighed.

"Oh, Catherine. I really don't know. But I will keep my opinion to myself, if your mind is made up. May I tell Darren about the baby?"

"Of course, Mom. But wait 'till I've gone home. I don't think I can stand any more emotion today."

"Do you want Darren to ask around about a good doctor in Arlington? You should look into that quickly."

"I think I'm fine. I liked the doctor I went to a few times back when I got my prescription for the pill."

Her mother looked at her skeptically, eyebrows raised.

"No, Mother. Obviously I'm not taking the pill now, and I wasn't six weeks ago. I stopped taking them when Bob moved out to live happily ever after with Rafael."

"Yes, well. I thought I had taught you properly about the birds and the bees, but it seems I must have left out a few pertinent details. And it's evidently a bit late to re-issue my stern motherly warnings. Would you like to invite him for Christmas?"

"Oh God. I completely forgot about Christmas. My mind's been in a whirl these last couple of days, and I totally lost track of time. But yes, that would be nice. I don't think he knows that many people around here. Although it's possible that David from work will invite him. They had him over for Thanksgiving. I suppose it's even possible his mom will fly over from France. I'll have to ask."

"He's more than welcome to come if he'd like, and I promise we won't make any reference to the baby. But I would like to meet him. He's the father of my grandchild, after all, even if he might never know it."

"Don't look at me like that, Mom. I'm trying to make the best decision possible given these totally bizarre circumstances."

"I understand, dear. Well, no, I don't understand at all, but I'll do my best to pretend that I do. Why don't you sit here and drink your cocoa, and I'll go see about getting dinner ready. Darren should be home soon, I hope. I don't want you driving back too late."

Catherine sat in the quiet living room, the light fading fast in the early December evening, and stared into the fire. She smiled as she remembered her mother's words about a summer baby but then closed her eyes and shuddered as an image from her recurring dream came back to her. She had been cold, clutching the baby to her and trying to keep them both warm as a sense of dread and terror swept over her.

Catherine shook herself with an effort and forced the nightmare from her mind. She would have a healthy baby in the summertime, in the 21st century. And maybe real life motherhood would finally drive the stupid dreams away.

CHAPTER FIFTEEN

"Oh Stephen, look! She's doing it again! She's smiling!" Anne was lying on the bed between them, having woken long before dawn demanding to be fed. Stephen had gotten up to stoke the fire, and now he came back to join them, hoping for just another precious hour before needing to get up and start the day.

Anne was twelve weeks old. Just the night before, when Katrina had been cooing over her after swaddling her for the night, Anne had looked her right in the eyes and smiled, a real smile, for the first time. Katrina's mother had warned her that most babies' facial expressions were flatulence, no matter how angelic they might seem, but this morning, there was no doubt. Anne was looking into her eyes and smiling at her.

Stephen rolled to his side and raised his head to look down at his happy daughter, whose tummy was full, her linens clean, and whose eyes were struggling to stay open as she looked up at her parents. "She has your incredibly big eyes, doesn't she? And they're turning brown, just as your mother said they probably would. Good morning, my little angel. Can you smile for me, too, before you fall back asleep?"

It seemed that Anne's smile grew even bigger as her eyes met Stephen's. Katrina laughed in delight. "Look how she loves her papa!"

"How is it that I am lucky enough to have the two most beautiful ladies in all America right here with me in this bed?" He bent his head and kissed Anne's forehead and then leaned over and lightly kissed Katrina's lips.

"Oh Stephen, must you go?"

"Yes, Sweetheart. I'm sorry. The general is most anxious for me to check on the situation at Fort Ticonderoga, as messages have been so infrequent of late. And after the disturbances recently in Massachusetts, he grows more concerned. But you will be safe with your parents, and I will return as quickly as I can."

Katrina nodded and tried to look nonplussed, but her heart was heavy. Stephen had been absent so often of late, and the fear that something would happen to him never left her.

Stephen kissed her again, and this time their lips clung as the kiss deepened. He raised his head and looked questioningly at her, and she nodded quickly. He had waited patiently for what had seemed like forever after Anne's birth, and although the first time had been painful, Katrina was overjoyed that they were at last intimate again.

Anne had fallen asleep, and Stephen very carefully lifted her and carried her to her cradle. He moved swiftly back to the bed, and Katrina reached up for him eagerly. He kissed her deeply and then pulled down her nightdress to kiss and lick her nipples.

"I love the little drops of milk after you've finished nursing her," he murmured, and Katrina blushed but arched her back in delight. She reached up and hungrily ran her hands up and down his back and then grasped his buttocks as she pushed herself up against his firmness.

"Come inside me quickly, Stephen, please. I do not want to wait another second."

He gladly did as he was bid, and they gasped in unison as he filled her. Their lovemaking was fiercely passionate, both aware, as they always were, of the dangers that lay outside their door.

Stephen's head stayed nestled in the crook of her neck for a moment or two before he rolled over and pulled her against him, her head tucked against his chest. Katrina lightly stroked the soft curls of his chest hair, still damp from the heat they had generated, and felt his breathing slow.

He did not doze though, and neither did she. After a few moments she whispered, not wanting to wake Anne. "What is it, Stephen? I can tell you are not at ease."

He pulled her more tightly to him and spoke quietly—so quietly that Katrina tried to still her own breath in order to hear him.

"Every day I put on my uniform and go out to fulfill my obligations to my general and to my king. I put on the damn red coat. I do not try to conceal who I am. I am not a spy; I am an officer in His Majesty's army. I am doing my duty to monitor activity in this, the royal colony of New York. I ride the roads and trails and watch and listen, knowing that I am seen as an enemy and possibly a target."

"But oh, God in heaven, Kat. I do not want to leave you, and I do not want to go searching for situations that will lead to more conflict. Never before have I questioned my duty. I took my commission with enthusiasm, and I assured my family that my sojourn here would be worthy and honorable, and that I would return home to them after a few short years, replete with tales of this wild and untamed land."

"Yet here I am, and my entire world now lies not out there

in the realm of honorable duty, nor back in my parents' home, but in this small cottage with you and Anne. I feel like I am being torn apart."

Katrina lay quietly in his arms, continuing to caress him but uncertain what she could say. Their discussions of late had gone back and forth over familiar territory, she defending the colonists' yearning for autonomy, and he steadfastly asserting the King's need for dominion over his land. But she knew that the recent colonial reports from Boston made him doubt for the first time the honor of his service. He took his officer's oath of loyalty to the King seriously, but every day he spent in this open, expansive land where the inhabitants worked with fervor from dawn to dusk, the more torn and confused he became. And now in the quiet darkness he voiced his hesitations to Katrina, who listened to him without interruption and asked questions that only served to deepen his unease.

"Why cannot parliament accept a delegation from the colonies? Every district in England gets to send representatives to London; why cannot each of the colonies do likewise?"

"I do not understand his reasoning any more than you do. I had no questions or reservations when I came here, and now I sometimes have nothing but doubts. Would we be good parents if we kept our children forever in the nursery and never allowed them to move into the schoolroom? Why even the birds on the riverbank force their young out of the nest so they can learn to fly on their own. I question what harm there could be in allowing you and your parents and your countrymen to judge best how your own land should be governed. And yet to think such thoughts is treason. You married an officer, not a traitor."

The pain in his voice brought tears to her eyes. She had fallen in love with him for so many reasons: his kindness, his humor, his intelligence and talents, but every day that she had spent with him had revealed how solidly good he was. It broke her heart that because of her he now doubted his own worth.

"Do not dare speak of yourself like that, Stephen. You are a good and honorable man. You are everything I could ever wish for in a husband and in a father for our child. I do not know what choices we may need to make in coming days, but I know in my heart that you will always do what is right and true. I just fear that others do not see you for who you truly are." Her voice cracked as she spoke, tears spilling from her eyes, and she clung to him tightly.

"Oh, my dearest heart, I am sorry. Please do not cry. This will all be over soon. It has to be. How I wish I could put you and Anne in a boat, take you down the river, and the three of us could sail home to England."

At his words, Katrina turned her head away, trying to quiet her own distress and not add to his. Yes, she wanted desperately for the three of them to be together in peace, but *this* was her home, not England.

Stephen kept his arms around her, his fingers running through the loosened tendrils of her braid. She tried to force her features to relax. The last thing he needed before setting off was for her to increase his anxiety. Maybe the arrival of spring *would* bring a return to sanity, and maybe. . . she gave up trying to pretend and instead focused on memorizing the feel of his heartbeat against her cheek.

"We must get up, my love. Let's get all of your things together in haste so I can see you to the tavern before I set off."

Katrina took in one last deep breath and then rose, washed, dressed quickly and poured some of the hot water over the chicory roots in the teapot. How she hated the bitter beverage, even sweetened with molasses, but she had steadfastly refused to let Stephen bring any more tea into the cottage, despite his pitiful hints that he could easily bring some up from the British supplies in New York. She had set out biscuits with ham the night before, and they ate them as they prepared their bags.

"Your mother will be happy to have you and Anne with them for a few weeks. And the weather will be getting warmer soon."

Katrina said nothing, and he gave up as his attempts at light conversation went nowhere.

"Promise me you will be careful, Stephen."

"I will, dearest. Do not fret. Your mother will enjoy spoiling you both so much that you will hardly notice my absence."

She gave him a mock glare and then glanced around the cottage one more time to make sure she had not forgotten anything.

"Very well, then, Major Howard. We will spend our days and nights frequenting banquets and balls in every corner of the Tarry Towns, and you will have to search from one townhouse to another to find us upon your return."

Katrina strove to keep her words light, but her insides clenched in dread at the thought of the several days she would have to live through, not knowing if he were safe. Reports of confrontations were coming in from several parts of Massachusetts, and the idea of him traveling the many hundred miles filled her with dread.

"Trying to make me jealous, wench? It will not work, you know. Even if your father turned the tavern into a second Almacks and invited every dandy in the colonies, I would not fear. You are mine, sweet Katrina, now and forever."

He, too, kept his tone light, but as he helped her into the carriage, she turned to him and pressed her head tightly into his chest, Anne carefully nestled between them.

"Oh Stephen. I love you so. Please *do* take care and come home quickly."

He tipped her chin up and looked intently into her deep brown eyes. "You know whenever we part, that you keep my heart with you. You have ruined me, dearest love, because I am only truly alive when I am with you. I will come back quickly, I promise."

Katrina nodded, trying hard not to cry again. Stephen drove Lord Philipse's carriage to the tavern, received a quick embrace from his mother-in-law and a curt nod from his father-in-law, and then, after a final swift kiss to Katrina's forehead, drove off back to the manor house where he would mount his horse to begin his journey north.

Susanna had swept the baby out of Katrina's arms and into the tavern, leaving her alone with her father in the early morning chill.

"He travels alone?" Johann's voice was gruff in the quiet.

"With a guide, I think, but otherwise alone, yes, Papa." She stared hard at him, trying to discern if he knew of Stephen's exact plans or of any specific danger that awaited him.

"You have a child now, so we must hope for the babe's sake that her father stays safe." He turned abruptly to walk off towards the well, but Katrina felt her heart lift and let out the breath she hadn't realized she had been holding. Surely his words would have been different if he knew of any pre-arranged obstacles to Stephen's trip.

"Thank you, Papa." She spoke to his retreating back, tightened her cloak around her, and turned to follow her mother inside.

CHAPTER SIXTEEN

"My mother said to tell you that she and Darren would love for you to join us for Christmas."

"That's kind of her, but I'd hate to intrude. Christmas is such a family-oriented time."

"For heaven's sake, Etienne! I wouldn't have asked if any of us looked on it as an intrusion. Can't you just for once see yourself as something besides a blind object of pity?"

Etienne stopped and turned his head in Catherine's direction. They had been walking with Jake along the path that paralleled the interstate. Catherine had suggested it the week before, saying that she knew Jake would enjoy it and that she needed to walk to build strength back in her ankle. Etienne had agreed with his now customary reserve, and they had taken a walk at noon every day the weather permitted. It was cold, but so far they had only been bothered occasionally by a chilly rain.

Catherine saw the muscles of Etienne's jaw clench as he no doubt struggled to find something diplomatic to say. For the hundredth time, she wished he didn't insist on the stupid glasses. If they were going to argue, she should at least be able to see his expression.

Oh God, what a bitchy thing to think. Idiot! Don't you think he'd like to be able to see your expression?

Feeling chagrined, she reached out and took Etienne's hand, interlacing her fingers with hers. He resisted for a moment, but she soon felt the answering pressure of his grasp through their gloves.

"I'm sorry." They both said the words at almost the exact moment, and Catherine laughed.

"Okay, that was horribly rude of me, and I apologize. But really, Etienne, I wouldn't have asked if you weren't welcome. Your mom's not coming over, is she?"

"No. She offered, but I persuaded her to stay home. I haven't told her yet that I'm hoping to have surgery next month. I just know she'll be online instantly to book a flight once I drop that bombshell."

They had turned by unspoken agreement and started walking again.

"What does your family usually do for Christmas?"

"We've more or less been making it up as we go along the last few years. My mom's parents are dead, of course, but before my Grandma died, we always celebrated Christmas dinner at her house, which is now my house, but it would be too weird to try to do Christmas there without her. Mom and Darren sometimes drive to see his family in Pennsylvania, depending on Darren's work schedule. In the past when I didn't go with them, I spent the day with Bob's family. But I think this year we're all just staying put, and we'll do it like we did last year: I went over early on Christmas Eve, we had dinner, went to church at 11, and then slept in and had a lazy breakfast and opened gifts on Christmas morning. That sound like something you'd enjoy?"

"Is your mother asking me to spend the night?"

181

Catherine heard the hesitation in his voice and felt a brief pang, realizing how each unknown outing had to be somewhat intimidating.

"Yes. I'm sure that's what she meant. I know she's eager to meet both you and Jake."

Etienne was silent for a moment and then smiled, a polite and most definitely constrained smile, but not a refusal.

"Tell her thank you for me. That would be very nice. I can Uber there if you give me the address ahead of time."

"*Please*, Etienne. Don't be ridiculous. Why in the world should you get a ride if I'm going there myself? If our simple Virginia ways prove too boring for your cosmopolitan French taste, you can always call for a ride and make your escape."

Etienne stopped again. "Catherine? Are we snapping at each other for some reason I've missed?"

Catherine heard the uncertainty in his voice and immediately felt guilty once again. She had no right taking her anxiety out on him, particularly as she was deliberately concealing the cause of her stress. Without thought she reached out and took Etienne's other hand as well.

"Stay, Jake," she said as she slipped the handle of the harness from Etienne's hand.

"I apologize, Etienne. I've been working hard on that article all morning, and I haven't been sleeping that well the last couple of nights. I'm sorry I've been so bitchy today."

As if of their own accord, Etienne's arms pulled Catherine close and he caressed her hair as he held her head nestled against his neck.

"Don't apologize, Sweetheart," he whispered. "I shouldn't be interrupting your work every day for these walks."

Catherine breathed in slowly and deeply, knowing she should pull away but wanting desperately to burrow closer. His arms around her felt so right, and even the slightly musky scent of his aftershave or deodorant seemed like a balm to her frazzled senses. She felt him spreading light kisses against her hair and wished she could stay wrapped in his arms forever.

Instead, she took in one more deep breath and forced herself to straighten up. Jake was looking up at them with his head tilted slightly to the side, tongue hanging out.

"Just ignore me, Etienne. I'm so happy to be out here with you and Jake, honestly. And I think it's been making my afternoons much more productive." An absolute lie, of course, since she was finding herself utterly exhausted and in need of a nap by two in the afternoon. But working from home made it possible, fortuitously, for her to lie down a while before trying to discipline her mind back to the article on deforestation. Her mom said fatigue was normal early in pregnancy, but she was definitely not going to share that tidbit with Etienne.

———

Two hours later Catherine forced herself up from the couch. She had to finish editing the article as she had promised David it would be done before six. Normally she enjoyed her work, turning the convoluted sentences the field reporters often came up with into the gently scholarly prose the magazine readers preferred. But focusing these days was proving to be a challenge.

She wondered how much she could ascribe to erratic pregnancy hormones and how much was due to the increasing mess that was her relationship with Etienne.

Was her mother right? Was she doing the wrong thing by not telling him? She hadn't known him all that long, but somehow she instinctively knew that learning of her pregnancy would send him into a tailspin of guilt and indecision.

But God, how good it had felt to be in his arms earlier today. It had taken all her willpower not to pull his mouth to hers when he was holding her, wanting, no *needing*, to feel his tongue dance with hers. Was pregnancy making her horny, or was it just Etienne? She had certainly never felt this burning desire for Bob or for the two or three guys she had gone out with way back in high school. Their kisses, with her back pressed against a locker when no teachers were around, had usually just left her wondering what all the fuss was about.

But every time she was near Etienne, she wanted to touch him. Wanted to feel his fingers and arms entwined with hers. Wanted to nuzzle against his neck and inhale him. Wanted to feel him grow hard against her thigh and . . .

"Snap out of it, woman!" She spoke the words out loud as she got up from the table and walked to the kitchen sink. She filled the kettle with water, put it on the burner, and got out a cup and teabag. She had to pull her mind out of the bedroom and concentrate. This baby at least deserved a mother who could earn a living, even if that mother couldn't seem to get her head on straight.

ETIENNE SIGHED in disgust as he once again stopped the news stream he had been trying to listen to. At least four times in the last half hour he had realized he had absolutely no idea what had been coming out of his laptop speakers. He knew it was a cold and cloudy December day, having not felt any warmth on his face while he walked Jake. Yet his imagination had Catherine wrapped closely in his arms in a sun-lit landscape, her breasts pressed tightly against him, his hands moving to encircle her buttocks.

Jesus. He shook himself. No wonder she had snapped at

him earlier. Was he giving off the same mixed signals to her as his stupid cock and his brain were giving to him? What was the matter with him?

Christmas. That was what had set off this latest line of fantasy. If he were going to spend Christmas with Kat and her family, he would have to bring presents. Somehow in wondering if a bookstore gift card might be best, his mind had leapt to lingerie, and it had all spiraled out of control from there. Surely, he thought wryly, that was a depressing and meme-worthy image: a blind man and a crazy dog in a lingerie shop, trying to buy something for a woman he had never seen.

What the hell was he doing? He knew, deep in his gut, that he should be, that he *was*, grateful to have survived the explosion in Egypt. His intellect scolded his whiny inner child that there were millions of people in situations much bleaker than his own. He had food, shelter, and access to the world at his voice commands via the magic of technology. He even had a faithful dog he trusted and was growing to love. He had a mother who yearned for nothing more than to be able to care for him and acquaintances who still treated him like a normal human being. And he had somehow been lucky enough to become friends with a wonderfully intelligent, witty, and caring young woman.

Friends. He found himself on his feet, pacing the condo without even realizing he had stood. Just thinking the word filled him with distaste. He didn't want to be Catherine's friend; he wanted to be her lover, wanted to wake up next to her in the morning and hold her close at night. He yearned for the ringing music of her laughter and the sense of home-coming he felt when her fingers were entwined with his. But he had no right to even think such thoughts in his present condition. He was useless to her. He would never be able to offer her support of any kind or be the strong, capable man she deserved.

The pain and yearning that washed over him was so intense that he crouched down on the floor, arms crossed across his chest as if to keep his heart from breaking. Where in the world were such crazy ideas coming from?

His preoccupation was cut short by a wet tongue licking his face and Jake's excited panting in his ear. The poor dog probably thought this was some new game, as Etienne had certainly never been on the floor with him before.

He put out his hands to pat Jake's head and took a deep breath. "I'm sorry, boy," he sighed. "I didn't mean to get you upset, too. I guess we're both in the same boat – yearning to be near Catherine when she's got her own life to live."

He felt and heard Jake's tail thumping against the floor and laughed. "Yeah, I'd wag my tail, too, if I had one. What do you say I call us a cab and we go set off in search of Christmas gifts?"

Unbidden, the mental picture of a black lace bra shot through his mind, and he sighed again. Thirty-one years he had lived, studied, traveled, and produced work he was proud of. He had always found it easy to get along with people and had enjoyed the company of women. He was confident that he had been a considerate lover and a thoughtful and engaged boyfriend during the few semi-serious relationships he'd been involved in.

Yet how was it this woman he had never even seen turned him on more than anyone he had ever known? His hands yearned to caress her, to draw forth the sighs and moans his mind kept replaying from their one intimate encounter, to bury himself deep within her and feel her tighten around him.

Jake gave a soft bark as if to remind him of their mission. Etienne groaned, reached down to adjust himself in his now far too tight jeans, pulled his phone from his pocket, and called in his request for a ride.

———

"WOULD you like me to go with you?"

It had rained hard all day, so they had skipped their walk. But Catherine had called to see if Etienne had been able to make the follow-up appointment with Dr. Abrams.

Etienne didn't answer immediately, and Catherine could tell he was trying to figure out the best way to put her off.

She knew he hated getting her involved, but it would probably be good to have someone there with Jake while they did the scan. At least that was the excuse she would give if he balked because she sure as hell didn't want him going alone. She was deceiving him big time—lying by omission and feeling overwhelmed with guilt as a result. Certainly hearing the doctor's words directly might reassure her she was doing the right thing—or persuade her to come clean.

"Are you sure you can spare the time?"

"You said the 21st, right? That's next week and four days before Christmas. No one's busy right before Christmas, except for holiday related stuff. And all that business is for people with big families and elaborate plans, so that leaves me free to do whatever I want."

Catherine waited, hearing Etienne's indecision in his silence, and then continued. "I'd be happy to go with you, Etienne, and I'm not just saying that to be polite. You know they always say it's better to have a second person listening to medical information. And if they use any crazy-ass words we don't understand, we can figure out what they mean together."

Etienne laughed. "Okay. You've got a point. I find myself

drifting off when I listen to research articles on brain functions, and the terminology all starts running together."

"Do you want me to drive, or should we take the metro?"

Etienne hesitated again, and Catherine rolled her eyes, figuring he was trying to determine which would be less of an imposition. *Enough already! He could play at complete independence on his own time.*

"I'll drive. Who knows what the weather will be like, and this way we won't have to worry about walking to the metro."

"You're sure it's not too much trouble?"

"I've got to tell you, Etienne. You carry this whole 'not wanting to bother anyone' a bit too far. Friends help each other out and enjoy spending time together."

Another moment of silence. Catherine pictured his brow furrowing.

"Thanks, Kat. We can talk about it tomorrow if the weather's better and we're able to take a walk. And as for the rest—I don't sit at home intentionally planning ways to come across as an asshole."

Catherine laughed, realizing with a start that she hadn't felt her features relax enough to smile in days. "Etienne, enough. You know that's not what I think. But one of these days you really are going to have to stop thinking of yourself as a defective product. As you are now is the only you I've known, and I'm not complaining."

"WHAT BOOK ARE YOU LISTENING TO?" Catherine was desperate to break the silence that had filled the car since she picked Etienne up. Jake had wagged his tail and stretched his neck for her caress, but Etienne's dry "Good morning. Thanks for coming for us," had been far from encouraging.

"A novel about the division of the Middle East after World War I. It's fascinating how the seeds for disaster were spread so haphazardly by a few condescending Europeans."

Thank God, Catherine thought. A thoroughly depressing topic, but at least when he spoke about books, Etienne seemed to relax and become less self-conscious. "You must hate the place after what happened to you."

"Not at all. Obviously I wish whoever blew themselves up at the pyramid that day hadn't done so, but I understand the frustration that eats away at people. I just don't see how any of it's going to be resolved anytime soon."

"How much time did you spend there?"

"The Middle East? My father was posted to Morocco when I was in first through third grade, but that's not really the Middle East. And then we were in Jordan for my sophomore and junior years of high school. After that I only returned when I was on some assignment or other. But even when I was little I couldn't understand how people so rich could ignore the poverty all around them."

"But that can't justify blowing up tourist sights."

"When people feel they have no options at all, they lose all sense of perspective. No one wanted to hurt me, to blind me. But whoever that guy or those guys were, they felt there was no other way to get the world to pay attention."

"That's amazing, Etienne. You're really not bitter towards them, are you?"

"No. I'm not. I'm mad as hell that I can't see, that I was in the crosshairs when they reached their breaking point, but I can only feel sorry for anyone pushed to such a level of despair."

"Wow. You're a better man than I. I try to steer clear of even thinking about international politics."

"Oh, come on. You work for *GeoMonde* and spend your days editing articles that concern activity in some of the most interesting places on the planet. You can't tell me you don't pay attention."

"Of course I pay attention. But I can't do anything about any of the tinderbox situations we cover. I'm not sure anyone can. I sometimes think we're all just pieces of flotsam caught on a tide we have no control over. And since I hate feeling impotent, I just choose not to think about any of it."

They rode in silence for a few moments.

"Do you want me to drop you off while I park?"

"No. We've got plenty of time. I know parking downtown always used to be horrible, so I can't imagine it's gotten any better over the years. If you can find a garage at or near the hospital, I'll pay for the parking."

Fifteen minutes later they walked into the large neurology department waiting room. Catherine knew he had managed the whole ordeal on his own before, so she was surprised to feel him reach for her hand and let her lead. But as they approached the desk, she hesitated. She didn't want to intrude or make Etienne feel she was butting in where she didn't belong.

"The desk is at 10 o'clock, six or seven feet away from here," she said, stepping back a bit.

Etienne turned towards her and reached out his right hand, Jake's lead in his left. "It's all right, Catherine. You've convinced me you want to be here, so let's stick together, okay?"

Catherine took his hand once more and laced her fingers with his, squeezing gently. "That's fine with me," she whispered.

In the small exam room, Catherine pushed the single chair as close to the wall as she could and pulled Jake between her legs. When Dr. Abrams came in, she noticed her look of surprise at seeing someone else in the room.

"Good morning, Etienne. I see you have company today."

"Dr. Abrams. This is my friend, Catherine Reynolds. Please don't hesitate to speak freely in front of her."

Catherine watched as the doctor shined her light into Etienne's eyes and thought again how riveting those eyes were. A distant memory suddenly came to her of her mother staring motionless in front of the television while they watched *The Sting* on the classic movie channel. "Those eyes," she had sighed, gazing at Paul Newman with adoration. Now Catherine finally understood her mother's fixation. It was a sin for eyes that blue to be hidden behind a pair of dark glasses.

Dr. Abrams continued her examination with the standard hammer to the leg and had Etienne balance briefly on alternate legs and touch his nose with one finger of each hand in turn. The doctor then helped Etienne back onto the table and proceeded to read a series of words, asking Etienne to recite them back to her.

Catherine's eyes widened, partly in admiration, partly in trepidation. She thought she had been paying attention, but Etienne remembered more of the words than she did. He then obediently spelled his name backwards, and Catherine silently thanked the gods that it was Etienne in the hot seat and not her.

"All right, Etienne. I'm finished torturing you for the time being. Normally we'd move into my office to discuss what I've observed today, but given that everyone seems comfortable, we'll just talk here."

"As I told you last time we met, I see no evidence of any neurological damage aside from the blockage or pressure on the ocular nerves. Your balance, stability, coordination— even your short-term memory—have improved in the last two months. We'll go ahead and do another scan to make sure nothing on the inside has changed, but I'd say you've made a remarkable recovery."

In the brief silence that followed, only Jake's quiet panting was audible.

"But I can't see."

"Well, no, but given the depth of penetration of whatever it was that hit you, the fact that you are able to carry out all normal neurological functions is truly extraordinary."

"But we spoke last time of the possibility of surgery to restore my sight."

Dr. Abrams sighed. "You're scheduled for the CT scan at 1:30, right?"

When Etienne agreed, she continued. "I'll most likely get the results tomorrow morning, but I'll be in surgery starting very early, and then the office will be closed for Christmas. Make an appointment for the first week in the new year, and we'll go over the scan and discuss our options at that point. Does that sound reasonable?"

"Yes, of course. Thank you, Dr. Abrams."

Etienne held out his hand and the doctor shook it and then gave Catherine a brief nod. "Nice meeting you," she said and walked out.

Catherine saw Etienne's deep intake of breath, and her heart clenched as he silently slipped the dark glasses back in place and assumed a neutral expression.

"Do you have time to wait around for the scan? Because if you're busy, Jake and I can make it home alone on the metro."

Damn. He was shutting down again. Shutting her out and retreating to his numbingly impersonal, grateful acquaintance persona. *Enough.* She was getting tired of the game they were both playing.

The doctor had closed the door behind her, probably automatically, even though Etienne had not needed to undress. She might as well take advantage of the privacy and lay at least a few of her cards on the table. She was not going to tell him just how consequential the question of surgery was to her, personally, but she could let him know that he had become important to her. She moved towards him and touched his hand.

"Etienne. Listen. I know you were hoping for more this morning. And we . . . I agreed we wouldn't bring this up, but there's something you need to understand because you're driving me fucking crazy. I spend time with you because I enjoy spending time with you. I care about you. You're not alone in this mess anymore." His head was turned in her direction, but the damn glasses were providing their annoying shield. She sensed, however, that he was listening intently.

"I thought we had agreed that we were friends. And even though we definitely agreed it was a mistake, I did go to bed with you. That's not something I do with every man I speak to on the metro. If I had a grain of sense, I wouldn't be telling you this, because it's really none of your business, but the fact of the matter is that you're the only person besides my gay ex-boyfriend I've ever slept with. I'm not telling you because I want a relationship or anything complicated— we've gone over all that already. But I wouldn't spend time with you if I didn't want to. Yes, I agreed it would be best to keep things casual, but I think you need to stop all this polite 'I don't want to bother you' bullshit.' I'm really getting tired of it."

Again, only Jake's breathing was audible, but as Catherine's eyes turned towards him, she laughed in spite of herself.

"Well, now that all that's off my chest, you should know that Jake's looking back and forth between us like he's afraid something bad is going to happen. Just stop being stupid, would you please? Let's go down and find some coffee while we wait for your next appointment."

Etienne was still on the end of the examining table, his top teeth biting into his lower lip. He was wearing a brown argyle sweater over a pair of jeans, and Catherine saw his shoulders relax as he took another deep breath.

"Thanks, Kat." He reached out his other hand and she helped him down off the table. She extended her arm around his waist and pulled him close to her, pressing her head into the crook of his neck for just a second. Then she bent down and put Jake's lead into his hand and opened the door.

CHAPTER SEVENTEEN

Stephen made a conscious effort not to glance towards the cottage as he brought the carriage back to the manor stable and got his horse ready. He refused to think about how much he would rather be back in bed with Katrina and Anne instead of leaving them for weeks. He rode through the woods and around town, not wanting to see the tavern again, and found his guide waiting for him just beyond the cemetery that fanned out behind the church where he and Katrina had wed just a few months back.

What changes the year had brought. It had been just this time last year, in a spectacular early spring, when he and Katrina met and his life was transformed forever. The weather then had been a glorious anthem to their instant attraction. This year spring was behaving like a petulant child, determined to keep everyone waiting as long as possible.

Even Kit, the Wiccopee Indian who was serving as his unofficial batman, guide, and bodyguard, looked cold as he walked around the clearing with his horse.

Unlike some of the Indians in the area, Kit, whose real

name had been shortened and simplified by his English contacts, had chosen to stay on good terms with the Philipse family and had even acted as a guide for the military during the French and Indian war. Now he had agreed to lead Stephen to Fort Ticonderoga, a journey that would probably take at least a week, given that they would not be able to change horses along the way.

Kit's saddlebags were full of supplies for the two men and horses, and he helped Stephen attach additional bags to his own mount. There would be a few inns and stables along the way, but most nights they would be out in the open air. His mission was not secret, per se, but neither Stephen nor his superiors were eager to attract the attention of New Yorkers eager for an altercation.

Stephen was grateful for the older man's company, but grateful, too, that Kit was not prone to idle conversation. They rode steadily through the overcast terrain, the temperature stubbornly refusing to rise. When what passed for daylight finally began to fade, they made camp and heated up some food and water over the fire that Kit managed to start in spite of the damp.

Stephen's muscles were used to long hours in the saddle, but getting comfortable on the rocky soil was difficult. He hoped that Katrina and Anne were warm in the tavern.

With luck, he and Kit would reach the Bird and Bottle Inn by the following evening, and then it would be two days of hard riding to reach Albany. After that they would experience little comfort until they reached the fort. He couldn't and would not count on welcome or hospitality from any small homesteads along the way. The population in the colony was almost equally divided between subjects who wanted to stay loyal to the crown and those who supported the agitators calling for armed rebellion. He fervently hoped that they would find everything at the fort well under control, with only understandable mishaps to blame for the lack of communication. Then he could head back home quickly.

Home. Katrina had filled his heart so completely that he now thought of their little cottage as home and England as a distant memory. He still daydreamed of how wonderful it would be to take Katrina and Anne back to England and introduce them to his family, but though he at times devoted considerable mental energy to trying to work out the logistics of such a voyage, he couldn't in truth see it ever happening.

Katrina's father's family was Dutch, and her mother had come over as a young girl from Scotland. But Katrina and her siblings were Americans through and through. Stephen was aware of the militia training that was occurring throughout the colony, and he knew damn well that Katrina's brother and father were actively involved.

Some days when he watched the training unobserved, he had to quash a yearning to ride in and give them pointers. Just two weeks ago he had observed from a distance as Martin tried to quickly reload his musket, and he had instinctively wanted to help. He worried for the young man's safety, as the vehemence and enthusiasm of Johann and his volunteers were still countered by the strong Tory presence in the colony.

Acting Governor Colden, or "Old Silver Locks," as he was affectionately called, was struggling to maintain peace in Manhattan, where the growing numbers of Sons of Liberty were at constant odds with the still numerous conservatives who urged loyalty to the King. The entire colony was splitting along divisive philosophical lines, and Stephen often found himself silently considering the pros and cons of both camps.

He had read accounts of Edmund Burke's passionate

speeches in parliament, urging the crown to halt coercive measures, and he desperately hoped that such sense would prevail before the violence escalated out of control. Riding through the small settlements dispersed among the various massive land grants, he knew that some watched his passage with suspicion while others were reassured by his presence.

They continued their trek north, the hours of daylight dutifully lingering due to the calendar but the chill in the air persisting. The hours in the saddle gave him little to think about save how he wished Katrina were by his side. Even at a distance, the thought of her smiling eagerness as she reached for him brought a stirring in his loins. How he wanted to give her a secure life with him, free from the constant threat of danger. It had been irresponsible of him to get her with child, but a part of him still selfishly rejoiced that their hands had been forced. He feared every day that something would happen to him that would keep him from caring for Katrina and Anne. Yet the joy and peace he felt when he was with them made his regrets subside.

They picked up additional supplies in Albany and then began the longest part of the journey towards Lake Champlain. Their final night was spent in the small settlement of Castleton, where Stephen felt stares coming at him from all directions as they rode out in the morning. It seemed support for the King waned the further he moved from heavily populated areas.

As they at last drew closer to the fort, Stephen expected scouts to apprehend them, but none did.

"When were you here last?" he asked Kit. "I expected there to be greater signs of activity by now."

"I traveled this far north last summer with an envoy from the governor. At that time soldiers were busy strengthening the fort."

"Let's hope they have completed their task and are secure within the walls. It does trouble me that no one is about."

When they finally reached the outskirts of the fortifications, no one appeared to challenge or greet them.

"Would you like me to go in first, Major?"

"No, Kit, of course not. But thank you. Let's go see what the situation is and hope that we can be on our way home again soon."

———

KATRINA GRITTED her teeth and tried to take a deep slow breath. If one more person gave her a furtive, suspicious glance, she thought she might scream.

She had lived in this village all her life and had served customers at the tavern since she was old enough to carry ale without spilling. Now people she had regarded as kinsmen quieted when she walked past.

She ached for Stephen and missed their cottage, a haven that had seemed like home the instant they entered it for the first time together following their wedding.

She even yearned for Hudson, who had been a demanding, distracting, but always reassuring and beloved companion on the too frequent nights when Stephen had been absent during the past several months.

"Absolutely not." Her mother's words had brooked no discussion when Katrina tentatively suggested bringing Hudson to join them. "Stephen will be back before you know it, lass. I cannot have a puppy running around causing problems."

Katrina had started to protest that Hudson would not cause problems, but even to her own mind, the words sounded unconvincing. Hudson was a bundle of non-stop energy, wanting to befriend every stranger he met, and his presence would most definitely disrupt the tavern's guests.

If only Stephen had not needed to travel so far north! During his normal trips to Manhattan, Katrina had stayed at their cottage, Hudson ferociously guarding her and Anne. The nights alone with the baby were long, but Katrina never minded terribly. She kept Anne in bed with her, nursing her comfortably whenever the little one awoke, Hudson adjusting his position against her legs as she moved with the baby.

She and Stephen had laughed over Hudson's devious determination to share their bed. Katrina had procured a rug just for him that she positioned near the fireplace, and he settled there happily during the chilly evenings when they were still up and about.

The minute they doused the candles and settled into bed, however, he jumped right up and made himself comfortable by Katrina's feet.

"My mother would have a fit if she saw him," Katrina had feebly protested.

"I am certain my own mother would whole-heartedly agree," Stephen had responded, smiling. "What is your wish, my love? Shall I exert my military authority and banish the rascal forcibly?"

"Please don't, Stephen. He is a great comfort when you are away, and he does no harm."

As Hudson always obligingly hopped down when sleep was not their immediate goal, his presence at night was now just part of their normal routine.

But nothing was routine here at the tavern. In less than a year she had become an entirely different person, and she no longer felt at home here. Her mother told her to run along whenever she offered to help, but there was nowhere to run *to*. Anne still slept more hours than she was awake, but with the weather so contrary, that was probably a blessing.

Restless and out of sorts, Katrina went again to the door to look out. The damp chill hit her as she stared into the gray mist, trying to decide what to do. It was early; she could walk the two odd miles to the cottage, visit the housekeeper at the manor house who had agreed to look out for Hudson, and spend a bit of time in the cottage before heading back. Anne would grow heavy during such a long walk, but Katrina did not want to leave her knowing how busy her mother and sisters would be during the mid-day meal.

Her mind made up, she went up the narrow stairs to begin bundling up Anne. She would put her own cloak on so as to cover them both, but she wanted the baby well-swaddled underneath.

Her mother looked askance as Katrina moved to pass her as she departed. "What in the world are you thinking, child? It is another heinous day out there. I declare, the weather these days reminds me more of the Highlands than it ever has before. Stephen wanted you here to keep you safe, not so you would be traipsing up and down the valley, catching your death of cold."

"We will not be gone long, Mama. But I must get out, or I will go mad. Please do not fuss."

Her mother shook her head in disapproval, but the sound of diners coming through the door distracted her, and Katrina took advantage of the commotion to slip out the back with Anne.

She walked steadily but cautiously over the slippery paths. How different it was from her mad runs down to the riverbank a year ago to see Stephen, the mysterious British major. Now she stepped carefully so as not to jostle their sleeping angel. Theirs! What miraculous changes the year had brought.

The handsome officer who had sketched her picture had proven to be a kind and thoughtful friend and a loving and passionate husband. But he was now off investigating the condition of a British stronghold, while the patrons at her family's tavern were discussing militia training and Sons of Liberty communications. When would this madness end?

Before Stephen's arrival, Katrina had never questioned her role in the arduous but secure routine the simple tavern provided. Nor had she questioned, in recent years, the spreading discontent with the injustices forced on them by a distant and obviously deranged monarch.

What was the foolish king and parliament imagining? That they could somehow continue to bleed the colonists dry and deprive them of any voice in their own governance? Such tyranny could not, would not, be endured, and King George would be well-warned that their days of compliance were at an end.

But where would this leave her beloved Stephen, and now herself and their child? Would his family ever forgive him if he forsook his professional duty and betrayed his commission? She knew that Stephen saw some merit in the colonists' complaints, but could he live with himself if he broke his vows? What would become of them in this ever-darkening future?

Katrina trudged on, head down in the mist, wishing desperately that Stephen would return soon and hold her close to quiet her fears.

WAVES OF FRUSTRATION swept over Stephen at the encroaching darkness. The appalling disarray at Fort Ticonderoga had shocked and frightened him. He needed to get south as quickly as possible, send secure messages to General

Gage and Acting Governor Colden, and then hope and pray that they would *not* send him back up to re-establish order at the fort. How had the men let things get so out of hand? Stephen understood that sickness and the harsh winter had taken their toll, but these were British soldiers!

Captain Delaplace, the fort's commander, seemed totally oblivious to the growing tide of rebellion sweeping the colonies. The men garrisoned at the fort appeared to be treating it like a rest home where they could grow fat and lazy and look after the 24 women and children now contentedly making their home within the compound. Only young Lieutenant Feltham seemed attentive to Stephen's sharp rebukes and exhortations to tighten their security.

What a bloody nightmare. It looked like any dream of having a prolonged reunion with Katrina and Anne would be just that—a dream. Would he ever be the husband and father he wanted to be? How could he call himself a man if he couldn't be there for the two most important people in his life?

Kit turned and pointed at the path they would take to head back towards Lake George, and Stephen pulled his cloak tighter around himself before urging his horse on.

———

KATRINA WEARILY LIFTED her eyes and breathed a slight sigh of relief when the lights from the tavern finally came into view. Anne had begun fretting long before they reached the cottage, and Katrina had felt guilt pangs shoot through her. She was too young to be carried through the cold mist for hours just because her mother couldn't bear her own family's censure.

She missed Stephen terribly. Missed his instantaneous smile whenever he looked at her and Anne. Missed his warm body pressed to hers at night, often in passion that never ceased to thrill her, and afterwards in warm comfort and tenderness. She missed their quiet conversations when they discussed literature and art and their fiery arguments when politics inevitably poked its angry fangs between them.

Should she give in to his suggestion that she go to England and await him there? Everything in her rebelled at the idea. These beautiful hills with their rich, fragrant woods and the ever-present reassurance of the river were her home. The hard-working, devout people that populated the Hudson Valley and farmed the land and worked the mills were her family. They had made her into the woman Stephen had fallen in love with, and she couldn't just abandon them.

She pushed open the back door of the tavern, the strong, yeasty scent of the barreled ale enveloping her. She took a deep breath, grateful to finally be out of the damp, and then tilted her head, surprised at the quiet. Usually at this time of day the building was awash in the sounds of conversation, tankards and cutlery clattering against the wooden tables, and her father and brother engaging in high-spirited banter with the diners while they worked.

But this evening conversation seemed muted, and she knew it was not because the tavern's occupants had caught sight of her—the wife of an enemy.

Loosening the folds of her cloak that wrapped Anne from head to toe, she shifted the now sleeping baby as she pushed her way into the still warmer kitchen area.

"Oh there you are, Katrina. I was worried when you were gone so long. Are you well, my child?"

"Yes, Mama. I am sorry to have distressed you. Is all well here? It seems more subdued than it ought."

"Six more villagers have fallen ill. The fever seems to be spreading rapidly, and obviously everyone is worried that it is the pox. Was anyone at the manor house ill?"

"I'm not sure. Mrs. Gantry was alone in the kitchen the whole time I was with her, and I suppose that, itself, is a bit unusual. But she did not mention anyone feeling poorly. Is it serious? I know many have been suffering from the ague in this dreadful weather."

"It does seem more urgent than the normal ague. Your brother said he saw Genny paying a visit to the Van Waert household with her bundle of poultices."

Katrina shivered despite the kitchen's humid warmth. She had foolishly hoped that spring would bring relief to the darkness that seemed determined to close around her and her new family. But this year spring seemed to hold nothing but shadows.

CHAPTER EIGHTEEN

The CT scan ordeal had seemed to last for hours, and Catherine knew Etienne had been glad of her presence, if for no other reason than to keep Jake company while he was ensconced in the coffin-like contraption.

They didn't talk much on the ride home, but when they pulled into the drive to Etienne's building, he turned towards her.

"Do you want to park and walk with us? It's been a long day, and I know Jake needs to move a bit."

"Sure. I'll pull into one of the visitor slots."

They got out of the car and Etienne reached for her hand. "I'm turned around from your parking, so I have no idea which way we're heading."

Catherine allowed him to lace his fingers with her own.

"See?" he continued. "Aren't you impressed? I *can* admit I need help once in a while."

"Ha. You're just kissing up because of the tantrum I pulled earlier."

Etienne stopped walking and pulled Catherine towards him.

"Kissing up? Is that what you call it? If you're going to throw words like that around, you'd better be prepared to back them up."

Catherine looked at him, unable to see his eyes but guessing from how his breathing had faltered that he felt guilty for the words the moment they left his lips. She went up on her toes, anyway, and brushed his lips with hers.

"It's late and getting dark. I know you can't tell, but I can. Let's get this walk over with and go inside and order dinner."

"You're not in a hurry to leave?"

"No, Etienne. I'm not in a hurry to go anywhere."

They spent ten minutes walking in the late afternoon dusk, and by the time they returned to the entrance, they were both shivering. The morning had been unseasonably warm, but December's early darkness brought a return of wintry chill.

"I don't know about you, but I need something hot when we get upstairs. I don't suppose you have tea, do you?'

"I've got a few bottles of wine, and I'm pretty sure there's some scotch and rum in the cupboard. Will that do?"

Catherine was silent for a moment. "I think I'm more in the mood for tea or hot chocolate. I'll be happy to hunt down the good stuff for you, though, if that's what you'd prefer."

"If it's tea you want, I'm sure you'll find some. My mother tried to stock the shelves with everything under the sun before she left, but since I can't read what's in anything, I've pretty much ignored it all. Tea sounds nice, though, so if you find any, I'll join you for a cup. They told me to drink extra fluids after that damn tracer stuff they made me drink, and I'm guessing they weren't suggesting alcohol."

"What shall we order for dinner?"

"Do you like Thai?"

"Sure."

"I'm used to my phone just reading the menu items quickly, so tell me what you like and I'll order it."

"Get whatever you like. I'm not picky."

"Come on, Catherine. You're always after me for not being up front about what I want. Tell me what you'd like and I'll see if they have it."

Catherine grinned in spite of herself. She had become self-conscious as they entered the apartment, not sure if staying was a good idea, but Etienne was making an effort, and she had to meet him at least halfway.

"Fine. Massaman curry with tofu. But they won't have it. So I'll have Pad-see-ew when they tell you they don't have the curry."

"Oh, ye of little faith."

Catherine left him to put in the order while she went to use his bathroom. When she returned, Jake bounded over to her out of his harness and with a rawhide in his mouth.

"Yes, I know, it's been so long, you silly dog."

She bent down to nuzzle him, and Jake fell onto his back at her feet, squirming his belly around as he rolled against the carpet.

"Are you and my dog carrying on again?"

"Guilty as charged."

Etienne walked over and came close to where Catherine was still kneeling over the dog.

"Where are you?"

She reached up her hand and pulled him gently down to the floor.

"Here," she said, taking his hand and rubbing it against the dog's belly. "Rub him right here and he goes crazy."

Jake's delirious pants were the only sound in the room. Etienne obediently rubbed his belly for another moment, but then he stood up, reaching for Catherine and pulling her up with him.

"How 'bout you, huh? Where do I have to touch you for you to go crazy?"

Catherine felt a flush spread across her entire torso.

"Etienne, you said you wanted to keep things Platonic."

His hands had found her face, and he gently stroked the sides of her temple, caressing her skin and hair.

""I guess I did say something like that, didn't I? Though I don't think I used such a fancy-ass term. And I know with absolute certainty that I meant it. But you keep proving ridiculously hard to push away."

"If you want to push me away, I'll go." Her words came out in a whisper, but even as she spoke, her body swayed against him as he continued his gentle caress.

"We're not very good at this, are we? Either one of us. You remember me saying 'friends only,' and I remember you agreeing with me." His hands had stopped their movements, but now his mouth was just an inch from hers.

She felt his soft breath against her lips and realized she had closed her own eyes as they moved closer to each other. And then his lips found hers, and she stopped thinking.

The kiss was gentle at first, as if they were getting reacquainted. His hands continued to cup her face, and Catherine found her arms around his waist. Her lips parted under his increasing pressure and their tongues met and welcomed one another. Once again Catherine found herself sliding into a sensation of utter contentment. Nothing existed but the luxurious haven of his lips, his tongue, and the rightness of being with him.

Nothing, that was, until Jake's whine and the feel of his nose pushing against the back of her leg interrupted her reverie.

Catherine pulled away reluctantly, Etienne's "noooooo" making her heart gladden. "We seem to have a jealous observer," she said, reaching down to pat the dog. "I think he wants in on the hugging."

"I knew there was a reason I should have gone for the cane instead of the dog," Etienne grumbled. "Noooo, don't," he implored as Catherine moved further away.

"I'll get plates and silverware out for dinner."

She moved towards the kitchen, but Etienne reached out and grabbed her arm.

"Kat, wait." He pulled her back against him, and her arms returned automatically to his waist.

"You have me all turned round again. Literally—I don't even know which direction the kitchen is at the moment. But I'm thinking maybe I don't really want to push you away."

Catherine closed her eyes and buried her face against his chest. He always smelled so familiar—a woodsy, earthy scent that made her want to inhale him as well as do other things to him.

She took a deep breath and straightened up again.

"All right. Let's have dinner and we can lay out new ground rules. Friends with benefits and by-laws."

Etienne laughed. "God, woman. You're going to drive me crazy. Tell me which way I'm facing right now so I can go in and wash up."

"You're facing me." Catherine laughed as he pursed his lips in mock disapproval. "I'm sorry. I couldn't resist."

Etienne had removed his dark glasses when they had first entered, and Catherine now stared into his sightless, but still beautiful blue eyes. Impulsively, she reached up and kissed him once more, but only fleetingly, on the lips.

"The doorway to your bedroom is directly behind you. Turn 180 degrees and you'll walk straight through it in three or four steps. Should I feed Jake while we're waiting?"

"That would be great. His food is in a container on the

floor to the left of the fridge. Just give him one level scoop, and leave the scoop inside when you close it."

Catherine fed Jake and set the table for two, being careful not to move anything out of place in the kitchen. She searched the cupboards and found three different teas: an Earl Grey, a mint, and an herbal blend labeled 'Quiet Bliss.'

She laughed and called loudly, "Hey Etienne, do you want some quiet bliss?"

"What?"

She moved to the doorway of his bedroom. "You have some tea here called 'Quiet Bliss.' Does that sound tempting?"

"That's my mother for you. But are you telling me I've had a box of bliss right here in my kitchen all this time and I didn't even know it?"

Catherine bit back the 'I guess tonight's your night' that sprang to mind. She wanted to think things through before jumping back in bed with Etienne. *Damn*, but this whole situation was complicated.

"I'll boil some water and we can test its audacious claim."

"Sounds good. Bliss and Thai – a winning combination." Etienne had come back into the room, and the buzzer sounded.

"That was fast. We must have gotten the order in early enough to beat the evening rush."

Etienne moved to the door, spoke through the intercom and buzzed the driver in. Catherine watched as he confidently handled the delivery, impressed both by Etienne's independence and Jake's quiet obedience to 'stay.'

Once the door was closed, she moved to meet him in the small kitchen. "I put plates on the table. Do you want me to bring them back in and we can dish out in here, or should we just bring the food to the table?"

Etienne handed her the bag. "You take this in, and I'll get some serving spoons. You're sure you don't want wine?"

"No, thanks. I'll stick with blissful quiet in a cup tonight."

They laughed together and moved to the table.

"I've never seen a dog not bark and run to the door before. Jake's more of a professional than I give him credit for."

"He really is. We joke about him, but he takes his job seriously. I was really lucky he was available."

Catherine opened up the paper containers.

"Etienne, there's Massaman curry here. How ever did you manage that?"

"I may be blind, but my telephone charm is still intact. My father was a diplomat, remember? I have deep recesses of negotiating skills."

"I'll say. Whenever I ask for it with tofu, I'm told it's not available."

Etienne smiled and Catherine was jolted yet again as he seemed to look straight at her.

"I hope it's good," was all he said.

THEY FINISHED their dinner and their tea, which had certainly been flavorful, if not bliss-inducing. They cleaned up together, Catherine watching carefully as Etienne showed her how he did things, returning the kitchen to perfect order so that everything could be found again easily.

"I don't know how to ask this without sounding condescending, but I'm really impressed. Were you always so organized, or have you had to learn discipline quickly?"

"I always tried to travel light, so I had to know exactly what I had and what I needed. And it was never hard to keep this place tidy, since I've always lived alone. I've had to speak with the management downstairs a few times about the cleaners, though. They give the place a thorough going over once a week, and have done so for years, but now I have to beg them not to move things around too much when they're working. Otherwise I knock things over or trip over things that appear somewhere I'm not expecting them."

He carefully hung the dish towel he had been using on the oven handle and turned in her direction.

"Come sit with me on the sofa. Unless you're in a hurry to leave? I know you've probably spent more time today than you planned."

"I've got nowhere I need to be tonight, so I have time. I finished the edits on a story last night, and the next one's not due until after Christmas, so I've got some breathing room for a change."

Catherine followed Etienne over to the couch and sat down sideways next to him, one leg tucked under her. While eating, they had kept the conversation light, Etienne recounting some of his many Christmas adventures around the world, first as a diplomat's kid and later as an itinerant photographer. But now he reached out his hand until he found one of hers

"You said something about ground rules."

"I did. And we need to set some. But Etienne, don't you need to focus on what Dr. Abrams said today? I really got the impression she wasn't in favor of surgery."

"I got that impression, too. But it's my life, not hers. If she has the skill and know-how to attempt it, I want her to try."

Catherine stared at the now closed expression on Etienne's face. She reached out with her free hand and pushed a bit of hair that was covering his eyebrow higher onto his forehead.

"Hey," she said. "You're going away. Can you come back to me? Can we talk about this without you getting all cold and distant?"

Etienne took a deep breath, and Catherine saw him consciously relax his features.

"I haven't gone anywhere. I'm right here. But Catherine, it's like this. I don't want you to fall for this slightly pathetic, unemployed shell of a human being. Except what I was before wasn't worth falling for, either. I've always been a barhopping photographer, who stays here or there for a few weeks, shows a girl a good time, and then moves on. I've never been particularly good at or interested in long-term relationships, let alone anything more serious. And now that my life has fallen apart, and I can't even function as an independent adult, I certainly don't want to be your Mr. Rochester. You deserve so much more."

"Wow. You've got a really screwed-up opinion of yourself, don't you? And of me, too, I guess, if you think my judgment so lacking."

"I never said your judgment was lacking."

"Well, yes, you did. Not in so many words, but you've obviously concluded that no visually impaired person in history has led a life worth living, and I therefore, would be foolish to 'fall for you,' as you so romantically put it, even if you were a decent human being to begin with, which you claim, you're not."

The stress of the day had caught up with her—her own admissions, his annoying magnetism, and her own inexplicable weakness towards him. And now he was back to giving her the hot and cold treatment in whiplash succession.

"You know what, Mr. Etienne Seton? You come across as a spoiled brat at times. I am so sorry you lost your sight. I really am. But you're sitting here, alive. You have full neurological capability, as Dr. Abrams pointed out today. People died that day. People died that day, and people have died on every other day since then. Lives were totally destroyed in that bomb blast. Lives have been destroyed since then elsewhere and in all kinds of circumstances. We could be hit by a bus tomorrow. Shit happens, Etienne. My father died in a car accident, and my mother had to pick up the pieces and go on. And you can go on, too. I can't answer to what kind of person you were before, but I've gotten to know you, and I disagree with your assessment. You're smart, you're witty, you're kind and generous, you speak God knows how many languages, and you have, in fact, learned to function with almost complete independence in just a few months."

She paused a moment and took a breath. "And you've got the world's best dog."

The silence in the room was like an accusatory observer, broken only by the low hum of the refrigerator and the world's best dog's quiet sighs. The condo was well-insulated, the windows shut tight against the December chill, and there was barely a sound from the outside world.

"You sure you don't want to tell me how you really feel?"

Catherine's posture had grown more and more rigid during her tirade, but at Etienne's salvo, she slumped back, rubbing her head momentarily against the back of the couch.

"I'm sorry, Etienne."

"Why should you be sorry? What's the point of being friends if we can't speak our minds?"

"So we're back to being friends again? Although friends probably shouldn't try to harangue each other to death."

Etienne was quiet again for a moment and then spoke.

"For the sake of argument, let's pretend for a minute that I was never involved in an accident. I'm back here in the States for a few weeks and we run into each other in the elevator at work. Would we have ended up having dinner together? Wanting to sleep together?"

Catherine groaned. "Life doesn't work that way. You can't just pretend something never happened."

"Humor me. Would you have spoken to me in the elevator?"

"Probably not."

"Why not?"

"Because I don't usually speak to people I don't know."

"Why not? You've never seemed particularly shy that I can sense."

"I'm not. But I just don't."

"Okay. I'll buy that. But again, assume we were alone in the elevator. I would have noticed you because you're cute, and I might have made some inane comment or other, just to get your reaction, and then we would have gone our separate ways."

"I know we're pretending, Etienne, but last time I checked, you were, in fact, still blind. So assuming I'm cute is complete nonsense. Cute is a horrible word, anyway."

"Cut the crap, Catherine. I can tell. But back to my point. We would have seen each other, spent a whole glorious five or six seconds sizing each other up, and then never given each other a second thought."

"You never speak to pretty girls?"

"Ha! I told you I knew."

Catherine groaned again and got up to walk over to the windows. She gazed out at the traffic on the street far below.

"Hey, come back. We're not done with our story."

"It's not a story. This is ridiculous, Etienne."

"Kat, come back. Please."

He held out his hand and she walked slowly back to him, reaching out to meet his hand and allowing him to pull her down onto his lap. They sat quietly for a moment, Catherine's head resting against the crook of his neck.

"Why don't you do more than toss out a line to women you think are attractive?"

"I've just learned over the years that I'm not a relationship kind of guy, so there's no point in starting things that might get awkward later on."

"That's a pretty lonely way to go through life."

"This from the woman who says she never speaks to people she doesn't know?"

"I didn't say 'never!'"

"The lady doth protest too much."

"Fine. You've made your point. Neither one of us would have gone after the other. But somehow we're here, now. You're still young, cute—pardon the obnoxious word—and smart, but you can't see. And I'm . . . " she caught herself abruptly. "I'm still me."

"Oh, so you can use the word 'cute' but I can't? Kat, I don't even know anymore what I'm trying to prove at this point. What I want to do is take you to bed and make love to you until neither one of us can move. But due to sheer stupidity on my part, I still don't have any condoms. So unless you've got a stash in your purse, I'm going to push you out the door. I probably should anyway, because I still don't want you to think I'm . . . courting you."

"Courting me?" Catherine snorted. "Courting me? First you compare yourself to Mr. Rochester, and then you talk about 'courting me?' Geez, Etienne, this has to be the most ridiculous conversation of all time. Buy some condoms. Who knows? You might meet the girl of your dreams any day now in another elevator somewhere."

Catherine struggled to get up, but Etienne held her firmly to him. "Didn't you hear what I said I wanted to do? *You* are the girl of my dreams. That's the problem. That's why you should run, now. I can't deal with dreams."

Catherine stared at him, wishing she had the guts to tell him the truth.

"I'm tired. Too tired to argue, and far too tired to run. But for tonight I'm going to go home. I'll come over on

Sunday at about four, so we can get to my mom's in time for dinner."

"We didn't resolve anything tonight, did we?"

"Sure we did. We're both introverts, and we want to fuck each other's brains out. But not tonight." She reached up and kissed him lightly, and then scrambled up before he could protest. She had to pee again, badly, but she'd wait till she got home, or at least down to the lobby.

FIVE HOURS LATER, Etienne was still restless and unable to sleep. The nights were no different than the days, and his mind often refused to shut down when the clock said it was time for bed.

Was Catherine right? Was he being an unreasonable jerk? He still didn't think so. Even if he woke up the next morning with his sight restored, would it be right to start a relationship and then take off again? He had never yearned to "settle down," much to his mother's chagrin, but now he found himself wondering if the conventional life he had always shunned might not be worth thinking about.

He had chosen to spend his life as an international photojournalist, a path that left him free of roots that could be torn loose at any moment. He made his living being in interesting places at critical moments and not worrying about fucking up as a family man. Because somehow he knew, deep down inside, that he wasn't reliable and that he would inevitably fuck up.

He had been a history major in college and enjoyed the reading and writing many of his classmates complained about. But he had spent countless hours taking pictures for the school newspaper and free-lancing for the city paper, and as his time at school had drawn to a close, he had slipped almost seamlessly into the life of a professional photographer.

He remembered the recruiters who had come to campus the fall of his senior year: Wall Street honchos, corporate headhunters, and intelligence agencies with an array of colorful brochures. One of the flyers had "Do you speak Arabic?" written *in Arabic* on the cover. He had laughingly picked it up and joked with the middle-aged man sitting at the table. "If I say 'yes,' do you hire me on the spot?" His Arabic was by no means fluent, but he certainly knew enough to read the simple question.

But the man had transformed instantly from tired-looking to attentive. He had stood up and gazed intently at Etienne. "We'd be delighted to talk with you and see if any of our career opportunities might be of interest to you."

Etienne had backed away, laughing.

"No, thanks. I'm too young for a government paycheck."

Now he wondered. The rehab center had sent him audio files about job training opportunities that he had ignored. Should he consider them? Might his experience and comfort with other languages possibly be of use to intelligence services? Was that work he might find interesting or of value? What in the world was he going to do with the next thirty-five years of his life if he didn't get his sight back? Or even if he did get his sight back, did he want to spend the second half of his life traveling from hotel to hotel like an overgrown hippie?

He thought of Kat sitting briefly on his lap just before she had left. He had been aroused, as always, by her proximity, but he had felt an enormous sense of peace as well. What if he could dare to imagine holding onto that peace—of holding Catherine—long term? He didn't need to see her to know she appealed to him in every way possible. Was there a chance they could build a future together? She seemed open to exploring a relationship with him—a blind man. Would she be less likely to want a relationship with a seeing Etienne who was eager to set off on his next assignment? If his sight were returned to him tomorrow, would he want to say good-bye and take off?

He didn't know how to be long-term. He could talk to his phone and pull up the career training files that were book-marked or listen more to medical information on brain surgery, but he didn't think there was much he could call up that would help him become worthy of commitment from a remarkable woman. Why did his gut keep telling him that Catherine was better off without him? Why was he so sure he'd disappoint her somehow?

Etienne sighed and turned over again. Jake thumped his tail eagerly against the bed, but Etienne's phone told him it was only 3:57. "Go back to sleep, you crazy dog. One of us has to be able to keep his eyes open tomorrow."

THE PHONE RANG, and Etienne groped for it, sure that it was just a few minutes later.

"Morning, Etienne. I'm not catching you at a bad time, am I?" David's voice sounded cheerily normal, making Etienne even more disoriented.

"No, not at all, David." He struggled to make his voice sound awake. "How are you?"

"I'm fine, thanks. But how about you? We haven't spoken in a while, and Sandra wanted me to see if you had plans for Christmas. I know it sounds last minute, but we'd love to have you."

"Thanks, but I already have plans. Tell Sandra I appreciate the offer, though. Thanksgiving was great. Are the kids getting excited for Christmas, or are they getting too sophisticated for that?"

"They'd better not be. I keep telling them Santa only delivers gifts to true believers. They roll their eyes, but they still agree we should leave out cookies, just in case."

Etienne laughed, still wondering what time it was but unable to get the time from his phone while David was talking. He could hear Jake panting off to his left and guessed the dog was anxious to get outside.

"David, I hate to be rude, but Jake seems to need a walk. Can I call you back in a few minutes?"

"Sure. But make sure you do because I need to talk to you about one of the people in your shots from Cairo."

Still foggy from sleep and more confused than ever by David's words, Etienne ended the call, promising to call back shortly. He moved quickly to the bathroom to take care of himself before hurrying to dress and take Jake outside. He was astonished to learn it was past eleven – the latest he had slept in years. No wonder the poor dog had been demanding his attention.

He tried to imagine what David could want. At Thanksgiving he had assured Etienne that the pictures looked great and that the issue was selling well and garnering impressive online clicks. Whatever David wanted couldn't be urgent, but Etienne was happy to have an excuse to keep Jake's time outside to a minimum. The cold had settled in, and he hadn't bothered to find gloves, scarf, or a hat before hurrying out. It felt cold enough for snow, and he bleakly wondered how much more difficult getting around on foot in snow and ice would be. Jake had been flown in from a center in California, so it would probably all be new to him, too.

Once inside, he made himself a cup of coffee and returned David's call.

"I know it's Christmas, and we normally don't come up with new projects or assignments over the holidays, but this made it to my email yesterday, and I wanted your thoughts. One of your pictures we ran last month was a shot of a young Egyptian offering tourists photo ops with a camel. Do you remember?"

Etienne closed his eyes and took a deep breath. For just a moment he could feel the relentless glare of the sun, the cacophony of car horns and hucksters, and the ubiquitous smell of body odor and diesel fuel. He remembered the wide grin on a teenager who was calling to tourists to "Come sit like a pharaoh, Mister!"

"Yes, I remember. Cute kid with a clever angle."

"Well, someone claiming to be his uncle sent a letter to us —to you, actually, in care of the American Embassy, and it just reached me last night. Apparently his leg was blown off in the explosion. Somehow or other they saw the picture, and they were hoping the kind American photographer could help them."

"Oh shit. The poor kid. How bad is it, do you know?"

David read him the letter that the embassy had copied, translated, and attached in an email. The writer said that 15-year-old Ahmed had been the main money-earner for the family, and that they were now destitute and unable to pay for a wheelchair.

"Fucking hell."

"I agree. But I've put out a couple feelers to the powers that be and wanted to run an idea by you. You know that when we ran the pyramid story with your pictures we included a brief note saying that you had been injured in the attack and would be on a leave of absence for a while. Here's what I was thinking: if you have any contacts over there who can verify his story, we might be able to put a piece together quickly, get it up on Facebook, Twitter, Instagram, and our homepage, and solicit funds over the holidays while people are feeling generous."

"The gods above would be okay with that?"

"Seems so. Guess some of that 'Good will towards men' stuff is contagious this time of year. Their only concern is that the story be accurate. What do you think?"

Etienne struggled to get his mind in gear. He had spent the last several months preoccupied with his own life, and until Catherine's remarks last night, had spared little thought for the others present during the explosion.

"Of course I'd like to help. Let me think. Scott Matthison from UPI had a great local translator. If you have contact info for Ahmed's family, maybe he could look into it."

"Okay. Any other suggestions? I'll send out messages, but given that it's the week before Christmas, we might need back-up options."

"The Deputy Chief of Mission at the embassy in Cairo was a friend of my father's. You told me in the hospital that he was the first one to call you after the attack. He might know some locals who can look into things."

"Good idea. I suppose I should have thought of him. But as he knows you personally, could you contact him yourself?"

"Of course. Give me a few hours. It's nighttime there already, so I'll get something off to him that he'll see first thing in the morning. Can you try and contact Scott?"

"Will do. Do you want me to come by on my way home?"

"No. I'll manage. Why don't you call again in a few hours and we'll compare notes."

Etienne hung up, showered, grabbed a granola bar, and sat down to work on his laptop. His voice recognition software was a godsend, but it still took far longer to get anything done than he was used to.

He had just begun to draft the email to Paul, the embassy DCM, when his phone rang again.

"Hey. Just wanted to see how you were doing."

The stab of pleasure that shot through him at hearing her voice made his breath stop for an instant.

"Hey yourself. I'm actually deep in trying to put words together in emails and a plea for help and sympathy. Too bad words are your forte, not mine."

He briefly explained the situation.

"Oh God, Etienne. The poor boy. Can I help? Would you like me to come over and work on it with you? I can pick up some sandwiches on the way."

He hesitated for just a minute. Should he stick with his resolve to keep her at a distance or give in to the inevitable pull that kept bringing them together?

"You're not busy?"

"Just finished the last of my online Christmas shopping and was trying to decide whether to brave the cold for a short run. This would probably be far easier on my ankle."

"Well, since your ankle's still partially my responsibility, I say give it a bit more rest and come over. Make a return to running part of your New Year's resolution."

Catherine was silent for a moment. "Among other things," she finally said. "I'll be over in about half an hour."

CHAPTER NINETEEN

It was late afternoon when they caught sight of the church spire, and Stephen felt a surge of joy encompass him. They had ridden hard the last several hours as he was anxious to gather up his ladies and get them home to the cottage before nightfall. He knew he would have to be on the road again early the next morning, but he was determined to have at least one night with them.

The Post Road had been curiously devoid of traffic the last several miles, and as they passed the Manor house on the right and rode further into town, few people seemed to be out and about. Curious, since the sun was shining for a change, although clouds continued to darken the sky periodically.

Going down Main St., Stephen saw only a few children out playing and heard no sound from the blacksmith shop.

"It is Friday, is it not?" he asked as they turned into the path that led to the stables behind the tavern.

"We left Albany on Tuesday morning, so it must now be Friday, indeed, sir. Is there something wrong?"

"I hope not." They dismounted and Stephen checked to

make sure he had all of his personal belongings from Kit's bags before handing him the agreed upon coins. "Thank you, Kit. Your guidance was extraordinary, as always. I sincerely hope I do not have to make the journey again soon, but if I do, I will send word."

Kit bent his head the slightest degree and slipped the coins into the small pouch around his neck. Stephen marveled at how tireless Kit appeared as he turned and rode back up the hill towards the Post Road. Having tied his own horse to the post, he turned and moved towards the tavern entrance, almost running in his eagerness. Passing through the door, he was surprised to see few patrons. The rich smell of roast pork filled his senses and his mouth watered as he realized with a start how very hungry he was. Swallowing, he looked around for Katrina but saw only a few faces he dimly recognized.

The bell on the door as he entered brought his mother-in-law out of the kitchen, a slight look of wariness on her face. Her eyes brightened when she saw him, though, and she smiled at him with genuine affection before darting a glance nervously over her shoulder.

"Stephen! What a relief it is to see you back safely. Let me fix some food for you to take back home with you."

He stared at her in confusion. "Take with me? Where is Katrina? Is she not here with you?"

"Oh Stephen, you must not have heard. Johann thought it wise she not stay here after the terrible news, and Katrina agreed it was better to take Anne back to the Manor. I confess I did not know how best to advise her. I know you bade her stay with us during your absence, but she feared so for the wee one. And . . . *things just became difficult*," she whispered, looking around as she spoke.

A great wave of foreboding descended on Stephen as he stared at his mother-in-law's careworn face. She was such a kind woman, but the years of constant toil had taken a toll on her, and she looked years older than his own mother, though he knew they were of a similar age.

"I would be very grateful, then, Mother Rynick, for some food to bring to Katrina. But please tell me what is amiss. Are you all well, I pray?"

"Yes, thanks be to God. But it is a fearful time, what with the tragedy in Massachusetts and the fever spreading. I scarce think what horror will come next."

"What tragedy in Massachusetts? What has happened?"

Her face was white and fearful as she looked around again. "Stephen, I am sorry. It is best we not speak of this. Be on your way to Katrina and Anne. I know she will be overjoyed to see you."

He waited uneasily while his mother-in-law quickly wrapped a parcel of food and placed it in a basket with a bottle she filled with ale, a cloth wound tightly around the stopper.

"I am that glad you are safely home, Stephen. But hasten to Katrina now." She stood on tiptoe to give him a quick kiss and then physically turned him to the door. A pang went through him to realize yet again how great a strain Katrina's marriage to him had put upon her family.

STEPHEN FELT a surge of relief pass over him as he at last half-ran along the path behind the manor house, a stable hand having kindly agreed to see to his horse. He saw smoke rising from the chimney of their small cottage, but then the high, intermittent cry of a baby reached him, and his relief was cut short. Anne seldom cried; when she was hungry, Katrina fed her. When she was tired or cantankerous, one of them gently played with or sang to her and she quickly grew angelic again.

He broke into a run, and Hudson's excited bark responded to his call. "Katrina! Katrina, love, I am home!"

The door opened and Katrina's slim body slammed into him. He dropped his bags and the basket and held her close, breathing in the smell of wood smoke and pine that permeated her thick brown hair. Her face was pressed tightly against his neck, but above his collar, Stephen could feel dampness from her eyes or nose.

"What is it, Sweetheart? What is amiss?"

"Oh Stephen. I am so happy you are home." Her voice shook as she struggled to speak through her tears. "Anne has been fussing and crying all afternoon, and I cannot bring her ease. I fear she is coming down with the fever. And I was so terrified that something would happen to you after the news came from Boston."

"What has happened? Your mother would not tell me though she looked half sick with distress."

"Have you not heard then?" Her eyes widened as she drew back to stare at him, an expression of pure misery passing over her as she struggled to take a breath. "It is war, Stephen. Our two countries are now at war."

He stared at her, a sense of dread passing over him like a cold rain.

"No. Oh please, no." But in the tears that streamed down her cheeks he saw the truth of her words.

"Oh God, Kat." He pulled her even closer to him and struggled to calm the sense of panic that threatened to overwhelm him.

"Is that why your father wanted you gone? Did anyone threaten you?"

Katrina pulled away, reaching for the linen handkerchief tucked in her sleeve, and ineffectively dabbed at her face.

Red and swollen, she had never looked so beautiful to him.

"Oh my love. I am so sorry. What have I done to you?"

"Do not dare speak thus to me. You have done naught to me but make me feel like the most cherished woman in the colony. I love you, Stephen. Do not ever doubt 'tis so."

Anne's cries grew more frantic, and Katrina turned from the door and moved quickly to the cradle. She picked up the woebegone bundle, her right hand moving to unlace the ribbon at her bodice.

"I keep hoping she will feel better after nursing, but she starts crying again almost the moment I lay her down."

"Let us pray it is not serious, my love. Babies sometimes fret. Could she be getting a tooth?"

"Stephen! She is barely four months old!"

"Of course. Forgive me, please. Whenever one of my cousins cried, my mother always said it was his or her teeth. Give her to me a moment. Maybe she will smile for her papa."

Hudson jumped at his legs as he came across the room, and Stephen distractedly reached down a hand to caress the excited animal.

"Calm yourself, boy. Wee Anne comes first, remember?"

There was more disarray than normal in the small space. Katrina's shawl was on the floor by the rocker, a plate with remnants of food was on the table, a half-full teacup next to it. The bedclothes were still mussed and the sour smell of soiled baby linens permeated the air.

Stephen could see the tears on his little daughter's red face, and an icy tingle of fear squeezed his heart. He reached for her and cradled her gently against his chest, pushing the thin wisps of hair back from her damp, furrowed forehead. She met his eyes and gave a gulping sigh but then nestled against him as he softly rubbed her back. "Shhh, my little love. Papa's home. Papa loves you."

Katrina had settled into the rocking chair and finished unlacing her shift to expose her breast. Stephen passed the babe to her and knelt on the floor next to them as Anne suckled for a moment and then turned her head away with a whimper.

"She has been doing thus all day," Katrina sighed. "Nothing seems to bring her comfort."

Stephen stroked Anne's head again and bent to kiss her. Then he turned as if drawn by a magnet and touched his lips lightly to Katrina's.

The peace lasted only a second or two as Anne turned her head restlessly, seeking the breast yet again. Stephen settled back on his knees and took a deep breath.

"Tell me what happened, please."

"We are at war. There was fighting at some place called Lexington outside of Boston, and then more fighting in Concord. Men were killed on both sides. Father said I must not tell you anything, but that is absurd. Militias from all the colonies are assembling and preparing to move against the British forces."

As she spoke, Stephen felt a coldness creep over him. He tried to take a breath but felt for a moment as if a vise constricted his chest. He had failed. He and his fellow officers had been assigned to maintain order and keep watch over the colonists' activities. Yes, they were soldiers—military officers—but they were not supposed to kill their fellow British subjects. And even if these colonists no longer wanted to consider themselves subjects, they *were* still his fellow countrymen. Much of Katrina's family had come from the Netherlands, but they were all Englishmen now, dammit. His family had feared his proximity to savages, but the closest he had come to knowing a "savage" had been the courteous, skilled, and companionable man he had just parted from a mere hour ago. And the colonists he had come to know were just as hard working, as pious, and often better educated in general than their comparable British counterparts. They were good and decent people the King should desperately *desire* remain part of his empire.

"Oh God, Katrina. I'm so sorry. I'm so sorry, my love." He reached out and put his arms around her. Tears were slipping continuously down her cheeks, and Anne was still emitting hiccup-sounding whimpers.

They were permitted only a few seconds of quiet before Anne's head turned again in search of Katrina's breast and Hudson's head butted against Stephen's hip. He got awkwardly to his feet and fondled the excited dog. His legs and hips were stiff from the many hours he had spent in the saddle.

"Yes, Hudson. I'm glad to see you, too, boy. Come, let us build up the fire and leave the ladies in peace. I've brought food from your mother, Katrina. Shall I set it out and make some tea?"

She glared at him in mock severity, tears still glistening in her eyes.

"NO TEA!"

"Does it really matter at this point? The tea is here, and the war is begun. I do not think at the moment one will have any real impact on the other, do you?"

Katrina stared hard at him and then gave a sigh that looked and sounded like defeat. "You are right, Stephen. A cup of tea will not make a difference any more. And it does sound lovely. Go ahead and brew a pot, and I will be grateful."

CHAPTER TWENTY

"**D**id you speak with him at all?"

"With Ahmed? No. He was just another interesting face I happened to notice while I was waiting. There were so many people there that morning. But then there usually are."

"Fewer now, from what I've read. People are frightened and tourism is way down."

"That's got to be hard. The guy from the ministry I was supposed to have met with that morning was doing all he could to make the world think Egypt was safe. I wonder if he got there before the explosion."

They both fell silent and Catherine noticed how dark the room had become. They had been working together for hours—Catherine reading aloud various first drafts of Tweets and copy that would be posted that night on the magazine's home page. Paul, the Deputy Chief of Mission and Etienne's deceased father's friend, had responded almost instantly with local contact information. They had reached out to the Red Crescent office in Cairo and even managed to set up appointments for Ahmed with transportation arranged for him and his uncle. The letter that had made its tortuous way to Etienne had included an email address, and Manu, Ahmed's uncle, had responded quickly to Catherine's first attempt to contact him.

Thanks to the miracles of modern technology, Catherine was able to instantly compare the pictures Manu sent electronically of the young man lying on a pile of cushions on a rug to the ones Etienne had shot in August.

"It's definitely the same kid," she confirmed immediately. "He's still smiling, but he looks like he's had a hard couple of months."

"Can you see his legs in the picture?"

Catherine gazed at the photo before her on the screen. The young man was wearing a worn T-shirt that hung loosely on his thin frame and a pair of baggy shorts. His left leg was crossed in front of him, but only a raw-looking stump ending above where his knee should have been was visible on his right side. Catherine stared at the image, her brain frozen by the sad tableau before her.

"Kat?"

"Yeah. I'm here. Sorry. His right leg's gone from above the knee. It all still looks pretty ghastly."

"Damn."

After that they had worked furiously, conferring with David, and before nightfall the magazine's homepage had one of Etienne's photos from the day of the accident that hadn't made it to print displayed next to the simple shot that Ahmed's uncle had sent. Catherine and Etienne had worked together composing a few paragraphs describing Ahmed's entrepreneurial energy before the accident and his current plight. A link was set up for readers to donate, and the UPI assistant Etienne had remembered was going to meet the family in the morning and get back to them after the initial medical appointments.

"I'm turning the lights on."

"I've kept you here late again, haven't I?"

"Yes, and it was extremely hard to work with you holding that gun to my head. Idiot."

Etienne got to his feet and moved towards her.

"Half the time I still turn on the lights when I walk in just from habit, so I never know if they're on or off. I suppose it's just luck that I haven't yet caused a spike in my electricity bill." He reached out to where he thought she was, and Catherine moved closer to him.

Her arms slipped around his waist. His went around her and she nestled her face in the hollow between his shoulder and his neck.

"What's happened to that poor kid really sucks, but it was good working together today, wasn't it?" Even as she spoke, Catherine wanted to kick herself. She wasn't supposed to be pulling them closer together.

Etienne was planting soft kisses on the top of Catherine's head, and she had a feeling he wasn't even aware he was doing so.

"Uh-huh."

"Do you want me to take Jake for a walk before I head home?"

Catherine squeezed her eyes shut while she waited for his answer, not sure what she was hoping he'd say. It really had been exhilarating working with Etienne. Despite his obvious impairment, they had communicated easily, and there had not been any awkwardness about who did what. Etienne's laptop and phone operated with voice control, but he seemed to have no compunction about asking her to look at something for him or do the actual typing when they were drafting together.

Etienne inhaled deeply, seeming to realize they were once again nearing a precipice.

"We'll walk you down. I could use the fresh air after being inside for so many hours."

Catherine stepped aside and went to get her jacket from where she had left it hours earlier, uncertain whether she felt relief or disappointment. If he had asked her to stay, what would she have said?

"You good for food tonight?"

"Yup. You?"

"I've got the leftover curry you sent home with me last night, remember?"

Jake was full of energy and moved quickly once they reached the path bordering the condo property. The wind seemed to whip right through Catherine's coat and she shivered.

"I'm glad I drove over. If temperatures stay this low, we might have a white Christmas for a change."

"You like snow then?"

"Doesn't everyone, at least at Christmas?"

"I guess. Most of our Christmases were spent in warmer climates, and even where my mother lives now it seldom snows."

Catherine shivered again and reached out to grab Etienne's arm.

"I want to hear about where your mother lives, but right now, even though I love snow, I'm freezing. I'm going to run to my car and pick you up tomorrow at four, okay?"

"Of course. Go get warm. But thank you, Kat. I couldn't have done even a fraction of what we did today without you."

She reached up on her toes and kissed him lightly.

"Good-night, Etienne. I'll see you tomorrow."

ETIENNE FINISHED BUTTONING his shirt and hoped that his black slacks and long-sleeved shirt would do. He couldn't remember the last time he had been in a church—probably for a friend's wedding several years ago. But he was pretty certain Catherine wouldn't expect a suit and tie. Before his mother had left she had helped put away everything except jeans and black slacks, assuring him that everything left in the closet would look fine with one or the other.

He had tried to take extra care while shaving, hating the need to rely on an electric razor, and he realized he really did need a haircut. Something else he'd have to figure out how to manage. Maybe they'd shave his whole head again for surgery and thereby alleviate that particular hassle.

The box of Belgian chocolates he had ordered from the D.C. shop was on the kitchen counter along with a large bouquet of flowers. His mother had called because she always called but also to wish him a Merry Christmas, checking to make sure he had procured the flowers and chocolate she insisted were appropriate gifts. He could hear the stress in her voice as she reminded him yet again how happy she would be to have him move in with her in Brittany.

"Catherine is a friend from work, remember?" he answered when she asked again exactly with whom he was spending Christmas. "Her family lives nearby and invited me to go to church, have Christmas dinner with them, and stay the night as Catherine will be doing."

"Is she married?"

"Catherine? No. She's just a nice person I've gotten to know, in part because she loves dogs. You remember what a friendly dog Jake is, don't you?" Etienne felt a slight twinge of guilt at minimizing his feelings for Catherine, but he didn't want to get his mother started.

"Are you sure it is fine with her parents to bring a dog to Christmas dinner?"

"He's my guide dog. He goes where I go, remember? But yes, I'm sure it's fine with them."

"*Bon.* Tell me once more when you expect to see the doctor again? I need to make reservations if you are going to insist on that terrible surgery."

"*Maman,* it's Christmas. Let's not worry about it tonight, okay? Have you made a *bûche de Noël?*"

"No. Your Aunt Thérèse made it this year. I am bringing the potatoes and the lamb. Shall I call again before I go to bed?"

"No. I'm not sure what time their church service is or what time we'll be eating. Though I'm pretty sure it won't be at midnight like you'll be doing. Give everyone my love and have a good time. *Je t'aime, Maman.*"

"*Je t'aime aussi, Etienne. Joyeux Noël.*"

Etienne sighed and wished for the millionth time in his life that he had siblings. It would be so nice for his mother to have someone else to worry about. After his father's fatal heart attack, his mother had thought about living in the States, but given how often Etienne was on the road, she had agreed that living near her sisters in her hometown in northern France was probably best. Until this year, she had limited her gentle remonstrances to his lack of a wife, but now that he couldn't see, she had moved into full-press worry mode. Yet another reason he had to have the surgery. If he had his sight back, his mother could return to her peace and quiet. And if things went badly, well, at least they'd both be out of this strange limbo.

He put Catherine's gift that the salesgirl at the bookstore had wrapped for him into his backpack on top of his clothes and toiletries and put the chocolates on top. This would be his first night away from the condo since leaving the rehab center, and he hoped that neither he nor Jake would embarrass himself. The dog's food and water dish were in another bag next to the door.

Ignoring the image of lacy underwear that stubbornly refused to vacate his mind, Etienne had decided on a poetry collection he had heard about on NPR and a bookstore gift certificate. He had gotten to know Catherine's taste in books, but he wasn't sure what she owned. Going into the bookstore had been a bittersweet experience as checking out the newest releases in stores around the world had always been a favorite pastime. He would often buy a paperback in one city and leave it behind when he moved on, hoping someone else would get to enjoy it. The busy chain store he had taxied to for Catherine's gift didn't have quite the sound and smell that his senses had craved when he walked through the door, but the salesperson who had come up to him shortly after they entered had been kind, finding the book he wanted and helping him maneuver the Christmas wrapping table and the checkout line.

The buzzer sounded, and Etienne slipped on his coat.

"Do you want me to come up and help with anything?" Catherine asked over the intercom.

"No, thanks. We're okay. Be right down."

He attached Jake's harness, slipped his backpack over his shoulder, and picked up the flowers and the dog's things.

"Huh. Maybe I should have asked for help after all," he said under his breath as he struggled out, sliding the handle of the harness over his wrist while he locked the door. "All right, boy. Let's go have a Merry Christmas."

***

"MY MOM HAS the door open already, and I haven't even turned off the engine."

The drive had taken about 45 minutes, with Catherine recounting a holiday trip she had taken many years ago with her parents before her father died.

"I was so afraid that Santa wouldn't know where I was that I barely paid attention to the fact that I was in Disney World. I'm sure my mom will find a way to mention it sometime tonight. It almost always comes up."

"But she'll probably fuss over you a while first," she continued. "I think my mother would have been happy with a bunch of kids, so she often seems to have a lot of mothering energy to spare."

"She and my mother would get along great, then. It's killing my mom to be so far away when she thinks I need someone to take care of me."

"Well, as they say on Star Trek, 'shields up.' We're in the driveway, and you can just cut straight across the grass to the door. I'll come back out to the car to get everything once we're inside."

Etienne had kept the flowers in his lap during the drive, and after about ten steps he felt warm air surround him as he heard the spring of a screen door opening.

"Welcome, Etienne. Three steps up and then one more here at the door."

"Merry Christmas, Mrs. . . . " He stopped, suddenly realizing he had no idea what Catherine's mother's last name was.

"I'm Ellen, dear. Ellen Marsten, but please just call me Ellen. And my husband, Darren, is just inside."

"Merry Christmas, Ellen." He held out the bouquet of flowers as he reached the top step.

"Oh, they are beautiful! Thank you."

Etienne passed through the door with Jake at his side and was immediately engulfed in the sounds and scents of Christmas. The beautiful strong smell of a real Christmas

239

tree was uppermost, but a sweet cinnamon scent was right beneath it, and there was Christmas music playing softly off to his right. Gentle but strong fingers grasped his hand for a moment and then he felt her reach for Jake's lead.

"May I hold your dog for you while you take off your coat?"

"Of course. Thank you. This is Jake, by the way."

"Hello, Jake." Ellen's voice changed slightly and Etienne guessed she was bending down to pat him. "I've heard so much about you."

Etienne laughed. "I hope it hasn't been all bad."

"Not at all. Come in, dear. We've got the fire going. Darren, this is Etienne and his dog, Jake."

Etienne reached out his right hand and felt it shaken in a firm grip.

"Nice to meet you, Etienne. I'm Darren Marsten. We're so glad you could join us."

"Thank you for having us."

"Merry Christmas, darling." Etienne heard Ellen greet Catherine and felt Darren brush against him as he, too, moved to greet her.

"Merry Christmas, Mom, Merry Christmas, Darren. Everything looks and smells wonderful. I'm just going to run back to the car and get the rest of our stuff."

"Let me help you," Darren said, and Etienne heard them exit.

"Etienne, come in and sit by the fire. It's gas, so it doesn't really give off much heat, but the illusion is good enough."

Ellen's voice was warm and kind, and Etienne felt himself relax, suddenly conscious of how stiffly he had been standing.

"Thank you. Can you see if my backpack made it in yet?"

"I suppose it's the large black one by the door, right? I'm pretty sure Catherine has nothing that looks like that."

Etienne was almost certain he heard laughter in her voice but understood no offense had been intended.

"Yes. That's it." He turned to move back to where he had come in, but Ellen stopped him, putting the heavy backpack into his arms.

"Thank you." He opened it and brought out the brick-shaped package that lay on top.

"This is for you and Darren."

"Oh, you silly boy. That wasn't necessary. You brought such beautiful flowers!" Then he heard her chuckle. "But I've heard of this chocolate shop. They are supposed to be the best, so I'm going to accept them graciously, while repeating that it absolutely wasn't necessary."

Etienne smiled. "They're my mother's favorites, so I hope you like them."

Etienne felt Ellen's hand on his arm again.

"Give me your backpack if you don't need anything else right now, and I'll put it away."

"Can you just get the wrapped gift out for Catherine and put it wherever you put gifts?"

"Of course, dear. I'll put it under the tree with all the rest."

She took his backpack and pushed him gently a bit to his left. "There's a nice armchair about six or seven steps that way and lots of room for Jake to lie down. I'll put this away and then come back and see if you and I can sneak a piece of this lovely chocolate before Catherine and Darren catch us."

Etienne found the chair easily and took a deep breath, commanding himself to relax. He was accustomed to Catherine's slightly guarded demeanor, but it was obvious that she had inherited her instinctive kindness, humor, and generosity from her mother.

Catherine and Darren came in laughing and Darren's voice came from immediately in front of him.

"Would you like a beer, Etienne? We've got scotch or

bourbon if you'd prefer, or wine. And the normal soft drinks and juices, I assume."

"A beer would be great, thanks."

"What about you, Catherine?"

"I'm the designated driver tonight, so I'll just get some juice."

Etienne felt Catherine's hand on his shoulder.

"Everything okay?"

He reached up and put his own hand on top of hers.

"Of course. They're wonderful. Thanks for including me."

He felt and smelled her move closer to him and then her lips touched his for just a moment.

"I'm glad you're here. I'm going to help my mom get dinner on the table, but Darren will be back in just a sec."

The evening passed quickly, with Catherine's parents treating him as if he were a normal friend they welcomed regularly. Even going to church with them turned out to be far less stressful than he had anticipated. Ellen demonstrated no compunction at squeezing in the back of Catherine's car with him and Jake, and the church service itself was a gentle Christmas celebration, heavy on carols and light on liturgy.

As they walked back to the car after the service, a cold wind was blowing, but nothing else seemed to be in the air.

"No snow, I guess," he said to Catherine as she walked next to him.

"I haven't given up hope. But at least it's not hot like it was last year. Global warming may be inevitable, but I'd prefer it leave Christmas alone."

Etienne decided it was best to keep his dread of snow and ice to himself. He didn't want Catherine's delight in the holiday dampened in any way.

"What's next? Will you go right to bed when we get to your mom's so that Santa can come?"

She laughed. "Not before dessert, that's for sure. And

don't think Darren and I don't want in on those chocolates. Mom's even put some champagne on ice, thinking it would make you feel more at home."

"Sounds wonderful. Your mother is a wise woman."

"She's always wanted to visit France but somehow has never made it. Knowing you're part French has gotten her all excited about finally organizing a trip."

"My mother would love to meet them. Brittany's a bit distant from most of the regular tourist haunts, but it's not far from Mont St. Michel."

"What's that?"

"A beautiful medieval monastery on an isthmus that gets cut off from the mainland during high tides. It's really worth seeing, but if you have any choice in the matter, seeing it at the spring or fall equinox is when it's at its most stunning."

They had reached the car, and as they settled in, Ellen joined the conversation.

"I'm listening and putting this all down on my phone. I've seen pictures of that place and it's always looked magical to me. I am definitely going to make sure it's on our itinerary."

"Let me know when you make definite plans, and I'll do whatever I can to help. And I know for certain that my mother would love to meet you."

Two hours later Etienne realized he had a slight buzz and a sense of relaxation he hadn't experienced in recent memory. Ellen had apologized that the Christmas log she had for dessert was from Whole Foods and not homemade, but it had actually tasted pretty good. The champagne had gone down quickly, and Ellen had made him repeatedly correct her pronunciation of *bûche de Noëlle* until they all ended up giggling hysterically. Darren had even opened up a bottle of cognac after the champagne was finished, and Etienne had found no reason to refuse the generous offer.

They talked about Etienne's proposed surgery, Darren freely admitting he knew little about neurosurgery but eager to hear all Etienne had learned. Etienne was aware that Catherine and her mom seemed to be arguing about something in the kitchen, but he sensed they were making an effort not to be overheard.

"I don't know about you two, but I'm ready to call it a night," said Ellen as the scent of her light perfume came back into the room.

"Coffee's all set for the morning, so the first one up just needs to press the button. Come on, Darren, we've got to get some shut-eye. Who knows how early these young people will be up clamoring to open their gifts."

Catherine laughed. "You're always the first one up, and you know it. I'm going to run Jake outside now, but if you see him first in the morning, I say you get to take him out for his constitutional."

"Don't listen to her, Ellen," Etienne interrupted. "You've done far too much already."

"If I'm the first one up, I'll be happy to take him out. It's been a long time since I've had a dog to walk in the morning. Besides, it will keep me from trying to sneak open the presents."

Catherine laughed again. "Poor Etienne didn't know he was coming to the home of an overgrown child. You have to ignore three quarters of what she says." Her last words were obviously directed at him, and he felt her approach and bend down for Jake's harness.

"You don't have to take him out. I can do it."

"Let's go together."

She brought his coat and they walked out into the cold, crisp night.

"Soooo," her voice stopped as if she were trying to pick the right words. "My mother's been up to even more antics than usual. Normally there's a guest bedroom, and the other room, which they use as an office, has a sleeper sofa. But she's telling me that they had to move too much stuff into the office to put up the tree, so the sofa can't be accessed. She just assumed we'd share the one bed in the guest bedroom."

Etienne wondered what Catherine was expecting his reaction to be. The idea of having her warm body against his on this, just possibly his last Christmas Eve, would be the perfect ending to an unexpectedly wonderful day.

"Are you waiting for me to say what a terrible idea that is? You might have a long wait, and it is pretty cold out here."

Catherine gave a prolonged mock groan.

"You are impossible. No sex, no commitment. Oh—wait. I've reconsidered. Sex is fine."

Etienne reached out, found her arm, and pulled her close to him, grasping her gloved fingers with his.

"I never said we had to have sex. Although if you insist, I won't object. And I did finally manage to get some condoms. But it's cold, it's Christmas, I've been well plied with alcohol, and thanks to your mother's diabolical scheming, we have one bed available. I'll offer to act the gentleman and sleep on the living room sofa, if that's what you'd really like . . . " he allowed his voice to trail off in a pathetic sigh.

Catherine growled.

"I give up. Let's get inside. You know Santa can't come if people are out wandering the streets, or sleeping in the living room, for that matter."

Once in the house, the tension between them seemed to slip away. Catherine led him to the guest bathroom, described where everything was, and brought in his backpack. When he made his way into the bedroom, he put his shoes and socks carefully beneath the bed and sat down on the edge.

"Go ahead and get comfortable. I'll be back in ten minutes."

Etienne listened as her steps moved away and the bathroom door closed again. He could still feel the cozy warmth of the cognac in his belly, but the room was chilly. He kept his boxers and undershirt on and slipped under the covers, wondering briefly if Catherine had a preferred side of the bed.

CATHERINE SLIPPED under the covers next to Etienne, bringing the evening's earlier tension back with her.

"There are times I could definitely throttle my mother."

Etienne rolled to face her and tentatively reached out a hand, coming to land on a flannel sleeve.

"Got your Christmas jammies on?"

"Yes, if you insist on knowing. I thought it would be like any other Christmas, and we'd all get up in the morning, have a leisurely breakfast, and open gifts in our pajamas."

"Huh. And now your mother, and I guess I, have done . . . what, exactly, to ruin that?"

Catherine gave out an indecipherable noise that sounded a bit like a snort.

Etienne let his hand drift up her arm, then moved it down her torso, confirming his suspicion that she was well covered, neck to toe.

"Your pajamas feel nice and comfy. What's the pattern?"

"Flowers." Catherine said nothing else, though Etienne waited.

"Ahh. Thank you. Such vivid description. Have you ever thought of a career using words?"

"Maybe I'll just throttle you, instead of her."

"Well, if that's what you want to do, don't let me stop you. You won't have absolute advantage now that you've warned me, but at least I won't be able to see you coming."

Etienne felt her move, and suddenly her breath was up close to his face.

"I'm sorry, Etienne. I know I'm being a bitch. I just didn't expect this tonight, and I don't know what I want."

Etienne reached out again and pulled her flannel-clad body close.

"It's late, and we're both tired. The bed is comfortable, our bellies are full, and we could both use a good night's sleep. Sound okay to you?"

She burrowed her head into his neck, and he thought he heard a 'yes.' He wrapped his arms around her and kissed her hair.

"Goodnight, Kat. Merry Christmas."

———

ETIENNE HAD no idea how much time had passed, but as he woke, he was aware of Catherine climbing back into bed. He reached out to embrace her again and realized the flannel was gone.

"That Santa is a mind reader."

A sound that seemed somewhere between a laugh and sigh reached him. She moved closer to him, and his hands caressed her warm flesh, his dick springing instantly to attention. He moved his head, searching for her, until their lips finally found each other.

Their tongues met hesitantly, but it took only seconds for passion to ignite. Etienne's hands unerringly found her breasts, and he felt a surge of desire and heat flood through him as she pressed their rounded fullness against his palms.

His thumbs moved over her nipples, hardened to pebbles against his fingers, and Catherine gasped.

He felt her press herself against his straining cock, and then her hands reached down and freed him from his boxers. The touch of her hands made him crazy, and he groaned as he pressed himself more forcefully into them. She wrapped her fingers around him and moved her grasp up and down in rhythm with her hips pushing against him.

"Catherine. Stop." He could barely get the words out. "Let me get a condom. I left one in the back pocket of my pants, just in case."

"It's okay, Etienne. Birth control's taken care of now." She was attempting to pull his undershirt off, and he lifted up quickly to toss it aside.

"Are you sure?" The feel of her naked body up close to him was unbearably hot, and he felt his hands pulling her more tightly to him, even as he attempted to maintain some semblance of control.

"Yes, I'm sure. Just come inside me. Please."

He did as he was told, pulling from her fingers, finding her warm entrance and slipping in, not even waiting to roll them from their sides. Her top thigh moved to rest on his hip and their bottom legs were extended together. Etienne pulled her fiercely to him, and for a second, or an hour, they just held tightly to one another, their genitals pulsing against each other in the sheer joy of finally being together again. Then suddenly unable to stop himself, he thrust deeper up and in, and they somehow rolled together so he was on top and her heels were locked around his thighs. In just seconds he felt her spasm around him, and with a huge groan, he felt his own release begin.

With a last exhausted exhale, he rolled over onto his back and pulled her to him, his hand moving up to gently stroke her hair.

"I told you I was a lousy partner, but I do, in theory, understand the concept of foreplay. I'm sorry if I kind of came across all caveman on you."

"You're not the one who needs to apologize. I think I kind of nailed the cavewoman part, myself. "

"What time is it, do you know?"

"It's about 3:30. I had to pee, and I decided I was just being ridiculous. It's not like I can't put my pajamas back on in the morning, right?"

"I wish you wouldn't. I'd be perfectly happy to spend all twelve days of Christmas right here like this."

Catherine giggled. The music of it stirred a warmth in him that went deeper than arousal, and he inhaled deeply, enveloped by the scent, sound, and feel of utter contentment.

"I'm afraid to fall back asleep and wake up to find this was all a dream."

Catherine burrowed more deeply against him.

"At least it will have been a really, really good dream."

She didn't speak again, and Etienne continued to move his hands gently through her hair as her breathing slowed. His words hadn't been in jest—the whole interlude had been akin to an extremely intense dream, his inability to see only intensifying the unreal aspect of it. But at last, he, too, felt consciousness slipping away, and his last thought was that as dreams went, it had, indeed, been a great one.

CHAPTER TWENTY-ONE

Their few hours together had sped by. Anne had continued to fret and Stephen had paced the small cottage, sometimes carrying Anne, sometimes just thinking aloud while Katrina tried to soothe the ailing infant. They agreed he should leave before first light in an effort to reach King's Bridge as quickly as possible, cross into Manhattan, and ascertain what, if any, orders had come from General Gage.

When Anne at last fell asleep, Katrina insisted Stephen lie down and sleep, too, and she placed the baby next to him in bed.

"I will sit and knit while you sleep, and that way I will be able to wake you up before dawn."

Stephen had started to argue, but Katrina had glared at him and refused to listen.

"You must rest. You wouldn't let your horse stay up all night and expect him to ride well in the morning, would you? If you are well-rested, you will ride faster and thus come home to us faster."

But what that homecoming would entail, Katrina could not guess. She wanted to hear more of his journey north, wanted some sense of normalcy in spite of the looming abyss. Had the people of Albany treated him as friend or foe? Communities up and down the Hudson River were split in their loyalties, but Lord Philipse was a strong public supporter of the King, making it known that the Sons of Liberty and other similar groups were unwelcome on his lands. Yet right here in the Tarry Towns, the majority of her family and friends were training in secret and stockpiling supplies. But what had Stephen perceived the mood to be in areas further north?

As much as she craved his news and to know all he had experienced, she suppressed her need for conversation. He had to sleep at least a few hours. And so she sat in her rocker and watched the two people she loved most in the world. Stephen's body was tucked around Anne's in sleep, his long, strong arm resting below her turned up bottom.

How could she bear it if he were told to take up arms against her fellow countrymen? How could she bear it if her own community turned more aggressively against him? Would she and Anne be in danger, serious danger? Would the young men she had grown up with turn their muskets against her or the man she loved so completely? Was there nothing she could do to keep them safe?

The clock on the shelf continued its relentless ticking and she once again heard the light drumming of rain on the roof. Katrina rocked back and forth, her mind and heartbeat racing as she imagined bloody confrontations and discarded one half-formed thought after another. Should she try to persuade Stephen to quit his commission and take her and Anne to England with him? The very idea seemed both overwhelming and fanciful.

Hudson shifted at her feet and she looked down at her

faithful companion. He had stayed close by her side ever since she and Anne had come back to the cottage after hearing of the troubles near Boston. A soft sob escaped her as she thought of having to leave Hudson. No matter which way her thoughts turned, she could see nothing but heartbreak.

Katrina rocked on and on, her arms folded tightly against her midriff, and inevitably, the hands on the clock showed the approach of dawn. She had promised to rouse Stephen no later than five, and she rose stiffly to her feet and added some wood to the fire before hanging the kettle to boil.

She walked slowly to the bed, reluctant to wake him but knowing she must. She reached out to stroke his hair and put her fingers over his lips as he woke and rolled towards her.

"Shhh. Anne is still sleeping," she whispered.

Stephen slipped out of bed and held her to him briefly before going to the door to slip on his boots and visit the privy.

By the time he got back, she had a cup of tea waiting for him and some of the meat and bread from last night wrapped in a small bundle.

Stephen dressed quickly, collecting his sword and fastening his rifle around his chest. He pulled her with him to the door, put down his bags, and held her face in his hands, his thumbs gently caressing her cheekbones.

"I will try to learn as much as I can about what happened near Boston and what is happening now, and then we will decide what to do next. Perhaps some sort of peaceful resolution can yet be reached."

"Please try not to worry," he continued, as tears trickled down her cheeks. "Oh God, Kat, I love you so. I am so very, very sorry I have to leave you again." His voice cracked, even though he was speaking in barely a whisper. "I do not know what will happen, but I will do everything I can to protect you and Anne. You are my life."

He kissed her fiercely one last time and then was gone. Katrina had been unable to say a word, simply nodding dumbly at him while she tried not to make a sound that might wake Anne.

Now she stood at the door and tried to keep him in view as he rode towards the bend in the path that would lead him away from the manor grounds. She thought she saw him lift his arm, but the pre-dawn mist swallowed him in seconds.

The air was cold and damp, and Katrina pulled the door shut. There were innumerable chores she could do, but she was more weary than she could ever remember being. Her first thought yesterday upon awaking had been, as it had for days on end, that maybe he would return that day. And return he had, and so pray God he would do so again, quickly.

After almost 48 hours of intermittent whimpering, Anne was now sleeping peacefully. Perhaps she, too, had simply been desperate for Stephen's presence. Stripping down to her shift, Katrina climbed into bed and inhaled deeply, Stephen's lingering scent filling her with both solace and longing. Would they ever be able to live and love in peace?

THE DAYS PASSED with excruciating slowness. Skittish about going into town, Katrina spent hours in the kitchen of the manor house. Sometimes Abbie took the baby and walked around with her outside, and Katrina would beg the cook to give her something to do. The first peas were up, as well as the early greens, and she sorted through them while Mrs. Gantry prattled on and on, happy to have a captive audience.

"My mother is a distant relation to his lordship, you mind, and she sent me over here when things were that hard at home. 'His Majesty loves his lordship,' she always said, 'and you'll do well to work hard for him and make a life for yourself.'

"And she was so right," she continued, barely stopping to take a breath. "The land here is rich and his lordship has been generous. I cannot understand what all the fuss is about, with those Liberty Sons or whatever they call themselves and good tea being harder and harder to come by. These upstarts will have to settle down sooner or later, if they're not wanting the King to round them all up and put them in the tower."

Katrina turned her head to hide her astonishment at the woman's simple assessment. But Mrs. Gantry had been kind to her throughout her pregnancy and during Stephen's many absences, and Katrina was grateful for the woman's gentle nature, even if her understanding of politics was minimal.

"Now just stop wringing your hands, young lady. Your handsome major will be back in no time, and all this fuss and bother will pass. You take care of that pretty little girl of yours, and don't let your husband see you with your face all red from crying."

Katrina's reply was a half-laugh, half-sob. If only a red blotchy face were all Stephen had to worry about.

Mrs. Gantry turned at Katrina's noise.

"You mark my words, Mrs. Howard. Take yourself outside and get some color in your cheeks. If your husband comes back and finds you all in pieces, he won't be able to concentrate on his duties."

Sighing, Katrina glanced to where Anne was sleeping in the large carrying basket near the open window. Whatever malaise had tormented her seemed to have passed, and Anne was napping peacefully.

"I won't go far. Call me as soon as she stirs, will you, please?"

"Of course, dear. The fresh air will do you good."

Katrina walked through the trees, listening to the sound of the river in the distance and the ever-present rumble of the mills. But the birds and insects were out as well, and Katrina took in a deep breath, realizing she was hearing the sweet sounds of spring for the first time that season. Had it truly been just a little over a year ago that she and Stephen had first gotten to know each other down by the water?

She thought about the cook's words as she walked. She was supposed to get rid of any redness on her face from crying and simultaneously bring some color to her cheeks, all while assembling a calm and welcoming visage so as not to add to Stephen's worries.

Part of her burned in indignation at the absurdity of it all, but she pushed the silly frustrations aside. Better to spend energy trying to find some kind of solution to their ordeal.

She had fallen in love with Stephen because he was all she could ever have dreamed of in a man. She had bound her troth to him before man and God, and now they had a daughter to care for.

As she paced, the constant cycling of her thoughts suddenly resolved into a moment of quiet clarity.

She had chosen Stephen. She had chosen him knowing what he was because of the more important truth of who he was as a human being. If his role as an enforcer for an evil tyrant was a problem, it was one they could weather together. He had never rejected the ideas she had presented to him time and time again. Instead he had listened and acknowledged their merit while calmly presenting the facts of the status quo and his need to meet his commitment to the established order. Perhaps he was right and they could find a way to honor both sides.

And Mrs. Gantry was doubtless correct in hinting that he didn't need an over-anxious wife to add to his worries.

Taking another deep breath, Katrina rolled her shoulders back and lifted her chin high to circle her head slowly in the sunshine. She, Stephen, and Anne were a unit. They would hold tight to each other and somehow make it through this storm.

For the first time, she began to seriously consider the possibility of traveling to England. If doing so could keep them together and make things easier for Stephen, maybe that was what they should do. And maybe Mrs. Gantry was right. Maybe the fighting would all blow over in a few months, and then they could return and build a new life for themselves.

Katrina made her way back to the manor house. The sunshine and fresh air had given her hope she hadn't felt in months. She would collect Anne, go home, and tidy things up before Stephen's return.

Two hours later she was just putting some soup on the hearth to heat when she heard hoofbeats drawing closer. Hudson began to bark excitedly.

Katrina moved to the open door and cried out with joy at the sight of a sweaty and exhausted looking Stephen dismounting. She ran to him and threw herself into his arms, almost knocking him over in her enthusiasm. Stephen's arms encircled her waist and lifted her off the ground as he held her fiercely.

Katrina raised her head and their lips met and clung. A moment or two later he loosened his grip slightly, allowing her feet to return to the earth.

"Now that was worth every damn minute on horseback," he whispered, rubbing his cheek gently against the top of her head.

Katrina smiled up at him. "I'm so glad you're home. Come inside. I've just put some soup on. You must be starving."

Stephen's arms squeezed her tightly one more time before releasing her.

"I'll see to the horse and run to the privy, and then I'll be right in."

CHAPTER TWENTY-TWO

Catherine's cell rang and she grabbed it, realizing she should have silenced it.

"Hey, Etienne," she whispered.

"Are you okay? Is anything the matter?"

"Yes. No! The dentist is coming in any second so I should have turned my phone off." The partial lie rolled easily off her tongue.

"Oh. Sorry. I'll call you later then."

"No, wait. What happened today? Are you doing it?"

"Yes. A week Thursday if all the pre-op goes well."

Shit. She couldn't think about this now. Not when her bladder was ready to burst from all the water she had been ordered to drink. They had better come in to start the ultrasound soon or they were going to have a real mess to clean up.

"I'll call you as soon as I'm out, okay?"

"Of course. Or come by on your way home. Whichever's easier."

"I will. See you soon." She disconnected and put the phone

on vibrate, trying not to think about the waves of panic that swept over her.

"Good morning, Catherine. Sorry to keep you waiting. You're here alone?"

"Hi, Dr. Calibri. And yes, it's just me today. This won't take too long, will it? I'm terrified that I'm going to pee all over your table."

The doctor laughed. "You wouldn't be the first. But don't worry. We'll be done quickly."

She rubbed an enormous amount of gelatinous goo on Catherine's just visible bulge and began to move the sensor around.

"There we go. A nice strong heartbeat. See it?"

Catherine bit her lip, overwhelmed at the sight of that pulsing gray section on the screen.

Dr. Calibri moved the wand with her left hand and pointed at the screen with her right.

"There's the head, the arms, the legs, and it looks like . . . " she moved it back and forth a few times, making Catherine wince with the need to pee. "It looks like it's a girl. Sometimes the boys make it hard for us to see things clearly until later in the pregnancy, but I'm pretty sure you have a little girl here."

Tears trickled out of Catherine's eyes. A little girl. A little girl she and Etienne had unthinkingly created together. And now he was going to have surgery that might kill him.

"Are you all right, Catherine?" the doctor asked. "She looks good at the moment, and all of your numbers seem on track."

Catherine nodded, unable to say anything.

"Are you having this baby alone? We have phone numbers and websites we can give you if you need support." She looked at Catherine, her eyes compassionate.

"Thank you. Things are a bit complicated at the moment,

but my mom is nearby and I have a good job. I'm fine for now."

"Make sure you check the list of upcoming prenatal classes. It's on our website, but I think they have printed copies at the reception desk."

———

TWENTY MINUTES LATER, Catherine sat in her car, unsure of what she was going to do next. A small part of her wanted to drive to Etienne's condo, throw herself in his arms, tell him about the baby, and beg him not to have surgery.

Another part of her screamed to avoid Etienne at all costs. She was scared he'd pick up on her conflicted emotions, scared he might change his mind about the surgery out of guilt, scared he might become more deter-mined to have the surgery, scared he might try to end things between them completely. And she was afraid she'd come apart completely if he did indeed take her in his arms.

Stalling, she picked up her phone, found her friend Maggie's name in her contacts, and tapped on her number.

"Catherine? Is that really you?"

"Hey, Maggie. Yeah, it's me. How's everything going?"

"Crazy, as always. I wish I could have talked to you more after the concert last month. Who was that cute blind guy you were with? Are you two together?"

"Oh God, Maggie. It's so complicated. And it was almost two months ago."

"Complicated? Hold on, Catherine."

"Jason, give your sister back that Lego, right now! Sorry, Catherine. As I said, crazy as always around here."

"No, Maggie, I'm sorry. You don't need to listen to my stupid problems."

"Actually, I'd love to hear someone else's problems for a

change. Trying to deal with these two, and juggling schedules constantly with Michael so that I have time to practice and get to rehearsals, I forget sometimes that other people are living normal lives."

Catherine's breath came out as a snort. "Then I definitely shouldn't be bothering you. My mess is about as far from normal as you could get."

Maggie's voice was quieter when she answered. "Hold on a second. Let me just stick something on the tv. It will buy us a few minutes of peace."

Catherine listened as Maggie put the phone down and negotiated a quick argument over whether to watch SpongeBob or Paw Patrol. A moment or two later she was back.

"Okay. Start spilling. Is it the blind guy? He really did look hot from what I could see of him. I meant to call, but then there were the holidays, and there was always something going on with the kids. Oh wait – your leg was broken, right? Is that okay now?"

Catherine laughed in spite of herself.

"Yes. It was my ankle, and it's fine now. I'd almost forgotten about that."

"So it's the blind guy that's causing the problems?"

Catherine half laughed, half sighed. "Maggie. Stop. First of all, don't call him 'the blind guy.' His name's Etienne, and you're not even supposed to say 'blind' anymore. You're supposed to say 'visually impaired.'"

"Oh my. We're getting serious here, then, I take it."

"Well, yes. I guess. But that's the problem. We're kind of serious and not serious at the same time, and I'm pregnant, and he doesn't know."

The silence was unbroken except for the distant sounds of the cartoon in the background.

Finally, "My God, Catherine. That is a mess. Do you want

to come over? Does your mom know? What can I do?"

"I don't know, Maggie. I'm not even sure why I called. I just got overwhelmed for a minute, and I wanted to hear your voice."

"Oh, sweetie, I'm so sorry. You can come over, you know. The place is a disaster, but I don't have to be anywhere until four. Although by the time you got here, I'd only have an hour or so. But you can still come by if you'd like."

"No, thanks. It's good just to talk to you and think about something else for a minute or two."

"Wow. You're pregnant. I can't believe it. How far along are you?"

"About sixteen weeks. I'm in the hospital parking lot right now. I just had my ultrasound, and now I'm sitting here in my car, adding time to my parking bill and probably annoying people looking for a space."

"Fuck 'em. Wow. So wait, are you guys together or did you make a baby and then split up? You said you were serious and not serious. What the fuck does that mean?"

Catherine smiled. Maggie had always been such a crazy bundle of contradictions: a deadly serious musician who treated her violin playing like a sacred calling, and a foul-mouthed partyer who could come up with a million ways to have fun on a whim. How she handled two young kids and a concert career was a tribute to her almost ceaseless energy and no-nonsense approach to whatever came her way. And to Michael, of course. The two loved each other like a pair of crazy teenagers, and had, ever since their cars literally ran into each other six or seven years ago.

"Good question." Catherine started to explain, but Maggie cut her off.

"And what kind of name is Etienne, anyway? Is he a foreigner? Do they make babies differently wherever he came from, and that's why he doesn't know you're pregnant?"

Catherine started laughing and found she couldn't stop. Why hadn't she called Maggie earlier? She could have saved herself months of self-inflicted isolation.

"What's so funny? Did I nail it? Or maybe he doesn't speak English? If you're at sixteen weeks, you should be starting to show. Just take his hands and rub them over your belly."

Catherine laughed until tears ran from her eyes.

"Maggie, stop. I'm going to have to pee again, and I don't want to go back into the doctor's office. They'll think I'm a lunatic."

"Okay. Get serious then. Tell me what's going on. All I've got so far is you're pregnant from a blind, ignorant, alien with a hot body. Wait, excuse me, a visually impaired alien with a hot body."

"You know what? Just talking to you for five minutes has made me feel better. I'm going to hang up and drive over to Etienne's. He's got shit of his own going on, and I should be there."

"Shit of his own?! Catherine, you said you just had an ultrasound. What did it show, by the way – boy or girl?"

"It's a girl. Listen, you've helped me more than you could know. Call me sometime after the kids are in bed, and I'll try to explain."

"Will this great doofus be there?"

"He's not a doofus, Maggie. He's really pretty wonderful. I think you'd like him if you got to know him. He definitely liked your violin playing."

Maggie huffed. "I'll reserve judgment. Wow. A little girl. You can have all of Katy's old stuff. I know some of it was hardly even worn. The little terror was determined to catch up with her brother right from the get-go, so she was barely a week in all of the little baby sizes."

"It's been way too long since I've seen them. I will try to come by one of these days."

"I'm going to hold you to it. All right, get going, so you can get to a toilet. I'll call you soon. But you call me first if you need me, you hear?"

"I hear you. Thanks, Maggie."

"Love you."

"Love you, too."

Catherine disconnected and started her car. Somehow talking with Maggie had made things better. She didn't understand how or why, but she now felt like she could see Etienne and continue her deception without falling apart.

CATHERINE BREEZED into Etienne's condo an hour later, determined to keep her wits about her and Etienne's hands and arms far away. She had stopped and picked up Mexican take-out and used the facilities, so she was good for a little while, at least.

"Sorry I couldn't go with you this morning. It's close to impossible, trying to change an appointment with my dentist, and I really needed to get a tooth checked." She wondered if this newfound talent for spouting lies had lain dormant all her life.

Etienne reached out to her as she came in, but she pushed past, making as much noise as possible in the small kitchen, rustling the bag and pulling out plates and cutlery, and then returning Jake's joyful greeting.

"I'm starving. Hope you are. I picked up burritos, chips, salsa, and guacamole."

"Yeah, I guess so. Thanks."

"Good. Let's eat and you can tell me everything."

She moved deftly past him again and put the plates on the small table.

Etienne's head was tilted as if he was trying to hear or

smell her mood, and Catherine felt a small pang of guilt that she resolutely decided to ignore.

"Come sit. I can only stay a little while because I promised my mom I'd go out and help her choose some new curtains." Catherine cringed at how preposterous the story sounded.

"Don't let me keep you, then. Thank you for bringing food. You didn't have to do that."

Damn. The polite wall was back in his voice. She hadn't meant to put him off that much. But what *had* she meant to do? Knowing she was playing with fire, but unable to stop herself, she got up and went to him, taking his hand in hers.

"Sorry, Etienne. It's just been a crazy day. A story I thought I was done with came back again with changes, and they want it finalized ASAP. But I'm here now. And I really want to know what's going on. Come sit and tell me."

His fingers were warm and strong in hers, and she caught her breath as his other hand came up to touch her face. He let go of her hand and brought his left hand up to join his right, his thumbs lightly caressing the tender skin under her eyes and brushing against her cheekbones. Could he feel any residual puffiness from her earlier tears?

"Which story?"

Her mind went blank. His fingers were so gentle and loving, and she felt herself swaying closer to him. He tilted her head up slightly and touched her lips with his own, then pulled back just a bit.

"Curtains? Really, Kat? Curtains? What's going on?"

Catherine sighed, closing her eyes and turning her face and stretching her neck so that her head moved side to side between his hands, just as Jake had done to her five minutes earlier.

"Oh Etienne, I'm sorry. I want to hear every word the doctor said, but a part of me wants to grab your hand and run as far away as we can get from that stupid hospital. I guess I'm just not coping very well."

"We never really got around to working out that running thing, did we? Maybe we'll try the surgery and see where that puts us. Who knows, maybe we'll end up training for a race together after all."

Catherine groaned and moved away restlessly.

"Do you really have to get going to work on the story? We can talk later if you do."

"No, it's okay. It's not all that urgent."

"And the curtains?"

"Yeah, all right. There are no curtains. Are you happy, smarty-pants?"

"Were you at the dentist? There is a kind of antiseptic smell about you."

"Yes." As far as lies went, this one wasn't so terrible.

"I haven't been myself in probably a year or more. Remind me if I'm still alive after the surgery to get an appointment."

Catherine made an impolite growl. "This is why I don't want to talk to you! Stop talking like that, please, Etienne?"

"Okay. Sorry. Let's sit and talk, and we'll stick to the facts. Both of us." He bent and kissed her again, lightly, before moving over to the small table.

"I'm scheduled to have the pre-op tests on Thursday, and if everything's good, which it should be, Dr. Abrams will operate Thursday of next week. I called my mom, and she's going to buy a ticket to fly in on Monday. I told her it wasn't necessary, but she wouldn't listen."

"For heaven's sake, Etienne. Can you blame her? You're her only child. Of course she'll want to be here. Does she think you're crazy, too?"

"Yes, she does. The two of you can gang up on me and blather on to your hearts' content about how wrong I am to tempt fate."

"Is that what my opinion is? What your mother's opinion is? Just blather?" Catherine put down her burrito, no longer hungry. "Maybe I'd better go, after all. I'm tired, and I don't want to get in another argument."

"No. Don't go. Please." He paused, seeming to think about his words for a moment. "But, you can go—you should go—if you want, Catherine. I know this surgery isn't something you can understand, but I feel in my gut that it's what I have to do. And from all I've learned from my research and from Dr. Abrams, even if it's a total failure, it will add something to the field of neurosurgery. Only a few operations like mine have been done, so they'll learn from it, regardless of whether it works or not."

Catherine had pushed back from the table, and she realized when Etienne stopped speaking that her hands had moved instinctively to cover and protect her belly.

"Is that what's most important to you right now? Advancing science?" Even to her own ears, her voice sounded shrill.

Etienne was silent again, and Catherine watched his face as he appeared to struggle with what to say next.

"Could you come here for a minute?" he finally said, moving his chair back from the table as if to make room.

Reluctantly, she walked around to him. He reached up and pulled her down so that she sat awkwardly on his lap.

"It's not the only thing that's important to me, but it's what I've decided, selfishly, I guess, to put first for now. I feel terrible about the fear I know my mother is experiencing. She has a good life, with a home she loves and lots of friends and family. But she loved my father deeply, and he was taken from her. You're right, I'm her only child, and I know she loves me with all her heart. I hate making her suffer, and I hate knowing how devastated she'll be if I die, or even if I end up in worse shape than I'm in now."

"And then there's you. Falling in love was the absolutely last thing I thought my new life would hold when I woke up in that hospital in Bethesda."

Catherine felt her heart seize, and tears came to her eyes. She moved closer on Etienne's lap and buried her face in his neck.

"But that's what happened, Kat. I've fallen in love with you." Etienne's voice grew husky as he spoke into her hair. "I don't want you to say you love me. I don't even want to think of that as a possibility, because I'm terrified at how I might be hurting you, too. I'd like to come out of this surgery better able to stand on my own two feet and then maybe woo you like a regular person. Does that sound better than court? You've made me dream of things I never even considered before, like settling down and maybe having a family with the woman I love."

Etienne's hand moved up and down Catherine's head, fingers tangling in her hair as tears streamed down her face and dampened his shirt.

"I don't know what, if any, future I'll have after the surgery, but I want to take this chance. And I don't want you to feel tied to me." His voice broke on those last words, but he cleared his throat and continued. "Not as I am now, and not how I might be if things go badly. I just want to hold you right now, and tell you that at this moment in time, I love you utterly. Part of me feels like nothing I've ever experienced in this life has meant anything because you were always missing. But you are young and smart and beautiful, and I want you to have the life you deserve. And if the operation fails, no matter how it fails, I want you to move forward and not worry about what could have been between us."

Catherine was convulsed with sobs, shaking her head in denial at the stupidity of Etienne's words. She tried to take a breath, tried to stop crying long enough to tell him what an idiot he was, but it took several moments to get her voice under control.

"I hate you, Etienne Seton. I hate you for being so damn stupid, and yes, so totally blind. There is no 'what could have been' between us. There's only what is. I love you, too, and I think I have since that first day when you carried me piggy-back in the park. I didn't want to fall in love with you, either. I didn't want to fall in love with anyone. I always felt deep in my heart that if I fell in love, it would end badly. And you've proved me right by being so damn stupid. You think I'm young and smart and beautiful? What the hell do you think you are? An ugly old man? No. You're the goddamn person I've spent my whole life trying to avoid. But you are stupid. Stupid, dumb, idiotic, and blind. You're so blind that I'm afraid even if you get your sight back, you still won't be able to see what's right in front of your face."

"And if you don't get your sight back, or even if you come out in worse shape than you are now, my love is strong enough to handle it. I don't need you to be financially supportive, or any of that traditional crap. I earn enough to take care of us both. It's you I need. You I love. The you that you've always been, that your life up until August made you, and the you you've become since then."

Catherine finally ran out of steam and continued taking hiccup-like breaths as she rocked back and forth in Etienne's arms, rubbing her dripping nose into his shirt and not even caring about the mess.

They sat glued together for what could have been minutes or might have been hours. Etienne's arms were around Catherine, and he continued to drop kisses against her hair. After a while Catherine became aware that Etienne had grown hard against her, and she was surprised to discover that she wanted him, too, quite badly. She shifted against him and pressed her face against his neck.

269

"Just ignore that guy down there. He has a mind of his own when you're around, I'm afraid."

"Maybe I don't want to ignore him." Catherine's voice came out in a croak and she sniffed again before loosening his hold so she could shift positions. She turned herself around to straddle Etienne and pressed into him, feeling him pulse against her in response.

"This is another really stupid idea, isn't it?" he asked, his hands sliding up under her shirt and pausing at the clasp of her bra.

"Yes. I think it most definitely is," she agreed, pushing harder against him as she reached to pull his shirt free from his pants.

He undid the hooks of her bra as his lips suddenly attacked hers, kissing her as if she were the only thing left to him in the world. Catherine moaned, her tongue meeting his just as fiercely as she shifted to press her aching breasts more fully into his hands. Her nipples were taut and sensitive, and she gasped as he teased them with his fingers. Suddenly unable to wait another minute, she shifted back and reached for the button of his jeans, and then eased the zipper down past his bulging erection. She ground against him, eliciting an answering moan from Etienne. It had been unusually warm that day, and she had put on a simple elastic waist skirt to wear to the doctor's and left her legs bare. Etienne's hands reached under her skirt and pushed the crotch of her panties aside with one hand while he lifted her bottom with the other and savagely sheathed himself inside her.

It proved to be too much for Catherine. Etienne had moved up and deeply into her only once before she clenched around him in spasms that made her cry out and arch back. Etienne held tight to her hips while thrusting hard, and then he, too, cried out, pulling her tightly to him and gasping for air against the side of her head.

They stayed that way for a few minutes, Catherine finally becoming conscious of Jake whining softly against her leg. She started to inch away, and Etienne sighed, his hands moving to cup her face for one last tender kiss before he released her.

"So. I guess we handled that discussion well, wouldn't you say?"

"Yeah. Maybe we should give demonstrations at the U.N. Show them what conflict resolution really looks like. Although I don't think we really resolved anything, did we?" Catherine's legs were stiff and felt like they might give way as she awkwardly climbed off Etienne's lap, holding on to his shoulders to steady herself. His arm moved instantly to encircle her waist, both to help her balance and to keep her close for just a moment more.

"This poor dog probably wishes he were blind by now. We keep behaving indecently right in front of him." Catherine reached down to pat Jake. "Do you want me to run him out before I go?"

"Do you have to go?" Etienne got to his feet and fastened his jeans.

"I don't know, Etienne. I don't really want to think about your surgery right now, and I don't want to yell at you anymore."

"Are you sure? You seemed to be on a roll." As if powerless to resist the force between them, he bent down and kissed her again, pulling her to him.

"Arghhhh. I meant what I said, you know. I hate you almost as much as I love you."

"I know. I'm sorry."

"And if you were trying to break up with me before, you did a really lousy job of it."

"Yeah, I know that, too." He continued to kiss her lightly

271

around the outlines of her face, as if he were attempting to memorize her features with his lips. "Should I try again?"

Catherine sighed. "No. And I take back what I said. I really do want to know about the surgery. Did you record what she said the way we talked about? I want to know every last, horrible, terrifying detail, so I can plan out my nightmares accordingly."

Etienne chuckled. "Of course I did. How about a compromise? We can listen to the recording together, go over the gory details, but then you sleep here, and I'll chase the nightmares away."

Catherine pulled away to look up at him. "God, we really suck at breaking up, don't we?"

"Was that a yes? Will you spend the night?"

"I don't have anything with me. And why are we talking about tonight? We haven't even eaten our lunch yet."

"Yes, but my watch dinged four o'clock a while ago."

"Oh, poor Jake. No wonder he's whining. Let's take him out and then come in and heat up this food."

"Will you stay?"

"What, are you pulling the pathetic 'I'm likely to die soon, so I need attention?' ploy?"

"Will it work?"

Catherine blew out her breath and shook her head at her own weakness. "Yeah. I guess it will. We're both pathetic. Let's take the dog out before he goes on Craig's List to look for a new human."

Neither one of them mentioned the four-letter word again, but it hung in the air, cocooning them as they put on their jackets and moved to the door, their interlaced fingers again expressing the feelings they wanted to ignore.

SEVERAL HOURS later Catherine came awake with a gasp, Etienne's hand on her head, brushing tendrils of hair from her forehead.

"Catherine, it's okay, Sweetheart. Everything is okay."

"What's wrong? What's happened, Etienne?"

"You had a nightmare, after all. I thought we were kidding earlier. Who is Stephen?"

"Who?"

"I don't know. I'm asking you. You were rolling back and forth as if you were upset about something, and then you yelled 'Stephen' twice."

"I don't know any Stephen. Are you sure that's what I said?"

"It was definitely 'Stephen.' Do you remember your dream?"

"No, I don't. Not this time. I have this one ridiculous nightmare that I've had over and over my entire life, but I don't know what I was dreaming right now. It's gone."

"Is there a Stephen in it?"

"I've never known who was in it. It's this stupid dream where I'm crying because someone is gone, and I don't know where he is. Sometimes it's raining and sometimes there's a baby crying, too. I just try and forget about it. I'm sorry I woke you. But don't be jealous. I don't know anyone named Stephen."

Catherine slipped out of bed and moved to the bathroom. "I'll be right back. I'm going to splash some water on my face. Go back to sleep."

She used the toilet quickly and went and peered at herself in the mirror. Was the guy she'd been looking for in her dreams for all these years named Stephen? And why had he showed up, or rather not showed up, again tonight? She held a washcloth to her eyes. She hadn't been lying to Etienne. She didn't remember what she had just dreamed, but it had to have been the same old nightmare. Her heart was beating fast and her brain still felt fuzzy. So now she had two names. Stephen and Anne. A lot of good it did her. Maybe she'd go to an exorcist and have it all flushed out. Her real life was nightmarish enough at the moment. She didn't need an alternative scenario haunting her at night.

Catherine turned out the light and went back into Etienne's bedroom. She could just make him out, sitting up in the dark waiting for her. He was so beautiful. So real. And she was sure he'd make a wonderful father. She sighed. She was bone tired. Catherine crawled into bed and tugged Etienne down. She pulled his arm over her waist and pushed back against him, trying to draw him around her like a blanket. She told herself to think of anything other than her normal nightmares or her current reality, but she was asleep before she could finish her plan.

ETIENNE LAY IN THE DARK, holding Catherine close. He wasn't sorry he had told her he loved her. She felt like his other half, like a part of himself that had always been missing but was now in place. If he could stay right here with her tucked into him for the rest of his life, he'd gladly forego the surgery and die a happy man.

After all the drama of the afternoon, he and Catherine had spent a surprisingly quiet evening together. He had answered her many questions about the planned surgery, and she had seemed to process the information calmly. They had cleaned up together, shared the bathroom, and gotten into bed like an old married couple, both of them exhausted after such an emotional day. He normally had trouble sleeping, but tonight he had fallen asleep quickly, Catherine's head on his chest. Her tossing and turning had woken him, and when she had cried out, "Stephen," he had answered, "I'm here," without thinking. She had called again, desperation in her voice, and that's when he had struggled to wake her.

She had told him not to be jealous, and he wasn't. He had responded to her call instinctively, sure she was seeking him and not some other man. But how could that be? And why did the idea of a crying baby fill him with such sadness? He had foolishly mentioned to Catherine earlier that being with her made him wish for a family of his own. An image of a smiling, beautiful little face crossed his mind, and he furiously tried to push it out. He would not, could not, think about anything like that. He'd have the surgery, and if, God willing, he came out of it in one piece, maybe even able to see again, he'd take Catherine out on a date like a normal person and think about what he should do with the rest of his life.

Catherine moved in her sleep, and he pulled her more tightly against him. She smelled so right, felt so right against him. He inhaled deeply and willed himself to relax and sleep. For just a moment before he drifted off, a thought flitted across his mind—as if there were something he had noticed but hadn't taken the time to think about. But before he could focus and try to figure it out, he fell asleep.

CHAPTER TWENTY-THREE

Katrina could tell by watching Stephen eat that he was exhausted. At one point he actually seemed to fall asleep with a piece of bread in his mouth. She was sitting on the stool close to him, nursing Anne while he ate, and she reached over and lightly jiggled his arm.

Stephen started and gave her a sheepish smile. "I'm sorry, Katrina. The captain General Gage sent down from Boston requested my help working with the local volunteers, training them to patrol the harbor, and we worked long hours while we waited for my orders to come in. I didn't have to wait too long because at least one of the messages I sent to Boston from Albany made it there in spite of everything else going on. Instructions arrived late last night ordering me to return to Fort Ticonderoga and take command until reinforcements can be sent."

Katrina's eyes widened in shock.

"You have to go back north again?" A wave of panic swept over her. "Stephen, no. Please."

"It's all right, Sweetheart. We shall all go. I discussed it with the governor and his wife, and they both think it's the best idea. Mrs. Colden says she has spent her entire life following her husband hither and yon, and that it has made all their children into resourceful and intelligent adults."

Stephen yawned and apologized again. "Oh heavens, I'm sorry, my love. Listen, the fort wasn't so bad as far as accommodations go, and there will be other wives, and," his voice faltered for a moment, "other women, many of them American, from what I recall. The trip will be difficult for Anne, but I know we can do it. I'm afraid we'll have to leave tomorrow because my orders are to report there posthaste."

Katrina looked at him in horror.

"Leave here tomorrow? Just leave?"

"Yes. I have a letter from the governor to Lord Philipse, explaining the situation and requesting the loan of a carriage, which I am sure he would have agreed to even without the letter." His voice trailed off as he watched Katrina bite her lip.

"If you think it better, of course, you can stay here, either in the cottage or return to live with your parents." His words were quiet, and he stared at her with tears coming to his own eyes.

Katrina felt as if she might crumple to the ground in spite of the stool she sat on. Anne had fallen asleep nursing, as she so often did, and her soft cheek was pressed close to Katrina's still damp nipple. Katrina looked at Stephen, whose eyes held such love, and she looked down again at her sleeping baby. She had never been more than a few miles from her home or family. How could she endure it?

The room was already growing dark, and she knew she should get up and add some wood to the fire and light the candles. These mundane tasks crossed her mind, and with a start, she realized that the three of them might never sit together like this again in their sweet home.

She forced herself to breathe and gazed back at her weary

husband. He had ridden hard for hours to reach her, and she knew she had no choice. She loved him. He was her life.

"Of course we will go, Stephen." She had to be strong.

"It should not be for too long. The hope is that the rebellion will be put down quickly, and General Gage will be able to send a company to replace the men currently at the fort."

"But it is not just a rebellion, Stephen, and I fear it will not be put down quickly."

His eyes were steady as he looked back at her.

"I know, Katrina. And I know how important this cause is to you. My task right now is to restore order to the fort until reinforcements can arrive. Let us do this together, and then we will decide what to do next. The fort is vulnerable in its current condition. I have been very fortunate in my career and have never had to fire at another human being. It is my hope and my prayer that my fortune will hold. If the fort's company is well-disciplined and everyone near the fort is aware of its strength, there is less chance of confrontation."

Even amidst his exhaustion and his commitment to obey orders, Stephen was trying to consider her loyalties and trying to find a path they could walk down side-by-side. Katrina took another breath and steadied herself. She could do this. They could do this together.

"Let's go to bed. You're so tired, and this will be our last night for God alone knows how long that we can sleep peacefully in our own bed. And I want to remember this spot. For all I know, you may drag me straight back to your castle in England when we leave Ticonderoga."

Stephen laughed. "How disappointed you will be when you eventually see for yourself that there really is no castle. But perhaps I will build you one."

"Now that is a plan I can support. But for now, let us sleep. We must rise early in the morning and set to work quickly."

Katrina got carefully to her feet and carried Anne to her cradle. The fair weather had abandoned them yet again, and she could now hear rain on the roof. She sighed. She and Stephen could make do with the chamber pot, but Hudson would bring in a mess after she let him out. The thought made her turn to Stephen abruptly.

"What about Hudson? Can he go with us?"

"Of course. He is a good dog, and I expect he'll be a fine traveler."

She went over to Stephen, who still sat in his chair at the table as if he were too tired to rise. She put her arms around his neck and held his head to her breast.

"I love you, Stephen. How lucky I am that you took that walk down by the river last year."

"And I love you, my darling. And I am so relieved that you don't look back on that walk and wish it had never happened."

"Hush. We were meant to be together." She kissed the top of his head. "Now take your clothes off and get some sleep. We have a new adventure to begin tomorrow."

Stephen rose stiffly and stretched. He stripped, washed quickly at the basin behind the screen, and was in bed before Katrina had finished covering the food and cleaning the table. She made her own brief ablutions and joined him in her shift, tucking herself next to her already softly snoring husband.

THE SOUNDS that jolted them awake seemed close at hand. They both sat up and Anne began to cry. It was raining harder now, but something else had pulled them both from sleep. Hudson was growling softly from the bottom of the bed.

"What is it, Stephen?"

"I don't know. Perhaps a tree was hit by lightning and came down. Or perhaps something at the mill? I'll go out and check."

"No. Don't. It's storming out there and we must rise early to pack."

Stephen went and picked up Anne, and kissed her on the head before handing her to Katrina.

"Let me just see what has happened and make sure nothing is wrong at the manor house. I will be back in a few minutes. You two can keep the bed warm for me. Go back to sleep, my love."

Stephen drew on his trousers and shirt and put his cloak around his shoulders while Katrina tucked the baby closer to her in the bed and began to nurse. She could just make out Stephen's profile in the dark, but then he lit the lantern with a taper from the embers and his face was dimly visible.

Katrina felt an inexplicable wave of fear pass over her. "Stephen, wait," she began, but he had donned his boots and hat and was unbarring the door. The dog ran over to him, eager for an unexpected outing.

"Stay here and take care of the ladies, Hudson. I'll be right back. Do not fret, Kat. Our night together here is not yet over; I promise. We have hours in the cottage still and then all the time in the world ahead of us."

Katrina started to speak once more, but he was gone. Hudson growled again and then slowly returned to the bed, his head turned mistrustfully towards the door.

"It's all right, Hudson. Stay here. Stephen will be right back." Her voice sounded shaky in the darkness, and Anne must have sensed her distress because she let go of Katrina's breast and began to cry.

"Shhh, Sweetheart. Everything is fine. Your papa will be back soon." She whispered the words and tried to get Anne to nurse again, but she herself continued to fret. What was the matter with her? She had agreed to their impending departure and convinced herself that they would manage somehow. They would stop at the tavern on their way out of town in the morning, and she would explain to her parents that they hoped their absence would be brief. What was the dread that was making her sweat while her fingers grew icy?

Anne seemed to have drunk all she wanted, though she continued to cry softly. Katrina climbed out of bed and laid her down in the cradle. She pulled on her shawl and went to stoke the fire. Stephen would be cold and wet when he came in and would need the warmth. She paced back and forth for a few moments while Hudson sat attentively by the door, watching her.

As long as she was up, she might as well start getting their things together. She pulled a valise from under the bed and set it on the floor but then returned to pacing. She went to the door and opened the top partway, and wet drops hit her face. She tried to see through the darkness, but nothing was visible.

He would be back soon. He had said so, said that their night was not yet over. Strange words, she thought, but maybe he had hoped they could make love one more time in their cottage. They had both been too tired last night after his long ride and their intense conversation.

Katrina continued to pace. What was taking him so long? A cold shiver swept over her and she clutched her shawl more tightly as she went again to the door and peered out into the storm.

STEPHEN TRIED to watch the path while he held his hat to his head in the wind. The rain was coming down hard, but he could make out faint light from the direction of the mill.

What in the world could be going on? He had foolishly failed to grab his rifle, expecting to see a tree down somewhere nearby.

But as he drew closer, he could hear voices, and they sounded like drunken voices. What in heaven's name were the village hooligans up to now?

"That old fool thinks he can cut down all our trees and send the profits to the goddamn king. He's going to regret acting like a little king himself around here."

"Ansel, the powder is too wet. It's not going to work tonight. Let's come back and try again tomorrow. We've already wasted too much time trying to blow this thing up in the rain."

"No. I've said we were going to blow up this blasted mill, and by God, we're going to do it."

A wave of irritation swept over Stephen. These drunken idiots were trying to destroy the source of income that provided for most of the population in the surrounding area. How in God's name was that going to help their drive for independence? He was wet and chilled, and he had to pack up his wife and child in the morning and tear them away from the only home they had ever known. He had no time for such bloody delinquents.

"Hey!" he yelled. "You boys go on home and stop behaving like fools. Your families depend on this mill."

"Whoa, it's our very own *lobsterback*. We'll show you what you can do with your damn army."

The blow came from out of the darkness. He had not realized he was so close to anyone. The blunt force of what must have been a wildly swung musket hit him squarely on the head, sending him reeling. He fell to the ground, dropping his lantern and clutching his head.

"Fucking dandy. You're nothing but a red-coated cock robin."

The words seemed to come from far away. His head hurt abominably, and as he struggled to push himself from the ground, he felt a wave of weakness sweep over him.

"Shit, Ansel. You've really hurt him."

"Yeah, and well he deserves it. We don't need any stinking Redcoats around here. They're killing our people in Boston, so let's get rid of this one now."

Stephen tried again to get up, but blows began raining down on his head and torso. He tried to cover his head, but the battering came too quickly. Pain exploded everywhere. He thought his eyes were open, but he couldn't see.

"Oh, Kat," he thought, just before the last breath was knocked out of him. "I'm sorry."

KATRINA WENT to the door again. Where was he? This time she pushed the top half back as far as it would go. The rain and wind lashed at her face as she leaned out, hoping desperately to see him returning through the storm. She turned, her eyes wide with fear, to glance towards Anne who was still crying feebly in the cradle by the hearth. She shivered with cold, knowing she should close the door, but loathe to abandon her vigil. *Where was he?* Tears mixed with raindrops running down her cheeks, and she tried to call out, but no sound came from her throat.

CHAPTER TWENTY-FOUR

All of Etienne's pre-op tests had gone fine.

Of course they had, thought Catherine. God forbid anything stand in the way of this crazy man's determination to test the boundaries of medicine in pursuit of some mythic 20/20 vision that would restore him to his true stature of manhood. How Catherine wanted to scream at the absurdity of it all.

She could understand, as much as any person not experiencing it firsthand could, how devastating it must be to lose one's sight. But what she could not understand, or sympathize with, was Etienne's conviction that he was somehow not a fully functioning human being without his eyesight. Didn't the fact that she had fallen in love with him convince him of anything? She hadn't even known who he was, aside from his name, before last fall. He, the person he was now, was the one she had come to love. For all she knew, once he had his sight back he might turn into some wild Lothario who had no interest in a quiet, suburban writer.

Catherine continued to grumble to herself as she made the beds in her guestroom. She had convinced Etienne that he and his mom should spend the nights before his surgery at her place. He had to be at the hospital by six in the morning, and since she had more space and would be driving them in anyway, it made sense for them to stay with her. And it wasn't as if she could even pretend not to care at this point. She had shown him her whole hand.

Not your whole hand, she reminded herself. She had left out that one, itsy-bitsy, life-altering fact that she was now carrying his baby. She turned and looked at herself in the mirror over the bureau. She had a loose turtleneck over some sweatpants and looked just a bit frumpy. But how would she come across to Etienne's mom, a well-traveled, mature woman, from France, of all places? Would she be elegant, Catherine wondered? Would she take one look at Catherine and question why Etienne was with her? Would she see that Catherine was pregnant?

Abandoning the guestroom, Catherine walked again to the closet in her own room. She had already spent time staring at the outfits that still fit, wondering what she would wear to the airport and in the days that followed. In light of all that was going on, it was a dumb thing to worry about, but she nonetheless continued to bite her lip. As long as it stayed seasonal, she could cover up with bulky sweaters, and she had a few of those that were acceptable, though probably not up to French standards. If the temperatures turned warm again—and who knew, with how unpredictable weather was these days—she would be in trouble.

By next week or the week after, she would definitely have to get some maternity clothes, as most of her pants no longer fastened. A shudder of fear swept over her. She didn't want to even think about next week. What if Etienne died on the table? She caught her breath and wrapped her arms around her midriff, rocking back and forth. The thought was like looking into a black abyss. She stumbled back towards her bed and sat down on the edge, trying to hold back tears. What had she done? How had she come to love someone so completely who might vanish from her life in a matter of days?

As she sat and rocked, she felt the strangest sensation just below her belly button, as if a butterfly were flapping its wings against the inside of her skin. The feeling stopped, and Catherine thought she must have imagined it. She had to get control somehow, she told herself, but tears continued to slide down her cheeks. The funny feeling started in her tummy again, and Catherine forced herself to sit up straight. Her hand went to rub her stomach, and the realization hit her like a brick. She was feeling the baby move. Yes, she had seen the image on the ultrasound, but this was the first time she had really felt her as a living, moving presence within her.

Oh God. How she wished Etienne were here and that she could put his hands on her belly and tell him their baby was there.

Five days, she told herself. Get through the next five days, and then you'll know whether there will even be a father in the future for this little girl moving within you. Five days, and she would know if the person she had somehow come to love so profoundly would even exist as part of her future.

She felt a pang of guilt as she got to her feet and forced herself back to the guestroom. She had focused so little attention on this precious life within her. She hadn't even looked at the books her mother had gotten her or gone to any of the gazillion websites that were out there for pregnant women. No wonder she hadn't recognized the sensation inside her at first. Whatever happened, she would have to start paying attention. If Etienne made it through successfully, she hoped that learning about the baby would bring him joy. If it didn't, she'd muddle through on her own. But she wouldn't think about any of that now.

She finished the beds and put clean towels in the guest bathroom. She'd go hide the pregnancy books that were on top of the bookshelf in her own room just in case Etienne's mom went in there. The fewer chances for questions at this point, the better.

———

"*MAMAN, écoute.* Catherine is driving me to the airport to meet you, and then we will be returning to her house. Please don't make a big deal out of it, *je t'en pris.*"

"This is the Catherine with whom you spent Christmas? Is there a reason I should make a big deal?"

Etienne sighed. He was damned however he played this. If he tried to convince his mother that Catherine was just a friend, he would hurt Catherine. Yet if he allowed his mother to know how much he cared, she would no doubt move into hyper-drive in her efforts to dissuade him from having surgery.

"*Maman,* she is a dear friend, who has been extraordinarily kind. Try not to think of her as a female, *d'accord?*"

There was a silence from across the Atlantic.

Finally, "*Bon.* I am very grateful to know that your friends have been so kind. I will always be thankful to David for the time and care he gave both of us in August and September."

David. Damn. He probably should call him to let him know what he was doing. They had been corresponding about the response to the Christmas story about Ahmed, but it had been several days since they had spoken. He'd have to remember to do so later that day.

"I'll see you on Monday, *Maman.* Have a safe flight. *Je t'aime.*"

"Je t'aime, aussi, mon fils. A bientôt."

As Etienne disconnected, he thought of the words that he had spoken so unthinkingly. Would he, indeed, *see* his mother soon? Or would he leave his mother and Catherine more shattered than they were now? He hated himself for allowing Catherine to become so vulnerable on his behalf. How could he have been so selfish? She would have been fine if she had never met him, or if they had stayed just friends. But now he was putting her happiness in jeopardy. And that nagging feeling that he was forgetting or missing something only made his guilt worse.

MRS. SETON WAS LOVELIER than Catherine had expected, making her feel unsophisticated and frumpy in her yoga pants and bulky sweater. Her own mother was fit and always dressed well, but Mrs. Seton exuded an air of quiet elegance. She wore an intricate blue print scarf over a lighter blue blouse, and her form-fitting black slacks just touched a pair of low heels. Her hair was a bit lighter brown than Etienne's, with a hint of gray at her temples. The camel hair overcoat she carried seemed the perfect intersection of fashion and practicality.

Catherine had worn her sneakers. Her ankle was still not 100%, and at the last minute she had faced a choice between her high-heeled dress boots and her bulkier bad weather boots and had just thrown on her running shoes. Now she wished she had taken the time to search out something nicer.

She reached to take Jake's harness when she saw the recognition in the petite woman's eyes. Catherine had been watching the passengers filtering out through the arrivals door, and she now took Etienne's arm and moved him with her to the opening in the barricades. Etienne's mother walked up to them, let go of her luggage trolley, and lifted her arms to encircle Etienne's torso. Etienne bent down and rested his cheek on the top of her head, holding her close.

The two were a quiet island of stillness in the midst of the chaotic waiting area. Catherine reached out to move the trolley further aside, not wanting to interfere. But as if sensing her unease, Etienne broke his embrace and reached out his hand.

"Catherine? Come meet my mother, Bernice Seton. *Maman,* this is Catherine Reynolds, my very dear friend."

Catherine moved closer and looked into a pair of blue-gray eyes. Mrs. Seton stared at her intently for a long moment and then moved to embrace her warmly.

"Catherine." Her accent gave stress to the usually silent second syllable of her name and sounded musical to Catherine's ears. "It is so good to meet you." She squeezed tight for an instant and then released Catherine and bent down to greet Jake.

"And how are you, my old friend? Remember we met a few months ago?"

Jake sat appropriately at attention, but he moved his head to meet Mrs. Seton's caress.

From her crouched position next to the dog, Mrs. Seton turned to stare intently up at Catherine with an assessing gaze. She then glanced at Etienne before returning her attention briefly to Jake. After a final pat, she stood.

"Do we have a moment to visit the toilets before we leave? There was a long queue near the customs section, so I chose to wait."

"Of course. We'll stay here with your things. Catherine, are we in the way here? Should we move?"

Catherine put the lead back in his hand and pushed the trolley closer to a row of seats. Mrs. Seton walked with her arm linked with Etienne's.

"We will be right back." She turned and took Catherine's arm. "You can show me the way, all right?"

Catherine was surprised but tried not to show it. "Of course. It's right this way."

She led Etienne's mother to the ladies' room. Once inside, Mrs. Seton released her arm and turned to face her.

"Catherine, my dear. Does he know?"

Catherine stared at the woman, unsure what to say. She realized her mouth was open, and she tried to compose herself.

"I'm sorry, Mrs. Seton. I don't understand. Does who know what?"

"Call me Bernice, please, my dear. Does Etienne know about the baby? And is it his?"

Catherine's eyes grew wide. She reached for the counter and tried to take a breath. She shook her head slightly and looked again at Etienne's mother, who was standing calmly next to the row of sinks. Two small vertical lines creased the space between her brows as she stared intently at Catherine.

"It is his, is it not?"

"Yes. No. It's mine. And no, he doesn't know. How in the world did you figure out that I'm pregnant?"

"I do not know. I just knew instantly when I looked at you. And forgive me. Of course it is your baby. But Etienne is the father, *n'est-ce pas?*"

Catherine continued to stare at the woman in confusion. Was she some kind of witch? Catherine had a loose jacket over her sweater, and she turned to look at herself in the bathroom mirror, just to be sure. She looked frumpy, definitely, especially compared to the elegant Bernice, but even her own critical eye couldn't see a bump that screamed baby.

She turned again to Bernice. "I don't understand."

Bernice shrugged and then smiled at Catherine, reaching out to hug her again.

"I can keep your secret, my dear, if that is what you wish. But are you sure this is the right thing to do?" She leaned back to look at Catherine, who was astonished to see tears in the older woman's eyes.

"I can't make this harder for him."

Bernice sighed. "I would not have thought this whole ordeal could get any more difficult, but I guess I was wrong. *Eh, bien.*" She glanced in the mirror, adjusted her scarf slightly, and moved to wash her hands, but then stopped. "We should use the toilets while we're here, no? I remember how it was."

Catherine shook her head in amazement and then switched to a quick nod. "You're absolutely right, on that account."

A few minutes later they were back together at the sinks.

"We will go back to Etienne, and I will say nothing." Tears were still visible in Bernice's eyes, but she smiled again at Catherine. "But I cannot promise to stay silent if all goes well this week, agreed?"

Catherine returned a wan smile. "Agreed."

Bernice took Catherine's hand and squeezed it. Then she linked her arm with Catherine's and the two returned to the arrivals waiting room.

ETIENNE'S MOTHER expressed no surprise when they spoke in the car of the plan for them to spend the coming three nights at her house. Catherine had made up the two twin beds in the guestroom, refusing to think about the incongruity of the situation. She had to swallow her instinctive snort, though, when Etienne whispered after her mother had shut the passenger door of the car, "It's probably best that she not know how close we are, okay? I don't want to give her any ideas."

"Of course," Catherine mumbled, her own nerves so frazzled by that point that she didn't even try to say more. But an hour later when she was showing Bernice to the room and indicating the two guest beds, Bernice had given her a slightly mocking smile, eyebrows raised quizzically.

Catherine had smiled back, knowing her face undoubtedly had a maniacal look to it, and Bernice had just shaken her head.

Etienne's list of tasks to finish in the next few days was daunting, as if the arrival of his mother had brought home to him the possible finality of his decision.

When they drove over to his condo on Tuesday morning, he asked them to name all the items in each room for him and keep a list of what should be done with them. His tone when he made his request was calm, but his mother grew more and more agitated as Catherine miserably attempted to do as Etienne asked.

"This is completely macabre. I do not, cannot, understand why in the world you are putting us all through such a nightmare. You want your piano to go to a good home? For God's sake, Etienne, you could play that piano right this moment. Why can you not be grateful for the life you still have and do something with it?"

Bernice's voice held the threat of hysteria, and Catherine had to turn away to try and get her own emotions under control. She forced herself to breathe and then walked over to slip her arm around the French woman's waist.

"I've met Dr. Abrams, Bernice. I have confidence in her. I think Etienne is just being overly conscientious. We should humor him now, and then we can make fun of him when it's all over."

Bernice turned and stared into Catherine's eyes. She pressed her lips and then turned more fully to embrace her.

"Of course, my dear. That is exactly the right plan." She pulled away slightly and turned back towards Etienne, the struggle to regain control evident in her voice.

"And now tell me, my great oaf of a son. You have been traveling the world for years now. Should you perish on the table on Thursday. . . " Bernice stopped to gulp in some air. "Should you perish or become even less sensible than you are now, what would you have me do if some child you never knew about appears one day out of the blue claiming you are his father?"

Catherine glared at Bernice, but Etienne laughed. "I think that's the last thing you'll have to worry about. But should it happen, I trust you will do whatever is best."

"Ah. How nice it is to know you still trust me for something." Bernice's sarcasm dripped like hot splashes of oil, but her hold on Catherine remained warm as she ignored the daggers Catherine's eyes were shooting her way.

"Fine then," she continued. "Let us make a well-annotated list. How much wine do you have?"

Etienne chuckled in resignation. "Okay. I give up. If I die, give my clothes to charity, my books to the library, and you, *Maman,* can drink all the wine. Catherine, you take whatever you want, including the piano. And now, to keep my mother happy, why don't we find someplace to go eat where she can enjoy a nice bottle of the wine she seems to need so desperately."

Etienne's words were light, but Catherine could tell he was keeping a tight hold on his emotions.

She looked from one face to the other and saw the resemblance in their hair color, their eyes, and the fierce way they compressed their lips when they were agitated. Etienne's hair was darker and his eyes a deeper blue. Distractedly, she tried to think if there was any recessive blue-eye gene in her that would allow her own daughter to carry on the beautiful color.

A massive wave of fear and sadness engulfed her. Was she to be left alone with a helpless baby and a heart that was broken?

"Excuse me," she whispered and moved quickly to the bathroom, closing the door and locking it. She stared at herself in the mirror for a moment, her own brown eyes large and brimming with tears. She had to pull herself together. She had to be strong for all four of them.

WEDNESDAY NIGHT they agreed on Mexican take-out. Bernice laughed as she recounted to Catherine how she and Etienne's father had bonded over their love for the then hard-to-find novelty when they were first getting to know each other almost forty years ago in France.

"He was so happy to meet a French woman who didn't love escargots. How he hated those things. That was when he taught me the word 'slimy.'" Her French accent drew out the two syllables, and both Etienne and Catherine started laughing.

"What?" She looked at them both in turn, her brow furrowed. "I know very well that is the correct word, is it not?"

They couldn't stop laughing, until eventually Bernice pushed her chair back and began reaching for their barely touched plates. "Enough, *mes enfants*. I will take what's left of the wine and go dispose of this remaining non-slimy food. It is almost eight, Etienne, and you must not have any more to eat." She paused. "Unless, of course, you may have changed your mind and decided to forego this nonsense?"

"No, *Maman*. I'm sorry." Etienne stood and reached towards his mother who moved to meet his gesture. She pressed her face into his chest.

"Then, God willing, my son, the next time you reach for me, you will see where I am standing. But you will do so with care, for I may very well reach out myself and wallop you for what you have put us through."

She moved to the kitchen area and Catherine watched her. She should probably get up and make Bernice sit down. Bernice was her guest, and this might be the last evening she got to spend with her son. But Catherine was so very tired, and the thought of standing up seemed impossible.

"Catherine? You're still here, right?"

"Uh-huh."

"Come sit on the sofa with me." He stretched out a hand in her general direction.

"I thought you didn't want your mother to think we were close." Her tone sounded sarcastic, even to her own ears.

"Oh, Kat. Come sit with me, just for a few minutes."

Slightly surprised that her legs worked after all, Catherine pushed herself up and took Etienne's outstretched hand. She led him to the old blue couch that she had kept after her grandmother passed, the couch where she and Etienne had first felt passion roar between them. The coffee table he had bumped into had long since been pushed closer to the fireplace, and Etienne's steps were now confident as he walked with her.

Etienne sat down and pulled Catherine directly onto his lap.

"Etienne, no! Your mother can see us if she turns around."

"It's fine. Don't worry. It doesn't matter anymore, does it? Besides, she told me earlier that I should spend time with you tonight and thank you for all the hospitality you've shown us." His hand was sliding repeatedly over her hair as he spoke, as if trying to gentle a skittish animal.

Catherine emitted an inhospitable grunt. "How considerate of her."

Etienne's hand stilled. "What is it? Have you and my mother had words?"

Catherine pushed her head more deeply against his chest. "No. It's nothing. I'm just crabby."

Etienne's hand resumed its caress.

Catherine sat quietly for a few moments, but somehow the agitation inside her seemed to ignite, rather than dissipate. She pulled away and looked up into his sightless eyes.

"Why, Etienne? Why? Remember everything they told you could go wrong? Vital parts could be nicked. You could have a spinal fluid leak. They could prick your carotid artery and you could die right there. You could stroke out and end up paralyzed as well as blind, or in a coma. Or maybe they'll just get out whatever the hell hit you in the first place, and your optic nerves will still be too damaged to work. Why risk any of that? Why?" She was crying by the end, unable to stop the tears that trickled down her cheeks.

Etienne moved his hands to frame her face, his thumbs moving back and forth gently over the soft valleys under her eyes and above her cheekbones.

"I love this part of your face. It is so soft. So beautiful."

Catherine groaned. "Why do you keep saying I'm beautiful when you can't see me? Maybe there was more brain damage than they've let on."

Etienne chuckled. "Nope. I'm just extraordinarily perceptive." He bent down and kissed the end of her nose. "Ooo, it's warm. It must be red, too, from those silly tears." His words were quiet, but Catherine could hear the strain behind them.

She sniffed, trying to get her tears under control. "Yes, it's probably bright red. And it's your fault. But you still haven't explained why we're going through all this."

Etienne inhaled slowly. "Catherine. I love you. No, don't," he said as she gasped and tried to pull her head away. "Listen to me."

"My life was fine before the accident. I had a job I liked and that I was good at. But in many ways, I was just going through the motions. Then those goddamn explosions went off, and everything that I was before was gone. I was angry and resentful. And then somehow in the middle of all that, I met you."

"You know those pictures you sometimes see that are all black and white with just a bit of color? I remember seeing one a few years ago that a German photographer had done. It was a bright red umbrella on a bridge or a walkway. Well, that's what meeting you was like. You were color in my colorless world. But I think you would have been, even if I could see. I've been taking pictures all my life, and you're the first color I've ever really known."

"Oh God, stop." Catherine had thought her heart broken before, but now it was worse. She struggled to make her words come out through her sobs.

"Etienne, listen to yourself. You're still an artist. It doesn't matter whether you can see or not. Beethoven didn't stop writing music when he went deaf. In fact, he wrote some of his best music after he lost his hearing. They call it 'Ode to Joy,' Etienne, not 'Ode to What Could Have Been.'"

He laughed. "And that's why you're the writer in the family."

They both froze for a moment. She knew he hadn't meant to say anything like that. How could they be a family when they were barely even a real couple?

Etienne took another deep breath.

"But you see, Kat, you've given me color, and now I want

to do something with it. Yes, I could live out a no-doubt long and perfectly adequate life as a sightless person. But I'm not Beethoven. I want to take this chance at having it all. I would like to be your equal partner in this world, and yes, selfishly, a part of me even wants to do my small part to advance medical breakthroughs. Dr. Abrams told me that almost all surgery near the optic chiasm is due to pituitary issues, but that medicine will almost certainly be called on to deal with more traumatic brain injuries as other fields advance."

"I don't want to finish my life only half-lived, if there's any chance of changing it. I want to be 100%. I need to do what I'm supposed to do, whatever that turns out to be, and I believe I can do it better with eyesight. I wish I could explain it better than that, but that's all I've got."

Catherine stared at him, wishing she could see something in his sightless eyes. The same sentiment went through her mind every time she looked at him, so how much worse it must be for him. She was denied the sight of his eyes seeing her; he was denied sight of everything. But he was still here. Wasn't that worth something to him?

Tell him. Don't tell him. *He deserves to know.* Don't make it any harder than it is already.

Finally she sighed.

"Okay, Etienne. I'm not going to try to change your mind anymore. But just know that there's no 'that's all I've got' as far as I'm concerned. I can be a red umbrella. And I'll still be one tomorrow night, if that's what you want, rain or shine, eyesight or no eyesight."

She moved her face forward the few inches it took for her lips to touch his, but her kiss was light and lasted only a second. She got up, quickly, before he could hold her.

"I'm going to go up to bed, unless you want me to take Jake out."

"No, that's okay, thanks. And thanks for taking care of

him tomorrow. Although that's a stupid thing to thank you for, given all you've done, but I mean it."

"No problem. And I'll make sure he's taken care of." She paused and then forced herself to go on, "if anything happens."

"I know you will. Good night, Catherine."

———

BERNICE WENT OUTSIDE with him when he took Jake out. Her hand gripped his arm tightly, but she said nothing.

"It's not like you to be so quiet, *Maman*."

"What would you have me say?"

"Tell me what the sky looks like. Can you see stars tonight?"

Bernice breathed in and out with what sounded like intentionally loud deliberation.

"Yes, my son. There are stars out. Can I tell you which ones? *Non*. That is not my area of expertise. But they are beautiful, and I truly wish you could see them."

She stopped walking and turned him towards her.

"Etienne, forgive me. I have been selfish. If there is a chance you will be able to see the stars again, I should not try to keep them from you." Her voice was quiet, and he had to strain to hear her.

"Don't apologize, *Maman*. I am sorry to put you through so much pain."

"Do you love her?"

Etienne inhaled sharply, stunned by his mother's directness. He thought fleetingly of dissembling but then surrendered.

"Yes. I do. Do you approve?"

Bernice snorted. "Now you seek my approval? I just apologized, but I cannot help thinking it is now late for me to approve of a young lady when your relationship may have an abrupt ending."

"I'm hoping that it won't."

They had resumed walking, but now Bernice stopped him and reached up to touch his cheek.

"I hope the same. And for the record: yes. I approve. I approve very much. And I hope you will do the right thing tomorrow night."

"Tomorrow? I'm not sure Catherine is ready for a proposal. If everything goes well, it may take a while for her to forgive me. And we've never had the chance to really spend time together like normal people."

"Tomorrow."

"*Maman*, even if the surgery is successful, I may not be conscious by tomorrow night, or at least not lucid."

"*Mon Dieu*. Do you have an answer for everything? *Bon*. Friday, then."

"Do I need to have a ring ready?" He laughed as he spoke.

Bernice gasped. "Etienne, do you remember the antique garnet ring that your father gave me after his grandmother died? I never felt quite right wearing it as his family always hated the fact that he married a foreigner. But it is a beautiful ring, and I am sure your Seton relatives would love to see it back on an American finger. I will call your Aunt Charlotte before I go to sleep and have her send it to me."

"No, *Maman*. Don't be silly. That will cost a fortune, and it's not necessary. Besides, wouldn't it be wiser to wait until after the surgery to call?"

Bernice uttered a quintessentially French sound. "Of course it is necessary. You are my only son, and this is the woman you love, *n'est-ce pas*? And if we have a plan in place, then the surgery will have to go well."

Better to give her something concrete to focus on, Etienne thought, *but still . . .*

They were at the bottom of the stoop to Catherine's front door.

"I do love you, *Maman*."

Bernice grasped his free hand again as they mounted the steps, and Etienne realized that she was actually using him to help support her weight. As they entered, her brisk, "You had better, my son. You are responsible for too many of the gray hairs that now cover my head," reinforced his awareness of her increasing frailty. *Terrific. Even more to feel guilty about.*

"I'm very grateful to you for making such a generous offer, but when and if I do propose, maybe a new ring that Catherine could help choose might be better." He spoke quietly, even though he was pretty sure his words wouldn't carry up the stairs.

They were inside now, and Bernice's reply was whispered but insistent. "I have gotten to know Catherine very well these past few days, and I believe she will love the ring. And do not give me any 'when and if.' You have already promised. Now go on upstairs, Etienne. I will be up in a few minutes."

Etienne climbed the stairs with Jake. He remembered the first time he had maneuvered them, one hand on Jake's harness and the other on Catherine's bottom as she hobbled on crutches. At the top of the stairs, he hesitated. He wanted desperately to turn to the left and seek out Catherine in her bed, but the saner voice in his head told him to let her sleep. Besides, his mother was revved up enough at the moment. No need to give her additional ammunition.

He sighed quietly and turned to the right. He doubted he would sleep, but he should finish with the bathroom so it would be free when his mother came up.

SEVERAL HOURS LATER, Etienne lay in the twin bed, unable to sleep. He could hear from the gentle breathing nearby that his mother had finally fallen asleep, for which he was grateful. Once again he thought of going to Catherine's room, and once again he dismissed the idea. He would no doubt bump into something, Jake would stir, and his mother would wake up. Better to let the women get some rest. He would be unconscious for at least several hours tomorrow while they would be awake and worrying.

He tried to quiet his mind, tried to remember beautiful places he had visited and photographed. But memories of the blissful hours he had spent with Catherine kept pushing other thoughts aside. From out of the blue, the gnawing sense of having missed something returned to him.

He thought of the first and only time they had made love in this house, and how the act of laughing with Catherine while loving had made the experience so different from anything he had known before.

He remembered how deliciously right she had felt sinking down on top of him, despite the cumbersome cast, making the whole encounter hilarious and sexy as hell. He remembered how unfamiliar but still gloriously satisfying it had been to find her breasts as she hovered over him—to find them and caress them and suck her sweet nipples without ever seeing them, and to hear her gasp in response.

His mind traveled over the other times they had made love, and how each encounter seemed to involve more and more of his heart as well as his body. And despite his now throbbing erection, he remembered how right it had felt to finally spend a night together in his bed last week without even making love. They had both been so emotionally exhausted and physically spent from their earlier encounter that just cuddling close had been as natural as breathing.

He remembered how her bottom had been tucked up

against his crotch and his hand had gently cupped her breast as she fell asleep.

Etienne bit his lip as the puzzle piece that had been haunting him suddenly took shape in his mind. Her breasts. He sat up in bed and struggled to concentrate. He tried to remember that first time, when they had started going at each other on the sofa downstairs. He had freed her breasts from her bra and played with them before they began their clumsy journey up the stairs. They had felt perfect, fitting nicely into his palms as he brushed her puckering nipples.

But then he thought of how she had felt on Christmas Eve and again last week in his bed. Her breasts were bigger, more rounded--he was positive. And her nipples had seemed extremely sensitive, his gentle nuzzling causing her to suck in her breath harshly. He heard the sound again in his mind and his dick stiffened in response.

Could she have had surgery? He dismissed the thought instantly. It was totally out of character for the Catherine he now felt he knew so well. Plus they had been in pretty frequent contact over the last several months, and even blind, he was fairly sure he would have caught on if she had been in major discomfort. And one way or another, he had managed to touch or brush against her breasts with determined regularity.

A cold sweat began to sweep over him. He thought of his mother's insistence that he propose to Catherine immediately. He remembered how she had told him on Christmas that birth control was taken care of. He had willingly accepted her words, never stopping to wonder if maybe she had meant something other than the obvious.

Oh God. What if she were pregnant? Could it be? Could she be keeping it from him because of the surgery? He tried to concentrate. She had been running to the bathroom a lot in the last few weeks, come to think about it. Had she had any alcohol at Christmas or at dinner last night? How the hell would he know? He was blind, God dammit! But she had insisted on drinking tea at his house the day of the CT scan.

Suddenly struggling to breathe, Etienne wanted desperately to get up and pace. He wanted to pace, he wanted to tear into Catherine's room, he wanted to look her in the eye and demand she tell him the truth.

"*Calm down,*" he screamed internally. "*Don't panic.*"

He tried to tamp down his rising fear. Again the thought that he mustn't disturb anyone's sleep forced him to stay in bed, but the waves of horror sweeping over him must have somehow communicated themselves to Jake, who began thumping his tail and whining softly.

"Shhhh." Etienne whispered. He wanted the dog to relax, but he himself thought he was going to explode. Holy Jesus, what had he done?

JUST FEET AWAY, Catherine sat huddled in the dark, trying to keep her wrenching sobs quiet. She had stayed awake long after going to bed, unable to concentrate on the words in her book, uninterested in television or the internet, but unwilling to go back downstairs and risk seeing Etienne or his mom.

When she had finally fallen asleep, her nightmare had returned. But this time, the mysterious missing man had had a face, and it had been Etienne's. As in earlier dreams, she had been in a doorway struggling to call out. In the next instant she was standing amidst trees, staring down at the battered face of a dead Etienne. She crumpled to the ground, pain slicing through her. Her husband, her love, her baby's father, was dead, and she was alone. A cry of agony broke from her throat, and Catherine jolted up in bed, gasping in despair.

This was infinitely worse than the disturbing but still shadowy dreams she had experienced in the past. This time the mysteries had been crystal clear: Etienne had gone out in a storm and he had never returned. His horrible death had left her alone with a baby, a little girl who would never stop crying for the father and husband who had been taken from them and was never coming back.

Catherine rocked back and forth, her knees drawn up almost to her chin, and tried to push the heartbreaking image of Etienne's bruised face and vacant eyes out her head. Had it always been Etienne who had disappeared? Or was this her current fears moving in to share space with amorphous nightmares that had always been there?

She saw again the gray pallor of his skin, and Catherine stumbled to her feet. She barely made it in time to the toilet before losing what was left of the little dinner she had eaten.

She forced herself to focus on breathing, sucking in gasping mouthfuls of air. It was just a stupid dream. She had to pull herself together. She had been having the damn nightmare for as long as she could remember, and it had nothing to do with Etienne.

Grabbing a washcloth from the linen closet, she splashed cool water on her face, rinsed her mouth, and then held the cool cloth pressed tightly to her eyes.

She went back into the bedroom and found her phone. 4:35. She had the alarm set for five, so there was no point in going back to bed now.

I may never willingly shut my eyes again, anyway.

The thought passed through her mind, and Catherine struggled to shove it aside, to push all memories of the dream into a box and put it far away for now.

She would shower and then go downstairs and make

coffee for Bernice and tea for herself. Etienne could have nothing, but she needed that cup of tea, and she needed it soon.

TWENTY MINUTES LATER, they were all downstairs. Etienne sat at the table, a blank look on his face and his dark glasses in place. His phone was in his hand, but it was silent.

Bernice stood near him, holding her coffee cup. She had said only "*Bonjour, mes enfants.*" Now she turned her head back and forth looking at them each in turn.

"Pardon my French, but you both look like shit."

Catherine choked on the tea she had been swallowing, almost dropping the cup. She put it down carefully and turned to look at Bernice.

Etienne, too, made a half-choking noise, and then he started to laugh.

"Tell me, *Maman.* Just how long have you been waiting to say those words?"

Bernice tilted her head as if silently counting.

"It must be almost forty years. I thought the expression quite absurd when your father taught it to me, but I see now it is most useful."

Catherine couldn't speak as noises that were somewhere between a laugh and a sob kept coming from her throat. When she finally got herself under control, her hand moved up to touch her cheek in wonder.

"God, Bernice, in a way that felt really good. I think my face had forgotten what it felt like to smile."

"Ahhh, you Americans are all about exaggeration. You laughed at my expense last night when I said the word 'slimy.'"

It proved too much. All three of them dissolved in laughter.

Catherine was trying yet again to get control of herself when the doorbell rang.

"What the fu . . . ? Ooops, sorry, Bernice. Pardon my French." They were all chortling uncontrollably as Catherine went to the door.

"Mother! What in the world are you doing here?"

"I was passing by and saw your lights were on and thought I'd stop."

"Yeah, right. It's five a.m. Seriously, is something wrong?"

"Of course not. Darren had an early flight to catch, so I drove him to the airport, and I thought I'd come by and see if maybe it would help if I took Jake home with me. He'd be good company while Darren is away."

"Oh Mom." Catherine reached out and her mother enveloped her in a warm embrace.

"Are you okay, Sweetheart? You look like shit."

Once again Catherine was overcome by hysterical laughter, which quickly turned to hiccupping sobs in her mother's arms.

"Shhhh. It's all right." Her mom held her tightly, rubbing her hand up and down Catherine's back.

After a minute Catherine drew in a breath and pulled free.

"Thank you, Mom. I'm okay. Come in and meet Etienne's mother."

Etienne stood up as Ellen came in.

"Good morning, Etienne." She kissed his cheek and then reached out a hand towards Bernice.

"You must be Bernice. I'm Ellen. As I just told Catherine, I thought maybe I could borrow Jake for a day or two if that's all right with all of you."

"Where are you, Ellen?" Etienne stretched out a hand and Ellen came over to him and met his fingers with her own.

He brought her hand to his lips and kissed the top of her knuckles.

"That would be enormously helpful. Thank you so much for thinking of it."

Ellen squeezed her fingers around his in acknowledgement and reached up to touch Etienne's cheek.

"It will be my pleasure. You can come get him whenever you're ready. Now I need to be going, since I guess you all will be setting off soon."

Catherine had moved to gather together Jake's food and bowls in a large canvas bag. She handed it to her mother and then went to put a leash on Jake.

"He's not wearing his service harness since I was going to leave him here and go back and forth during the day to walk him for however many days Etienne needs to be in the hospital. Since he won't be working with you, there's no need for him to wear it."

As CATHERINE and Ellen went outside, Etienne felt his growing sense of urgency and frustration bubbling over. He had wanted to get a moment alone with Catherine and confront her with his suspicions without his mother hearing. If he was wrong, he certainly didn't want to plant ideas in her head. And if he was right, it was a conversation that demanded privacy. Now he didn't know if he would get even a second alone with her.

"Etienne, we must be going. What do you need me to get for you?" His mother's voice had lost any of the mirth from just a few moments ago.

"Nothing, thanks. I brought my bag down with me and put it near the door."

"Very well, then. As soon as Catherine comes back in, we should go."

The door opened as she spoke, and Catherine spoke to them from the entryway.

"I'll be ready in two seconds. I just need to grab the bag I packed upstairs."

"Did you two get any breakfast?" Etienne asked. "We still have a few minutes."

"We'll have all day to eat," Catherine replied. "I don't think my stomach could take any food right now, anyway. Do you want anything, Bernice?"

"Not at all. The sooner we are on our way, the sooner it will all be over."

CHAPTER TWENTY-FIVE

Katrina stood staring down at Stephen's lifeless body. It was not possible. It could not be possible. They needed to be on their way in just a few minutes to head north. He had gone to check a noise. He could not be lying here on the muddy ground, a puddle of blackened liquid under his head.

Lord Philipse's stable master was holding on to her arms, but she pulled free and dropped to her knees, her hands reaching out to brush the hair back from Stephen's bashed-in forehead.

"Stephen, please wake up. Please look at me." His eyes were open, but there was no focus to his gaze, no life in their still beautiful blue depths. She bent down and kissed his lips. They were cold and dry, despite the dampness of the morning air.

"Please, Mrs. Howard. Please come with me." The stable master tried to pull her up, but Katrina resisted, holding Stephen's face in both her hands and trying to will life between her palms.

"Stephen, please. You must wake up. We must be on our

way." Tears streamed down her face, but she refused to acknowledge what her eyes, hands, and lips were telling her.

"Stephen!" She leaned down again to put her cheek against his. "Stephen, please. I'll go to Ticonderoga. I'll go to England. I'll do anything you want. Just please, come back to me."

"Come now, Ma'am. Let me bring you back to the manor, and I will get some of the boys to come help me with the major's body."

"No! We cannot leave him here. It is too cold and damp."

"It's all right, Mrs. Howard. I'll come right back and see to him. I promise. You must be getting back to your young one."

"Anne!" Katrina looked about wildly, as if she expected the baby to materialize before her. "Anne mustn't see her papa like this. She will be frightened."

She reached out again as if to try and pull Stephen up, but the stable master grabbed her firmly and pulled her to her feet.

"Do not fret, Mrs. Howard. Let us go back now, and you may tend to your young daughter so she does not take fright."

Katrina at last allowed him to lead her away, but just before they reached the bend in the path that would put Stephen's body out of sight, she turned back.

"Oh, Stephen," she whispered. "We were supposed to make everything work, remember? We were going to prove we could overcome the obstacles, not let them overcome us."

She turned then and pulled her arm from the stable master's grip. She was alone now. She and Anne were alone.

———

KATRINA HAD STOOD at the door for hours, rain and mist coming and going through the early morning hours. Her hands had grown icy with fear, and when she went to pick up Anne, the baby cried out at her cold touch.

She walked the baby around for a moment or two and then laid her down, hearing her cries but more consumed by Stephen's continued absence. When at last the sky began to lighten, she wrapped Anne in a blanket and ran with her to the manor kitchen.

"Mrs. Gantry, thank goodness you are here. Would you take Anne for a few minutes? I must find the major. He went out last night and didn't return."

"Don't you go running out there alone, Mrs. Howard. There was trouble about last night. I'll send young Abbie to find Michael from the stables, and he can go with you."

"No, I cannot wait. Stephen might be hurt. I must find him."

Busying herself at the hearth, Mrs. Gantry managed to delay taking Anne from her arms until the stable master arrived.

Now Katrina stood again in the kitchen. It was only eight in the morning, and the sun was shining through the windows still wet from last night's rain.

"Sit down and have some tea, my dear. You can drink and warm yourself while you feed this poor little girl. She's been wailing and wailing for you. I gave her a cloth soaked in sugar water to suck, but she wouldn't be comforted."

Katrina sat as ordered and put Anne to her breast, taking a sip of the sweetened tea as Anne gradually quieted. The liquid was hot and welcome. She stared into the china cup, so unlike any of the sturdy and utilitarian cups she had grown up with in the tavern. Stephen had loved tea. And he had wanted her to find pleasure in it despite the colonial prohibitions. Such a silly thing to fight over.

She continued to stare into the steaming cup, and tears trickled down her face. What was she to do now? Who was she now? She had parted from her family and friends to marry the enemy, and now he was gone. Her Stephen. Her friend, her lover, her artist, was gone. Katrina closed her eyes as her tears continued to fall. Why couldn't they have gone together?

HER MOTHER ARRIVED with her brother an hour or so later.

"Katrina, my dear daughter. Let us get your things together and we'll go home."

Katrina stared at her mother in confusion.

"Leave? How can I leave? I cannot go home, Mother. The people have made it clear that I am not welcome in town. And they killed my husband." Her final words came out in a strangled cry.

"My husband, Mama. They killed him. He never harbored any ill will towards anyone here. He wanted peace, not war. And now they have killed him."

"Oh, Katrina, lass. Your Stephen may not have wanted war, but war is upon us now."

Katrina stared at her mother, seeing the face of an aging woman who had always treated her with love and who had extended kindness towards her son-in-law.

But Katrina had turned her back on her mother's love for the love of an English officer. And now that love was gone. Everything was gone. She couldn't go back. She had nowhere to go. Stephen was gone. The love that had swept her away and made her put all else aside was gone.

She looked bleakly at her mother.

"I am sorry, Mama. I do not know yet what I am going to do, but I cannot go back with you."

THE NEXT AFTERNOON Katrina stood in the shadow of a tree a few feet away from the church in which she had been wed. The pastor had agreed to bury Stephen in a private service, but he insisted that no identification be put on the small stone.

"These are dangerous times, Miss Rynick. I will not risk vandalism on this sacred ground."

Katrina stared at him coldly. "My name is Mrs. Howard, Pastor. Remember? You married us on a beautiful September afternoon."

"Forgive me, Mrs. Howard. And yes, I do remember. I was not sure then that I was doing the right thing, and I am still not sure. But I give you my condolences for your loss."

Katrina turned away. His condolences were worth nothing. There was only pain.

She shifted Anne in her arms and walked away from the fresh grave. Her parents were standing a few steps away, watching her with uncertainty in their eyes.

As she approached, her father spoke.

"My daughter, I am sorry for the distance that has existed between us for so long. Will you not come back now to your family?"

Katrina looked at him. The years of hard work had taken a toll on her father, and today he looked like an old man.

"Thank you, Father. But I cannot. I am sorry. I have decided to take Anne and go to Manhattan to visit Mrs. Colden, the acting governor's wife. She has invited me in the past and has shown us kindness. I must get word to Stephen's family, and I must do what is right for Anne."

"It is right for your daughter to grow up with the love of a family, Katrina." Her mother's voice sounded strained, but Katrina stood firm.

"Anne and I are a family, Mother. And Stephen's kin in

England are her family, too. Perhaps I will return, but for now, this is what I must do."

Katrina walked to the carriage that the staff at the manor had insisted she use. She turned before she climbed in and looked one last time at the church where she had felt such joy and hope. She had been foolish to believe that their unlikely love could prevail. Stephen was gone, and she would not risk her heart again.

CHAPTER TWENTY-SIX

Damn! It looked like any chance at speaking to Catherine alone was slipping away.

She had dropped him and his mother at the hospital entrance and gone to find a parking spot. For a major hospital in the middle of the nation's capital, parking was about as inconvenient as it could get, and he doubted she'd catch up with them for at least 20 – 30 minutes.

After her last-ditch efforts of the night before, his mother now seemed unusually calm and quiet. Unlike Catherine, Bernice was not used to walking with him alone, and their progress was awkward as they made their way, first to the check-in counter, and then to the waiting room.

"I hope you brought a book or something. It's likely to be a long wait even before anything gets started."

"Don't worry about me. I have my Kindle. Besides, I'll have Catherine for company, and if that fails, I can just stare at my phone for hours on end the way so many of you young people like to do."

Ah, there it was. The acerbic tongue he knew and loved.

"Yikes. Maybe I really shouldn't have the surgery. After

all, right now that's at least one infraction you can't scold me for."

"Humph. Not that I blame you, but since you lost your eyesight, that damn thing is in your hand now more than it ever was before."

Etienne gave her a moment to relish her verbal victory.

"How crowded is the waiting room?"

"It looks like there are probably three other patients here, with their assorted family members."

His mother enjoyed talking with strangers. Maybe she'd get involved in a conversation with one of them and he'd have a minute to talk with Catherine privately. *Where was she?*

"Etienne Seton?"

He heard the female voice and felt his mother stiffen next to him.

"If you'll just come this way, we need to make one final check of your information before we take you back."

He rose to his feet and his mother's hand clamped on to his forearm. She might be the one who could see where they were going, but her grip conveyed the level of her anxiety.

Etienne turned and brought his hand up and searched until he found her face. He patted her cheek gently. "It will be okay, *Maman.* And you will be okay, too, whatever happens. *Je t'aime.*"

Bernice's grasp just tightened further, and she moved jerkily forward. After a short distance, she stopped.

"There's a chair here for you to sit in while they do whatever they have to do."

"Is there one for you, too?"

"Yes."

The woman's voice came again. "Good morning, Mr. Seton. Do you have a picture ID with you?"

His mother took the small backpack he had been carrying

and rifled through it, finding his Virginia driver's license after he explained which pocket to search.

"You drive?" The woman sounded surprised.

Etienne laughed quietly.

"I did. And I hope to, again. That's why I'm here. But the license is still valid."

She checked his insurance information for what had to be the billionth time, and then verified his next of kin information. At his pre-op ordeal the week before, he had impulsively added Catherine's name. He hadn't asked her first and had told the technician to put 'other' when he had pressed him to identify their relationship.

Now he heard his mother's intake of breath when the woman before them read both names and attempted to verify their contact information.

"Catherine Reynolds will be here any moment," Etienne interrupted. "Her phone number is the one you have, and it's local, unlike my mother's. Will they be able to go back with me?"

"Yes. They'll be able to stay with you until you're taken to the operating room."

"So you'll bring her back to us the minute she comes in? She's trying to find parking."

"Yes, don't worry."

Good and bad, Etienne thought. He'd have one last chance to speak with Catherine, but there would be fewer distractions for his mother.

Just then he felt and heard movement behind him, caught a whiff of the scent that always lightened his heart, and then Catherine's hand was on his shoulder.

"Sorry it took so long," she whispered.

He reached up and squeezed her hand, and their fingers intertwined, regardless of the awkward angle.

"Okay, come around to the right, and I'll lead you to the surgery prep area."

Etienne stood up and felt Catherine's arm move to encircle his waist. He turned and breathed in the citrusy cloud of her hair, trying somehow to capture it in his mind. Then she let go of his waist and pulled away slightly.

"Can I go with you, or do I need to stay here?"

"You're Catherine Reynolds, right? You're on the list, so you're fine."

She led them down a corridor, and then into a partitioned room with curtains around each sectioned-off area.

"All clothes except your underwear in the bag. Do you want it labeled and kept with us, or will your next of kin hold on to it?"

"We'll take it," Bernice said.

"Put on the gown that's on the bed, opening at the back, and Dr. Abrams will be here shortly to speak with you. There are chairs right out here if you ladies want to step out."

"Miss, would you be so kind as to show me where the lavatory is?"

Etienne turned his head towards his mother in surprise. He had never known her to need public restrooms as much as she seemed to have needed them this week. Maybe women always needed to go to the bathroom more frequently than men, and he had just never noticed before?

"Are you well, *Maman*?"

"Ah, *oui*, of course. But Catherine can help you undress, and I need to powder my nose."

Catherine gave a small laugh as Bernice moved off with the hospital attendant.

"You were right about your mother being a schemer. Her eyebrows were going up and down, and she was giving me laser glares as she trotted off to the 1950s powder room."

Ah, no bladder infection. Just my mother trying to help, yet again.

He undressed quickly, Catherine matter-of-factly taking his clothes from his hands as he disrobed and helping him on with the cotton hospital garment.

She backed him up so his legs were against the bed, and he sat down, trying to pull her down next to him, but she resisted.

"It's okay. I'd rather stand. They said the doctor would be here in a moment."

And just as she spoke, Dr. Abrams was there, pulling back the curtain.

"Good morning, Etienne."

He felt her touch his shoulder.

"How are you this morning?"

"Fine, thanks. And you?" All totally perfunctory and ridiculous when what he desperately needed was a moment alone with the woman he loved who might be carrying his child. "Doctor, you remember Catherine?"

"Yes, of course. Good to see you again."

The doctor moved to his side and he felt her putting the blood pressure cuff on his arm.

"They just did that."

"Yes, I know. But I like to double-check everything myself. We were often short-staffed in military hospitals, so I got used to doing things for myself, and old habits are hard to break."

She listened to his heart when she was done taking his blood pressure and then stepped back.

"You've had nothing to eat since last night, correct? The nurse will be in in a moment to give you a shot that will help you relax, and then we'll be taking you back in about fifteen minutes."

Her next words seemed to be directed at Catherine.

"Will you be staying here today? You know it will likely be several hours before you can see him again."

"Yes. His mother and I will both be here. She's coming right back. She just stepped out for a minute."

"Well, as I said, it will be a while, and at least three or four hours before I'll even be able to give you any kind of update. Feel free to go out and get some breakfast and fresh air. We have your contact info, right?"

He assumed Catherine had indicated assent because Dr. Abrams reached out to touch his shoulder again.

"We've discussed the possible outcomes, including the fact that there are risks of things going wrong that I haven't even thought to mention. Do you have any last questions? And if you want to change your mind, you still can. Once we give you the anesthesia, there will be no going back."

"No, I'm ready."

"Then I hope we'll talk again this evening." Once more her hand touched his shoulder, and then she was gone.

Etienne turned towards where he thought Catherine was standing and stretched out his hand but met only air. He couldn't know that she had her arms wrapped tightly around herself and was sitting on the chair, rocking back and forth.

"Catherine, I need to talk to you. Could you come closer, please?"

It was hard for him to make out her reply as her voice sounded garbled, but he thought she said, "No, I'm fine here."

"Kat, please?"

"Why do you insist on calling me Cat?" Now her voice was loud, and Etienne heard the horrible anxiety—the anxiety he was inflicting on her, along with God only knew what else.

"Catherine, please come here. I need to hold you and I need to ask you something." Even to his own ears, his words had a frantic tone to them.

321

He heard the slight sounds of her movement and then felt and smelled her presence near, but not touching him.

He reached out a hand.

The curtain opened. "Good morning," came a cheery male voice. "I'm here to give you a little something to relax you before we head into the O.R. My name is Phil, but I doubt you'll remember me later."

Phil's laugh was friendly and confident, and Etienne wanted to throttle the kind man. Phil took his arm, and Etienne knew that Catherine had again slipped further away.

"Is that going to put him to sleep? Because his mother will be right back, and I think she probably wanted to speak to him."

"Not to worry. This is just a little benzodiazepine to take the edge off. They won't be taking him back for ten minutes or so. But as I said, he probably won't remember any of this."

Etienne heard Phil's last words as he felt a slight prick and burn in his arm. He groaned in frustration.

"Oh, I'm so sorry, Mr. Seton. Did I hurt you?"

"No, no. It's fine, thanks." He had to talk with her, had to know if she was pregnant, had to tell her again that he loved her.

"Okay, then. Someone will be by to get you shortly. Hope you all have a great day!"

The incongruity of Phil's words evidently struck Catherine, too, because he heard her choke.

"Catherine, please." *The hell with pride*. He really was desperate now, but then the damn curtain moved yet again.

"I hate seeing you in a hospital bed once more." His mother's voice was soft. "I hope and pray that after this is over, none of us will have to look at white sheets again for a long time."

Etienne wanted to scream, but he forced himself to inhale

deeply. He could feel his head getting fuzzy. He needed Kat, needed to talk to her about something important.

He felt his mother's lips brush his brow and her hand touch his face. *"Je t'aime, mon amour. Je t'aime."*

"Toi aussi, Maman." He reached out to grasp her wrist and brought her hand to his lips and kissed it. "Bring Catherine here, please?"

His mother kissed him once more and then moved away.

He heard Catherine's quiet, ragged breathing, but couldn't feel her, couldn't see her. He turned his head from side to side, forcing his eyelids open as far as he could in a desperate attempt to catch some glimpse of her, but of course there was nothing.

He heard her choked sob and then felt her hands on his face, her lips against his and the warm drops of her tears against his skin.

"Kat, my sweet Kat." He kissed her but felt like he was already in a dream, not able to do what he was supposed to do, or say what he was supposed to say.

"I won't leave you, I promise." He couldn't remember what else he had needed to tell her. "I love you."

"I love you, too."

He thought he heard her, but he wanted to concentrate on the softness of her hair under his fingers, the feel of her nose nuzzling against him, and the warm beautiful sensation of all that was his love.

BY MUTUAL AGREEMENT, Catherine and Bernice rejected the doctor's suggestion of fresh air. They sat or paced in the impersonal waiting room, where the white walls were decorated by large, framed photographs of stunningly beautiful sunsets, cliffs overlooking the sea, and an eagle in flight, none of which interested them at all.

Yet at maybe her 100th trip around the perimeter of the room, Catherine noticed a picture of the Hagia Sophia in Istanbul that reminded her of a similar shot hanging in Etienne's condo. She stopped and stared at it for a long moment, fear, dread, and hope all battling for supremacy. Would Etienne ever be able to take photos again?

It had already been four hours. Bernice had forced her to go with her to the cafeteria and eat and drink at least a little.

"You may not want it, but that does not matter. You have a baby to think about, and she needs you to take care of yourself."

Catherine noticed that the fruit cup Bernice had taken for herself sat untouched on the small round table, but she didn't say anything. The toast felt like sawdust in her mouth, but she forced herself to swallow a few bites and to sip the weak and barely tepid liquid that masqueraded as tea.

Their stress levels almost perfectly synched, they pushed back from the table at the same time. It was far too early to expect anything, but they needed to be back in the surgical waiting room.

The hours dragged by. Catherine had brought a book, but she couldn't read. She opened her phone's email a few times, but minutes later her glance would fall on the black screen in her hand, and she would realize it had again gone dark from lack of activity.

Her mother called at eleven, and Catherine was grateful to hear her voice. Jake was doing fine, Ellen assured her. "How 'bout you, Sweetie? You holding up okay?"

"Yeah. I'm fine. Thanks." She wasn't, but there was no point in saying so. Her mother knew, anyway. That was why she had called.

"We're thinking about you, honey. Darren called from

Chicago, and he told me again that everything he was able to learn about Dr. Abrams was good."

"I know, Mom. Thanks. I'll call you later if there's any news. And thanks again for taking care of Jake."

She slept for a while without meaning to. She had just closed her eyes for a minute while resting her head against the wall behind her, but she jolted awake when she felt Bernice sit down next to her.

"I'm sorry, *ma chère*. I didn't mean to wake you. I have been trying to find someone who can check on him for us, but no one will help. They keep saying we will be called as soon as there is an update. Is your phone still working?"

Catherine groggily touched her phone, and all the appropriate indicators lit up.

She showed the screen to Bernice, not bothering to say anything. She understood all too well the woman's feeling of helplessness and frustration.

Bernice sighed again. "Can I bring you some water or some juice?"

"No, thank you, Bernice. I'm fine."

"Well, I am not." Bernice stood again and walked to the wall of windows that looked out over a busy city street.

Catherine stretched in the chair, trying to get the kinks out of her neck, and then rose to join Bernice. This day was just another nightmare, but at least in this one there was no rain.

HE GAZED down into the tunnel-like opening below him and saw the brightly lit room with numerous people dressed in blue and green, some of them bent over a supine figure. He shifted his gaze to the side, and other tunnel-like openings appeared, each one showing different figures against varying tableaus. Some were clearer than others, but he didn't struggle to bring any of them into focus.

He turned his attention again to the busy room. Detached thoughts drifted in and out of his mind. That was Etienne, and he was being operated upon. He shifted his attention slightly and saw two women standing together. Catherine. She looked exhausted and frightened. He wanted to reach out to her, to comfort her, but he knew there was no way he could help her. Her features became clearer for just an instant, and he felt a pang of anguish at her worry.

The tunnel to his left caught his attention, and he saw Catherine again, standing in a doorway with tears on her face. More pain, more fear, and he was again helpless. He focused more intently on the woman in the doorway, and her whole story appeared before him. It was Catherine, but it was Katrina, searching for him, for Stephen. He saw them meet, fall in love, marry, and then from a distance he saw the smiling face of a little girl. He wanted to go to them—to Katrina and Anne, to take them in his arms and make them whole again. But he couldn't move. The scene dissolved.

Everywhere he looked he saw figures he dimly recognized, names flying through his mind. Lives lived, love profound and everlasting weaving its presence through story after story.

He looked once more at the scene that seemed to pull him most urgently. There was tension in that bright area around the man on the bed. Was that he? Was he supposed to be there in that bed, or did he belong here, torn away once more from the woman he loved? He concentrated his focus and saw Catherine sit down next to an older woman. Bernice. His mother. She had known great pain in this life as well.

He glanced around at the kaleidoscope of images swirling around him. The scenes that glowed brightest showed a man and woman together, sometimes working, sometimes playing, but always turning to each other.

He searched and found Catherine once more, and suddenly a wider picture opened before him. He saw another little girl, a smiling child with blue eyes and silky reddish-brown curls. He saw Etienne and Catherine walking hand-in-hand, the little girl now joined by two more children.

He looked back at Katrina standing in the doorway. He had wanted to do so many things with her. He, Stephen, had loved her, but violence had torn them apart. Violence had come again this time, to Etienne, but it had led him to Catherine. Perhaps he was going to be given another chance. He looked at the pathways radiating out in all directions. Their apertures were closing, one by one, until all he could see was the operating room below. Now he could hear sounds coming from that room. They were distant at first, but then he could make out the hiss of an oxygen machine and a voice saying, "Okay, his pressure's coming back. I think we've got him."

He smiled, and a feeling of peace and joy swept over him. He was getting another chance.

It was after five when Dr. Abrams came into the waiting room. Catherine felt exhausted, but to her tired eyes, the doctor looked equally spent.

"Good news. Etienne is in recovery, and we're hopeful that he'll be fine. He gave us a bit of a scare for a few minutes, but he rallied and all his vitals now look good."

"Can he see?" Bernice spoke the words as Catherine tried not to hyperventilate.

"We don't know yet, and I can't even tell you how long it will be before we do know. There was considerable inflammation around the optic chiasma even after we extracted this little gem."

She held out a tiny scrap of non-descript metal. If Catherine had seen it on the street—but she would never have seen it. It was too small to notice, smaller than a pea but not as nicely rounded.

"This is what blinded him?"

"Yup. One chance in a billion. From what I saw of Etienne's records, it left barely an entry hole. It just made a beeline for the one spot in his brain where it could block his vision and yet not harm anything else. Now we have to wait and see whether the nerves themselves were damaged, or if his sight will return once the swelling goes down.

"We've got his head and eyes bandaged. You know that, right?" She looked from one anxious face to the other. "We had to do a craniotomy – peel back part of his skull—to access the optic chiasma. He should heal fine, but the bandages make it look worse than it is. We'll uncover his eyes tomorrow in a darkened room and see how he does. It's possible that he'll only see variations in light for a while and that his vision will improve as the inflammation decreases. It's conceivable that he'll see everything as soon as we uncover his eyes. But I have to warn you: it's also completely possible that the damage to the nerves themselves was irreparable and that his sight will not return. I'm hopeful that there will not be other repercussions from the surgery, but again, we'll have to wait until he wakes to know for sure."

Bernice reached out and took the doctor's hands. Dr. Abrams looked surprised, but she didn't pull away when Bernice then bent forward and kissed the doctor on both cheeks.

"Thank you, Doctor. We knew that was a possibility going into this. We are just grateful he made it out of the surgery. You are our hero."

Dr. Abrams smiled and blushed ever so slightly. Catherine realized that the woman was probably only a few years older than she was. She had no doubt seen all kinds of unimaginable horrors, but she likely had little experience with effusive French mothers.

Catherine gave a shaky laugh. "Etienne had complete confidence in you going into this, and I guess his feelings were justified. Thank you so much, Dr. Abrams. Can we see him now?"

"Someone should be out to get you in about a half hour or so. I know you've been waiting all day, but we like to see patients stable in the recovery room for a little while before we admit family. Keep in mind he'll be very groggy and might not make any sense, assuming he's awake enough to know you and talk. We'll know much more tomorrow morning."

They thanked her again, and she went back down the corridor. Bernice turned to Catherine and pulled her into her arms.

"I heard him promise to come back to you, *ma fille.* Etienne was always a good boy who kept his promises. It will all work out, regardless of whether he can see or not."

"I know it will, Bernice. At least I hope it will. I still don't want him to feel trapped by the baby."

"Oh, *ma petite.* I have known him his whole life, and I have never seen him as he is now. He loves you. I think that is why he was so determined to risk the surgery. He loves you like he has never loved anyone else, and I think he wanted to be whole for you."

"That doesn't mean he wanted to start a family, especially if it turns out he still can't see."

"I think if he knows he did everything possible, it will be easier to come to terms with whatever the outcome of the surgery is. I do not believe the idea of a baby will sadden him. *Au contraire,* I think it will bring him joy."

Catherine relaxed into the warmth of Bernice's arms, marveling that after so many hours, the woman could still look so lovely and smell of lilacs.

"Thank you, Bernice. I fell in love with your son almost as soon as we met, and now I think I'm falling in love with you, too."

Bernice laughed and kissed Catherine three times, alternating cheeks. "*Mais bien sûr*, my new daughter. When a mother only has one son, she, too, must fall in love with the woman her son chooses. Otherwise she would risk losing everything. Now let us go freshen up before we see just how 'groggy' that young man is."

Catherine laughed. "Groggy" sounded so funny in Bernice's accent, and suddenly, she felt as if the weight of the world had been lifted from her shoulders.

HE TURNED towards a presence he felt near his face and a slight weight on his chest. *Lilacs.* His mother. He was alive, then, or else the afterlife smelled like his mother's perfume.

"*Maman?*" His voice was a croak.

"*Oui, mon amour.* You still have many tubes in you, so do not try to move. We are here, Catherine and I, and all is well."

"Kat?" His tone was still hoarse, but he felt a sudden stab of fear. Was she here? Was she all right?

"I'm here, Etienne. I'm right here."

He felt a shift in the touch on his torso, and now it was Catherine's delicious scent that reached him. He inhaled and realized how heavy his head felt. He moved his arm slowly, finally making contact with her hand resting lightly on his chest.

"I'm sorry." His words were slow and quiet, but he needed to tell her. "It didn't work. I still can't see you."

Catherine laughed, and the sound sent a cascade of pleasure vibrating through his leaden body.

"Your eyes are bandaged shut, silly. We don't know if you can see yet or not. The doctor said that maybe we'll know tomorrow."

"Is the baby all right?'

The weight from his chest was abruptly lifted.

"What did you say?"

"The baby. Is she all right?"

Neither woman spoke, and Etienne wondered for a moment if they were gone.

"Everyone is fine. You need to rest, *mon fils*. The doctor said you gave them all quite the scare today."

The words drifted in and out of his consciousness. They were here. Catherine's voice sounded happy, so the baby must be fine.

"I love you," he whispered and fell asleep.

THEY SAT by his bedside for a few more minutes, but he seemed to be sleeping calmly.

"You're welcome to stay if you really want to, but he probably won't be awake again for a while. Assuming he remains stable, they'll move him to a room in three or four hours. I'd recommend going home and getting some sleep yourselves. When you come in in the morning, they'll be able to tell you downstairs which room he's in."

The recovery room nurse looked competent, and her tone was reassuring.

"You'll call us if there's any problem?"

The nurse looked at her tablet. "You're Catherine

Reynolds?" She verified Catherine's number. "You're good to go. Really."

When they didn't move, she looked at them each in turn. "I've been doing this a long time," she said. "The bad part is over for now. What he needs is sleep, and what you need is sleep. I'll be on duty 'til seven tomorrow morning, by which time he'll probably be in a nice room grumbling for breakfast. But if anything goes wrong, I'll call you. I promise."

Catherine and Bernice looked at each other and word-lessly agreed. They each bent and kissed Etienne's small amount of exposed cheek and thanked the nurse, gathered their bags and coats from the anteroom, and slowly walked out of the hospital.

It was cold and dark outside. Catherine looked around, momentarily disoriented.

"I forgot how long we've been here. It was dark when we got here this morning, and it's darker and colder now. Thank goodness my mother came and took Jake because I probably would have forgotten to walk him like I had planned."

"Yes. We must call her and thank her and give her the good news."

"It is good news," Catherine agreed. "At this point I couldn't care less if he can see or not."

"I agree. But let us still keep some hope. It would be nice if he could see his baby. When did you tell him?"

"ME? I thought you must have told him. I certainly didn't say anything."

"Hmmph."

They walked the several blocks to the parking garage.

"Bernice? You really didn't tell him?"

"Absolutely not. I told him that if he loved you, he should marry you, but I said nothing about the baby."

Catherine emitted a strangled snort. "You told him he

should marry me? Isn't that a bit . . . I don't know . . . a bit presumptuous?"

Another French sound came from Bernice's throat. "He loves you. You love him. You get married, and *voilá*, I will have my grandbabies. I do not see a problem."

Catherine could only laugh. It had been the longest day of her life, and now she had a mother-in-law in waiting to tell her what to do. No husband, at least not yet, but a very dear, very wise, mother-in-law. As they drove the now quiet roads back to Arlington, she couldn't help but wonder. How on earth did Etienne know about the baby?

CATHERINE WAS ASTONISHED the next morning to realize her appetite had returned with a vengeance. Bernice laughed as she watched her spread peanut butter and honey on two pieces of toast. The elegant French woman was, of course, content with her black coffee—"Oh, *mon Dieu*, it is hard to understand how anyone drinks this facsimile"—and a single piece of barely buttered toast.

Once they were on their way, though, Catherine felt her anxiety return. Would he be able to see? Would he mention the baby again?

They found Etienne sitting up in bed, the lights in the room dim, his bandages still intact, and only a single intravenous line left of the multiple tubes that had seemed to cover him last night.

"*Bonjour, mon amour. Comment ça va?*" Bernice walked briskly to his bedside, picked up his free hand, and kissed it.

"Good morning, *Maman*. I'm okay, I guess. It's hard to tell, actually."

He tilted his head just a bit, and Catherine recognized his question.

"Morning, Etienne." She bent down and touched her lips lightly to his, still self-conscious in front of his mother, which was most certainly ridiculous considering everything they had said to each other.

Etienne found and grabbed her hands before she could move back, drawing her back down.

"Careful," she said instinctively. "Don't move. There's so much of you bandaged. I'm afraid you'll hurt yourself if you move."

"Then come closer and don't make me move."

Catherine smiled. The success of the surgery might still be uncertain, but Etienne was himself. They hadn't lost him.

"Pretty demanding for a man who looks like he's auditioning for a part in the next 'Mummy' movie," she said teasingly. Their fingers were communicating on their own, as always, and she spoke with her mouth hovering less than an inch above his.

It couldn't stay there, though. The pull between them was too strong, and she found herself dropping kiss after kiss around his mouth and chin. Etienne responded with what sounded like a purr, and all three of them laughed.

"Later, *mes enfants*. Etienne, tell us. What have they told you?"

Catherine stood up, but her fingers remained laced with his.

"A resident was here a little while ago, and he said that Dr. Abrams would be here by eleven. Do either of you have my phone? I have no way of knowing what time it is."

Catherine emitted a guilty groan. "I didn't even think to bring it this morning, Etienne. I'm sorry."

"Ah. Only a day without me, and my mother's anti-phone propaganda is getting to you."

They all laughed again, but then Etienne demanded, "Well? Can't one of you tell me what time it is?"

"Manners, please, *mon fils*. It is now 8:45, according to this marvelous piece of antique technology on my wrist. Time for me to go downstairs and see if I can find anything that resembles real coffee. Are you allowed to eat and drink?"

"They brought in something a while ago, but I don't think the person who delivered it knew or cared that I can't see. The nurse asked about it when she came to check everything again a while ago, and I told her you'd probably get me something. I have water here, though." He gestured vaguely to a portable table to the right of his head.

"*Bon.* I will find myself some coffee and hunt down something appealing for you. I may be a while, but I am sure you two can find something to talk about."

She breezed out of the room, winking at Catherine, who burst out laughing.

"I have to come clean, Etienne. I've fallen in love with your mother."

"Yee gads. If the two of you start ganging up on me, I'll need more than a service dog to protect me."

Catherine just looked at him for a minute, overcome with relief that he was alive and still himself. If it turned out he could see, that would be icing on the cake, but she was happy just to have cake.

"Catherine, be an angel and come sit with me, please?" He moved slowly and cautiously, trying to make room for her.

"Etienne, the railings are up. I don't think they want us to put them down."

"I don't really care. Can you see how they work?"

She reluctantly bent and studied the array of metal and plastic, not wanting to do anything that would set off an alarm.

Etienne seemed to understand her hesitation. "Come on, be brave. I'll take the blame if we get in trouble."

Catherine sighed and surrendered. There didn't seem to

be any point in arguing with him today. She pressed the levers she hoped would do the trick and laughed when the railing descended.

"Yes!" Etienne rejoiced and reached out his hand. "Come here."

Catherine sat down and then cautiously swung her legs up and fit herself carefully alongside Etienne. He urged her head on to his chest and sighed deeply when she relaxed against him, his arm enveloping her.

"We have a couple things I think we need to talk about."

Catherine lifted her head, but he gently pushed it back down. "Just listen for a minute. This is going to sound crazy, but . . . " he stopped briefly, as if searching for words.

"I saw things yesterday, Catherine. I saw things that don't make any sense, but somehow they do. You know that nightmare you told me you've had all your life? I saw it."

This time Catherine succeeded in pulling up to stare at his face. Of course with all the bandages, there was only part of his nose and his mouth to stare at. A sliver of her consciousness noticed that his lips were chapped, and she made a mental note to put something on them before she left.

"You saw my nightmare?"

"Yes. I know that sounds impossible, but it's true. There were two people—their names were Stephen and Katrina, and they fell in love when the world said they shouldn't. They had a little girl, and they loved her dearly. But Stephen was killed, and he left Katrina alone. I saw it, Catherine. I saw it all."

Catherine continued to stare at him, now propped up on one elbow, her eyes wide in disbelief. She had told him some details from her recurring dreams, but she certainly hadn't spoken of the dead man she had seen the night before his surgery.

"But you can stop worrying about it now. It's not going to happen again. I'm here, and I'm not going to leave you. And our little girl is going to have two parents who love her."

Catherine reached out trembling fingers to touch his lips, unable to believe the words he was uttering.

"But how? How do you know about the baby?"

Etienne stretched up his arm with the IV attached and held her fingers where they were, moving them only slightly so he could kiss each digit in turn.

"I guessed before the surgery, but I never got a chance to ask you about it. I know . . . I hope . . ." He stopped.

"What I mean is, that I hope you don't mind. Because I don't mind. It's maybe not the best thought-out way to start a life together, but you are the one I want to spend my life with. My forever with, Catherine. You saved my life. What I had before I met you wasn't really worth living, even with 20/20 eyesight. And now you're growing another life inside you that's part of both of us."

She couldn't take her eyes from his mouth, unable to think of a single coherent response. She took a breath and put her head back on his chest. She stayed there, breathing in and out slowly, trying to take in this stunning change in perspective.

"Are you okay, my love?"

Instead of answering, she reached around for the hand that was on her hip holding her close to him on the narrow bed. She pulled it up and over her, pressing it tightly against her belly.

"I don't think you can feel anything yet, but she's moving right this minute. I wanted so much to tell you before the surgery, but I was frightened. Forgive me, Etienne."

"Oh, my dearest love. There's nothing to forgive. I'm sorry I put you through such hell."

They lay there for a few minutes, simply sharing the joy

of being together. Finally Catherine lifted up again to look at his face.

"I am more happy that I could ever have hoped to know you're excited about the baby, but I don't get what makes today so different from two days ago. We still don't know if you can see, and that was all you cared about."

"Oh Catherine, no, that was never all I cared about. Yes, I wanted to see again, desperately. I still do. But I guess it took me seeing what I saw yesterday—and yes, I know it sounds crazy—but I did see it, just like I described it to you. Before yesterday, I was afraid that as a blind person, I couldn't be the man you deserved. And to be honest, a little part of me still feels that way. But what I saw yesterday convinced me that we are somehow more than just two people living today. I've called you Kat since I first met you without knowing why. I still don't understand it, but that guy Stephen loved Katrina with every fiber of his being, and when I met you, I somehow felt that same love."

Etienne's fingers were still spread across Catherine's belly. She pulled free of his embrace and climbed carefully onto her knees, straddling him and then grasping both sides of his face as she bent down to kiss him ever so lightly.

"I love you, Etienne. And I'm willing to buy into the idea that I loved Stephen, too. I don't really care, as long as you're done with all that 'I can't be the man you need' crap."

Their lips met again, and it was like coming home. Quiet, fervent love flowed between them, and Catherine felt like she could remain in that awkward position until the end of time, as long as Etienne was there with her.

But their reverie was cut short by the burst of French energy that came through the door.

"He will never be able to eat any breakfast with you on top of him like that, my dear."

Catherine pulled away quickly, laughing at Etienne's moan of protest.

"You will both be happy to know I did, indeed, find a close imitation of a cup of coffee, and I have brought you that miraculous invention you Americans call a breakfast sandwich. And even more exciting, *mon fils*, is the fact that the package I asked your Aunt Charlotte to send me arrived this morning."

"You must be joking. That's not possible."

"I did not spend twenty years traveling the world with your father without learning something about getting things from one place to another. But we will talk more about my package after the doctor has come."

Bernice helped Catherine climb down from the bed and handed the egg sandwich to Etienne. He ate slowly, and both women smiled to see him enjoy his first food in two days. They were all laughing over Bernice's descriptions of the people she had observed in the cafeteria—"they all seem to take their consumption of great quantities of bad food very seriously"—when Dr. Abrams appeared at the doorway.

"Well, I'm glad my invitation to the party had the right room number on it. I was afraid I was going to have to spend my morning visiting hospital patients."

"Good morning, Dr. Abrams," Bernice said. "I apologize that these two children have been making so much noise."

The doctor laughed. "I'm just happy to see that Etienne is up and alert. It takes some patients a while to recover from long periods of anesthesia, while others bounce back quickly. Let's hope the rest of his recovery goes equally well."

She walked over to Etienne and felt his pulse and checked the notations on her tablet.

"How are you feeling?"

"My head feels heavy, but there's no real discomfort."

"Good. We're going to keep you on pain meds for another

day or so and blood thinners for at least a month, and I want to see you in my office next week. I have two sets of bandages on you now. The top one is simply covering your eyes, and we'll take that off this morning. The other set will come off next week. Until then, please limit your activity. If all goes well today, I expect that I'll be able to discharge you tomorrow, but even then, you'll need to take it easy and just rest. Your brain's been through a lot and it needs time to get everything back in order."

As she spoke, she moved to cut the strip of bandages that encircled Etienne's eyes.

"Now Etienne, when this comes off, I want you to open your eyes slowly. Do not panic if you don't see anything right away. We might not be able to determine immediately whether there's been any improvement since the inflammation may continue to exert pressure on your optic nerves. Do you understand what I'm saying?"

"Yes. I understand. Don't worry; I promise not to panic."

Catherine looked at Bernice, who smiled grimly and then closed her own eyes, unable to watch. Catherine moved over to stand on the other side of Etienne's bed. She reached over the railing and took his hand in hers. Etienne turned his head in her direction and then nodded, signaling his readiness to the doctor.

Dr. Abrams unwound the strips she had cut and stepped back. Catherine stared intently as Etienne opened his eyes and then she gasped. For the first time since meeting him, she saw recognition in his gaze. He looked at her, and an expression of utter joy passed over his face.

"Catherine," he whispered. "My Kat. It's you. It's you."

EPILOGUE

"**M**ommy, Mommy, Jake met a lady dog in the park and they played ball together!"

"That's great, Annie. Was Jake a good boy?"

"Yup. They both ran really fast when Daddy threw the ball."

"I'm glad, Sweetheart. Now go wash your hands, and we'll get some snack."

Catherine looked to the doorway where Etienne was wiping dirt from Jake's paws.

"Tough day at the park?"

"Those two seem to get more rambunctious every day. I think I'll need to start taking extra vitamins when the baby's born."

"Oh, you poor old man. Come here and help me up, and we can hobble together into the kitchen."

Etienne came over and tugged gently on her hands until she was standing before him and his lips could easily meet hers.

"Just a few more days, and I'll be able to hold you tight again without this little monster between us."

"Don't call your son a monster. Not yet, anyway." Catherine's words were said with a smile. Etienne was the gentlest, most loving father she could imagine.

The last four years had swept by as if propelled by a toddler's unflagging energy. With Bernice's smug approval, Etienne had formally proposed to her right there in the hospital room, his head still wrapped in bandages to hold his skull in place. And in defiance of all international laws of bureaucratic delay, he had slipped an exquisite antique garnet ring on her finger that Bernice had miraculously had delivered directly to her at the hospital.

They had married shortly thereafter, with a small crowd of friends and family on hand to cheer exuberantly.

David had worn a huge smile on his face. "I did this, you know. I get the byline. You two would never have met without my intentional engineering."

David's wife had cuffed him on the head, and Catherine and Etienne had just smiled at each other.

The mysterious visions Etienne had seen during his surgery remained a part of their history, something they wondered about and discussed occasionally, but no more frequently than they laughed over their crazy first venture together to the dog park.

Etienne had done some research and finally found the marriage records of a young woman named Katrina Rynick in Tarrytown, New York, who married a British officer named Stephen Howard, and there was a baptismal record for a little girl. But the trail had gone dead beyond that point, at least for now.

Sometimes late at night they speculated on what might have become of Katrina and her baby, and Catherine would send out a silent prayer that she had found peace.

Catherine's nightmares had never returned, and for that respite alone, she would be forever grateful to Etienne. But their lives were now fuller than she could ever have imagined, and there was little time to dwell on the past.

As soon as he was released from the hospital, Etienne resumed contact with Ahmed and his family in Egypt. After just a few weeks of working with him in the evenings, Catherine resigned her position at *GeoMonde*. They now worked tirelessly together for the charity they had founded to set up rehabilitation centers for victims of terrorism around the world. Etienne still traveled occasionally to photograph some of their projects and the people they were assisting. Service animal training centers had been started in areas where they had never before existed, and personnel were taught to individualize animal training to match the needs of the victims. Jake often traveled with him as a working ambassador.

Etienne had become an expert in web design and development, and Catherine had learned more than she would ever have wanted to know about fundraising, writing grant proposals, and battling bureaucratic obstacles. Unfortunately, the demand for their services never waned, but they found satisfaction in knowing that fewer lives were being permanently destroyed by acts of violence

Bernice came and went. She and Ellen engaged in friendly rivalry for the position of grandmother-in-chief, and their fierce competition meant that each wanted to spend as much time with Annie as possible. Since they were already vying for first babysitting rights for the new baby, Catherine and Etienne could only marvel at their good fortune. Bernice insisted that summers in Brittany were far superior to those of Washington, but her visits the rest of the year were often lengthy, and she insisted on conversing with Annie exclusively in French. "She'll have to be fluent, after all, since she'll be spending her summers with me, *n'est-ce pas?*"

Catherine and Etienne just looked at each other and

smiled. The nature of their work allowed them to carry on anywhere there was good Internet service, so if Bernice wanted them all in France, they'd no doubt all go to France. And if Bernice wanted Annie without her parents, and maybe the rest of her grandchildren down the road as well, she'd most likely get her way. Ellen would no doubt volunteer to escort them on their journey.

And that was fine with Catherine and Etienne. They had their family, and they had each other. Again, now, and forever, they had each other.

HISTORICAL AND MEDICAL
NOTES

Except for the existence of Major Howard and his assignment to Tarrytown, all historical material is factual to the best of my knowledge. Support in the colony of New York for the crown varied greatly from region to region, but the Philipse Manor in Tarrytown remained a loyalist bastion until it was seized during the course of the revolution.

The church where Katrina and Stephen married, "The Old Dutch Church," still stands, one of the oldest, still-operating churches in the country. The graveyards surrounding it hold markers dating back to the 1600s, and Washington Irving's grave can be found there, surrounded by other prominent New Yorkers.

Conditions at Fort Ticonderoga were, indeed, deplorable, and had command been reassigned and the area fortified, it might not have fallen as quickly as it did to the American forces in 1777. Acting Royal Governor Colder was, amazingly, 86-years-old in 1774, still in full command of his senses, and the father of ten surviving children and numerous grandchildren.

I am enormously grateful to neurosurgeon Dr. Angela

Viers for patiently answering all of my questions regarding head injuries and brain surgery and to Dr. Tamara Worlton for general medical and surgical information. The details concerning Etienne's injury, prognosis, and surgery are all within the realm of possibility given today's medical capabilities. At the end of our last conversation, Dr. Viers said wistfully that it would be nice if my fictional doctor could be a female, and I was delighted to comply!

ACKNOWLEDGMENTS

As always, I am enormously grateful to my husband and to my sister for being my first, last, and most loving editors and critics. My words would never leave my notebooks without their support and encouragement, and I thank them from the bottom of my heart.

One on the east coast and one on the west, my son and my brother continue to answer my scatterbrained cries for technological help. Thank you again, and what was that thing you told me not to forget?!

I am also grateful to the volunteers at the Historical Society serving Tarrytown/Sleepy Hollow in New York. Since this book has been several years in the making, I doubt anyone there remembers my visit, but they were enormously kind and generous with their time and access to the research material on their shelves.

As I write these words, I have not yet had to call on the incomparable J.T. Bock, writer and graphic designer extraordinaire, in panic, begging her, yet again, to help me figure out the incomprehensible language of book cover design and configuration. I'm crossing my fingers everything goes smoothly this time. Because I know it won't, thank you, Jen!!!

Lastly, I wanted very much for a dear friend, Elizabeth Kitsos Kang, to read here how grateful I was that she showed patience and kindness while I peppered her with bothersome questions about brain scans. Sadly, the cancer that cruelly attacked her brain took her life and left the world a less vibrant place. So I hope her family: Stan, Jamie, and Eli, know that I am grateful and will never forget her.

If you've flipped to this page first, I hope you'll find time to go back and read the story. If you've come to this page after finishing the book, I hope with all my heart that you have found moments of joy. Write me at MegNapierAuthor@gmail.com and let me know your thoughts, and if you have a moment, share your delight in a review wherever you buy or chat about books. Thank you!

ABOUT THE AUTHOR

Meg Napier knows beyond a shadow of a doubt that love stories form the basis for everything that matters in life. Not a fast or furious writer, she is nevertheless intent on sharing the stories that find their way from her pencil to her notebook and finally to her keyboard. Her hope is to bring joy, excitement, and a sigh of satisfaction to readers everywhere.

ALSO BY MEG NAPIER

Second Stanza

A young man dies, and a young woman's heart breaks. Years later the woman's life is threatened, and in the midst of chaos, she believes that same beloved man saves her life. So begins a search: for him, for truth, and for the chance to reclaim a love that refuses to die. Breathtaking romantic suspense that will keep you holding your breath from the first page to the last.

Second Act

New York Times bestselling author Sherry Thomas says: "Meg Napier devises an ingenious plot," and in SECOND ACT, romance and suspense go toe to toe when a ballet dancer dies onstage and a NYC detective must determine if the beautiful ballerina is a murderer or next in line to be killed.

Love At Dawn

Remember waking up with the first blush of a new romance filling your morning with joy?

Meg Napier joins with six uniquely talented authors to bring you a medley of love stories that will quicken your senses, lift your hearts, and make you imagine love in whole new ways. Spanning the scale from gentle and sweet to spicy hot, each entry brings a fresh look at love in all its variations along with the perennial promise of morning's renewal. ALL proceeds go to the charity feeding people in need here and in every corner of the globe: World Central Kitchen.

Second Draft

A short and flirty love story about a romance writer whose characters insist she's got her priorities mixed up.

NEWSLETTER SIGN-UP

Sign up for my newsletter here, and get a copy of "Second Draft" for free! I'll send you updates only occasionally, and promise to share news of other great books I've been reading!

https://www.megnapier.com/megs-mailing-list/